Praise for
The Ruby Notebook

★ "A complex and satisfying novel that is both a mystery and a tender, wise meditation on love and self-identity. Characters are rich and vibrant. . . . Readers . . . will likely be clamoring for the third [book]." —*Kirkus Reviews*, Starred

"Anyone who enjoys detailed settings and thoughtful narratives will be rewarded with this story." —*School Library Journal*

Praise for
The Indigo Notebook

"Observant, aware, and occasionally wry, Zeeta's first-person narration will attract readers and hold them. Resau . . . offers another absorbing novel with a Latin American setting." —*Booklist*

"The characters fairly brim with life in this thoughtful, poignant novel filled with cultural details. The writing is simple but evocative. . . . A remarkably engrossing, layered work." —*Kirkus Reviews*

"An entertaining and suspenseful read." —*School Library Journal*

"Readers looking for inspiration and impetus to get out and see the world will find this a satisfying outing." —*The Bulletin*

Also by Laura Resau

The Indigo Notebook

❖

The Jade Notebook
Available February 2012 from Delacorte Press

THE

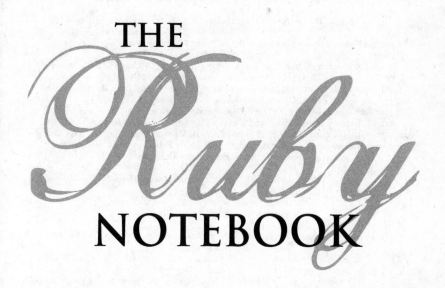

Ruby

NOTEBOOK

LAURA RESAU

EMBER

Text copyright © 2010 by Laura Resau
Cover art copyright © 2010 by Ericka O'Rourke

All rights reserved. Published in the United States by Ember, an imprint of Random House Children's Books, a division of Random House, Inc., New York.
Originally published in hardcover in the United States by Delacorte Press, an imprint of Random House Children's Books, New York, in 2010.

Ember and the colophon are trademarks of Random House, Inc.

Grateful acknowledgment is made to the following for permission to reprint previously published material:
Coleman Barks: Excerpts from *The Essential Rumi,* translated by Coleman Barks, copyright © 1995 by Coleman Barks (HarperSanFrancisco, an imprint of HarperCollins Publishers).
Les Éditions José Corti: Translated excerpt from "Prendre Corps" from *Paralipomènes* by Ghérasim Luca, published by Les Éditions José Corti.
Spirit One Music: Lyrics from "I'll Be Your Mirror," written by Lou Reed, copyright © Oakfield Avenue Music, Ltd. US and Canadian Rights for Oakfield Avenue Music, Ltd. Administered and Controlled by Spirit One Music (BMI) World excluding US and Canadian Rights. Administered and Controlled by EMI Music Publishing, Ltd. International Copyright Secured. Used by Permission. All Rights Reserved.

Visit us on the Web! www.randomhouse.com/teens

Educators and librarians, for a variety of teaching tools,
visit us at www.randomhouse.com/teachers

The Library of Congress has cataloged the hardcover edition of this work as follows:
Resau, Laura.
The ruby notebook / by Laura Resau. — 1st ed.
p. cm.
Summary: When sixteen-year-old Zeeta and her itinerant mother move to Aix-en-Provence, France, Zeeta is haunted by a mysterious admirer who keeps leaving mementoes for her, and when her Ecuadorian boyfriend comes to visit, their relationship seems to have changed.
ISBN 978-0-385-73653-4 (hardcover) — ISBN 978-0-385-90615-9 (lib. bdg.) —
ISBN 978-0-375-89761-0 (ebook)
[1. Secrets—Fiction. 2. Interpersonal relations—Fiction. 3. Mothers and daughters—Fiction. 4. Single-parent families—Fiction. 5. Aix-en-Provence (France)—Fiction. 6. France—Fiction.]
I. Title.
PZ7.R2978Ru 2010
[Fic]—dc22
2009051965

ISBN 978-0-375-84525-3 (tr. pbk.)

RL: 5.2

Printed in the United States of America

10 9 8 7 6 5 4 3 2 1

First Ember Edition 2012

Random House Children's Books supports the First Amendment
and celebrates the right to read.

ACKNOWLEDGMENTS

Glimmers of ideas for this book appeared fifteen years ago, while I was living in Aix-en-Provence with Annie and Alain Thille, my fun-spirited and generous host parents. *Merci mille fois* to you and your family for sharing your love, your home, and your amazing meals with me both when I was a college student and on recent visits. Conversations with the Aixois artist Juan Carlos Gallo in his exquisite gallery-courtyard gave me endless inspiration. *Grâce à vous,* Juan Carlos, this book (and my life) are infused with a bit more magic and mystery. A big *merci* to my *hyper cool* friends Jean-Christophe Prin and Megan Daily for their help with French language details.

Once again, my editor, Stephanie Lane Elliott, and her assistant, Krista Vitola, were instrumental in shaping and shining this manuscript. I'm deeply grateful for their patience and confidence in me, and for all the dedicated behind-the-scenes support everyone at Delacorte Press has given to my books. My energetic agent, Erin Murphy, deserves heaps of thanks for bringing the Notebooks series from an idea to a reality. Old Town Writers' Group has kept me sane and smiling—thank you, Carrie Visintainer, Kimberly Srock Fields, Leslie Patterson, Molly Reid, and Sarah Ryan. Special thanks to Coleman Barks, phenomenal

Pour Annie et Alain Thille

Rumi translator, for his generosity in letting me quote so much from *The Essential Rumi*.

Most of all, I thank my mother, who—when I felt overwhelmed and lost with this manuscript—showed me the way again, step by step. I suspect that you *do* have a magic wand after all, Mom. Dad and Ian, thanks for picking up our slack when Mom and I dropped everything in a scramble to finish this book. And Bran, thanks for your toddler joie de vivre in Aix-en-Provence as we rode the carousel and danced to street music and splashed in fountains!

ONE

It's true. There's something about the light here. It's hazy golden, as if it's moving through honey. I've seen all kinds of light. Wet green glow in the Amazonian jungle, squid luminescence in the Pacific, indigo dawns through a waterfall in the Andes. But this particular light—this southern French light glinting off my tiny espresso cup—this is something else.

It hits me now, the familiar urge to e-mail Wendell. It's a hunger that needs to be satisfied every three or four hours. A split second later, the rational part of my brain kicks in, and I remember he'll be here in a week. June twenty-fifth, the day filled with unabashedly giddy hearts and exclamation points on my calendar. He'll be here, in Aix-en-Provence, in this square, and we'll actually be touching, and this light will be settling on his skin. He'll be hopping up to snap pictures through the fountain spray, catching the cloud of pigeons alighting on an old man's shoulders, a miniature dog nonchalantly making a large pile of *merde* as the owner, unaware, studies a dress in a shop window.

Across the café table, Layla picks up her little bowl of lemon *glâce* and tilts her head back to pour the last melted drops in her mouth. Not the kind of thing the well-mannered French people surrounding us would even think of doing. I know my mother so well, I can guess why she does it. It's not just because everything's so expensive in Aix—although that drop of *glâce* is probably worth ten *centimes*. That's just Layla, savoring the tiniest droplets, sucking every bit of sweetness from life. Which is maybe why we move to a different country every year. Sixteen countries in my sixteen years on earth. It doesn't take her long to lick a place clean.

She gazes over my head. "Doesn't everything here look edible, Zeeta?"

"Edible how?" I can't help smiling. We've been here a week, already over the jet lag but still marveling at every novel detail. It's amazing; not a single sarcastic comment has emerged from my lips all week. Layla and I have been like sisters adventuring together, probably because I'm insanely happy about Wendell coming.

Best of all, he'll be staying in our apartment. I'll see him every day for two months, enough to make up for nine whole months apart. While I was getting his room ready this morning, I had a goofy smile on my face, just imagining breakfast together at our sunny kitchen table, dinner on our roof patio. Almost too good to be true.

"Look at those buildings, love." Layla waves her arm, her bracelets clinking. "They're like sugary, buttery desserts."

I nod. "Crème brûlée." All the buildings—shops, cafés, bakeries, post office, town hall—are painted in the same dessert palette. This honey haze has oozed into everything, even the people. They're draped in pale creams and lemons and silvers. They even talk in milky hues, their lips pursed and cheeks sucked in to form sexy French vowels.

Layla leans in. "Don't you love that we're living in a place pronounced 'X'? Like X marks the spot. Like there's a hidden treasure here! Like it can be whatever we want it to be! *C'est magnifique!*" She blows a kiss at the sky.

"He'll like it here," I say. Layla knows the *he* I'm talking about. For nine months, she's heard me find roundabout ways to work Wendell into every conversation.

"Is his room ready?" she asks.

"Clean sheets, empty chest drawers, space in the wardrobe, a shelf in the medicine cabinet. All set." He'll be moving into my room, and I'll sleep on the sofa bed in the living room.

"Hyper cool," she says, pronouncing it the French way. "Eep-air" cool. A few months ago in Ecuador when I told her my plan to have Wendell stay with us this summer, she just said, *"¡Que pleno!"*—"Cool" in Spanish. The idea of my boyfriend sharing our apartment didn't faze her one bit. She's more like a sister than a mother, young-looking

• 3 •

enough that people often ask if we're doing our junior year abroad together, pretty enough that random college back-packers turn to ogle. Even on windless days, her blond hair flies wild behind her, trailing along like a comet's tail. "It'll be good to have him around again," she says. "Other artists inspire me."

Just what kind of artist Layla considers herself is hard to get a handle on. Life is her canvas, each country a brush-stroke of a different color. Wendell's another type of artist—a photographer, slow and thoughtful with his craft. But what I love most about him is just him. His presence. How it feels to be near him. I imagine kissing him goodbye as he leaves for classes, and meeting him in the afternoons to wander the town together, meandering through the markets, hanging out at cafés.

Still, there's a piece of me that's wary, sure that this *is* too good to be true, a piece of me prepared to have my heart torn apart. My heart has been torn apart, over and over, every year, every time we say goodbye to our home. Still, somehow, over the course of a year in the new home, my heart heals and hopes and loves . . . only to be torn apart again.

• • •

One afternoon when I was eight years old, in the high-lands of Guatemala, I spent hours playing with my best friend, Paloma, at our magical waterfall fort in the woods. As we headed home I remember feeling at the pinnacle of happiness, flying through the door with her, rosy-cheeked and breathless and laughing. Layla gave us both big hugs and said, "Oh, love, I have good news! We're going to Morocco next week!"

And with those words, Paloma and my magical waterfall fort were snatched away. It was a heavy, falling, crushing feeling. A giant tree smashing to the ground.

The worst part of leaving Guatemala was saying goodbye to Paloma's father, who I'd come to think of as my own, even calling him Papá. He doted on me, telling Paloma and me how much we looked alike. And we did. My skin was just a shade lighter than hers. Our eyes were wide and brown, our hair black and straight and long, and our cheekbones high. We fantasized that we really were sisters. . . .

Saying goodbye to Paloma's father made my lack of a father grow into a huge, empty void. That's when I first started bugging Layla about my own father, when I learned that I was the product of a one-night stand on a Greek beach. She didn't even know his name, only the initials J.C. And that's when she told me that my chances of meeting my father were zero.

Over the years I searched for his face in every crowd. I had no idea what he looked like, but I assumed I'd magically recognize him. Little by little, with each face that wasn't his, I realized Layla was right. I'd never know him. I'd have to accept it.

And I have. Except for a tiny piece of me, a piece located

not in my mind but in my stubborn heart, the piece that skips a beat whenever I meet a J.C., the piece willing to risk being torn apart once again.

• • •

Across the café table from me, Layla tilts back her head, letting her blond hair cascade down the back of her chair, closing her eyes like a cat, relishing the warmth. She knows how to be happy. Her happiness isn't clouded by the sense of impending doom that mine is. No, she dives into the moment, forgets the past, doesn't worry about the future. Which is what she appears to be doing now, bathing in sunlight, full of lemon *glâce.*

"Beauty constantly wells up," she murmurs, *"a noise of spring-water in my ear and in my inner being."* It's Rumi, her favorite thirteenth-century mystic. She quotes him so often I feel as if he's part of our family—adored by her, tolerated by me.

And then, as though she's conjured it up, a sound bursts forth like springwater, like a fountain suddenly turned on. Music, a rushing, churning, chaos of music, spurting out from under a tree next to us. It's like a carousel song that flew away and crashed into a gypsy caravan and burst into flames of polka. There's a whirlwind of accordion, trumpet, and bongos, each one shooting out notes like squiggly fireworks. The melody swirls around slowly at first, gathering momentum, and then explodes.

The musicians' clothes, all in shades of red, are patchworks of satin, corduroy, velvet, and silk, sewn with an odd assortment of items—feathers and beads and little plastic dolls and tiny cars and bottle caps and paper clips and shells. These people do not match the milky-smooth surroundings. Not by a long shot.

They seem to be around my age, maybe a little older. One girl is spinning, her long scarlet skirt swirling, her hips and arms undulating, her dark hair flying. Gazing at her, a lanky guy in a crimson top hat plays the trumpet, with a tuba at his feet. A redheaded girl dressed in a leotard and tights and a short skirt, the deep reds of cherries, sways cross-legged on the ground, beating bongos. Sunlight catches the brass buttons and sequins randomly sewn on her clothes.

Beside the band, a mime in a puffy white shirt, loose white pants, and a black skullcap is leaning against a tree. He holds so motionless it's as though he's part of the tree. His face is painted white, with black diamonds around his eyes and a black teardrop on his cheek. I can't tell if he's part of their group. Probably not, since he's not playing any instrument and he's not in red.

And then there's a guy playing accordion. You'd think it would be hard to look hot playing an instrument associated with dancing monkeys, but he pulls it off. The muscles of his arms ripple as he squeezes and releases the accordion. His hair is a mass of loose black curls that fall over his eyes, grazing his thick lashes.

"Vâchement cool!" Layla says. Literally, "Cow-ly cool."

I nod. *"Super cool!"* We've been using French slang for a week now, so it comes quickly to our lips.

Layla's eyes widen. *"Hyper super cool!"*

Already, a crowd is gathering and kids are clapping and coins are flying into the open tuba case lined with a pooled-up raspberry red scarf. After a few songs, the group takes a break, passing one another a carafe of water. The redheaded girl dances around the crowd holding out a top hat. In her other hand, she holds cherries. One-handed, she pops one after another into her mouth, spitting the pits over her shoulder with abandon.

She whizzes by our table, doing a backflip just a meter from us, and holds out the hat. I drop in a few coins. Then, with a smile, she's skipping on to the next table. Once she's finished her round, she announces, in a musical voice much bigger than her elfin body, "We! Are! *Illusion!*"

It takes me a moment to realize that Illusion must be the name of the group. They do seem too bright and eccentric and red to be real, like something my mind has conjured up. One thing I'm sure of: I want to be friends with these people. As much as I complain to Layla about our gypsy lifestyle, I always find kindred spirits in people who exist on the fringes.

From Café Cerise, I head toward Cybercafé Nirvana, since it's been a few hours since I last e-mailed Wendell. On the way, I swing by the bookstore to buy my first notebook in France. Since I was eight, in each country we've lived in, I've written in a different-colored notebook. I started with a purple notebook in Guatemala, filling only half of it with big, awkward letters, a jumble of English and Spanish. More recently, I've filled four or five notebooks per country, mostly in English with a smattering of words in the local languages. Ecuador was indigo, Thailand was white, Brazil red, India yellow, Laos green, Chile blue, and Morocco orange.

My notebooks—enough to make a small suitcase bulge— are the only sentimental things I bring from one country to another. They're brimming with interviews, musings, observations, questions, and the occasional rant. When you're constantly moving to a new place, adapting to new ways of life, it takes extra work to make sense of it all. Thus my rainbow of notebooks.

As I stand in front of the shelves, one notebook leaps out at me, practically does a flip, and lands in my hand. It's ruby red with bits of golden sparkles that make my heart race. If it had a sound track, it would be the wild, soul-sparking music of Illusion.

TWO

The sun's setting as I walk to Cybercafé Nirvana. The sign on the door advertises air-conditioning, which is why the door and windows stay shut, but that just makes it stuffier. Inside, it feels like a dimly lit oven filled with whirring, humming machines and grunge rock. There's a stale cigarette smell from years of smoking before it was outlawed indoors. A few flickering fluorescent lights give the room a dull gray pallor.

As the door swings shut, jangling a bell, I silently curse Layla for rejecting technology like cell phones or laptops, for making it such an ordeal to communicate with Wendell.

"Essalam alikoum," Ahmed says with a wave. His eyes flicker away from the game on his computer screen.

Apparently he's internationally notorious in the online-gaming realm of KnightQuest.

"Essalam alikoum," I echo. We always switch between French and Arabic, which keeps me on my toes. I learned both languages in Morocco, but it's been seven years since I lived there, back when I had my orange notebook.

Ahmed's friendliness makes up for what Cybercafé Nirvana lacks in atmosphere. He's Moroccan, and he started giving me discounts once he heard my rusty Arabic. This place is right down the street from our apartment in the North African neighborhood, and sometimes, if I close my eyes and smell the tagine in the air—that pungent blend of lamb and almond and cinnamon—I feel as if I'm back in Marrakech.

Well, except for "Smells Like Teen Spirit" playing on repeat on Ahmed's computer. Nirvana is his favorite band. He's always asking me to translate the lyrics, and doesn't believe me when I assure him they make just as little sense in English.

Ahmed swishes his head around, as though it's a mess of stringy blond locks rather than his close-clipped, gelled helmet of silver-streaked black hair. "Oh, my. Two entire hours have passed since you e-mailed Wendell." He glances up quickly with a teasing grin. He's a neat man, decked out even on sweltering days in white, long-sleeve shirts, which complement his dark skin nicely, but make him look oddly formal. He wears a fancy gold watch that he never looks at since the time is always in the corner of his eye on the computer screen. He's the age my father would probably be—midthirties to early forties. Whenever I meet someone like Ahmed, I imagine for a sliver of a moment that I could be his daughter.

Ahmed smiles. "And what is the love of your life doing now?"

"I think he's at a pool party." I like that I know where Wendell is at all times, even though he's across the entire Atlantic. I've never been to his home in Colorado, but from what he's described, I can imagine the sunshine and mountains. We met last summer in different mountains, on a different continent altogether—the Andes in South America. He'd been adopted from Ecuador as a baby, and sixteen years later, had returned to search for his birth parents.

Ahmed gives a wistful shake of the head. "Oh, how I partied back when I was younger," he says, deftly maneuvering his custom KnightQuest mouse. "Even played in a grunge band. We toured around a little."

"Really?" I have a hard time picturing Ahmed wearing anything other than his pressed cotton pants and button-down shirt.

"Now I just listen to music," he says. "The only remnant of my old life." He blinks and shakes his head, as if waking himself up. "So, when will *l'homme de ta vie* be here?"

"A week." I can't help smiling when Ahmed offhandedly refers to Wendell as the love of my life. One thing about living in a different country every year is that you have to jump in and make friends as fast as you can. And you can't be too discriminating about age or gender—you just search out whoever has that spark, a certain je ne sais quoi. After only a week, Ahmed and I already joke around like old friends. He's talented at showering me with attention while still kicking butt in KnightQuest.

"Well, go and write," he says, flicking his hand at me cheerfully. "And tell *l'homme de ta vie* that Ahmed says hello."

I settle into the chair at my favorite computer in the corner. It's just beneath the travel poster of colorful houses crowded onto cliffs on the Italian coast.

Wendell's sent me five photos from his phone. In all of them, I'm standing on a big boulder, on the top of a mountain in the Andes. The wind is tossing my hair around, and each photo captures it in a different position, like it's a moving sculpture. It looks as if the air could pick me up and carry me away. That's how Wendell has always made me feel—on the verge of flying. The pictures move in closer and closer, and in the last one, my eyes fill the photo. And you can tell that my eyes are looking at something amazing—the vast patchwork of fields and trees and red-tiled roofs spread like a blanket below me.

His e-mail says:

```
I'll be your mirror,
Reflect who you are
In case you don't know.
I'll be the wind, the rain, and the sun,
```

```
The light on your door
That shows when you're home.
```

They're the lyrics to a Velvet Underground song he played me in Ecuador. I remember flipping through these photos and listening to the song and feeling his arm around my shoulder. And once the song ended, I thought, *He knows me. He sees who I am. He can always remind me.* A rare and precious thing.

I kissed him and breathed in his cinnamon smell and absorbed the feel of his muscles and hung on to his long braid, wrapping it around my hand as if it were a rope to hold him with me.

And all I could think was *My God. I am lucky.*

I stare at the computer screen. The lyrics are all he's written, except for the end.

No matter where you are, you are *la femme de ma vie.*

I linger on those last words. *The love of my life.*

I smile, knowing he's half kidding but enjoying the fact that he's half serious, too. He's been signing off that way since I told him that Ahmed calls him *l'homme de ma vie.*

There's the ding of a chat request. He's online, probably on his phone. His words appear on the screen. "Hey, Z—call me?"

I only have a few euros, so this will have to be short. Ahmed moves his gaze from KnightQuest long enough to flip to Wendell's number in his little notebook, and nods when he hears it ringing. I go into the phone booth, close the flimsy wooden door behind me, and perch on the stool.

As I pick up the phone, a tingling thrill runs through me. "Hey, Wendell. It's me." It still feels incredible that I'm someone's *me*. That "me" is all I have to say. That I have the *me* spot in his life.

"Hey, Z." His voice is muffled, barely audible over music and shouts in the background.

"It's hard to hear you, Wendell."

"Yeah. I'm at this pool party." More noise, splashing, heavy bass.

I press the phone to my ear, straining to hear, barely catching his words.

"Listen, Z," he says. "There's a change of plans."

I swallow hard. "What?"

"I won't be staying with you."

My heart stops. "But are you still coming to France?"

"Yeah." His voice is garbled and lost in the noise.

"I can't hear you, Wendell." I press the phone to my ear again, put my hand over my other ear. "What?"

He shouts. "I'm staying with a host family there."

Why would he do that? Why wouldn't he want to stay with me and Layla? "Why?"

"My mom and dad thought it would be a good idea."

I try to find words. "I don't understand, Wendell."

"They thought it would be good for my French if I live with French people."

I stare at the pattern of scratches in the door, the bits of graffiti, names, doodles. "But I can speak French with you," I say. "And you'll have French teachers, and you'll be surrounded by French people and—" I pause, trying to keep the edge of desperation out of my voice.

"Yeah, but they think—"

"What? I can't hear." I close my eyes, focusing. I want, suddenly, to kick something.

"They think it might be too much pressure on us."

"Pressure? What are you talking about?"

"It might be weird at first to be together again. They think I should have my own space."

I rub my eyes, press them hard, until I see constellations of stars behind my lids.

"Z? You still there?"

"Yeah."

He keeps talking, as if to fill the spaces of my silence. "At first I didn't like it either, Z. Then I started thinking about it. And I saw their point."

Now I actually do it, kick the wall. Ouch. Not a good idea in sandals. I rub my toes and curse under my breath.

"Z? You okay?"

"I don't know." I look at the clock above the phone and calculate how many euros I have left. Probably enough for another minute. "Listen, Wendell, I have to go."

"Hey, I'm sorry, Z." His voice is sincere, tender even, but a little distracted.

"I don't have any more time. I'm out of euros."

"You still picking me up at the airport?"

"Your host family isn't getting you?"

"I told them you would. I mean, if—"

"Yeah. I'll be there. Bye." I hang up before he can say I love you. For a long time, I sit on the stool, staring at the scratched wall.

When I emerge from the phone booth, Ahmed looks at me with concern. "Everything okay?"

I nod but say nothing. At times like these, I wish I had a father. Not a temporary substitute, but a real one. Sure, there's always Layla. But I know exactly what she'll say about Wendell's change of plans. She'll give me a hug and a kiss on the forehead, quote Rumi, and assume I'll get over it in no time. I always imagined my father would be the one who would understand that the words of a thirteenth-century mystic aren't universal Band-Aids. He'd understand that not every disappointment can roll right off you, that sometimes you need someone to mourn with you.

But there is no father, and there never will be, and all I can do is take these small kindnesses, like Ahmed's, where I can. I offer him a weak smile and reach into my bag for the two euros to pay him. As I'm searching for my change purse, my hands touch the cool, smooth plastic of a CD case.

Strange. I don't remember putting this in my bag. The case is translucent red, and inside is a silver disc with the words *Make every day a song* scrawled on it in French.

That's one of Layla's mottos. Sometimes when she breezes out the door in the mornings, she calls that phrase over her shoulder. She *has* been known to surprise me with odd little homemade gifts before.

But with a closer look, I see that the handwriting isn't her distinct, swirling script. It's more masculine, small and neat. And now that I think about it, the CD wasn't in here when I paid for my drink at the café earlier. Someone must have put it in my bag within the past hour. Someone at the café? Or maybe Ahmed? Maybe it fell from the counter into my bag.

"Ahmed," I say, showing him the CD case. Evening sunshine pours through the window, reflecting a circle of light onto the wall. "Is this yours?"

"No. Did someone forget it in the phone booth?"

"It was in my bag."

"Bizarre," he says.

Mystified, I pay him two euros, tuck the CD back into my bag, and step out into the breezy air. I feel a strange gratitude to whoever put the CD in my bag. It's as if somehow, this person knew what I needed.

• • •

When I walk through our apartment's door, breathless from three flights of stairs, Layla's in the kitchen, baking. Her violet cotton tunic is covered in flour, and her hair, slipping from an orange silk scarf, is splattered with bits of cream. A paper-thin sheet of dough is spread on the counter, surrounded by mixing bowls and bags of sugar and flour.

"Hello, love! I'm making *mille-feuilles*. Pastries with a thousand leaves!" She holds up a ball of dough in one hand and a pastry roller in the other. This kitchen is better stocked than any other we've lived in, and Layla's determined to figure out what every last utensil is for and use it. "Want to help, Z?"

"Nope." I dump my bag on the snow-white sofa. Our apartment matches the town—creams, buttery yellows, silvers, pale pinks, whites. This is one of the only furnished apartments we've lived in, probably because it's the richest country we've ever lived in. In the past, our apartments didn't even come with toilet seats or stoves, for fear the tenants would run off with them. This apartment has all the bells and whistles, from lemon zesters to stacks of glossy art magazines to framed prints on the walls. The closet is full of fluffy white towels and neat plastic caddies for cleaning supplies and toiletries.

I was proud to offer Wendell such luxurious accommodations, but now it doesn't matter. I pull my clothes from the antique chest of drawers in the living room and carry them by the armful to the bedroom.

"What are you doing, love?"

"Moving my stuff back into the bedroom." I work quickly, wanting to get it over with. "Change of plans. Wendell's staying with a host family."

"Why?"

"His parents wanted him to." I keep my voice flat, emotionless. "Something about too much pressure."

"Oh. I'm sorry, love." Layla sweeps into the living room, gives me a floury hug, and kisses my head.

I stiffen. "Every time I'm happy, something happens to end it. It never lasts." I grab an armful of shirts from the bottom drawer. "I should be used to it by now. I don't know why I thought this thing with Wendell would be different."

Layla gets on her Rumi-quoting face—raising her eyebrows slightly, half closing her eyes, giving a spacey hint of a smile.

Before she starts talking, I'm already rolling my eyes.

"You must have shadow and light source both," she says. *"Listen, and lay your head under the tree of awe."*

"I'm not laying my head anywhere," I snap, slamming a drawer shut. "I'm going to start listening to my head instead of my heart. Getting rid of any delusions I had about things going perfectly this summer."

As Layla lowers her eyelids and opens her mouth to respond, I add, "And no more Rumi, please."

She closes her mouth, walks back into the kitchen, and rolls out the dough on the counter, spritzing it with a little water bottle. After a moment, she says, "Well, maybe it's best he has his own place."

I snatch a stray sock off the floor and stare at her. "You actually agree with his parents?"

She pushes a strand of hair from her face with her wrist

and squeezes doodles of white cream onto the sheet of dough. "It's been nearly a year. People change. It might take some—"

This is an unexpected twist. She hardly ever takes the responsible, maternal route. "We e-mail five times a day, Layla! I know him much better than I did last summer."

So much for getting along like sisters. Although, maybe this is how sisters get along. As the sisterless, brotherless product of a one-night stand, I wouldn't know. Since that fateful night, Layla has only once come close to a long-term relationship. And thanks to Layla, I have absolutely no idea what it's like to have a romance that lasts more than a month. I can't help mustering up some sarcasm. "I forgot. A hundred flings in a decade makes you queen of love advice."

She shrugs and smooths the cream with a spatula.

I toss the clothes into the wardrobe in the bedroom, not bothering to fold them. Then it occurs to me. I walk out of the room and look at Layla. "What if Wendell's worried I'm like you?"

"Huh?" She licks cream from her finger.

"That I just flit from one guy to another." Breathless, I clear out the last drawer and pile the pants and jeans into my arms, stomping into the bedroom.

"I don't think he thinks that," Layla calls.

I cross my arms, slump against the doorframe. "Why else would he do this?"

"The reason he gave you." She gives a resigned smile. "Just roll with it, Z. He'll still be living in the same town as you."

She holds out a spoonful of sweet cream. "This'll make you feel better. Have some."

I shake my head and take a long breath, trying to put this into perspective. It's true, Wendell and I can still spend all our time together when he's not in class.

"Hey, Z!" Layla tries again. "Why don't we blast some monk chants and just be happy he's coming, okay?"

"Fine. But not monk chants." I grab the little clock radio/CD player and flip through our case of bootlegged music. Most of our music is homemade by Layla's ex-boyfriends. The didgeridoo player in India, the yodeler in Thailand, the whistler in Brazil. I'm trying to decide between those last two when I remember the mystery CD. As I rummage through my bag, I call out, "Layla, did you put a CD in my bag at the café today?"

"Nope."

"Well, whoever put it there stole your motto." I read from the case, "Make every day a song."

"My kind of guy."

I pry open our ancient CD player, hoping it will work. Layla bought it at a flea market in Chile, and we've dragged it around six countries since then. It's on its last legs, but we can't afford any new music-playing devices. In Ecuador last year, we vowed to save nearly half of our income for college, investments, retirement, and emergencies—which leaves little money for luxuries. I put in the CD and press play.

The music starts slowly, one delicate guitar note plucked

after another. Behind my eyelids emerges a single star, then another, then another. Each note is pure and bright, each as huge as a sun and as tiny as a snowflake all at once. And then comes a cascade of crystalline notes, and then the chords, deep and wide and resonant. The crescendos send me flying, weaving through galaxies, spinning like planets.

It's only one song, no words, but at the end of it, I realize my eyes have closed and I'm holding my breath. In the silence after the song, I press pause and look at Layla.

She's leaning against the kitchen doorframe, a far-off look in her eyes. "Whoever gave you that must be completely smitten."

"What?"

"That music exudes love. It's made of love. Someone's got it bad for you, Z."

"I don't think so."

Layla looks skeptical.

"I have a boyfriend, Layla, in case you've forgotten. I haven't even looked at another guy." As I say this, I realize I'm not being entirely truthful. There was that unusually handsome accordionist. But everyone was looking at the band, not just me. He'd have no reason to think I noticed him.

"When did you find it?" Layla asks, spinning the pastry roller thoughtfully.

"In Nirvana. But someone could've put it in my bag on the square." I flip the case open and closed, frowning. "I don't think it's an admirer."

"Then who?"

I search for a more logical explanation and, giving up, say with a wry grin, "A *fantôme.*"

"A ghost?" Layla spreads another thin sheet of pastry on the *mille-feuilles* and shoots me a mischievous smile. "Then Monsieur le Fantôme chose the perfect music to reach right into your heart."

THREE

Someone is watching me. I'm sure of it. And I'm guessing it's the *fantôme*. I glance around, then stir four cubes of sugar into my tiny espresso cup with a pinkie-sized spoon and take a baby sip to make it last. That's what French people do—savor small sips of small servings in small cups. Layla's at an English teachers' training today, so I'm on my own at Café Cerise. I've written down my goals for today in my notebook.

1) Find the fantôme.
2) Buy more yogurt in those cute little jars.
3) Make some friends.

Usually after I've spent a week in a country, I've managed to form some friendships. The sooner I make friends, the longer I have with them until Layla and I move on to the next country.

The band Illusion starts playing about five meters away, just under the tree by the edge of the café tables. Their outfits are different today but still blaze red and gold with tiny ornaments glinting the sunlight—old coins, soda-can tops, beads. Their melodies suck me in, like a whirlpool, making my insides spin and dance.

I look around again. I'm not usually paranoid. But now that I think about it, why wouldn't I feel I was being watched? The Place de la Mairie is like one giant stage at the heart of town. Everyone is watching everyone else. In fact, the main occupation here at Café Cerise seems to be watching. And now, most eyes are focused on Illusion.

People in Aix-en-Provence love street performers. Accordionists, drummers, singers, jugglers, harpists—you name it—make their rounds around town, usually lingering here in this square. It's a prime, sunny spot, in front of the café tables that line two sides of the square like theater seating. There's an expanse of space, perfect for performing, just between the fountain and the ancient city hall building and the historic post office. Peering out over each of the arched windows are carved stone faces bursting with expression—jovial, devilish, grumpy, snooty, angelic.

The fountain is the centerpiece; it's circular, with a round column shooting up high, topped with a stone ball. Water spurts out from four sides, and short, wide steps lead up to it, covered with kids and pigeons. The fountains scattered throughout town are why we chose Aix. The fountains and the light. The only thing Wendell has ever told me he saw in our future was this: a place with amazing light and fountains everywhere.

Back in Ecuador, when we mentioned these features to Layla, she said she knew just the place. She unfolded seven crumpled, weather-worn sheets of lined yellow paper that had survived for seventeen years and seventeen moves. Her List—one of her most treasured possessions—records all the places travelers have urged her to visit over the years. She has declared them the coolest places in the world. Whenever she's getting restless and ready to leave a country, she peruses the List to find our new home.

There's not too much logic to where on the List we go next; it's usually some place drastically different from the one we're in. Sacred sites are always a plus for Layla, especially if water rituals are involved. Last year she chose Ecuador after she heard about bathing in the Peguche Waterfall to make wishes come true. When she found out that Aix-en-Provence was built over a network of springs, she was sold. And when she learned it's just an hour from the miraculous cave springs of Lourdes—which we visited the jet-lagged day after we got here—she was in heaven.

Aix-en-Provence is near the top of page one of the List, which means someone must have recommended it a long time ago, before I was born. Next to it, in purple pen, Layla wrote, *fountains, light, art, ruins, underground springs, cafés, music.* And as fate would have it, there were a few summer-abroad art programs here for Wendell to choose from. It was a good choice, but for me, anywhere would have been fine, as long as Wendell was there. I can easily blend into any scene, quickly take stock of how people act, and slip right in, unnoticed.

Which is why I can't stop thinking about why my *fantôme* picked me out of the crowd. I open my notebook, write, *Who gave me the CD? And why?* With questions on a fresh page, my powers of observation sharpen. I take another look around, sure that my *fantôme* must be out there.

There's that mime again, frozen against the tree trunk, eyes closed as though he's asleep or dead. *A mime,* I write. Of course, I would have noticed a mime slipping something into my bag. He's pretty conspicuous.

Above him, just inside a tall, ceiling-to-floor window above Café Cerise, sits an old woman, peering outside. The French doors are open wide behind a twisted wrought-iron railing. The woman lifts something to her eyes. Binoculars? Yes, they must be. They're cream colored and look old-fashioned, like opera glasses. No one but me seems to notice. Then I realize they're pointed in my direction.

I write, *There's a lady in a window with binoculars.* She shifts the angle higher, gazing at something else, beyond me. My eyes dart around to see what she could be looking at. By the fountain, an old man—covered head to toe in pigeons—waves to her, and she waves back. I jot down notes on the binoculars lady and the pigeon man. *Maybe they saw my* fantôme.

My espresso is nearly gone now. I resist sipping the last drops, and instead, nibble on the square of dark chocolate that came on the saucer.

Looking around to signal the waiter for another espresso, I catch a glimpse of the old woman in the window. She's waving again, this time straight at me.

Startled, I wave back.

• • •

As Illusion plays the last notes of their set, the red-haired girl tosses up the hat, does a backflip, and a split second after landing on her feet, belts out, "We. Are. *Illusion!*"

Wiping sweat from their foreheads, the band members pass around a carafe of water. The tuba player is all loose limbs, with a relaxed smile that grows bigger when the gypsy dancer sidles up to him, slips her arms around his waist, and whispers in his ear.

The other girl is busy pirouetting around the square, collecting money in the hat. When she dances up to me, I toss in some coins and shake off my twinge of nervousness. The only way to make friends fast is to jump right in and start talking. "Your band's great," I say.

"Merci." She eyes me carefully, then says, "There's something different about you."

"Different how?"

"You're not quite a local, but you're not quite a tourist, either."

I smile, curious. "How can you tell?"

"You're an insider and outsider all at once. You fit right in, but stay at a distance. A girl of contradictions. Like me."

I laugh. I like her. "I'm Zeeta," I say.

"I'm Amandine," she says, her eyes dancing. "Always nice to meet another traveler our age, isn't it? We stick together, *non?*"

I nod.

She holds the hat as if she's forgotten about collecting money. "How old are you, Zeeta?"

"Sixteen."

"Me too! I just had my birthday last month."

I'm surprised. She looks younger.

"When's your birthday?" she asks.

"March seventeenth. I'm a Pisces."

"Water's your element, then." She does a backflip, not in a show-offy way, but more like it's a restless habit, the way some people might jiggle a knee. And somehow, she doesn't drop a single coin from the hat as she does it. "Air's mine," she announces, then says abruptly, "You think I look young, don't you?"

"A little," I admit.

"Life circumstances have made me old for my age, even though I look like I'm twelve."

"Life circumstances?"

She nods. "The wandering life. Lack of parents."

The accordionist comes over, offers Amandine a swig from the carafe of water.

After sipping, she does another backflip, as effortlessly as if she were scratching her nose. They obviously know each other well, well enough that they don't need words.

The guy's lips are wet with the water. His mouth stays in a sensual pout even as he smiles at me. He runs his hand through his black curls, revealing, for a second, a thick white scar across his forehead. Then the curls fall back into place, just grazing his eyebrows.

"I'd better finish collecting the money," Amandine says, pecking my cheeks and skipping away as people shower coins into her hat. Apparently in Aix, people kiss once on each cheek in greetings and salutations. I've noticed it can take a long time for a large group of people to greet each other here, with all the kissing going on.

I turn to the accordionist. "Where'd you learn to play?"

"My stepfather." He smiles again. "I'm Jean-Claude."

"Zeeta," I say, registering his initials, J.C., out of habit, although of course he's way too young to be my father. Just a couple of years older than me.

"*Enchanté*, Zeeta," he says formally, shaking my hand. Enchanted to meet you. Not pleased. Not glad. Not happy. *Enchanted*. Magic seeps into even the most mundane inter-actions in this language.

"*Enchantée*, Jean-Claude," I say, turning to a fresh page in my notebook. It's a relief to look away from his eyes. They're disconcerting, like two perfect circles of sky.

"I noticed you sitting at the café yesterday," he says.

He noticed me? I wonder if he could be my *fantôme*. I

decide to take him by surprise. "Yesterday, in the square, did you notice someone slip a CD into my bag?"

He cocks his head, amused. "You attract mystery, *non?* Could it have been from an admirer, perhaps?"

I shrug, a little embarrassed. "Just a *fantôme.*"

"Ghosts can be tricky," Jean-Claude says. "They're good at not being seen." He raises an eyebrow. "Where are you from?" he asks, thankfully changing the subject.

"Everywhere and nowhere." One of my standard responses to a standard question.

"So that's why I can't pinpoint your accent."

"It's mostly Moroccan. That's where I learned French. My mom and I lived there a few years back." I'm very conscious not to let my gaze linger on his face. It's disturbingly handsome, especially those eyes that pull you in like blue pools. "How about you?" I ask.

"I too am a wanderer. All of Illusion wanders."

I twirl my pen. "Tell me about Illusion."

"We are each a bit of kindling." His eyes skim over the others in his band as they stand around talking and putting away their instruments. "Our music is our fire."

As I jot down his answer, he doesn't question what I'm doing. Not only does he not question it, he whips out his own notebook from his back pocket, a small spiral one. No one has ever matched my notebook with another notebook.

There's an instant bond between us wanderers, I've noticed. An understanding of how to leap into conversations, to grab hold of the day with passion, to hurl yourself into adventure—because you know that once you move, everything changes. And then you have to do it all over again. Which is why there's also a hint of sadness in wanderers' eyes, the exhaustion of being a cup that's emptied out when you leave a place and filled again in a new place only to be emptied again.

Jean-Claude is scribbling now, his eyes closed. His notebook is so tiny you'd think he could only fit about seven words per page. And how can he follow the lines and keep from running off the page with his eyes closed? I try to peek, but his handwriting is minuscule.

He shuts his notebook, glances up, and smiles. The sun catches a bottle cap sewn onto his sleeve as he waves at someone over my shoulder.

I turn to look. It's the mime. The man breaks his frozen posture to wave back.

"A friend of yours?" I ask.

"*Oui.*" Only he says it "*Ouais,*" like "Yeah," the cool way to say yes. "His name's Tortue."

"Tortue?" Turtle's an odd name. "As in the animal?"

Jean-Claude nods. "Tortue's like a father to me and Amandine."

"She's your sister?"

"Like a sister."

"What about the stepfather you mentioned?"

After a beat, he says, "My parents are part of my old life.

The life I've left behind." He rubs the scar on his forehead, as if trying to erase it. "And your family?"

"Just me and my mother. Layla. We're more like sisters. The kind of sisters who fight a lot," I add with a cynical grin. "You probably noticed her—the blond one?"

He nods. "I thought you two were friends." He squints at me. "How old are you?"

"Sixteen. And you?"

"Nineteen."

"Don't you miss your home?" I ask. "And your parents?"

"Not at all. It's *liberté absolue*. Ultimate freedom."

His name rings through the noise of the square. "Jean-Claude! *On y va!*" It's the gypsy dancer girl, calling to him.

Jean-Claude blows out an *"Ouf!"* through his pursed lips, then kisses both of my cheeks. Even though that's how everyone here says hello and goodbye, my face burns.

"There will be a *fête* Friday night, Zeeta. For the summer solstice." He scribbles an address on the inside cover of a small, old book. Looking back up, he runs his hand through his dark curls, once again revealing the scar, the only flaw on his otherwise perfect face. When I know him better, I'll ask him about it. Stories about scars are always good notebook material. People can pick and choose their memories, but they're stuck forever with the ones linked to their scars. The reminder's there every time they look in the mirror, or take a shower, or rub their hand absently over their skin.

I trace the tiny, nearly invisible scar on the back of my hand. In Guatemala, I was spending the weekend with

Paloma's family in her grandparents' village, and as we were cutting firewood in the forest, my machete bounced off a stone and slashed my hand. When I showed my bleeding hand to Paloma's father, he tore off his T-shirt and wrapped it tightly around my wound. It didn't hurt too much. Despite its depth, it was a clean slice. He carried me three kilometers through the woods back to their pickup truck.

Strangely, it was a good memory, him carrying me, worrying about me, murmuring to me that it would be all right. I glimpsed what it would be like to have a father, his smell of sweat and soil and pine wrapping around me, the warmth of his chest under my cheek. He stayed with me at the hospital as the doctor cleaned the wound and stitched it up. She told him, "Señor, your daughter will be fine, but she will probably have a small scar." He didn't correct the doctor, simply nodded and held my good hand, and I closed my eyes, not in pain, but bliss.

I try to study Jean-Claude's scar more, but hair is hiding it. He presses the book in my hand. "*Viens*, Zeeta. Come to the *fête. S'il te plaît.*" Please.

I look at his scrawl. After the street address, he's noted that it's beneath Café Eternité. In a *cave*. Before I realize that *cave* means "basement," I think of a real cave, imagining the cave Wendell and I were in last summer.

And then I remember Wendell. I'm supposed to be an expert at fitting him into any conversation. I push this fact from my mind and focus on the address in my hands. "*Merci,*" I say, not committing to anything yet.

"Return the book at the *fête!*" Jean-Claude calls over his shoulder, then follows his friends out of the square.

I watch Illusion leave, a mass of glittering red, growing smaller and smaller and disappearing down the street. I check *Make some friends* off my list. Now all that's left are the cute little jars of yogurt and finding the *fantôme*.

FOUR

A few hours later, after a quick trip to the *boulangerie* for a baguette and the *charcuterie* for chicken, I swing by Nirvana. Ahmed is dabbing his forehead with a handkerchief, gazing longingly at turquoise posters of seascapes taped to the walls, the only splashes of color in the room. They're the kind of posters you might find free at a travel agency—Mediterranean ports with painted fishing boats, whitewashed domed chapels on hills, colorful houses built into cliffs over the sea.

"This heat is *insupportable!*" he says in greeting.

"Why don't you take a day off, Ahmed? Go to the beach? It's only an hour away."

"Oh, too much work."

I look around. "I'm the only one in here."

He grins. "Exactly. It's hard work keeping you in constant communication with the love of your life." He looks back at his screen. "Anyway, that young, crazy part of my life is over."

I laugh, trying to envision Ahmed as young and crazy, then settle down at my computer and open my e-mail.

Wendell's sent me another photo. He must have sent it during the pool party. The photo is artistic, even though it was taken on his phone—a red rose blooming in the foreground with a blurred pool scene in the background—wet skin and bikinis and sparkling hair and hot dogs and shiny cans of soda and a green lawn. He's written a few lines. *Sorry about the change of plans, Z. I love you. I can't wait to see you. Love, Wendell.*

Nice rose, I write. I'm at a loss for what to write next. *So,* I begin. *How long's your hair now?*

I've wondered this recently. If hair grows at the rate of a centimeter a month, Wendell's should be nine centimeters longer now, practically down to the middle of his back. He wears it in a braid, like the men of the Ecuadorian Andes, where he was born. Of course he's sent pictures of himself over the past year, but never a backview with the braid. It's these little things I'm curious about, these small surprises.

Do you still use that cinnamon soap? Do you still go through a tin of Altoids a week?

This is shaping up to be the world's most boring e-mail. I take a deep breath and write about what I really want to know, what I'm circling around. *Someone dropped a CD of guitar music into my bag. It's weird. I wish you were here already to talk about it. Have you*—I hesitate, let my fingers rest on the keyboard, imagining his reaction to what I'm about to write. He'll sigh, close his eyes, shake his head. And he won't answer my question. I write it anyway. —*had any visions of a mysterious CD?*

He doesn't like when I ask him to tell the future. Call it what you will—fortune-telling, divination, prophecy. For years this power scared him, but last summer he found a teacher in Ecuador who showed him how to use it. And for a year Wendell's been practicing. Some people would find this thrilling, but he insists it's more a curse than a gift. He's promised he'd warn me if he ever saw Layla or me in physical danger. But in relationships, he refuses to let his visions get involved. They're more likely to screw things up, he says. I can't help but wonder if he saw something in a vision that made him freak out and decide not to live with me and Layla.

Biting my lip, I add, *Or visions of anything else this summer?*

• • •

At home, Layla's at the table making mobiles out of bits of glass and pebbles and old metallic chocolate wrappers. My *fantôme*'s guitar music is blasting so loud, Layla doesn't even hear me come in. "Layla!" I shout.

"Z!" She looks up and turns down the music. "Did you find out who your admirer is?"

"If you mean the *fantôme,* then no."

She twists a piece of wire with her pliers. "Hey, you know what this music reminds me of?"

"No idea."

I'm expecting her to quote Rumi, or recount a weird dream, but instead she says, "The music your father played me that night on the beach."

I blink. "Does the music jog your memory, Layla? Help you remember anything else? Like his name? What J.C. stands for?"

She snips a strand of wire with scissors and twists it around a pink pebble. "Mundane details like names didn't seem to matter that night . . . with that music and the ocean. Remember, I was drunk on the moon's reflection."

"Right," I sigh. "The moonlight-induced altered state of consciousness. I forgot."

In Morocco and Chile and Laos, I was sure I'd run into my father any day on the street. I assumed he'd track me down and we'd all three live happily ever after. When I got older, I eventually accepted that it wouldn't happen. Last summer's search with Wendell gave me a renewed glimmer of hope. But at least Wendell knew the geographical region where he'd find his parents. My father, on the other hand, could be anywhere in the world, one of billions of men. So I've put the idea of a father into a coffin. Buried him. Mourned for him. Gone through all the stages of grief—denial, anger, bargaining, depression—and accepted that it's just me and Layla, forging our way in this world.

The few times I've brought up my father with Wendell, he says that what matters most is the people—in my case, person—who raised you and loved you . . . the ones you want when you're scared or hurt or sad. It's been a big role for Layla to fill, and she's done the best she can, considering her flightiness. And I try, with my notebooks, with my friendships, to fill in all the gaps.

The CD ends and Layla pauses in her wire-twisting to press play. Again the music starts, and she smiles, as though she's settling into a hot bath or biting into a steaming baguette. "You know what this music does, love? It opens the window in the center of your chest and lets the spirits fly in and out."

"Tell Rumi my window's stuck shut."

"Oh, Z. That's impossible."

"Better yet, tell him the window's not really there. It's painted on, like those trompe l'oeils." I saw one on a building earlier today at the edge of *le centre-ville*—downtown. From a distance the painting looks like a real window, but once you get close, you see it's a mural, tricking your eyes into thinking there's depth.

Layla holds her mobile to the window. "Ta-dah!" she announces. The light catches the foil and glass, bits of trash transformed into art. It makes me think of the glittering costumes of my new friends, Illusion. Of my invitation to the *cave* party. Of the poetry book in my bag. And of the boy who gave it to me, who knows nothing of Wendell.

• • •

After a late dinner of spinach quiche, I climb up the tiny staircase to a glass door that opens to a little rooftop patio. It's dusk and the air smells like cinnamon and cumin, wafting up from the Moroccan restaurant down the street. Yellow lights flicker on one by one in the windows below. I open Jean-Claude's book. It's French poetry by Luca, who I've never heard of. I flip to a page marked with a gold string.

> I transparent you
> You half-darkness me
> You translucent me
> You empty castle me
> And labyrinth me

It doesn't make sense. Parts of speech are jumbled, with nouns and adjectives where verbs should be. I read the verse three times, at first wondering if my French is rustier than I thought. Finally, I begin to suspect that the words are supposed to confuse you, catch you off guard, make you *feel* the poetry more than think about it.

Each poem lasts for pages, nonsensical language that leaps over rules of grammar and flouts standard parts of speech. But the words give me a sense of something mysterious. A sense that life is a dream we drift through, no past, no memories. I read more and more and sink into this feeling as dusk turns into night and I can no longer see the words.

From inside, I hear snatches of starry guitar music. The

notes drift through the open windows, melt into the night. My *fantôme*'s gift makes no sense either, but like the poetry, it gives me the feeling that I'm walking a dimly lit path at night, and before me is an empty castle, waiting to be explored.

I think back to Jean-Claude's answer about the CD. *You attract mystery. . . .* Now that I think about it, he didn't deny putting the CD in my bag. Maybe he is my *fantôme*.

• • •

Routines are essential to surviving in a new country each year. In Phuket, there were sunset volleyball games on the beach. In Marrakech, nightly drumming and dancing in the square. Here in Aix, there are my daily, tiny, sugary espressos at Café Cerise in the Place de la Mairie. Today, over my espresso, I'm reading more of the poetry book Jean-Claude lent me. I find myself glancing up from time to time, looking for Illusion.

Instead of Illusion, I catch a glimpse of Layla heading my way. She's absorbed in conversation with a woman carrying a stringed wooden instrument unlike any I've seen before. It looks like a small harp, adorned with intricate carvings of Celtic knots. The woman is wearing a long tunic of red cloth, obviously hand-dyed and sewn with coarse, uneven stitches. Leather strings attached to homemade sandals climb her ankles like vines. A brass snake winds around her upper arm. From a cord at her neck hangs a brass pendant of three interconnected spirals.

In a city where nearly every woman is ultrachic, straight out of *Vogue*, dressed all in white or black or pale yellow or gray, Layla *would* find the one who treats life as a costume party.

She announces, "This is Sirona!"

"*Enchantée*," I say. "I'm Zeeta."

"*Enchantée.*" Her hand feels solid, with callouses at the fingertips. I have no idea how old she is. One moment she looks thirty, younger than Layla, the next she looks old enough to be Layla's mom. Tiny laugh lines fan out from the corners of her eyes. I can tell right away she's one of those people who always seems to be smiling.

Layla kisses my cheek and plops down. "Hello, love!" She turns to the woman. "Sit, sit, Sirona!" She waves her arm at the waiter, who rushes over. Layla has that effect on men. It took him ten whole minutes to notice me. This is why, with Layla around, it's hard to determine whether my *fantôme* could be out there—because a half dozen men's eyes are glued to our table. And she does look especially stunning today in a dress of raw pink silk from Thailand and a wreath of daisies on her head.

Layla beams at the woman in the odd tunic and says, "Sirona plays the lyre!"

"*Hyper cool,*" I say. It doesn't take Layla long to sniff out the fringe elements in a new place. The only thing missing now is a clown boyfriend. Of the dozens, possibly hundreds, of boyfriends she's been through, most have been travelers like us—bards, gyspies, troubadours—mostly penniless, usually musicians, artists, clowns, or some combination thereof. Layla's a clown magnet. Someday I'd like to know how many clowns there are in the world, because chances are, Layla's had flings with the majority.

She drapes her arm over Sirona's shoulder. "And Sirona's named after a goddess of the hot springs in southern France!"

No wonder they've become instant friends. Layla has some kind of sacred water goddess radar that beeps in her head when she encounters a like-minded soul.

"Sirona knows everything about the history of this place." Layla's flushed pink with the elation that comes with making a new best friend in a new country. "Tell her, Sirona!"

"*Eh bien,*" Sirona begins. Her voice is low and calm, soothing to the ear. "Aix. It's a sort of nickname for Aquae Sextius. Sextius was a Roman general." She shudders. "Terrible man. Until him, a couple thousand years ago, the Celtic tribes in this area were holding their own against the Greeks and Romans. But he sweeps in and sets up an army camp and claims these springs are his. The Celts were fantastic warriors, but Sextius defeated us, the little worm."

"You're Celtic?" I ask, glancing up from my notebook, where I'm scribbling notes.

"My ancestors were the Salluvii—a Celtic Ligurian tribe that lived around here. Sextius and his warriors slaughtered our men. To escape slavery, the women killed their children, and then, themselves." She winces and lowers her gaze to the lyre in her lap. "A horrible, sad, bloody time."

"Then how are you here?" I ask.

Sirona looks at me, puzzled. "What?"

"I mean, how can you be a descendent if all the women and children died?"

"You're sharp." Her fingers glide over her bracelets, making a clinking sound. "A few of the Salluvii survived, hidden, preserving the ancient traditions of our people." She plucks a few strings of her lyre. "*Alors,* a few centuries later, the Christians conquered the Romans. Over the centuries, people added new neighborhoods, new architecture, new art, layer after layer of civilization."

I click my pen against the table. The city must feel tired, always reinventing itself, piling on new identities. "So what's the thing that makes Aix, Aix?" I ask. "Has anything stayed the same over the millennia?"

Sirona doesn't hesitate. "The springs. They are its essence, its soul, its timeless core. "People's ideas about the waters have changed over time, of course." She shakes her head. "These waters have survived a lot."

"Like what?" I ask, my pen poised.

"*Ouf!* People were always fighting over the springs, trying to own them, making stupid rules. Those Romans built their fancy bathhouses two thousand years ago." She makes a face. She obviously doesn't think highly of Romans, as though they were bullies from elementary school she still resents. "And then," she says, "when the Christians came along, they claimed the waters were the site of pagan rituals—'diabolical activities,' they said—and forbade the use of them." She rolls her eyes. "And later on, during the prudish phase, the rulers decided that the waters encouraged debauchery, so they forbade women to use them. And when there were plagues and diseases, everyone blamed the waters." She shakes her head.

Layla says, "Sounds like a dark time."

"It was," Sirona says, sighing. "It was. Luckily, there are those of us who've loved the waters through the years, *non?* We see past the fountains and wells and bathhouses and baptismal pools. We know that deep underneath all those layers is what truly counts. The source." She sweeps her hand over the square, stopping at the huge fountain, where the pigeon man is standing amid a mass of feathers swirling and wings flapping.

"Here comes my family!" Sirona announces as a woman and two men arrive, toting a collection of odd instruments and wearing hand-dyed tunics and rough-hewn leather sandals like Sirona's. "We're also a band. We're called Salluvii."

"After your ancestors' tribe?" I ask.

She smiles. "You pay attention, don't you?" She introduces the man with the silver-flecked beard as Grannos, and the younger one, her son, Bormanus. His girlfriend is Damona, whose brass bracelet snakes up her arm like Sirona's, and blond hair encircles her head in a braided rope.

They say *"Enchanté"* and *"How do you like France?"* and the basic pleasantries, and then go off to start playing. Sirona picks out a few notes on her lyre; then Damona starts blowing on a long, oval instrument, curved like a mountain sheep's horn, with a bar across it that rests on her shoulder. Next, Grannos comes in with a bone flute, and finally, Bormanus with an instrument that looks like a long trumpet.

In the next song, Sirona and Damona shake tiny bird-shaped clay bells as the men play. The ancient melodies sound almost eerie, entirely unlike anything I've heard before. It's an unexpected combination of sounds, almost jarring. It's not until I've heard a few songs that I begin to understand the rhythms, the patterns of notes. The band is obviously well practiced, with each person coming in at just the right time, without even any eye contact, as though they've been playing together forever.

• • •

While Salluvii is in their second set, Layla leans across the table. "Hey, Z, you think your *fantôme* is out there some-where?"

I shrug. "No sign of him."

She tucks a strand of hair behind her ear. "He has phe-nomenal taste in music. I wouldn't mind a few more albums of that instrumental guitar."

My eyes skim over the square, searching for *fantôme* sus-pects. My gaze lands on the old woman in the window above Café Cerise. Her binoculars are aimed at me. She raises her hand in greeting, as if we're old friends now. If she were in the square, I'd definitely ask her whether she's seen my *fantôme* and interview her for my notebook. But she's always up in that window. She's a spectator of life rather than another actor onstage like the rest of us. I simply raise a hand, mirroring her greeting.

My gaze continues to sweep across the square. There's a group of grinning German tourists, the mime frozen and leaning against the tree, a bunch of children playing tag, a violinist performing classical music, and finally, the pigeon man. My gaze rests on this eccentric old man, another fixture in the square who might impart valuable information. *If I can barrel my way through the horde of pigeons to reach him.* Somehow he notices me through the chaos of birds around him and waves.

I wave back and write down, *Plan to find my fantôme—ask the binoculars lady and the pigeon man if they've seen anything.*

I consider asking the mime, too, but I doubt he'd be helpful. He seems lost in his own silent, still world. He's just a few meters from our table, so I can clearly see his eyes, the only part of his body that's moving. When his gaze lands on mine, I smile. His eyes dart away and fix on a point in the distance.

I move my head toward Layla's and whisper, "You must be turning over a new leaf, Layla. It's the second time we've seen the mime and you haven't seduced him yet."

I shouldn't have said anything. Layla flashes a devilish smile in the mime's direction.

"Layla!" I roll my eyes. "I was kidding! Can we please get through one country without a clown? Please?"

She winks at him, trying to get some response.

The mime stays still as a statue. Now even his eyes are unmoving. He doesn't seem to be breathing.

Layla murmurs, "Don't worry, love. Not my type of clown. No spontaneity. No playfulness."

We listen to a few more songs, and when I look up again, the mime has disappeared.

"Nice work, Layla," I say, grinning. "You scared him off. And I was going to ask him about my *fantôme*."

She sighs. "You don't give my clowns enough credit, Z. There's more to clowns than meets the eye. They're psychologically complex. All over the world, they're mixed in with the sacred. Nonsense is one road to wisdom, you know. There's the Sufi concept of the wandering wise fool, intoxicated by the ecstasy of the Absolute . . ."

I've heard all this before, every time she brings home a new clown. I interrupt. "I'm going to interview the pigeon man now, Layla. See if he knows anything about my *fantôme*." But when I look again toward the fountain, the old man is gone. Only a flock of pigeons remain, pecking at birdseed he must have left for them on the ground.

FIVE

"Wendell!" I say suddenly.

"What about him?" Layla asks, sipping her third espresso.

"I haven't e-mailed him yet today!" Usually, it's one of the first things I do in the morning. And now the sun's overhead, which means it's already noon. Layla and I must have been idling here at the café for a couple of hours now. I have no excuse for forgetting about my boyfriend. I drop some coins by my empty espresso cup, say goodbye to Layla, and hurry toward Nirvana.

As I enter the dim room, the bells jingling, Ahmed glances up from the computer. "Oh, I'm glad you're all right, Zeta." He sips his sweating can of Coke with a bendy straw. "You're normally here much earlier. What will the love of your life think?"

I give a friendly shrug, then settle into my chair, which reeks of old cigarette smoke. Three e-mails from Wendell. I skim them. He's obviously trying to smooth things over, keeping his responses to my questions light and sweet. His hair is four to four and a half inches longer, depending which side you measure, due to a crooked trim at Econo-Hair. He's cut back to a half-tin of Altoids per week, down from a full tin during final exams.

And then, to my amazement, in the third e-mail, he tells me about a vision. Maybe as a peace offering. I slow down and read more carefully.

> I haven't seen any CDs, Z. Just a vision
> that makes no sense. It's dark and we're
> both soaking wet, like we've been
> swimming. But it's weird because we're in
> our clothes. And I'm not completely sure
> it's you, since it's so dark, and the
> dress you're wearing isn't your style.

I send him a short reply. *Well, let's hope the girl's me.* ☺ I stick a smiley face in so he won't think I'm jealous or mad. Then I write, *And by the way, my style changes from country to country. You've only known the Ecuador Zeeta.* ☺ After I reread it, I toss in another smiley face for good measure. I end with, *Can't wait for you to come!!! Love you!!!* with an excess of exclamation points to drive home the point that I'm not holding a grudge.

Next I answer a dozen other e-mails, IM for a while with an old friend in Brazil, e-mail some little girlfriends in Ecuador, then Google Illusion. They have a pretty basic Web site, just photos and tour dates and a blog that hasn't been updated for three months. I sign up for their newsletter, then plug in earphones and listen to a few songs.

Suddenly, I realize I have nothing to wear to the party tonight. Nothing dazzling, that is. Illusion's sparkling outfits make my own clothes—mostly from markets in Ecuador and Thailand—seem dull and rustic.

I log out, jump up to pay Ahmed, and dash next door to the secondhand shop. It's musty and dark inside, with low French reggae playing. I shuffle through the racks, not sure what I'm looking for, until my hands rest on a soft red dress, an airy blend of cotton and silk. It looks about my size, although I'm not sure how sizes work in France yet. When I try it on behind a thick velvet curtain, it fits me perfectly, close enough that it skims my curves, loose enough that it won't suffocate me in this heat. It's held up by slim spaghetti straps, and seems to float around my body. It stops midthigh, which is shorter than most of my dresses, but it's liberating to have my knees uncovered.

It's not until I'm standing in front of the mirror that I remember Wendell's wet dress vision.

Not your style.

Whatever my style is at this moment, this dress seems to fit it. The French Zeeta. *La Zeeta Française.* I press the fabric to my face. It smells like roses, maybe the perfume of whoever owned it before me.

At the cash register, my stomach tightens, as it always does when I make a rare frivolous purchase. Our checking account has been nearly wiped out after the deposit on our apartment and a week's worth of groceries. And Layla's first paycheck will go to next month's rent. I'll have to start tutoring right away. Last year, I made Layla swear that we'd put away money for savings, and now I'm the one breaking the promise.

I take a deep breath and lay fifteen euros on the table, our food budget for the day.

Outside, I lean against a wall and make a few quick signs in my notebook. *ENGLISH TUTORING by a Fluent Speaker with Six Years of Tutoring Experience.* I tear out the pages, tuck the flyers beneath my arm, and head toward the university to hang up the first batch.

When I'm inside the university's main foyer, by the bulletin board, I reach into my bag to pull out the flyers. My fingers graze something small and smooth and cylindrical. A little jar of lip gloss or face cream? I don't remember putting anything like that in my bag. I pull it out, curious.

It's a small jar that fits perfectly into my palm, made of clear glass, worn and scratched. Sand is inside. And on a white sticker label is written, *That night meant the world to me.* It's the same compact scrawl as the writing on the CD.

I glance around, scanning the faces of tourists and locals streaming by. Nothing unusual. No one paying any attention to me. Someone must have put this in my bag while I was on the square. It was crowded enough that it could have been done inconspicuously. I review where I've been. It couldn't have happened in Nirvana—that place was empty except for me and Ahmed. Maybe at the secondhand shop while I was looking at dresses. But it wasn't crowded in there. I would have noticed.

As I walk home, turning the possibilities over in my mind, I suddenly stop in my tracks. *That night meant the world to me.*

The *fantôme* must already know me.

• • •

"Look, Layla," I say, pulling out the jar of sand and setting it on the café table. "My *fantôme* slipped this in my bag." I rest my bag on an empty chair, tempting him to leave something else but keeping a close eye on it, in hopes of catching him in the act.

Layla shields her eyes from the glaring sunlight and reads the note, then gazes at the jar in her palm. "Undeniably romantic!" she announces. "I told you he was smitten, Z. Any ideas who it is yet?"

"Well, it's obviously someone I've met before. And spent time with." I pause, contemplating the grains of sand. "Or the *fantôme* could be mistaking me for someone else."

"True," Layla admits, twirling her finger around a lock of hair. "But what if it really is someone from your past, Zeeta?"

I make a face and say, "I haven't exactly had many unforgettably romantic nights, Layla." Then, flushing slightly, I add, "Except with Wendell."

Layla's eyes twinkle. "The universe will reveal its secrets with time, love. In the meantime, enjoy the mystery!"

I keep staring at the sand, as if it holds answers. "The sand must be a clue. Maybe it's from one of the beaches we've lived near."

"Thailand?" Layla says, lighting up. "Oh, wait! There was that cute French boy you met in Brazil. What was his name?"

"Olivier." His name gives me a little jab of pain. My first fling. He was on vacation in Brazil, where Layla and I lived three countries ago. Olivier and I surfed together, took some hand-in-sweaty-hand walks on the beach at night. But then he went back to France and after a few months stopped answering my e-mails. "He was the one who ended things with me," I remind Layla. "It can't be him."

"Oh, but maybe that's why he isn't showing himself. He's ashamed. Regretful! Karma has brought you together again. Now he can find redemption."

I shake my head, remembering how Olivier broke my heart, how I lay on the beach for hours on end blasting our music in earphones and crying. Of course, I always imagined he had some reasonable excuse for not e-mailing: A virus infected his computer and erased my e-mail address. His house burned down and his family was barely surviving on the streets. And the best, he was murdered.

"I don't know, Layla," I say. It's way too messy to think about Wendell and Olivier being here in the same town. I look over her shoulder, toward the fountain, where the pigeon man has reappeared and is scattering more birdseed. "Listen, I'm going to ask that old guy with the pigeons if he's seen my *fantôme*."

Layla kisses each cheek, adopting the Provençal style. "*Bon courage,* Z!"

I grab my bag and hand her a bunch of flyers. "Can you hang some of these up?"

"With joy," she says, tucking them under her arm. I hear her voice calling after me, "Make your day a song!"

• • •

Holding the jar of sand, I walk across the expanse of stones, toward the flock of pigeons. This man looks like a pigeon himself, dressed in shades of silver. Around his neck a green-purple iridescent scarf mimics the colors of a pigeon's neck. He walks like a pigeon, wobbling along, jutting his head forward. Even his potbelly echoes the roundness of a pigeon's midsection.

The main difference between him and the pigeons—apart from belonging to different species—is his gray beret. He's the only person I've seen in this supposedly beret-adorned country actually wearing a beret. He climbs onto the edge of the fountain and, standing there, reaches out a tin cup, fills it with water, then takes a long sip. He even drinks from the fountain like a pigeon. It's strange to see him perched up there, the blue sky behind him, a mysterious smile in his eyes, the breeze carrying a few stray feathers from his shirt. The children around him are chasing the pigeons as they hop and flutter a few feet away. The man seems amused and hands the kids some birdseed to toss. Catching my eye, he waves to me, then climbs slowly down.

I walk up the low steps. Up close, his face looks jaunty. His pink-tipped nose and rosy cheeks make me think of Santa Claus minus the beard. Water drips from the points of his white mustache.

I sit down beside him and open my notebook. "*Bonjour, monsieur.* I'm Zeeta."

His cheeks form little balls when he smiles. "I'm Vincent."

"*Enchantée,*" I say. "I like your pigeons."

"*Merci, mademoiselle.*" He looks pleased. "If only everyone felt the same way as you." He clucks. "The city put those pins on the stone heads over the doors so my dear pigeons can't rest there." He leans forward conspiratorially. "But I think those old heads look better with a bit of pigeon *merde* on them, don't you?" He gives a hearty laugh.

I smile appreciatively, then get to the point. "You saw me earlier today at that café table, didn't you?"

Vincent squints at the table, smiles, and says, "You're observant, *mademoiselle.*"

I pass him the jar of sand. "*Monsieur,* did you see someone slip this into my bag?"

He weighs it in his hand, studying the grains, as if their texture and color might hold some clue.

"I think the same person slipped a CD into my bag a few days ago," I add.

He hands back the jar and raises a bushy white eyebrow. "Ah. A mystery. How I love a good mystery." He chuckles. "But no, *mademoiselle*, I cannot offer you any clues to your mystery. Tell me, do you have any suspects?"

I stash the jar back into my bag. "Maybe this boy I knew in Brazil."

"And he followed you here? Is this *le grand amour*?"

"No!" I say. "It was definitely *not* true love. Just a silly fling. Anyway, I have a boyfriend now." I skim my fingertips over the water, watch a few feathers float and sink and rise again in the rushing water. Just calling Wendell a boyfriend makes him seem so temporary, as if he could easily go the way of Olivier. But *l'homme de ma vie*, as Ahmed would say, sounds way too dramatic. I snatch my hand from the water, pull out my notebook and pen, and impulsively say, "Vincent, tell me about the love of your life."

"The love of my life!" He laughs, a big, belly laugh, looking at the pigeon on his shoulder as though he expects it to laugh, too, as though they share an inside joke. *"Eh bien, dis donc!* Why do you ask?"

"So I can remember you after I leave here in a year." I pause, then add, "Plus, I'm curious." Then I admit, "And maybe a little confused."

Vincent laughs again. Another real laugh, a genuine bubbling of joy from deep inside. He takes his time laughing, a full thirty seconds, until the laugh runs its course.

"And how, may I ask, did you choose me, *mademoiselle*? Do I have true love written all over my face?"

I study his face. He has something written on it. Playfulness. Liveliness. Jolliness. But something deeper, something secret, something he's holding back. "I noticed you and your pigeons. And you seem like a person who knows a thing or two."

Vincent rubs his chin. "I like you, *mademoiselle. Alors* . . . the love of my life." He reaches down and picks up a pigeon, white with gray spots on its wingtips and tail, and a band of green-purple iridescence around its neck. A tiny clear vial is tied to one of its spindly, salmon-pink legs. "Maude," he says, gazing at the pigeon.

"Maude?"

"My true love."

"Is Maude your . . . wife?" I venture.

He gives another deep belly laugh that shakes his whole body. "In France there exist many kinds of amorous unions, but never have I heard of a man marrying a pigeon." He whispers to the pigeon. *"Ma Maude, ma petite Maude."*

It takes a moment for this to register. "This pigeon is Maude? And she's the love of your life?"

He's smiling now, a wistful smile. "Maude's been living with me for, oh, fifty years now. Since just after my wife died." He looks at me merrily. "My human wife," he says. "She died in childbirth a year after our marriage."

"I'm sorry," I say.

"Oh, it was so long ago," he says. "I was twenty. She was beautiful. Hair black as yours. Skin like yours too. She was from the Canary Islands. Maybe she could have been the love of my life, but she was gone before I could find out. I started getting to know the pigeons, feeding them birdseed." His voice turns serious. "Birdseed is better than croissant or baguette crumbs. More fiber. Produces nice piles of *merde* that wash away easily. The street cleaners appreciate it. Now, croissants and baguettes, they make hard balls of *merde*, little sticky green things that won't come up." He holds out a handful of birdseed for me to inspect.

I nod politely and jot down, *Birdseed—good pigeon* merde. "*Alors, monsieur,* how did you know that . . . Maude . . . is the love of your life?"

"She was there for me when I needed her. She stuck with me. I let her fly, but she always came back, roosted in my alcove. I need her. She needs me. We understand each other. She makes me feel like myself. And I know she'll be with me forever, until death do us part."

"You never get tired of her? Wish for another pigeon?"

"*Ouf!* The new generations of pigeons are a dime a dozen. I like the ones who've been with me a long time. These little ones"—he points a finger at each one—"Yves, Irène, Marie— they're nice, but not like Maude. There's just something comforting about Maude, how she looks at me. All the things she knows about me."

"What's that vial on her leg for?"

"Ah! It holds messages. She's a homing pigeon, you see." He turns to Maude, stroking her feathers. "You work for your birdseed, don't you, *mon amour*?"

I survey the mass of birds, pecking and waddling. "How can you tell them apart?"

"*Eh bien, dis donc!* How can you tell me apart from your mother? Why, they look completely different! Different colors and patterns and beak size and feather shape and, oh, just that magical thing, that soul thing that makes each creature special. And with Maude, why, I could recognize her even if I were blind. Look! She only has three toes on her left foot! And the way she wobbles on her three toes touches me right here." He puts his hand on his chest.

He really, truly loves this pigeon. It's touching. I scribble all this in my notebook.

"And you, *mademoiselle*, what brings you here?"

"We live in a new country every year, my mom and me. This year's France."

"Where were you last year?"

"The Andes of Ecuador."

"*Ah bon?*" Vincent looks excited. "Did you see the Peguche Waterfall?"

I'm surprised he's heard of it. "As a matter of fact, Layla and I bathed in it with rose petals. To make our wishes come true." I leave out the parts about its being a near-death experience. "Have you been there?"

"*Mon Dieu! Non, non, non!* I've never left France. My son, now, he's sailed around the world, lived all over the place. He just came to town a few days ago to make sure I'm still breathing!" He winks. "But back to the waters. You could say that sacred waters are a bit of a . . . hobby for me." He leans in, eager. "Now tell me, *mademoiselle,* did the waters of Peguche work?"

"Well. Sort of."

"Tell me! Every detail!"

I describe how you walk down a forest path to reach the waterfall, how icy cold and tumultuous the water is, how sparkling it looks in the early-morning sun.

Vincent is a sponge, soaking it all up, wide-eyed. Once I've finished, he says, "So, *mademoiselle,* you believe in the powers of sacred waters, *non?*"

I shrug. "I've been dragged to sacred waters all over the world. My mom's a water-ritual junkie."

A radiant smile spreads across Vincent's face. He strokes Maude's neck feathers. She makes a warbly purr. Finally he says, carefully, "You are the kind of girl who could uncover secrets. Uncover them yet keep them hidden. Aren't you?"

I try to think of secrets I've uncovered yet kept secret. Nothing immediately comes to mind, but I say, "Sure."

"And you are also the kind of girl who notices things, unusual things."

"That's true," I say. I do have a suitcase full of notebooks to show for it. "I noticed you, *monsieur*. I noticed the lady with the binoculars."

With a chuckle, he glances at the window and waves. I can't tell if she waves back. "The exquisite Madame Chevalier. The famous artist. She was my playmate as a child."

"You think she might have seen someone slip mysterious gifts into my bag?"

"Quite possible. I'll ask her and get back to you."

Before I can ask more, he whispers, "You know the woman who plays the harp in that Celtic band, Salluvii?"

"It's a lyre, actually. And her name's Sirona. Why?"

"Well, here's one more thing for you to notice. That woman and her band. Study them. Write about them in that notebook of yours. Remember them."

"Why?"

He moves his head close to mine, lowers his voice. "Because, *mademoiselle*, they have a secret deeper and older than you could possibly imagine." He looks at me, rubbing his chin, as if musing about something.

I wait another moment, to see if he'll explain, then I say, "Well, I'd better hang up the rest of these posters."

He glances at them. "You teach English?"

I nod. "Six years of experience. No certificate, but I've picked up lots from my mother."

"I will hire you."

"Really?"

"I own an antiques shop. One must be able to converse with tourists." He sighs. "Of course, my son speaks English, and many other languages, but he has no patience to teach me!"

"Well. All right."

"Come to my antiques shop by the fountain on the Place des Trois Ormeaux. How's tomorrow afternoon?"

"Parfait."

He presents me with a silver pigeon feather, and then turns back to Maude, the alleged love of his life.

Six

"So what's this *fête* you're going to tonight?" Layla asks, adjusting her flower crown. She's already dressed for her own party, wrapped in flowing yards of white cotton, with sparkles over every bit of bare skin. It looks as if she got tangled up inside a fabric store and fell into a vat of glitter. We're headed to Nirvana for a quick stop before going to our separate solstice parties.

"That group Illusion invited me," I say. "It's in a *cave*."

"Hyper cool!"

I nod. "I think I might become friends with that acrobat girl, Amandine." I don't mention Jean-Claude, or clarify that he was the one who invited me. I don't mention his poetry book that makes me think of pathways to castles, either.

"Well, you look magnificent, Z!" Layla eyes my red dress. "It's good to change your style once in a while. Experiment."

I force myself to stop tugging at the dress. When I changed into it this afternoon, it suddenly seemed too short, too red, too low-cut. And my old leather sandals from Ecuador look as though someone chewed them up and spit them out. "Here's the place," I say, glad we're cutting the conversation short. I jangle open the door. "Nirvana."

We duck inside the dark, stale-smoke-laced room. I wave to Ahmed. *"Essalam alikoum."*

Ahmed gapes at Layla. Not an unusual reaction to my mother, although I didn't think anything could make Ahmed abandon his online gaming. But my mother does look striking now, all dressed up in her goddess garb. Beautiful and ridiculous at once.

"Layla, Ahmed; Ahmed, Layla," I say quickly, and add, "Layla's my mom."

Forcing his mouth closed, he nods.

"Enchantée, Ahmed," Layla says, offering a glittery hand around his computer monitor.

"En-enchanté," he stutters, looking as though he doesn't want to let go of her hand, as though he's completely forgotten the existence of KnightQuest. Truly enchanted.

"So, do we just grab any computer?" she asks.

He comes to himself. "Ah, yes, *allez-y, madame.*" "Come As You Are" is playing softly on his little speakers. "Zeeta, your computer's open." He nods with his chin, but his eyes haven't left Layla.

"Actually, I'm just making a quick phone call," I say.

"To the love of your life?" he asks, already punching in the number he keeps on a sticky note by the phone. His eyes follow Layla as she floats across the room to a computer in the corner.

"Yup."

"Fantastic chairs!" Layla calls out, swiveling like a kid. *"Très amusantes!"*

Ahmed looks pleased. "You may sit on them whenever you like, free of charge."

Layla laughs and turns her attention to the computer screen as Ahmed watches, smitten.

I pop into the phone booth, shut the flimsy wooden door, and perch on the stool. Waiting for Wendell to pick up, I open Jean-Claude's poetry book, letting my eyes skim over a random page.

Wendell's voice is a little breathless, as if he's just been running. "Hello?"

I slam the book shut, stuff it back into my bag. "Hey, it's me."

"Zeeta, hi." His voice drops to that soft tone, the one that always makes me melt. All last year in Ecuador, we used to talk until late at night, him on his cell in bed and me on the plastic stool in the little phone booth that I'd gotten to know very, very well, every crack in the ceiling and chip in the paint and stain on the tile floor. "What's up, Z?"

"I bought a dress yesterday. Red. Short. With spaghetti straps."

He says nothing.

"Is it the one in your vision?"

After a moment, he says, "Yeah."

"Weird stuff is happening, Wendell. Remember how my *fantôme* slipped me a CD?"

"Your phantom?"

"My ghost. Well, now he's slipped me a jar of sand." I pause. "Are you sure you haven't seen anything else?"

He speaks, his voice eerily serious. "One thing I learned, Z, is that I can only tell you the future if, for some reason, you need to know it."

"I need to know it." I run my fingers through my hair, frustrated. "First you change plans, then this *fantôme* starts giving me things, and—I don't know, I want to know what's really going on." I look at the ceiling, and add quietly, "And not just with my *fantôme*, but with us. You and me. Will things be different? Will . . . ?" I let my words fade.

He hesitates. "I've just seen glimpses of things, Z. Things that don't make sense. Colors and lights, nothing distinct. Some people, but no one I recognize."

I sense in his voice that I won't get anywhere, so I leave it be. Outside the thin wooden booth, I hear Layla chatting with Ahmed. I can't hear their words, but it's obvious from the rise and fall of their voices that Layla is charming him and he's becoming putty in her hands.

"Hey, I should go," I say. "I'm trying to be frugal until I get some tutoring jobs lined up."

"Okay," he says.

"Love you," I whisper.

"Love you too," he whispers back. And then, so faintly that I wonder if I've imagined it, he says, "No matter what."

• • •

Illusion seems comprised of the kind of people whose parties wouldn't start until nine or ten but would then last until dawn. It's nine-thirty, and I'm walking along a dark, deserted street, hoping I won't be too early for the *fête*. I'm in the medieval part of town now, the oldest *quartier*, where the roads are extra narrow. One street is called Fly's Elbow in the old Provençal language; it's so narrow that even a fly buzzing through would get its elbows stuck.

Following my map, I make three rights in a row, spiraling into an ancient part of town I've never been to before. A medley of fantastical faces carved in stone peer at me from nooks over doorways—angels, demons, monsters, mermaids, saints, bearded men, lions, dragons, cherubs.

When I reach the address, the shades are drawn; they're red velvet, like the curtains of a stage before the first act. A small sign in the window reads CAFÉ ETERNITÉ. I push on the heavy door. It creaks open.

I step inside.

I've never been to an opium den, but this is how I picture one. Shadowy corners, little pools of candlelight through red glass orbs. A golden-red luminescence. Low, Middle

Eastern music playing. Hookah smoke drifting, each breath a different flavor—cherry, vanilla, clove. Burgundy carpets draping the walls. Pillows with gold tassels and silk brocade scattered around low tables. A few people sitting cross-legged on the fringed rugs, drinking tea and murmuring, reclined on sequined cushions.

I clutch my bag, which contains Jean-Claude's poetry book and my ruby notebook. I want to sit in a corner and write about this place, but I force myself to keep moving, into the next room, where the smoke forms a thick veil. Toward the back, I can barely make out a narrow spiral stair-case that descends into what must be the *cave*. The metal stairs quiver beneath my feet as I walk down.

The *cave* actually does feel like a cave. A low ceiling caps rounded, half-crumbling stone walls, and a few tapestries are hung in odd spots, over what are probably holes. An old man is playing his violin like a fiddle, the notes bubbling and bouncing like champagne fizz. People are dancing and clapping and jumping around him. Some of them are perform-ers I've seen on the streets—a harpist, a contortionist, a magician.

The tables have been pushed aside to make room for the dancing. Around the edges, a troupe of muscular hip-hop dancers are eating cake. Next to them, two puppeteers are passionately kissing, their puppets abandoned on a cushion. In the far corner, a juggler squats, tossing lit candles and teacups in the air. From what I can tell in the dim light, most of the people are a few years older than me.

Through the gyrating crowd, I spot the members of Illusion. The gypsy dancer girl and the tuba player are swaying in an embrace, their lips all over each others' necks. Amandine is swirling alone, barefoot, wearing a red dress that is actually shorter than mine.

I wave to her, but her eyes are closed in a blissed-out state. I look around for Jean-Claude. There he is, at a table in the corner. "Zeeta! You came!" He smiles and stands up, weaving through the dancers to greet me. He kisses me on both cheeks and leads me back to his table in the shadows. "And the poetry? It touched you?"

I pass him the book, hoping my sweaty hands haven't left marks on the cover. "I love it. I didn't understand much, though."

"You're not supposed to understand it." He waves his hand. "Simply experience it. Like smelling the moon."

"Right." I look around. "Nice place."

"Isn't it? The owner of Eternité lets us use it for our *fêtes*. I live on the second floor with the rest of Illusion." He smiles. "You should come by sometime. The apartment's our base for playing music this summer. The hub of our wheel. The center of the daisy. The pit of the cherry."

"Where do you live the rest of the year?"

"We wander. Mostly around the Mediterranean. Near sea light. Warm places call to us. Spain, Italy, Portugal."

I open my notebook to a fresh page. "Why red?" I ask, twirling my pen. "For the costumes, I mean." Now I've forgotten about my shabby shoes and too-short dress. With a pen in hand and an open notebook, I'm instantly in my element. I can ask anyone anything.

"Rouge." He meets my gaze. "It's the color of passion. Of blood. Of joy. Of anger. Of the ripest, richest, juiciest berry. Of our music." He sips his tea. It's chai, with a warm ginger-clove smell that mingles with his spicy cologne. "We set people's souls on fire with our music. Like a bite of chili, you know?"

I jot down his answers in my notebook. As I write *fire,* my skin feels as though I'm sitting too close to a flame.

Someone plunks a tiny cup on the table. Jean-Claude pours me some chai and swirls in milk from a little brass pitcher.

I take a sip and say, "Tell me about your family, Jean-Claude."

"My old family was a weary dandelion that I blew and scattered into many pieces. My new family is Illusion."

"Earliest memory?"

He pauses to think. Our heads are close now, since the music is loud. Finally, he says in a dreamy voice, "Hundreds of silver fish on shaved ice. Cold scales, glistening. The smell of the belly of the sea."

"Where?"

"In Marseille, the market near my childhood home."

Marseille is the port city just south of here. According to my guidebook, it's full of drum music and warm spices and bright fabrics from North Africa and other Mediterranean countries.

"Enough about me." Jean-Claude's head moves even closer. "Tell me, Zeeta, what first set your soul on fire?"

Just the kind of question I might ask someone for my notebook. But not a question I want to answer. I raise one shoulder in a shrug and say, trying to sound mysterious rather than dull, "Who knows."

Suddenly, I'm aware of how hot it is in this *cave,* with so many people dancing, sweating. Despite my wisp of a dress, heat is rising inside me. Clutching my notebook, I stand up and say, "*Excuse-moi,* Jean-Claude." Without explanation, I move away, through the dancers, wishing I had my indigo notebooks with me. They're filled with Wendell. This ruby notebook contains nothing about him. And the remaining pages want to be filled with new fiery things.

Why didn't I pick beige?

SEVEN

I interview a jovial capoeira dancer, a pale celloist, and a wild-haired fire-eater, then move on to Jean-Claude's friends in Illusion. Since the gypsy dancer and the tuba player are inseparable, I interview them at the same time. Sabina is Romanian, nineteen years old, with a throaty, warm voice and gentle brown eyes. She's wearing a golden tank top and a flaring crimson circle skirt that skims her ankles, which are adorned with silver charms.

Her Parisian boyfriend, Julien, is a bit older, his sun-pinked skin covered in a smattering of freckles, his hair a ruddy shade of red, cropped close to his head. His capri pants are made of patched-together scraps of velvet and satin, with sequins stitched at the cuffs. He and Sabina tell me that they've both traveled all over Europe, that together, they speak eight languages, English included.

I turn to a fresh page in my notebook and ask, "How do you know who you are?"

Sabina and Julien give me puzzled looks. "What do you mean?" she asks.

"If you're always changing, always moving?"

They look at each other. "Julien reminds me," Sabina says. "And I remind him."

"But how do you know you'll still get along? I mean, in all these different places?"

Julien doesn't hesitate. "You are what you love. I love Sabina and my sister and my music. That won't change." It's amazing how in French, you can say these things, and they don't sound sappy but simply like a statement of romantic facts.

Just then, Amandine bounds over in her red dress and perches at the edge of the table. "*Bonsoir,* Zeeta!"

As she kisses my cheeks, I catch Jean-Claude approaching out of the corner of my eye. He slings his arm around her shoulder and tousles her hair.

Amandine glares at him and smooths out her hair, which is loose and tumbling to her waist.

I smile and close my notebook. Amandine's even prettier in this *cave,* the candlelight making her red hair glow, setting off her green eyes. Her hair must be heavy, but she holds her head high, like a ballerina.

While her gaze stays on my face, her hand darts out and messes up Jean-Claude's hair.

"Eh!" He jumps back.

She grins at him impishly. "That's what little sisters do, *non?*"

As he runs his fingers through his curls, I can see traces of some kind of product, a gel, maybe. He must have taken time to style it, arranging the waves just so, making them appear casual, effortless. "Do that again," he tells her, "and I won't make that *tarte aux fruits* for dessert tomorrow."

Amandine ruffles his hair again, teasing, "And I'll take back that vest I spent two weeks making you."

It's an old tuxedo vest, faded red and covered with iridescent beads. He wears a white tank beneath that shows off his arm muscles. Somehow cute French guys get away with wearing clothing that other men in the world wouldn't touch for fear of appearing girly.

"You made that vest?" I ask Amandine, impressed.

"Sabina and Amandine are the geniuses behind our costumes," Julien says.

"Not true," Sabina insists. "Amandine is. She designs them. I just help sew them." She raises her eyes to Julien. "And you give me moral support, *amour.*"

Amandine imitates the romantic gaze, making goo-goo eyes at Jean-Claude, tossing aside her hair. "And you, *amour,*" she says with an exaggerated eyelash flutter, "sit around eating *tartes aux fruits,* watching us work."

Jean-Claude rolls his eyes and reaches his hand toward her, but she ducks away.

There's something Peter Pan–ish about these young people forming their own family, goofing off and surviving together, dancing and playing music and roaming the streets all day.

Suddenly, Amandine's eyebrows furrow. "Has anyone seen Tortue tonight?"

The others shrug, shake their heads.

"He said he'd come to the party. I hope nothing's wrong." In a flash, Amandine moves across the room, leaps a meter high, grabbing the railing of the upstairs floor, and swings her feet up and over the edge, disappearing from sight.

It takes me a minute to remember who Tortue is. Then I remember. Turtle. The mime. I turn to Jean-Claude and ask, "What's Amandine worried about?"

Jean-Claude lets out a long breath. "Tortue feels like a piece of wet wood tonight."

"Wet wood?"

"He must dry out again before a spark will ignite him. And when it does, he'll be able to make any instrument burst into flame." Jean-Claude runs his fingers through his black curls. There's that scar again. It's slightly curved, like a sliver of moon. "It's like this with him," he continues. "Tortue's specialty now is being perfectly still and silent. Like a piece of wood drying in the forest. We wait for him."

"Why?"

"He's like a father to us," Julien says. "Especially to Amandine, after what happened to our own father."

After a pause, he heads upstairs after his sister, with Sabina trailing behind him, leaving me and Jean-Claude alone.

The music grows louder, and around us, the crowd is dancing, pushing us against each other. It's too loud to talk. The only thing left to do is dance together, so I force myself to say, "I think I should go home now, Jean-Claude."

"I'll walk with you."

"Oh, no—"

"I insist." And he takes my elbow in a gentlemanly gesture from our grandparents' era and escorts me outside.

• • •

The night air is clear and cool. From the distance floats music from bars and restaurants, blending with the hum of far-off motorcycle engines. The street is deserted except for Jean-Claude and me, and a few pigeons cooing in an alcove above.

I extract my elbow from his hand and try to set a fast pace, but Jean-Claude saunters. His profile is breathtaking in the silvery moonlight, as though it's draped in a thin veil of silk.

I look away. A black cat creeps across a rooftop. The silence is dangerously romantic. I start talking in a too-loud voice. "I've always identified with cats," I say. "Their nine lives."

"Ah bon?"

"Only for me it would be sixteen lives. A new life every year. A new Zeeta."

"The joys of being a wanderer." Jean-Claude spreads his

arms, as if embracing the world, a gesture that would look silly for most people but that makes him look radiant.

I hug my arms tight across my chest, holding myself in. "The *woes* of being a wanderer."

He tilts his head back, face to the sky. "But don't you love it? Always creating a new you?"

"No!"

"Why?"

"A zillion reasons."

"What's one?"

"Well . . ." I think. We walk through a pool of yellow lamplight, past a small, gurgling fountain. A smooth stream of water pours from the mouth of a copper snake. I listen to the rhythm of my breathing, my sandals slapping the pavement. "For instance," I say finally. "How can you be in love with someone if you're always changing into a different person?"

He considers. "Perhaps *le grand amour* is for other people, settled people. Not us. We wanderers go where the breeze takes us, enjoy whatever lovely feathers and leaves are blown our way."

"That's terrible!"

As we walk, his arm brushes against mine. If I had pockets I'd stuff my hands in them now. I'm too aware that his hand might slip into mine and stay there. I take a sharp breath, but I don't move away.

Pausing in the middle of the street, he whips out the tiny notebook from his back pocket. He scribbles something.

"What are you writing about?" As soon as I ask, I wish I could snatch back my question.

"Your eyelids."

Feeling dizzy, I'm suddenly conscious of my eyelids.

He scrawls a little more. "They are the flicker of fireflies." He reaches his hand to my face, and his fingers graze my eyelashes.

"*Attends.*" Wait. I step away and sputter, "I—I have a boyfriend."

He lets out a long, slow breath between pouting lips. "Where?"

"In America. But he'll be here soon."

Jean-Claude looks at me for a moment with a thoughtful expression. A little sad, maybe. Then he raises a shoulder in a resigned shrug. "You should bring him over for dinner to our apartment."

That's the last thing I expected him to say. "Really?"

"*Bien sûr.* If friendship is what you have to offer, I'll take it."

A block later, we've reached my apartment, and he gives me a kiss on each cheek. "I'm glad we met, Zeeta." Then he adds, "You're one of us, you know."

"One of you?"

"Someone who makes every day a song."

I give him an odd look. "Layla says that all the time." I study his face. "And it's the phrase that was written on that CD."

"It's from a story about a troubadour."

"I know the story well. The man uses his music to save himself." I stare at him, bewildered. "Where did you hear it?"

"*Ouf.* Who knows? It's just a story that we travelers pass around, *non?*" He smiles. "Like I said, you're one of us."

• • •

Streetlamp light pours onto my twisted, crumpled sheets. My open window lets in a faint night breeze, but the air still feels too hot, heavy, pressing down on me. My travel alarm clock glows 3:00 a.m. with fiery red numbers. Most of the time, I can handle anything that comes my way. There was the pickpocket I chased down at Carnaval in Brazil, the bus breaking down in the desert in Morocco, the angry hyena in Tanzania.

But at this time of night, when I'm most alone in the world, every fear emerges. They rush out of hiding in full force, especially when the apartment is new and doesn't feel quite like home yet. The worst part is I can't always put my finger on the worries. They're looming monsters that shift shapes once I think I've seen their outlines. They make my insides twist and my heart race, but they're shadowy, elusive.

I wish I could talk to Layla. She doesn't mind being woken up in the middle of the night for a chat. But she's still at her solstice party on the Celtic ruins, which she warned me would last all night. She and Sirona and the others are probably dancing naked around a bonfire about now.

Instead, I conjure up a good memory with Wendell— stretching out beside each other in a garden in Ecuador, hand in hand. Usually this relaxes me, lets me drift to sleep.

But not tonight. I climb out of bed, walk barefoot across the cold tile floor, and open the red CD case. I stick it in the mini stereo and press play. Closing my eyes, I let the music grab hold of me, spin me away.

Make every day a song. I try to remember the original version of the story, the one Layla first told me years ago. My mind has always spun its own variations, depending on where we lived. The forest morphed into a desert or jungle or beach, and the guitar changed to congas or didgeridoo or whatever instrument we were into at the time. The story goes something like this.

There was a troubadour—a singer, poet, musician—who led the wandering life, like us. "Make every day a song" was his motto. Every day a new adventure. A new lifetime. A new poem. He would wander around, playing his music, singing his poems. This is how he made money for food to eat, a place to sleep. And if, one day, he had to eat only nuts and berries, that was fine. Or if he had to sleep on the ground one night, that was fine too. He had his music to nourish him. The songs in his soul. All he needed was his guitar and he was happy. (Layla loved telling me this story when, as a kid, I complained about our lack of well-rounded meals and our inconsistent bedtimes.)

One day in the forest, the troubadour encountered a band of criminals, men with hard hearts, tough pasts. When they found he carried nothing of value, they decided to kill him.

"May I have one wish before I die?" the troubadour asked. The criminals laughed at his request. "Yes," they said, expecting him to ask for a cigarette or jug of wine. Instead, he said, "Let me play one song."

They agreed.

The troubadour closed his eyes and held his guitar like a precious child and plucked out the first notes. They were the most beautiful notes: sparkles of sunshine on water, the perfumed hum of bees on the first days of summer, dewdrops, nectar, trails of comets.

One by one, the criminals sat down on the mossy forest floor.

And then the troubadour began to sing, the words from the deepest place in his soul, the farthest reaches of the ocean, the bluest space between stars. The song was a spring bubbling up through rocks. A cool glass of water in a desert. The sweetest fruit dripping from your lips. The troubadour sang and the earth seemed to quiver with his voice, to pulse with each note. On the last note, the troubadour stretched out his voice, and finally, it faded like dawn. He put his guitar on his lap, ready to die.

For a moment, there was silence except for the birds and insects. Then the criminals found their voices and said, "One more song."

Again the troubadour conjured up the deepest, highest, brightest, darkest song from the most secret treasure-filled place inside him. He played with all his soul.

When it was done, the criminals cried, "Another one. Another one!"

All night he played. One by one, the criminals sank into

the soft earth and drifted off into the sweetest dreams. And by dawn, they were all asleep, with smiles on their faces.

The troubadour, too, had a smile on his face as he picked up his guitar and walked off into the rising sun, ready for a new day, a new poem.

Sometimes, instead of "See you later," Layla says, "Make your day a song, love!" That's what she takes from the story. I've always loved the story's assurance that when we find ourselves lost in a dangerous slum or a thick jungle or a parched desert, if we reach deep enough into our souls, we can survive anything.

But tonight this story doesn't comfort me.

EIGHT

Now, after Layla's third espresso at Café Cerise, she's finally waking up, jumping straight from lethargic to hyper. "Z, it was so amazing at my solstice *fête!*" She rambles on and on about the ceremony, which involved jars of olive oil, goblets of springwater, candles, chanting, dancing, singing, feasting, and general merriment under the moon. She didn't come home from the Celtic ruins until dawn. Apparently, she and Sirona and her family and friends hopped the fence around the ruins and had their all-night party in secret. Typical Layla. I wonder if she'll ever outgrow this stuff.

"Hyper cool," I say without enthusiasm, rubbing my eyes. I put my hand back on my bag and scan the square, determined that the *fantôme's* hand won't sneak by me so easily again.

Layla ties her hair into a knot. Already the heat of the day has set in. "Look, there's Sirona!" She waves, a flick of the wrist that jangles her dozens of copper bracelets.

Sirona and her family wave back at us as they set up not far from our table.

I open my notebook, looking at each member of Salluvii closely, remembering what Vincent said about some secret. *A secret older and deeper than you can imagine.* I list my observations:

- *They all dress oddly.*
- *Their instruments are unlike anything I've seen before.*
- *Their music sounds strange and old.*
- *They have Celtic ancestry.*

I strain to hear them talking, listening to the rhythms and intonations. They're not speaking French or any other language I've heard before—and I've heard dozens. The closest familiar language would be Gaelic, which an Irish colleague of Layla's spoke.

- *They speak a strange language, similar to Gaelic.*

In the sun, Sirona's brass pendant flashes, the triple spiral. And then I notice they're each wearing the same kind of necklace.

- *They all wear triple-spiral necklaces.*

Sirona's coming over, so I quickly turn to a blank page. After we greet one another, she sits down beside me, and I ask, "What do those spirals on your necklace mean?"

She rubs the pendant. "Whatever you want them to mean. Water, cycles of life, ending and beginning, renewal, rebirth, eternity."

I jot this down and ask, "Why does your whole family wear them?"

"They remind us who we are," she says, and counters my question with her own. "And who are you, Zeeta?"

I'm tongue-tied.

Layla jumps in and answers for me. "A seeker! That's what her name means. And that's what you do in your notebooks, right, love?"

"How fitting," Sirona says, looking delighted.

I'm determined to foil her attempt to switch the focus to me, but it's tricky. The thing about secrets—especially old, deep ones—is that by definition, you don't go around talking about them to people you've just met. Instead, I ask her details about what town she's from, how she and her husband met, where she lives, why she speaks a Gaelic dialect. Her answers are gracious but a little cloudy. "We're from around here, but we're often on tour." "We live in a quiet, old part of town." "Grannos and I met ages ago on our travels." "We've always been good at languages."

I'm getting nothing interesting, so I change tactics and ask about local Celtic history. With this, Sirona opens up completely, answering questions in intricate detail, recounting vivid stories of her people. Her face lights up as she describes the array of festivals—the festival of light, summer's end, the winter solstice, the spring equinox. Then, shaking her head and wincing, she tells about the loud carnyxes that people blew on the battlefield, dozens at a time, creating an ear-splitting, earthshaking noise that terrified their enemies. She laughs. "Some of those Romans cried out for their mothers, they were so scared!"

Finally, Sirona stands up with her lyre. "I'd better go warm up with Salluvii now." We kiss goodbye, and she says, "It seems you're interested in Celtic history, Zeeta. I'd be happy to give you a tour of Entremont. It's the ruins of the Salluvii town on a hill outside Aix. Where Layla went to our celebration last night. My family and I go there often."

"We'd love it!" Layla says. "Right, Z?"

"Sure," I say, watching as Sirona leaves, gracefully toting her lyre. I can understand how Vincent might think someone like Sirona holds ancient secrets. Still, I don't see anything that sets her apart from some of the other unusual people I've met on my travels.

After Sirona rejoins Salluvii, Layla turns to me. "And how was *your* party, Z?"

"Fine." I pause, considering how much more to say. "I talked with Jean-Claude. The accordionist from Illusion. He told me we're alike, that we're the kind of people who make every day a song."

Layla's eyes widen. "You think he's your *fantôme*? Jean-Claude?"

I shake my head. "But I've never met him before, so the jar of sand wouldn't make sense. And he claims that the troubadour story is just one that travelers pass around."

"Hmm." She doesn't sound convinced. "He's almost always in the square with his band. And before your *fantôme* left both gifts, Illusion was nearby, right?"

"I guess." My hand is still on my bag, guarding it.

"Well, love, perhaps you should keep an eye on this accordionist." Layla stands up, stretching, and craning to look at the time on the clock tower. "More teacher training meetings. See you tonight for dinner?"

"Right. I'm making *pistou*."

"Yum." She kisses my cheeks. "See you, love."

As she disappears into the crowds of tourists, I search in my bag for my notebook. My hand lands on something soft. Fabric. I pull it out. It's an old, worn T-shirt, faded black. There's a decal of a dreadlocked guy playing a guitar. I hold it up and squint at it. Jimi Hendrix is my guess, although some of the image has crumbled away. The shirt is riddled with holes, nearly threadbare. Tentatively, I press it to my face. It smells clean, freshly laundered.

Why would the *fantôme* give me a ratty old T-shirt? And

how? I've had my hand on my bag practically the whole time. How could he have gotten past it? How could I not have noticed? Maybe he *is* a ghost.

I frown. It could have happened at the *fête* last night. With all the distractions, I wasn't watching my bag the whole time. Or it might have happened even before that, on the street last night, going to or from Nirvana. The streets were bustling.

I look around in frustration. Nothing suspicious. And Vincent the pigeon man isn't even there, so he couldn't have seen anything. Speaking of Vincent, he's probably waiting for me at his shop for our English lesson. I fold the T-shirt and stuff it back into my bag, more annoyed than mystified.

• • •

On the way to Vincent's shop, I swing by the market, grab a head of garlic and a bundle of fresh basil for the *pistou,* then hurry through the maze of side streets. Here and there, people slip in and out of heavy wooden doors. As the doors swing closed, I peek behind them, down the hallways. Some passages offer glimpses of hidden courtyards with trees growing inside, their leaves poking over the buildings. Some courtyards are visible from the street, with only wrought-iron gates blocking the entrance, making it easy to peer right through. Of course, I want to know what's behind the closed, locked doors.

Why is it that the forbidden always holds so much allure?

On the Place des Trois Ormeaux, I pause by a circular fountain, water bubbling up from the center, a few pigeons hopping around the edges. Just on the other side is Vincent's antiques shop, its sign nearly hidden by a cloud of flapping silver feathers. The sign is wooden, and shaped like a pigeon. LES SECRETS DE MAUDE, it reads in gold calligraphy on a black background, some of the paint chipping off. I smile, imagining what kinds of juicy secrets Vincent thinks his beloved pigeon has.

The wrought-iron gate is open. Trying not to step on any pigeons, I walk back into the cool shadows of a narrow courtyard, navigating around leaves from potted plants and overhanging tree branches. Tucked into the foliage, like ruins in a jungle, antiques peek through. They're stashed haphazardly against the stone walls—old gilded picture frames, a dusty velvet chair with stuffing coming out, an ancient wooden chest. The furniture seems to be overflowing from the shop entrance at the rear of the courtyard.

I'm taking so much care not to trip over any pigeons or antiques, I nearly collide with a man in a pink polo shirt.

"*Désolé, mademoiselle,*" he says.

"Oh, my fault."

"Well," he says, "actually, it's my father's fault for attracting vast quantities of birds and furniture."

I study him, confused. He has light brown skin—or else a very deep tan—and doesn't look much like Vincent. Then I remember that Vincent's wife was from the Canary Islands. It's ironic. People are always questioning whether Layla's my mother, simply because we have different complexions. And now I'm making the same wrong assumption.

"I'm about to visit Vincent now," I say. "Tutor him in English."

The man laughs. His laugh is similar to Vincent's, deep and hearty. "*Bon courage, mademoiselle!* My father is not exactly a linguistic genius." He extends his hand. "I'm Jean-Christophe."

"*Enchantée,*" I say, taking his hand, which is calloused and muscular, maybe from pulling and knotting the ropes of a sailboat. Another J.C., I can't help noting. Of course, *Jean* seems to be a prefix to lots of guys' names here in France. Vincent mentioned that his son sailed around the world. He looks it—his face is worn from the sun and wind, deep wrinkles fanning out from the corners of his eyes, probably from squinting at the bright ocean. "I'm Zeeta."

"Young to be an English teacher." He grins. "Impressive."

"Well, my mom's the certified one. I just picked up some things from her. Layla drags me to live in a different country every year."

"Exciting life, no? You must be very happy."

"More or less," I say.

He's about to say something when a pigeon flies onto his head, making him jump. He grabs the bird and looks into its eyes. "Juliette! Don't scare me like that."

I smile at his first-name basis with his father's pigeons. "I should tutor Vincent now," I say, walking toward the shop. "*Au revoir,* Jean-Christophe."

"*Au revoir,* Zeeta."

He walks out onto the street, and I head to the back of the

courtyard, into the shop. The throngs of pigeons reluctantly move aside, giving me a little space to stand. It's a small room, packed ceiling to floor with feathers and antiques. Everything seems balanced precariously, as if touching one thing might cause the rest to come tumbling down. There are statues of saints and the Virgin of Lourdes; dark oil paintings of people in old-fashioned dress; glass beads and rosaries; heaps of lace spilling from falling-apart trunks; cracked leather books wedged into every possible space; clocks of all shapes and sizes; golden pendulums swinging and hands ticking. I stifle a sneeze at the dust and mold, which is strong enough to overpower the sharp smell of basil in my bag.

Through piles of ancient canvases and mirrors and glass, something moves. A page, turning. The yellowed page of a book. And a yellowed, age-spotted hand turning it. Vincent is hunched over the book, peering through thick glasses through an even thicker magnifying glass. He looks utterly lost in whatever he's doing. He's motionless now, and if it weren't for that page having turned, I'd believe he was a statue. Maude, of course, is nestled on his shoulder, nuzzling her beak behind his ear.

I'm wondering whether I should interrupt him or come back later, when he raises his head and sniffs, like a dog tracking a scent. He sniffs and sniffs and turns his head and rests his gaze on my bag.

"Basil!" he announces. "I knew it! *Bonjour, mademoiselle!*

Come in!" He gestures toward a rocking chair, nearly hidden among a pile of old velvet coats and minks.

"*Bonjour,* Vincent," I say, stepping around more pigeons, hugging my bag to my chest to avoid knocking over heaps of pink crystal beads, bowls of silver and brass buttons, leaning towers of china plates and teacups.

As I sit down, the chair creaks and swings backward. I right myself and pull an English textbook from my bag. Hopefully, he won't be as challenging a student as his son suggested.

Vincent sits on a stool across from me, looking eager. "Did you figure out the Celtic band's secret?"

"I tried, but I'm not sure what I'm looking for."

He nods and digs around in a crate, pulling out a book. "Why don't you take this home and read chapter nine?"

It's a small book, bound in burgundy cloth, ancient-looking, with gold-edged pages. *Curiosités d'Aix-en-Provence,* it reads in ornate script.

He hands it to me. "Madame Chevalier and I discovered this book here in this very shop, back when it belonged to my father, when we were children. We found chapter nine particularly interesting."

I flip to chapter nine. " '*Les Eaux Magiques.*' " The Magical Waters. The alleged secret must have to do with Vincent's interest in sacred waters. I'm not sure what it has to do with Salluvii, though.

Vincent is just smiling at me, not offering any more

information but obviously bubbling over with excitement. He sees life as a treasure hunt. A quest. Why not? I'll play along. I tuck the book into my bag for later. "Sirona's taking me and my mom to some Celtic ruins tomorrow," I say. "I can try to find out more then."

Vincent looks thrilled, nearly jumping up and down in his chair. "Ah! *Oui!* Perfect!" He gives Maude a peck on the head. "Hear that, Maude? Closer every day!"

I'm not sure what he's talking about.

Vincent leans forward. "Have you discovered who is leaving you the mysterious gifts?"

I shake my head. "But I got another one. A black T-shirt."

"He is persistent, isn't he?"

"Oui." I get the feeling Vincent is stalling our lesson. I smile enthusiastically and open the book. "Ready for some English?"

"In a moment, *mademoiselle*. Listen. Madame Chevalier has invited us to her apartment on Monday. Perhaps she has information about your mysterious giver of gifts."

"Has she said something to you about it?"

"No, but she sees everything from up there. She's got the eyes of an eagle."

"Good," I say in a measured voice, careful not to pin my hopes on an eccentric old lady who fancies herself a spy. I open *English for Everyone* to chapter one and say in English, "Let's start."

• • •

The lesson drags at an excruciating pace. As Jean-Christophe warned, Vincent is not exactly a linguistic prodigy. Afterward, Vincent ceremoniously pulls out a little piece of whisper-thin paper. Then he digs out a fountain pen from beneath rolls of yellowed lace and uncovers a jar of ink from behind a heap of rosary beads. "One moment, one moment, *mademoiselle*," he mumbles, peering through his spectacles at his script.

I stash the English book back in my bag and stand up, ready for some fresh air. And I have to get home to make the *pistou* for tonight's dinner with Layla. My basil is already wilting. Curious, I peer over his shoulder. "What are you doing, Vincent?"

"Sending a little note to Madame Chevalier telling her you've accepted her invitation for Monday." He blows on the paper to dry the ink. "She doesn't get out much these days. She likes to know what's going on outside the square."

"I can drop it at her house on my way home," I offer.

He chuckles, rolling up the paper and stuffing it into the tiny vial on Maude's leg. "Oh, *non. Merci, mademoiselle,* but Maude can deliver it much faster than you or I." He pats Maude's head with a fingertip. "Remember? She's a homing pigeon. Microscopic bits of magnets in her brain tell her where to go, and how to get home." Maude stands patiently still as he screws on the cap. "See how I put the vial on the leg with the missing toe? I constructed it to weigh exactly as much as a pigeon toe! She flies better with it, so I leave it on.

And it's waterproof! After decades of sudden storms and birdbaths, no water's ever leaked inside!" He smiles, satisfied.

Maude hops around, looking happy to be of use. Vincent tosses her in the air and she flies out of the shop, into the courtyard.

I run outside, following her flight path with my eyes, watching her go. She catches the wind and soars over the rooftops. "How long will it take her?"

"Only a minute! She can fly one hundred kilometers per hour."

"She always goes straight to Madame Chevalier's?"

"*Bien sûr!*" He gives me a mischievous grin. "Well, sometimes she takes a detour. Stops at her secret places on the way back." Chuckling, he says, "Oh, how she loves Madame Chevalier. Who else feeds Maude cookie crumbs and lets her sip tea?" He shakes his head. "Birdseed, I tell her. For the *merde!*" He turns to me, his eyes wide. "*Viens!* I'll show you something."

As we walk inside, some pigeons flutter from his arms to the ground as others rise to take their places.

He bends over and sorts through piles of stuff—glass fishing floats, ancient books, maps, statues. "*Ouf!* Here we go."

He reemerges, sneezing and holding an old photo album. Eagerly, he opens it and puts on his glasses. The pages are clear plastic, encasing tiny paintings on tissue paper. He flips through hundreds of pages, each filled with a dozen minuscule watercolor paintings. "We correspond almost every day," he says. "When Madame Chevalier is in town, that is."

"For how long?"

"Oh, since—why, I suppose since my wife died. Since I got Maude."

I peer over his shoulder. Each painting features something different, but always something you might see on the square—Salluvii, cherries, a tuba. Each tiny masterpiece is intricately detailed.

"I send Madame Chevalier little messages and she sends these back!" Vincent says proudly. "It's an honor, you know. She's a brilliant artist. She's traveled the world. Her work is in the best museums all over Europe and America. Probably on every continent! I'm just an old school friend. She's nice enough to amuse me with these little messages." He runs his hand over the album, smoothing the plastic and chuckling to himself over some of the paintings.

I comment on Madame Chevalier's fine artwork, then glance around the room, trying to imagine a lifetime packed with so much junk and so many pigeons. "Do you ever get tired of all this stuff? Do you ever wish for something new and different and exciting?"

"*Mais non!*" He glances around, as though the objects might take offense. "I love my treasures. This is who I am. These things reflect my soul. I still discover new things every day. Look at this!" He digs in a cedar chest, pulling out an ancient shaving set, an old-fashioned doll with curled black lashes, and finally a carved box of dark wood. He blows off the dust and rubs it with his shirt. "Don't remember where I even got it—a flea market somewhere. Maybe even a trash bin! Every few years I take out this box, polish it, clean the velvet inside, set it on a shelf to see if anyone will buy it. Secretly, I hope they don't!" He grins. "One year I discovered a spring inside, and little metal gears. So I got out my magnifying glass and headlamp and music box manual and fixed it. And wouldn't you know it, it played *'La Vie en Rose!'*"

He hands me the box. I lift the lid. The melody starts and spirals out of the red velvet, like a rose unfurling, like a thousand petals bursting out. I close my eyes and listen as he sings along in a raspy, earnest voice. *"C'est lui pour moi. Moi pour lui ..."* He's for me, I'm for him ... *LA la la la la la LA la la la la la LA la la la la la LA ..."*

The song ends and I close the box. *"Super cool,"* I say, really meaning it.

"Oui! Imagine! I discovered this music hiding inside! This, after years of looking at it!" He clucks. "No, Zeeta, the things I choose have lifetimes of hidden mysteries."

I hand it back to him.

There's a flap of wings and he says, "Oh, look, here she comes!" Maude darts back into the store and lands on Vincent's shoulder. The expression on his face is truly one of *le grand amour.*

NINE

"Mmm. Your *pistou* is extraordinaire, Z," Layla says, twirling the green-flecked pasta into her mouth. The evening sunlight illuminates the feast I've made, spread out on the table on the roof patio—*pistou,* endive salad, and potatoes au gratin.

"Merci," I say, pleased. There's still a thin coat of sweat on my face from rushing around the kitchen and darting up and down the stairs carrying the dishes. My hand's still aching from smashing the basil in the mortar and pestle. Deliciousness comes at a price.

Beyond our patio table, patchworks of red tile roofs stretch far into the rosy orange sky. Treetops rise from hidden courtyards, little islands of translucent green. It's golden and comfortable up here above the city, the slightest breeze whispering through my hair.

"Hey, are we on for the Entremont tour with Sirona tomorrow?" Layla asks, spooning more *pistou* onto her plate.

"Sure," I say, remembering how pleased Vincent was at this news.

My eyes rest on the jar of sand from my *fantôme*, which I've stuck a candle in to form a centerpiece. The flame whips in the breeze but is protected enough by the glass that it stays lit. "Oh!" I blurt out, suddenly remembering my latest gift. I forgot about it in my rush to make the *pistou*. "Layla, my *fantôme* left me something new!"

Her eyes widen. "Let's see it!"

I jog downstairs and grab the T-shirt from my bag. Back up on the patio, I hand it to Layla, breathless, and settle back down in front of my *pistou*. "I found it after you left me at the café."

Layla takes the T-shirt, stares at it, and pokes her fingers through its many holes. Held up to the light, it looks practically transparent. "This is weird, Z."

"I know. Why would someone give me a grubby old T-shirt? It's kind of icky. But at least he washed it first."

Layla has a strange look on her face. "That's not what I mean, Z. It's that—I had a shirt exactly like this . . . years ago." She rubs the fabric against her cheek. She seems to have forgotten her *pistou*. "I'll never forget it. When I was backpacking around Europe, I only had three shirts and a pair of old jeans and a skirt and cut-off khakis. I hardly ever washed the clothes. They were like a second skin. I was so bummed when I lost my Jimi shirt."

I take another bite of *pistou*. "Where'd you lose it?"

She closes her eyes, thinking, and then, with surprising certainty, she says, "Greece." For a moment she strokes the worn fabric, lingering in some memory. Suddenly, her eyes fly open. "I gave it away. To J.C." She pauses, her face pale, and then speaks again, in a bewildered voice. "That night, he came out of the water and pulled a guitar from a nook in the rocks. He played for me, and we talked, and . . . you know. At some point, he was cold. I searched in my bag and gave him my Jimi Hendrix shirt. It was nearly sunrise. He fell asleep on the sand, wearing my shirt. I blew him a kiss, then left. It was the last time I saw that shirt. The last time I saw J.C."

I've dropped my fork. I'm staring at Layla, practically speechless. "My father? He's my *fantôme*?"

She looks at me, her eyebrows knitted together. "Zeeta, love. The odds of us being in the same place at the same time are minuscule. It can't be the same T-shirt."

My words tumble out. "My father could have been the first person who told you the troubadour story."

"Don't do this to yourself, Z."

I keep talking. "The sand could be from the Greek beach."

"Z. Let it go." Her voice sounds almost desperate. "Please."

"You're the one who's always talking about the universe making things happen."

"I thought you'd let this father thing go, love." She twirls her hair up in a knot, then loosens it again. "Why would we want some man coming in and complicating our lives?" She hands me back the T-shirt. "Hopefully, this is the last thing you'll get. Let's forget about it and just enjoy life here." She scoops up a forkful of pasta, but as much as she tries to act casual, her hand is shaking.

• • •

The next morning, in the bus on the way to Entremont with Layla and Sirona, I clutch my bag tightly in my lap. I almost didn't come today, but even though I'm still annoyed at Layla, I don't want to miss Sirona's tour of Entremont. And it will be good to get out of the city, walk in nature, distract myself from my confusion over my *fantôme*, Jean-Claude, Wendell.

I haven't been e-mailing Wendell as much lately, but he'll be here in two days. Thinking about his arrival ties my insides in knots, so I try to avoid it. I've also been pushing away any thoughts that the *fantôme* could be my father. Layla's right, I've decided. It's too unlikely.

Through the window, I watch the green hills and occasional farmhouses and red-tile-roofed houses outside of town. Meanwhile, Layla and Sirona are deep in conversation in the seats ahead of mine. Sirona is decked out in a blue raw cotton tunic, belted with silken, braided rope. She's gotten a few stares from other passengers on the bus but doesn't seem bothered by it in the least.

I pull out the book Vincent gave me. *Curiosités d'Aix-en-Provence.* I take a moment to appreciate the book—its cover of deep red cloth, frayed at the corners. The lettering is gold, with a gilded border of swirls and vines. It smells ancient and musty, like an attic. The binding is loose, the pages uneven, coming unstitched at the center. Carefully, I flip to chapter nine.

In ornate script, the chapter title reads, *"Les Eaux Magiques."* The Magical Waters.

It takes concentration to read, with the bus bumping along the highway. And the book's written in old-fashioned French, somewhat stiff and convoluted, with unfamiliar conjugations. In Morocco, I learned to read and write French well, but I was only nine at the time, so we never reached old, formal French. I squint at the page, moving my finger along like a child, whispering the words.

> *One is certainly aware that the glorious Aix-en-Provence is notorious for its magnificent fountains and the ancient springs which feed them. Indeed, these are the very springs in which the barbaric tribes such as the Celts and Ligurians bathed, the very waters from which they drank, and at which they worshipped. Yet one may hear rumors of an enchanting secret that has flowed*

underground for thousands of years, like the waters themselves. It is claimed that this bewitching secret offers the fantastical key to immortality, the fountain of youth, eternal life on earth.

According to the tales, versions of which date back to pre-Roman times, if one drinks from a particular spring at frequent intervals, one will live forever. With but a single sip of these powerful waters, any illness shall be cured, any wound healed, no matter how dire. Legend says that for those already in robust health, these exceptional waters shall bestow clarity of mind and pureness of heart.

It is said that the location of these magical waters has been lost with the passage of time. There are a few who insist that there exist guardians who come together to imbibe the waters, bathe in them, and perform pagan rites, which perhaps are remnants of the barbaric tribal traditions of the distant past. These guardians are rumored to be millennia old, and it is said that they may be jealous and ruthless, going to great lengths to protect their sacred waters. . . .

I close the book, tuck it into my bag, and ponder the back of Sirona's head. I consider her odd clothes, her Gaelic dialect, her intimate knowledge of Celtic history. Does Vincent think that Sirona and her band know the secret? Does he think they're the immortal guardians? Is that why he's interested in Salluvii? Is that why he chose me? Because he saw me with Sirona?

Sirona turns her head and says, "We're nearly there!"

Layla and I follow her off the bus, stepping into the soft, honeyed country air. We're the only people around. Once the bus leaves, it's quiet except for cicadas clicking, their rhythms rising and falling. Peaceful. As we walk on a path up a hill, through the open gates that read ENTREMONT, we don't see a soul. We follow the path through a sunlit meadow, the grass tips waving in a light breeze. Silently, we pass ruins of old stone farmhouses nearly swallowed by vines and bushes and clumps of olive trees. For the first time in days, I feel calm, free of the confusion that's been sending my mind reeling.

"How lucky that hardly anyone comes here on weekdays," Sirona says. A quiet radiance has swept over her face. Her eyes scan the landscape, blissfully soaking it in.

Layla murmurs in agreement.

We cross the field, stopping at the edge of the hill, where there's a view of the valley, the red-roofed villages around Aix in the distance. Somewhere down there, Jean-Claude is playing accordion. Amandine's leaping and dancing around. And the *fantôme* is doing whatever he does.

Sirona spreads her arms, as if hugging the view. "Some places feel timeless, don't they? A summer's day is a summer's day. But in the city, things are always changing." The sunlight illuminates her hair, catches tiny insects and butterflies as they drift and buzz and meander through the afternoon air.

"Here it feels like anything is possible," Layla agrees. "Like you could fly, doesn't it?" Of course, she can't resist quoting Rumi at times like this.

> "You knock at the door of reality,
> Shake your thought-wings, loosen
> Your shoulders,
> And open."

My cue to keep going. Rounding a bend, I see a maze of low, uneven stones spread out before us, what look like the foundations of ancient homes. "Imagine how it used to be," Sirona says in a wistful voice just behind me. "The houses, people bustling along the streets. Children laughing, dogs running around, chickens pecking. Sheep grazing in the pastures. The sounds of warriors training in the distance, their horn cries."

We walk along the labyrinth of streets as Sirona points out highlights, telling us about the healer who lived here, the musicians who lived there. She explains how the women used to walk down a long path, all the way to Aix, where they'd collect springwater in their vessels and then tote them back up here and dump the water in a communal cistern. "Let me tell you," she says. "We women had bigger muscles than the warriors, from carrying the water uphill for kilometers!" I scribble her remarks in my notebook, glad at my talent for writing and walking at the same time, while hardly ever tripping.

"How do you know so many details?" I ask.

She shakes her head, as if coming out of a trance, and smiles. Her gaze lands on my necklace. She reaches out a graceful hand to touch the beads. "What a lovely necklace, Zeeta. Seeds of a tree?"

I nod. "Wendell got it for me." I'm acutely aware that she's just changed the subject.

"He's the one I told you about," Layla tells Sirona, idly grabbing a leaf from a low-hanging olive tree. "Her boyfriend. The one who's coming, what, in two days, Z?"

"Yup."

"You must be excited to see him after so long," Sirona says.

"*Oui,*" I say, feeling sick to my stomach. Now it's my turn to change the subject. "What's that, Sirona?" I ask, pointing to a large enclosure.

"The olive presses!" she says, delighted. "Nothing better than the smell of fresh olive oil. Oh, and here's where we gathered for the market. Over there was the poorest part of town. We'd always slip those children some fruit or a bit of bread."

"We?" An odd choice of pronoun for the ancient inhabitants. I imagine what Vincent would say about this.

"Well, the Salluvii," she clarifies. "My ancestors."

"Hmm." I move on to more philosophical topics, which comes naturally since I've been doing this for years with my notebooks. "So," I ask, "what do you think about eternal life on earth?"

Sirona raises an eyebrow and tilts her head.

After a pause, Layla says, "Time is relative. You can make a moment last an eternity with the right attitude. If you truly exist in the moment, you already have eternal life."

I ignore Layla and look directly at Sirona. "Do you think it's possible for a person to *literally* live forever?"

"Maybe," Sirona says, brushing her hands along the ancient stone.

Before she can say more, Layla jumps in. "But it's irrelevant, Z. There are other, easier ways. Rumi said,

"Make peace with the universe. Take joy in it.
It will turn to gold. Resurrection
Will be now. Every moment,
A new beauty."

I turn again to Sirona. "What about those stories about immortality? Like the Holy Grail? The fountain of youth?"

Sirona lifts a shoulder in a kind of shrug.

"Metaphorical, not literal," Layla says. "It's about discovering a different way of being in time. Sink into the infinity of every moment."

I turn to Sirona, looking at her expectantly. Finally, she says, "Your mother is right, Zeeta. It's best to simply live in the moment. Because whether you're immortal or not, moments are what make up a lifetime, *non?*" She puts her hand on my shoulder and squeezes. "Remember, Zeeta, seeking eternal life on earth has brought most people nothing but trouble."

TEN

The chimes of the clock tower slip into my dreams, and I find myself counting them. Eight, nine, ten . . . and then I remember it's Monday, and I have my meeting with Madame Chevalier and Vincent at ten-thirty. Usually I'm an early riser—a necessity when you're responsible for making money, grocery shopping, fixing things, and performing a dozen other duties that quickly fill the days. I look at my clock, and sure enough, it's ten already.

Groaning, I roll over, right onto *Curiosités d'Aix,* whose corner jabs into my ribs. Last night, I stayed up late reading it after we got home from the Celtic ruins. I skimmed through the entire book, which was interesting enough, but chapter nine—*"Les Eaux Magiques"*—was the best. I must have fallen asleep with it still in my hands.

I splash water on my face, throw on some clothes, run a brush through my tangled hair, and hurry downstairs. Luckily, our apartment is just a couple of blocks from the square, so I'll be on time to the meeting at Madame Chevalier's apartment. As I race down the street, my bag flopping against my leg, the melodies of Illusion drift down the street. I whiz by the band on the Place de la Mairie, giving them a brief wave, and they nod and smile in my direction. Jean-Claude's smile lingers, I can't help noticing.

Then I turn around the corner to the narrow side street behind Café Cerise, stopping at a polished wooden door, scanning the names next to the buzzer. *Mme Violette Chevalier. 2eme étage.* Literally, the second floor, but since the French don't count ground floors, it's actually on the third story. The outside door's unlocked, so I let myself in and walk up the flights of worn red-tiled stairs until I reach the door labeled *Mme Violette Chevalier* in fading handwritten ink. I knock, and a faint *"Entrez"* floats from behind the door. I draw in a breath, turn the knob, and push the door open. I catch a whiff of sweet vervaine and mint and old velvet and furniture wax. *"Bonjour?"* I call out tentatively. "Madame Chevalier?"

"Entrez, entrez!" she calls again.

I follow the voice through a long hallway lined with framed paintings and sketches that cover every centimeter of wall, ceiling to floor. Most feature beautiful women of all ages. They have chestnut hair and bright brown eyes and elegant necks and each has a different style of clothes. One woman sits in a tropical fruit market, her hair piled in a bun woven with flowers. In another picture, a woman with a pixie haircut in a cute sixties dress is silhouetted against a shimmering ocean. Another wears a palm hat, her face hidden in the shadows, with colorful African-print fabric hanging in the background. Farther on, the subjects of the painting look older. The oldest has chin-length gray hair and big copper disc earrings and looks like she's been caught laughing at a bawdy joke.

Now the hallway opens into a small living room, tastefully decorated with antiques—an overstuffed sofa, a faded blue velvet armchair, a few cedar chests, glass vases, and, in the corner, an empty artist's easel. Off to the right is a closet-sized kitchen with a half-fridge and a two-burner stove top and tiny sink and enough counter space to hold a single plate. To the left is a bathroom, containing a single toilet, with space for nothing else. Beside it is the washroom, not much bigger, barely fitting in a sink, mirror, and tub.

And there, silhouetted against the window, is the woman with the binoculars. It's not until I see her that I realize the paintings in the hallway are not of different women. They're all the same woman. All self-portraits of the live version here in front of me. She is as still as her portraits, only in three dimensions, with the Place de la Mairie through the window as the background. Her expression holds an odd mix of weariness and curiosity. Her body seems to weigh on her, even though she's bird-thin, yet her eyes are alive, clever.

And they brighten even more when I offer her my hand. "Madame Chevalier?"

"Oui, ma petite." Those caramel-brown eyes pierce into me. It feels as if dozens of eyes are watching me, eyes of all the ages she's been, looking at me, into me. Dozens of different people that are somehow one person. I'm not sure how I can tell, because her skin has shriveled and become spotted with brown patches, her muscles have diminished, her hair has turned coarse and gray, her eyelids have drooped, and her shoulders have shrunk.

"I'm Zeeta."

"Enchantée, Zeeta."

"Enchantée." Her shawl is red velvet, faded by the sun. She wears large earrings, dangling, silver filigree like ones I've seen in South America. Around her neck hangs a heavy necklace made of bits of hand-worked metal, a style common in the markets of Morocco. Old-fashioned ivory binoculars hang from her neck. Her shirt is Mayan—and her skirt, long and simple black. Her shoes are worn leather thongs that look handmade, revealing knotted toes.

"Sit down, sit down," she says. "Vincent will be a few minutes late. He sent word with Maude. He's with a customer now." She leans forward. "Now, you, *ma petite,* you've got a bit of everything in you. The way you move, you talk. I can't put my finger on where you're from."

"From everywhere and nowhere," I say, and I reel off the sixteen countries I've lived in.

"I've spent time in quite a few of those places," she says in a thoughtful voice.

"You were in all those places you painted?"

"I was. My whole life I've spent noticing things and putting them on canvas." She pauses. "Until recently, that is."

"Why?"

She waves away my question with her hand. "You're a girl full of questions, aren't you?"

"*Oui,*" I admit, pulling out my notebook. "Madame Chevalier, you've watched me in the square. Have you seen someone dropping things into my bag?"

"Well." She strokes the leather cord around her neck, where the binoculars dangle. "I notice a great many goings-on in the square. And although I haven't seen anyone actually slip something into your bag, I know who I'd place my bets on."

"Who?"

She smiles. "That red-headed acrobat girl."

I stare. "Amandine? The girl with Illusion?"

"*Oui.* That one." She points a bony finger out the window, toward Amandine, who's skipping around from one table to another, offering the top hat as people toss in coins.

"Why do you think it was her?"

"She's taken an interest in you, *ma petite.* And she's agile. She jumps and flies and flips all over the square. She has mastered the art of charming people to distraction."

"You think she's sneaky? Deceptive?" I study Amandine through the window.

"Oh, she's never pickpocketed anyone, but she'd be good at

it, I can tell. Trust me, *ma petite*, there's more to that girl than meets the eye."

"Wow." I open my notebook and jot down notes. Her theory's interesting, even though I have a feeling my *fantôme* is male, and most likely someone I've known before.

"And another thing I've noticed," Madame Chevalier whispers mischievously. "The accordionist is drawn to you and you're trying not to be drawn to him. But you can't stop."

I flush, looking quickly at my feet.

She goes on. "I notice that you have confidence walking around markets, through crowds, talking to strangers. Yet there is part of you that feels lost."

I blink. How can she tell?

She points a ring-bedecked finger at my notebook. "Most of all, I notice you writing in that notebook. I notice that you noticed me. I notice that you are a person who notices."

I take a long breath. No wonder I've felt I was being watched.

She twists the binocular cord around her fingers thoughtfully, like an observant, retired spy. "Most people in the square only notice what their tour guide points out. They notice the statues and carvings mentioned in the guidebooks, or the displays in the storefronts. They notice the prices of things. They notice what they want to buy. They notice beautiful women or beautiful men. They notice what would make a pretty photograph. They don't notice an open window. They don't notice the old lady inside it. But you do, *ma petite*, you do."

Once in a while you stumble across a person like Madame Chevalier, the best kind of person for interviews, the kind who could fill a whole notebook. I jump right in. "Madame Chevalier, can love last a lifetime?"

She jangles the silver charms of her necklace, thinking. "Not for someone like me. I was always running off to paint new pictures in some new place. I loved the thrill of it, the newness. I was like your young accordionist friend, always moving from one *amant* to another."

"You mean Jean-Claude? How could . . . ?"

She smiles. "This is not the first time he's been here. He and his band have come and gone over the past few years."

Suddenly uncomfortable, I shift the focus back to her. "So you've never had one true love—*un grand amour?*"

"Perhaps. But love isn't always returned. When it is, you're very lucky." She stands up slowly. "I'll make some tea." She shuffles into the kitchen, hunched over as if in pain, with a slight limp. I can't tell how old she is. Her mind seems sprightly, but a cloud of exhaustion hangs over her. She has to be the same age, more or less, as Vincent, since they were school friends, but she moves like someone much older. And she's thin, thin, thin, as though she's disappearing up here.

A book sits on the table, a handmade album of gilded leather. I open it and there, pasted to the pages, are scraps of thin paper covered in small, formal handwriting, written with an old-fashioned ink pen. They must be messages from Vincent, delivered by Maude. Many of them are funny little things, nonsensical rhymes. Once in a while there's a reference to Salluvii or simply *les Eaux*—the Waters. It's as though he and Madame Chevalier are still children playing detective, a game they never outgrew.

Madame Chevalier comes out with the tea, struggling under its weight. The cups are rattling and the tray looks about to fall. I jump up and rescue the tray.

Embarrassed, she looks away, and sees the open album. "Oh, you found my little book. We have fun together with little Maude. I adore that bird."

She strokes her binoculars. Her fingers glitter with rings, a mélange of silver, brass, copper, and gold, studded with cut stones of all shapes and colors. "Now, Vincent said you believe in the powers of sacred waters. Is this true?"

"I'm open to the possibility. I've seen lots of amazing things."

"Such as?"

"Last summer, a crystal led my friend to his birth family."

"This was in the Andes?" she asks.

Vincent must have told her about the Peguche Waterfall. I might as well tell her about Wendell now. She'll see him through her binoculars soon enough. "This friend, well, he's my boyfriend, actually, and he'll be here tomorrow."

"*Eh bien, dis donc!* Better than a soap opera," she says with a sparkle in her eyes. "Tell me about this boyfriend."

I tell her about last summer in Ecuador and Wendell's birth family and the crystal cave. She listens so intently that before I know it, I've let something slip. "And last summer," I say, "he saw us together in France."

Immediately, she asks, "What do you mean, he saw you in France?"

Her eyes are piercing into mine and I can't think of a rational explanation fast enough. It seems safe to tell her. She obviously believes in sacred waters. Wendell's powers wouldn't be much of a stretch. "He can see the future," I say, pausing to gauge her reaction.

"*Ah bon?*" She leans forward. "What exactly does he see this summer?"

"Me and him, soaking wet. I'm in a dress."

"*Très intéressant,*" she murmurs, staring into space, as if her mind is whirling. "What else?"

"He won't tell me anything more," I say. "I'm worried he sees me with—" I force myself to continue. "Someone else." I bite my lip. "Or maybe he sees us not connecting. Maybe I'm not the same Zeeta he knew in Ecuador."

She makes a sympathetic cluck, then launches into questions about Wendell's powers. She wants to know the kinds of things he's predicted, how specific he can get, how easily he can see the future on demand.

The more I answer her questions, the more I wonder why she's so interested. There's an intensity to her questions. An inexplicable urgency blazes in her eyes, as if my answers, somehow, are a matter of life and death.

• • •

By the time Vincent finally arrives downstairs and rings the buzzer, I'm thoroughly confused. Is Madame Chevalier wise? Or a tad crazy? Or maybe both? I remember what

Layla says about clowns and fools—that craziness and wisdom go hand in hand.

"Would you get the door, *ma petite*?" Madame Chevalier smooths her hair, her shawl, her skirt. "That must be Vincent." As she says his name, she lights up.

I open the door, waiting for Vincent to climb the stairs. It takes him a minute, and when he appears, he's a little breathless. A light dusting of feathers covers his coat, and Maude is perched on his shoulder. He's wearing old-man cologne that blends nicely with his natural smell of birds and old cedar. As he enters, he takes off his beret, revealing white hair that's been recently combed with some kind of oil. He fiddles with the beret in his hands.

" 'Ello, Meez Zeeta!" he says in English, punctuated with a laugh.

"Hello yourself," I say in English, and head down the hall. He follows slowly, lingering over the self-portraits on the wall, as if he's in the Louvre. The first is when Madame Chevalier was about sixteen. My age. I wish I looked so poised and elegant. He stands in front of the painting. *"Comme elle est belle!"* he whispers in an awed voice. How beautiful she is!

He waddles along like a pigeon, craning his head forward and peering at the paintings that grow older and older, oohing and aahing over each one. Sometimes he reaches out his hand, as if he's about to touch the portrait, and then, at the last second, withdraws it, shoving it in his pocket.

"I never grow tired of looking at these," he murmurs. "No

wonder she's world famous." He lowers his voice. "Now you understand why she intimidates me. She's a genius."

We continue walking past all the faces of Madame Chevalier, growing older, portrait by portrait. At the end, Madame Chevalier, in the flesh, sits facing the window. Vincent greets her with a burst of energy—*"Bonjour, madame!"*—and pulls a wicker chair to our chairs by the window.

Madame Chevalier reaches out to him, and for a moment I think she's going to embrace him, but instead she takes the pigeon from his shoulder, kisses her on the head, and tucks her into her lap, stroking her. *"Maude, ma petite Maude. Ça va, mon amour?"*

Vincent watches Maude for a moment, smiling, then turns to me. "So, have you read chapter nine?" He's as excited as a little boy.

I'm direct, even though I feel silly saying the bizarre theory out loud. "You two think that the members of Salluvii drink from the sacred waters? You think they're the immortal guardians?"

Vincent smiles at Madame Chevalier.

She nods, beaming, as if I've passed some test. *"Oui,"* she says, "just like Maude here."

"What?"

"Remember when I told you that Maude takes occasional detours to her secret places?" Vincent says, his eyes twinkling.

Madame Chevalier's eyes grow starry too. "We suspect

she's sipping from the waters. How else could a pigeon live for fifty years in perfect health? Most pigeons barely make it to thirty-five."

These two really, truly believe in a fountain of youth. Right here in this town. For years, they've been encouraging each other, playing this game together, until they've begun to believe it in their hearts. It's undeniably weird. But they're both so eager, so genuine, and they light up when they talk about these sacred waters.

I can't help indulging them. And it does make great ruby notebook material. So I press my lips together, holding in my smile, and ask, "And how do I fit in?"

Vincent puffs up his chest like a pigeon. "Madame Chevalier and I have decided we can trust you." From his bag, he pulls a small album with the word SALLUVII embossed on the leather cover, opens it, and says, *"Regarde."*

There are a series of paintings of two men and two women who wear clothes and hairstyles similar to Sirona, Damona, Grannos, and Bormanus.

Vincent taps the album with his fingers, flipping through the pages, letting me look at each one. Finally, he says, "We're seventy, born and raised here in Aix. Those people in the band Salluvii—they've been coming to town since we were children. The same necklaces. The *same* people. They never grow older. They look exactly as they did sixty years ago."

I study the album. Each painting is dated, the oldest from 1956. It's true, the people in the paintings look similar, especially the jewelry, tunics, and hair, but then again, these are quick sketches, just splashes of color, not detailed enough for me to make out facial features.

Madame Chevalier peers at the album over my shoulder. "The members of Salluvii keep to themselves, mostly. They must think that no one will remember their faces, but we do."

"So," I say, "these sacred waters—where do you think they are?"

Vincent smiles. "That's where you come in, *mademoiselle.*"

"We'd like you to find them," Madame Chevalier says, as though she's just awarded me a prestigious, highly coveted job.

I blink, searching for words. "If you've spent your lives searching, what makes you think I can find them?"

"Well," Vincent says, "we weren't serious about the search until now. It was a game for us." He takes a long look at Madame Chevalier. "But now, circumstances have changed." He lifts his palms to the sky, a pleading gesture. "And now we're too old to search. We need your help."

My doubt must be written on my face, because he adds, "You must wonder if we're *fous, mademoiselle.* Going on about eternal life. But trust me, we're not crazy."

I bite my lip. "Why me? Why did you choose me?"

Madame Chevalier answers. "You notice things. You have a connection with Salluvii. And now, what you've told me about your boyfriend! Well, this makes it even better." She nods. "You're a seeker, that's clear."

"Seeker." That's what my name means. But right now I'm up to my ears in unsuccessful seeking. Seeking the real Zeeta, seeking the *fantôme,* seeking the reason for my creeping anxiety around Wendell's arrival. Now doesn't seem the time to get entangled in a search with two sweet but slightly deluded old people. I try to let them down easy. "I wouldn't even know where to start looking."

"Pas de problème," Vincent says. No problem. "For the moment, you must simply gather information from Sirona and report to us."

Madame Chevalier turns to him and murmurs, "Her boyfriend has powers of divination. And he saw Zeeta and himself in a vision, here in Aix, soaking wet." She gives Vincent a meaningful look.

His eyes widen. "Soaking wet," he murmurs. "As if they've just discovered the magical waters!" he says.

"What?" I say, bewildered at how he leapt to this conclusion.

"This is perfect!" Vincent cries.

"Isn't it?" Madame Chevalier agrees.

I try to get a word in. "Wendell can't exactly control his powers," I say. "He doesn't even like talking about them."

Madame Chevalier smiles. "Oh, when he hears of our quest, he'll be glad to help you." She speaks with a childlike faith, certain Wendell will be her knight galloping in on a white horse.

I look at their hopeful faces and say reluctantly, "He'll be here tomorrow."

"Magnifique!" Vincent exclaims. "We can't wait to meet him!" He raises his teacup in a toast. Madame Chevalier raises her own cup and looks at me expectantly.

I swallow my misgivings and clink my teacup against theirs.

ELEVEN

When they're really into a song, Illusion seems to transform into fire, flames leaping, sparks shooting, sweat flying, sunlight glinting off the odd, tiny ornaments sewn to their outfits. They're in this fiery state when I leave Madame Chevalier's apartment and encounter them in the square. I sit down at a nearby table, where the music is so loud I can feel its heat.

After the song ends, Amandine leaps up from her cross-legged position behind the bongo drums and calls out through the applause, "We. Are. *Illusion!*" Then she skips through the crowd with her red hat, headed toward me. When she reaches my table, I toss in some coins, noticing that the hat is halfway full of money. Illusion does well. She kisses my cheeks, breathless. She smells like cherries, tart and sweet, and her lips appear stained red, not with lipstick but with something like berry juice.

"Sit for a minute, Amandine," I say, offering her a chair and pushing my untouched glass of water toward her. "Help yourself."

She perches on the seat, tucking one leg under the other. Her natural state is movement. She seems restless sitting still, even for a minute.

I pull the T-shirt from my bag. "Recognize this?" I ask, studying her reaction, just in case Madame Chevalier is right about her.

Amandine raises her eyebrows, surprised, and reaches for the shirt. She holds it up and asks, "Where did you get it?"

"Someone put it in my bag. Do you know who?"

She shakes her head.

"I think whoever it was left me a jar of sand too. And a CD of guitar music."

"Bizarre," she says.

We're at a standstill. And really, what would be her motivation for putting this stuff in my bag anyway? What I want to do, I realize, is confide in her. She's the closest thing I have to a girlfriend my age here. "Amandine. I think it might be from my father."

She furrows her eyebrows. "Your father? Why?"

I tell her the story of Layla's night in Greece, and the few bits of things I know about my father.

She listens closely to my rambling. Afterward, she stares at me for a while, and finally, she says, "If you're right, at least your father is alive and out there. Just be happy knowing that."

"It's not that easy. It's hard not having a father—" I catch myself, remembering too late that Amandine lost her parents. "I'm sorry. I forgot—" And I stop, embarrassed.

"I *do* have a father," she says. "Tortue's like my father."

I nod, wishing I could take my foot out of my mouth.

"They died four years ago," she says. "When I was twelve and Julien was eighteen. We only had distant relatives, so Julien became my guardian. I was really into ballet and gymnastics, and his passion was music. So we started doing street performances, first in Paris, then all around France. We hooked up with Tortue in Marseille, and it felt like I had a father again. Someone wise, someone who cared about me, gave me advice. Someone who made sure we were organized and had a place to live and food to eat and gigs lined up."

"Really?" I've thought of the mime as silent and frozen, always leaning against the tree. "He doesn't seem the type."

She tilts her head. "What has Jean-Claude told you about Tortue?"

"All he said was something about wet wood."

She giggles, a tinkling bell sound. "Jean-Claude's a nut."

It's funny that she says it so matter-of-factly. I laugh too.

"Tortue has bipolar disorder." She looks at me, waiting for a reaction.

"What does that mean?"

"It's basically manic depression," she says. "Sometimes Tortue gets in a supercreative phase, helping us come up

• 129 •

with new routines, new songs. He plays music with us—brass, strings, keyboard, you name it. At those times, he's a whirlwind of energy. He books our shows and sets up recording sessions and plasters Illusion posters all over. Other times, there are weeks when he can barely get out of bed. He doesn't talk and hardly eats. This month he's pretty down, but I've been able to convince him to at least get in his clown costume and come out with us. All he has to do is stand there, I tell him. We try to take care of him. He's so good to us, when he's able."

"Does he take medicine?" I ask.

"Well, sometimes he decides he doesn't need it. Especially when he's feeling good." She sips the water, studying its transparent shadow.

We're quiet for a moment as I jot down the notes about Tortue.

When I look back up, Jean-Claude has come over. "And what are you ladies gossiping about?" He asks it casually but looks the tiniest bit worried. He thinks we're talking about him, I realize.

"Not about you, Narcissus," Amandine snaps, sitting up a little straighter. "We happen to be discussing Tortue's bipolar disorder."

Jean-Claude grins. "Ah, what limitless talent contained in such a small girl. The acrobat psychologist can diagnose us all, can't she?"

"The doctors diagnosed him," she slings back with a glare.

"I just do Internet research to figure it all out. Unlike some of us, who just ramble incoherently about wet wood."

Jean-Claude smiles. "Amandine is Illusion's personal, on-the-road psychologist."

She flips her braid, whacking him in the face. "Only I don't get paid or appreciated."

"Come on!" He grabs her braid and tugs. "We're about to play another set."

Lifting her chin, she says, "I think I'll sit this one out, actually."

With a roll of his eyes and an exasperated *pppptttt,* Jean-Claude goes to join the other band members.

Once Illusion starts playing, Amandine leans in and says bluntly, "You like him, don't you?"

"Who?" I ask, knowing very well who.

She motions toward Jean-Claude with her chin.

I will myself not to blush. "I have a boyfriend."

"I know. Jean-Claude told me."

"He'll be here tomorrow." Why is my stomach clenching?

She nods. "I'd understand if you like Jean-Claude."

I look at my espresso cup.

"I mean, he's pretty seductive," she says.

I lift a shoulder, trying very hard to seem nonchalant. "Even though he's a nut?"

"Especially because he's a nut." She grabs her toes, extends her foot toward the sky. "Try to keep a cool head around him."

"We're just friends."

"I know. But he kind of has a . . . reputation, especially with girls like you."

My head snaps up. "Girls like me?"

Sunlight dances over her red hair. "*Hyper cool* girls."

"Oh." I'm not sure what to think about this. "Do you warn all the girls about him?"

"No. Just you."

When in doubt of what to say, turn the tables. "What about you, Amandine? Do you have a boyfriend?"

She shifts, crossing and uncrossing her legs.

I wait, sort of enjoying her discomfort.

"It's impossible," she says. "Jean-Claude and Julien think I'm a little girl. Tortue's the only one who treats me like an adult. Which is funny, since he's the one who's most like a father." She takes a sip of water. "Try being on your own from age twelve. It drives me crazy when people look at me and see a little girl."

In a way, I can relate. I've always been the responsible one, making sure Layla and I have food and shelter and clothes and savings. But at least she treats me as an equal. I study Amandine's face, her copper hair, the freckles scattered across her nose. A cute elfin creature sitting across from me, a child who leaps and flips and dances. It's not until you talk to her that you see she's lived a more intense life than many adults. She's complicated, smart. Madame Chevalier was right about that much.

There's a rustling in the leaves above us. We both glance up.

Tortue is perched in the branches, still and staring, his foot paused midswing.

Amandine smiles, hops onto her chair, and springs up a full meter, grabbing onto the tree limb and perching beside the mime. He's trying to stay frozen, but she grabs a leaf and tickles his nose. He bursts out laughing. And I can see it clearly. Tortue melts in her presence. The cold, snowy mask dissolves and he is indeed an adoring father.

TWELVE

It's here. The big day. The day of Wendell's arrival. I barely slept last night.

On the way to the stop for the *navettes*—shuttle buses— I'm so distracted I trip or stub my toe a few times every block. Maybe it's from guilt. I've only sent Wendell one e-mail a day over the past few days, a big change from our usual five a day. Ahmed mentioned it last night, and I got defensive. I argued that too much has been going on here for me to keep Wendell in the loop.

The quick e-mails I've sent have barely filled him in on the Jimi Hendrix T-shirt, Vincent, Maude, Madame Chevalier, Sirona, and our trip to the ruins of Entremont. I haven't told him much about Illusion. And nothing about Jean-Claude.

The *navette* ride to the airport is less than an hour. And Wendell's plane gets here in less than two hours. I catch my reflection in the shop windows. My shoulders are hunched and tense, my eyebrows furrowed. My lemon-yellow sundress is rumpled already, even though I ironed it this morning. I hardly ever wear makeup, but I've put a little on today. My nail polish has already chipped and I suspect my mascara has gotten smudged from sweat. Already, this is not going well.

Even in their sparkling red outfits, I don't notice Illusion coming down the street until they've spotted me. Amandine reaches me first, bounding ahead of the others, doing a cartwheel and landing smack in front of me.

I gasp. A few passersby applaud.

About ten meters behind her, Jean-Claude catches my eye and smiles. Sabina and Julien are in their own little whispery, kissy world and don't seem to notice me.

"Hey, Zeeta!" Amandine gives me a quick peck on each cheek. "Where's your boyfriend?"

"Not here yet. I'm meeting him at the airport now."

"*C'est excellent!* You should bring him to eat over at our place tonight."

"*Merci, mais*—" The thought of Wendell and Jean-Claude in the same room makes me break into a sweat. "He'll probably be too jet-lagged."

"Then how about tomorrow?"

"Tomorrow?" I stall, wracking my brain for an excuse.

Why does the prospect of Wendell and Jean-Claude meeting seem so uncomfortable? "He'll probably have to hang with his host family then."

"All right. Then Saturday."

I hesitate, wondering why Amandine is so set on Wendell and me coming to dinner.

"The dinner will be *trop top*," Amandine assures me, as if that's the problem.

"Well, all right. Thanks."

By now Jean-Claude has reached us. He plants two kisses on each cheek. As Sabina and Julien briefly tear apart from each other to give me air kisses, Amandine announces, "Zeeta and her boyfriend are coming to eat with us on Saturday."

Jean-Claude doesn't blink. He just smiles and says, "Your tongue will melt into our food. We are all *gourmands*."

Gourmands. People who love to eat. It's a word I've heard often during my short time in France. We don't have a single, everyday word in English that really captures the meaning. Definitely not pigs. More like people who engage in eating as a hobby, eating experts.

"Well, I'll be on my way." And without going through the whole ritual of kissing goodbye, I give a quick wave and half-run away.

"See you Saturday!" Amandine calls. "Seven o'clock!"

• • •

Now, at this moment, Wendell is somewhere in this airport. Maybe passing through customs. Maybe just behind that wall, less that fifty meters from me. It's no longer a matter of days but minutes. Every time I glimpse anyone with dark skin or long black hair, I jump.

I sit on the edge of the baggage conveyor belt. This is ridiculous. I fling open my notebook and write, *Why am I a nervous wreck?* I can't think of anything else to write. I slam the notebook shut, stuff it in my bag, and pull out Jean-Claude's book of poetry. I read a few pages, and when I look up, there's Wendell, coming out of customs.

He's already spotted me. I fix my gaze on his face through the crowd, and he walks closer. My heart is pounding, and now the sweat is dripping down my torso. He's got his backpack on, the same worn blue one from Ecuador. I wipe my hands on my dress. In my fantasies, I've thrown myself into his arms, planted a long kiss on his mouth, pressed my body into his, clung to him, his arm, his back, his broad shoulders, and walked arm in arm with him through the airport, stopping to kiss every few seconds.

But now I feel suddenly shy. Shy, with this boy I've been e-mailing five times a day. Well, except for the past few days. He knows practically every thought I've had over the past nine months. And now I feel shy. He's moving closer. The corner of his mouth is turned up in a half-smile. You can tell there's a much bigger smile underneath.

He wraps his arms around me and I wrap mine around his waist and breathe in his smell. It's the same, cinnamon soap and Altoids. It's so familiar and good. I sink into it. I don't lift my face to look at his. I just bury mine in his shoulder. I'm afraid he'll see something different in my eyes. I'm afraid he'll ask me what book I was reading. Finally, he pulls away and takes my chin in his hand and kisses me. Part of me feels like melting into him, but I step back.

"How was your flight?" I ask. What a dumb question. The kind anyone could ask anyone else. Two people who don't even know each other. Why can't I think of something real to ask him? I'm supposed to be the expert on deep questions. I have notebooks full of them.

"Good," he says. "Slept, mostly. And watched a bunch of bad romantic comedies."

My laugh spurts out, sounding jittery.

"God, I'm happy to see you," he says.

"Me too."

And then, as if it's too much to look at him, I turn to the baggage circulating on the belt. "So, you see your bags?"

"That big dark green one," he says. "And the matching smaller one. Christmas presents from my dad." He gives an embarrassed laugh. "I couldn't fit all my art supplies in, so my mom packed for me. She put red ribbons on them to make them easy to spot."

I smile. A red ribbon is how his parents explained their spiritual connection with him before his adoption. On one hand, I love that I know what the ribbons mean, and I love that he knows I know. But at the same time, I can't help comparing him to Jean-Claude.

I can't in a million years imagine Jean-Claude owning matching forest-green suitcases. His would be shiny vintage, lacquered with bits of strange fabric. Wendell's clothes are all subdued earth tones, sandy beige pants and a shirt the pale blue-gray of an overcast sky. The only flash of real color are the tiny red ribbons on his suitcases. Not a single sparkle. Nothing shines. Last year, Wendell matched the adobe and woods and fields and rivers in Ecuador. He matched me. But something's different now.

And there's more. Jean-Claude's nineteen, only two years older than Wendell—three years older than me. But next to Jean-Claude—who's been on his own for years already—Wendell seems like a little boy. Of course, he doesn't *look* like a little boy, with his broad shoulders, which are even broader and more muscular now. And I can tell he's grown a few inches. I have to raise my eyes to look into his.

On the way back to Aix in the *navette,* our conversation starts and stops in little fits. I don't say much as he tells me about the end-of-the-year parties. I mention Illusion's dinner invitation, then change the subject so I won't have to mention Jean-Claude and get flustered.

Wendell seems content just gazing out the window, commenting here and there on the landscape. His profile is beautiful. *He* is beautiful. His face has grown more angled and strong over the past nine months. But Jean-Claude's face is in a different realm altogether, the lose-your-breath realm.

Stop comparing them! I order myself.

"So," I say, "Aix was inhabited by Celtic tribes thousands of years ago," and I proceed to give him a history lesson, something throughly impersonal. Nothing to indicate that this is the love of my life. I ramble on about the Celts and Romans as he listens and nods politely.

After a while, we fall silent again. How can it be that we have nothing to say?

A half hour later, in Aix, we get off the *navette* and are greeted by an enthusiastic middle-aged woman and her whole extended family. The woman holds Wendell's photo, printed out from a computer, and gives him a big hug. The others—a small crowd of men, women, and kids—proceed to hug him, shake his hand, or kiss his cheeks, each nearly bursting with excitement. They talk to him slowly and clearly so he can understand their French, and they laugh at his attempts at jokes. He's using all his energy to try to communicate with them. I hang back, feeling invisible in the exhaust from the *navette*.

When Wendell introduces me, I raise a hand and fold my arms over my chest, keeping my distance from the greeting frenzy. The host father heaves Wendell's bags in the trunk, and then everyone piles into two small cars, the kids sitting on each other's laps. The host mother offers me a ride to *le centre-ville*, but there's clearly no room for me in either car. I decline, and wave goodbye to Wendell.

"I'll meet you in *le centre-ville* tomorrow, Wendell?" I call through the open window. "On Cours Mirabeau?" I name a café far from the Place de la Mairie, where there's not much chance of running into Illusion.

"Sure, Z. Three o'clock?"

I nod, and watch the cars putter away, the laughter fading,

leaving me feeling suddenly alone. I stare at the ground most of the way home, trying to figure out what just happened.

* * *

The leafy tree branches lining Cours Mirabeau form a translucent green tunnel over the wide street. Wendell and I are sitting at one of the cafés along the Cours, beneath a striped awning, engaged in less-than-riveting conversation about the French *lycée* system. Spending the morning tutoring students gave me a taste of what's to come when high school starts for me in the fall. It's always a little jarring to delve into a new school system, year after year.

I explain to him how in France, the non-college-bound students stop school to train or work around age sixteen, and the rest continue for two years, preparing for the *bac*—a giant, important standardized test. The students I taught this morning have a whole year until they take the *bac*, but their parents are already willing to dole out tutoring money in hopes that they master the English section. If they do poorly on the test, they might have to take an entire extra year of high school.

"Sounds stressful," Wendell says.

"Well," I conclude, "I'll be living in a different country when I'm eighteen, so no *bac* for me."

"Lucky." Wendell's still in a dazed, jet-lagged state. Now he's staring, mesmerized, at a dripping, moss-covered fountain in the center of the street, which motorbikes and tiny cars are weaving around.

"Natural hot springs feed into that fountain," I say, glad to find a new topic of conversation. "Supposedly, in the winter, the fountain steams. That's why the moss can grown on it year-round." Great. I'm back in historical tour guide mode. I bite my tongue and stir my café au lait, glancing at Wendell. We used to have hundreds of things to talk about.

"Chouette," he says, trying to show enthusiasm. He looks worn out. The good thing about this café is its prime people-watching location, which covers awkward gaps in our conversation. He takes the last sip of his second espresso, which isn't even touching his jet lag.

I let my gaze rest back on the fountain. So much moss clings to it that you can hardly tell the shape of the stone underneath. You can't even pinpoint where the water's coming from. It just seems to emerge from the moss and fern leaves and drip into the pool below. It's like a remnant of another age, something you might find in the middle of a forest.

I give Wendell a sideways glance. "You know the pigeon man I wrote you about? And the elderly binoculars lady?"

He nods.

"Well, I've been hanging out with them lately. Tutoring Vincent, and having tea with Madame Chevalier. But here's the weird thing. They're convinced there are magic waters around here. Healing waters. Immortal waters."

He raises an eyebrow. "Where?"

"That's their quest. To discover the location." I take my last sip of café au lait. "They're cute, like two little kids playing spy, all wrapped up in this secret mystery. Want to go meet them now?"

"Another time?" He glances at his watch. "I told my host family I'd go out to eat with them tonight."

"How about after that?"

He gives a sleepy half-smile. "Well, as I learned last night, their meals tend to last till midnight."

"Tomorrow, then?"

"Sorry, Z. They're taking me to hike Mount Sainte-Victoire. And at night we're going to a concert."

"Oh. Okay." I look at him closely, trying to figure him out. "Are you—" I swallow, unsure how to say this. "Do you not want to hang out with me? Did I do something . . . ?"

"No, Z. Look, I'm sorry." He does look sorry, but mostly sleepy, his lids heavy. "They have everything planned out for my first week here. They're just really nice and excited and want to show me around. And it's good for my French to hang out with them. You could come along—"

"You don't get it, Wendell!" I feel like smashing my cup on the ground. "Two months. That's all the time we have." I drill my eyes into his. "I'm used to this. I'm used to things ending too soon. Used to making the most of these little windows of time with people. You act like we have all the time in the world."

"Z, I'm sorry," he says softly. He pauses, looking a bit bewildered at my outburst. "I shouldn't have waited till the last minute to duck out of living with you. But it's not a big deal, Z. After this summer, there'll be other summers, and then, after we finish school—"

"Wendell. Anything could happen. We have to be together while we can. Forget your itinerary."

He tucks a loose strand of hair behind his ear. "Z, I can't be rude to my host family. This Saturday I'll see you for that dinner party, right? With your friends?" He reaches his hand across the table and lets it rest on mine.

I calculate the days in my head. Saturday is four whole days from now. And he acts as though it's nothing. "It's like we live in different worlds, Wendell." I pull my hand away, wrap it around my cup.

After a pause, he starts ripping up his sugar-cube wrapper.

I wonder what's really going on here. If he thinks I'm like Layla, flighty and fickle and flaky. If he thought I'd abandon him. And instead, he's abandoned me.

His expression is sleepy and distressed but still tender, and I want, so badly, to move forward and kiss him. To hold him. To just be with him, smell him and taste him and feel his warmth—all the things I was dying to do during the past nine months.

Instead, I drop five euros onto the little plastic tray, stand up, and say, "Well, see you around."

He doesn't reach for my hand again, or even try to stop me. He just adds a few coins and stands up and says, "See you Saturday, right?"

"Right. Bye." I turn and walk down the street alone, thinking it's strange that in the past week, I've kissed Amandine's and Jean-Claude's cheeks more than I've kissed my own boyfriend's.

After a few seconds, on an impulse, I turn back to see if he's still watching me. No, he's moving away, his faded jeans and brown shirt easily blending into the crowd. I stand and watch him disappear, then sink down onto a bench. To make matters worse, Rumi sneaks into my head, unwelcomed. It's the quote Layla tosses out whenever we're leaving our home for a new country.

> Look as long as you can at the friend you
> love. No matter whether that friend is moving
> away from you or coming back toward you.

• • •

Of all the people who could walk by at that moment, it's Jean-Claude. His accordion is slung over his back, his dark curls bouncing with his steps. He sits down beside me and pushes his hair away. His eyes are shockingly blue up close. "What's wrong, Zeeta?"

"Nothing," I say. No way am I going to cry on his shoulder about Wendell.

Jean-Claude nods, then says, "Know what I do when I feel terrible?"

"Write secret, morbid poetry in that tiny notebook?"

He grins. "Sometimes. But sometimes, I do this." He grabs my hand and pulls me up, leading me down the street.

"Where are we going?"

"You'll see."

Jean-Claude is running down the sidewalk now, dragging me along, weaving around all the people in creamy-hued outfits, and crossing the street, darting between little cars. We stop, breathless, in front of the carousel.

I give him a look full of questions.

He grins and buys six tickets at the kiosk.

"Six?" I ask.

"Three for you, three for me." He grabs my hand again and helps me onto the carousel. We're the only people over four feet tall on here. "Take your pick," he says, flinging his arm wide. "Zebras, lions, airplanes . . ."

I climb onto a black horse, feeling silly.

Jean-Claude gets on the zebra beside me.

The music starts—horn, accordion, tuba—and the carousel spins and our horse and zebra go up and down. I can't help laughing.

"*Excellent!*" Jean-Claude says. "See? I told you it works."

For the first round, I feel slightly ridiculous, passing all the parents waving at their children. After that, the ticket man comes around and collects our second tickets. Parents help their kids off and on, and there's a scramble for their creatures of choice.

"Want a different animal?" Jean-Claude asks.

"I've grown fond of my horse, actually," I say. This time, when the music starts, I get into the rhythms of going up and down and around and around. I forget my self-consciousness. I actually start smiling despite myself.

After the second ride, in the commotion of the kids getting off and on the carousel, I say quietly, "I don't think Wendell gets me." I don't look at Jean-Claude as I say it, just stare at the brass pole in front of me.

"Why?"

"I've been living this nomadic existence. Like you. And you know how you have to have a certain intensity in your relationships? Because within a year you'll be saying good-bye?"

He nods. *"Tout à fait."* Exactly.

"Wendell doesn't understand that." I press my head against the cool metal. "He's completely wrapped up in his host family."

"Ouais. It's hard for people to get us gypsies." The music starts again and Jean-Claude throws back his head, making his curls fall back in a wild mane. The moving lights make his vest sparkle.

"That doesn't make you dizzy?" I ask.

"Embrace the dizziness, Zeeta!"

I throw my head back too. Now everything is backward and upside down, a mishmash of lights and colors, and nothing makes any sense, but yes, in its own way it's beautiful, and I hang on tight, just letting the spinning lights and colors wash over me.

THIRTEEN

The tiny bells ring as the door swings open and I step into Nirvana. The stuffy, stale air smells almost homey after my absence of the past few days.

"Zeeta!" Ahmed cries. "Where have you been?"

"Wendell's here in Aix now, remember? I don't need to e-mail him as much."

"Ah, *oui!*" He beams. "And how is it finally being with *l'homme de ta vie?*"

I muster up as much enthusiasm as I can. "Great."

"And Layla?" His eyes flicker back to the screen. He's making an obvious effort to sound nonchalant. "She'll come back again soon, I hope?"

I sigh. So many men's hopes raised, then shot down. "Ahmed, trust me, Layla's not your type. She gravitates toward poorly groomed artists and musicians and clowns. She's never had a boyfriend for more than a couple of months. Forget about her."

He's quiet for a moment, then says, "You know, the Persian mystic Rumi mentions a Layla in his poetry."

"You read Rumi?" I can't hide my surprise.

"I have a doctorate in Middle Eastern literature." He smiles. "There are many things about me that you don't know. Do not always judge a person by how he appears." Laughing, he turns back to his game.

"Do me a favor and don't mention Rumi to Layla." The Rumi thing might let Layla overlook the fact that Ahmed is well groomed and financially stable. And the last thing he needs is to form a Rumi bond with Layla, then get his heart broken.

"Listen, I just need to make a quick call to Wendell," I say, handing Ahmed a slip of paper with the host family's number. Wendell canceled his cell phone for the summer to save money.

Ahmed dials the number as I head into the phone booth.

The host mother picks up. She whispers that Wendell's sleeping, exhausted from jet lag and the family's latest outings. I stare at graffiti on the wooden door as she chats about Wendell's jam-packed itinerary for the next few days. They're planning to take him to the major tourist attractions. First Mont Sainte-Victoire—the mountain Cézanne adored painting—then la Sainte-Baume—a cave where Mary Magdalene supposedly lived in her later years—and then the pretty little beach town of Cassis. All the places that Layla and I crammed in during our first week, before her teacher trainings started.

Finally, I interrupt. "Madame, I have to go. Can you tell Wendell I called?"

"*Bien sûr.* Does he have your number?"

"I don't have a phone. But he can e-mail me."

"Can I give him a message?"

I think. What is it I want to say? I don't know. I just want to be close to him. Just be together, comfortable together, like we were in Ecuador. But we're no longer in Ecuador. We're no longer *who we were* in Ecuador.

Of course, this is not the kind of thing you leave in a message. "*Non. Merci, madame,*" I say. "*Au revoir.*" I set the phone in the cradle, leaving my hand there for a moment, feeling, with that click, that something has ended.

• • •

Beneath white awnings, long tables stretch before me, covered with yellow cicada-print tablecloths and filled with bags of crushed herbs and spices, heaps of dried red sausages, soft white sheep cheeses, jars of amber honey, bottles of olive oil, shining like liquid sunshine. Sirona and Layla and I have been wandering up and down the market aisles, sampling baguette dipped in fresh olive oil or spread with cheeses. Sirona looks cheery in an orange tunic, her hair woven in a network of intricate braids. She did Layla's hair the same way.

The outdoor market is packed with people, the perfect

time and place for my *fantôme* to slip me another gift. I'm keeping a close eye on my bag, hoping to catch him in the act. It's easy to get distracted, though, with all the people to look at, the food to taste. We're just sampling an array of olives when Layla says, "Look! That mime's actually moving for once."

It's true, he's doing a performance, acting out a skit in pantomime. We pop a few more olives into our mouths and wander over to the crowd that's gathered around him. One moment the mime is crying, looking mournful in his skull-cap, with the black tear, clutching his hands over his heart. The next moment, he changes character, throwing on a bonnet and prancing around like a playful, silly girl, skipping arm in arm with someone. Next, he tosses off the bonnet and puts on a colorful vest with a patchwork of rainbow diamonds. He must be the girl's companion now—a frolicking, distractible clown, elbows linked with the girl's, pointing at this and that. Seamlessly, Tortue switches among these three characters. Although I don't understand the story, it's fascinating to watch.

Sirona whispers to us, "It's the tale of Pierrot."

The French people around us appear to be familiar with the story. They're laughing and clapping and clucking in sympathy at the right times.

At the end, Tortue bows as everyone applauds, tossing money into his hat. Once the crowd disperses, he collapses onto a bench, looking exhausted.

Layla says, "Let's go talk to him."

"Why?" I say. "So you can start meeting your clown quota for France?"

"No, Z! To have him explain the story."

Sirona says, "Good idea. He could explain it better than I could."

I trail behind them, cringing inside.

"Bonjour!" Layla says as she approaches him.

Tortue looks up, surprised. *"Bonjour, madame."*

"We loved your performance."

"Merci, madame." His voice is soft, almost shy.

"Could you explain the story?"

"Oui," he says hoarsely, as if he's not used to talking much. "It's the tale of Pierrot and Harlequin and Columbine." I can't put my finger on his accent. A Latin language, maybe. Italian or Spanish or Portuguese. "There are many different versions of the story, but here's the one I like. Harlequin was a colorful clown, dazzling, bright, fun. He traveled in a little caravan, having sunny adventures, charming people with his words." Tortue pauses, looking nervous, swallowing hard, as though this is the most he's talked in ages.

He continues. "Pierrot was a clown who was quieter, deeper, wore white and black. He baked bread in a wood-fired stove, by the light of the moon. He had always loved Columbine, but she was drawn to the bright colors of Harlequin. And so she went off with him. Pierrot was sad, but patient. He waited. When winter came, and the world grew cold and harsh, Harlequin had no food to give Columbine. They had no heat, no fire, no light. Columbine realized her mistake and returned home. Pierrot let her into his warm kitchen and nourished her with bread and love."

"Ohhh," Layla says. "Now I get it."

Suddenly, Amandine appears, slinging her arm through the crook of Tortue's elbow. "So. You met Zeeta and her mom!"

He gives a slight shake of the head. "Not officially."

"Well," Amandine says, "this is Zeeta."

I nod in greeting.

"And I'm Layla," Layla says, holding out her hand. "I'd do the kiss thing, but I wouldn't want to mess up your makeup." She laughs.

With a tentative smile, Tortue shakes her hand with his gloved one.

"And this is my dear friend Sirona," Layla adds as Sirona offers her hand.

Amandine smiles, satisfied, and turns to me. "Tortue will be at the dinner on Saturday. You're still coming, Zeeta, right? With your boyfriend?"

I nod and say nothing. I don't even want to think about the dinner.

Amandine looks around. "Where is he, anyway?"

"Busy with his host family. They're sightseeing this week, since he starts art classes on Monday." I try not to let my voice quaver as I say this. Come Monday, I'll be even less likely to see Wendell. He'll probably be at class for most of the day, then do homework in the afternoons and spend evenings with his host family.

"We're off to find some chocolate samples!" Layla says, rescuing me. "There has to be a chocolate section around here somewhere!"

We wave goodbye and Layla pulls us away, tugging on Sirona with one hand and me with another, back into the sea of tarps and crowds and market stands. I look back at Amandine. She and Tortue are staring after us. I remember what Madame Chevalier insisted. *There's more to her than meets the eye.* The only thing I'm sure of is that Amandine cares deeply about Tortue.

Layla doesn't seem very interested in the mime, which is surprising considering her history of clown boyfriends. Although, now that I think about it, most of Layla's dozens of clown boyfriends would be the fun-loving Harlequin types. Tortue, on the other hand, is most definitely a melancholy Pierrot.

• • •

Making our way slowly through three pots of linden flower tea, Madame Chevalier and I exchange stories of our travels over the course of the afternoon. We've been to some of the same countries—Senegal, Brazil, India—and can thoroughly appreciate each other's misadventures. At times, I find myself laughing so hard at her stories, I'm crying. It's rare and delicious to meet people who can share these kinds of memories with me.

I don't realize how long we've talked until it's nearly too dark to see her face. Once I turn on the blue glass table lamp, I see that Madame Chevalier's eyes look happy but tired. I wish her goodnight and kiss her goodbye.

Outside in the cool, dusky air, I realize I'm starving. Layla's at a teachers' meeting, so I'm on my own tonight. I swing by the *boulangerie* and pick up a mini quiche Lorraine for dinner. On the way home, munching on the quiche and crossing the Place Richelme, I run into Illusion.

Jean-Claude greets me with an energetic "Zeeta!" and kisses me soundly on each cheek.

I notice unlit torches piled beside him and the pungent smell of kerosene. A few meters away, Sabina is twisting Amandine's hair into a bun, and Julien is warming up on the drums. "What are you up to?" I ask.

"Dancing with fire," Jean-Claude says, a daring gleam in his eye. "Very dangerous, Zeeta. Don't let your soul get too close. It might burst into flames."

"I'll take that risk," I say, sitting on the wall of the fountain and finishing off my quiche.

It turns out that Illusion is holding an impromptu fire-dancing performance, something they don't do often for lack of permits. "If the *flics* come, we'll have to bolt," Julien says nervously.

"We'll be fine," Sabina assures him.

"But we'll have to be quick," Amandine says. "Fifteen minutes, tops." She douses the wicks with kerosene and lights a match. After a moment, the torches flare.

Julien begins pounding a primal beat on the bongos.

Amandine twirls two torches around her head in figure eights, then shimmies into a back bend. She tosses the torches into the air as she does a flip. Landing gracefully on her feet, she catches the torches just before they hit the ground, one in each hand.

People flock toward Illusion, oohing and aahing, drawn to the flames. Amandine looks especially young in the firelight, bending her tiny body in all directions. I can see why Jean-Claude would feel protective of her. Still, she possesses a fierceness, an intelligence that makes her much more than a needy little sister. I watch, hypnotized, as her body fades into the darkness and my eyes focus on the orange fireballs spiraling as if of their own accord.

What first set your soul on fire? The question Jean-Claude posed at the *cave* party. I could have answered *Wendell.* Why didn't I?

I let thoughts of Wendell drift away, and lose myself in the smell of smoke, the drumbeat, the whirl of Amandine's skirt. Jean-Claude is warming up in the background, casually juggling torches as though they were oranges, tossing them high, then spinning on his heel to catch them. His face glows in the flame. I suck in a breath every time a torch moves near his black curls.

Amandine skips away, letting Sabina take center stage. She moves like a belly dancer, swaying her hips, gyrating her torso, swirling the torches, painting the night air with fire. Her stunts aren't as impressive as Amandine's acrobatics, and there aren't as many gasps from the audience, but she's entrancing. The crowd is clapping now, in sync with the flicks of her hips and shoulders.

The flame briefly illuminates a part of the street that was in darkness, lighting up Tortue, in his Pierrot costume, leaning against a doorframe, perfectly still. I wonder if he's worried about Amandine, his daughter, playing with fire. Or simply proud. Or a mix of both.

Sabina tosses the torches to Jean-Claude. Now that Amandine has rested, she skips onto the scene again. Jean-Claude tosses her the torches. He and Amandine throw the torches back and forth, high and low, both of them leaping and spinning as the flames arc between them. They maintain nearly constant eye contact, anticipating each other's moves and cues. As Julien's drumming grows faster, louder, rising into a wild fervor, Amandine runs to Jean-Claude, leaps onto his shoulders, swirling her torches overhead as he stands up.

It's breathtaking. The audience explodes in applause.

Afterward, I sit with Illusion by the fountain. We're all floating from the rush of the fire dancing. Sabina is talking with Amandine about some new costumes they're designing, while Julien taps out complex rhythms on the bongos with his fingertips. Jean-Claude sits next to me and pulls his little notebook from his back pocket. I take out my ruby notebook. Together, we write, occasionally looking up to smile at each other, and then lower our heads to write some more.

I write about fire. Who knows what he's writing about.

Once, he looks up and says, "Your wrists are ocean waves."

"What do you mean?" I whisper.

"The way your wrists skim your page as you write. The invisible pulse inside, the hidden movement that keeps you alive."

I look back down at my notebook, aware now, of the rhythm of my hands. It's really too dark to see the words between scattered puddles of streetlamp light. It's better this way. No chance that Madame Chevalier is reading this through her binoculars. I glance up at her dark window. Maybe she's asleep. Or maybe she's watching us in the darkness. I imagine her trading her binoculars for night-vision goggles once the sun sets.

As I look back down at my notebook, I feel Jean-Claude watching me for a while, then scribbling something in his notebook.

"What are you writing about?" I whisper.

He motions with his chin to my neck. "That necklace makes you look like you've just emerged from a tree hollow."

My hand rises to my neck. It's my seed necklace from Ecuador. *"Merci."*

I don't tell him that Wendell bought it for me. Just a few weeks ago, I could fit Wendell into any conversation. But now, here, with Jean-Claude's poetry, in the afterglow of fire dancing, Wendell feels like something that didn't quite fit into my suitcase, something I left behind, along with my navy blue skirt with too many holes and my moss-green tank that had bleach splashed on it. Something with no place in my life now.

Of course, that's not true. Wendell is here in this town, and tomorrow he and Jean-Claude will be in the same room, at the same table, and I can't imagine that scene without feeling my throat start to close up.

• • •

Later, outside my apartment, my hand is fumbling around in my bag, looking for the key, when I feel something odd. A large envelope filled with something. I suck in a breath. Another mystery gift. How could my *fantôme* have slipped it in there? I've been so careful with my bag in crowded places.

My heart pounding, I hold the envelope up to the yellow streetlamp light. The front is marked *For Zeeta and Layla.*

Any lingering possibilities that the *fantôme* mistook me for someone else vanish. I open the envelope carefully, leaning against the stone wall. Inside are a bunch of folded-up light blue papers, and on the top, a piece of torn-out notebook paper, white and graphed, as most French notebooks are. On this top paper is a letter, written in French.

Chères Zeeta and Layla,
 I'm sorry I cannot give these letters to you in person. I'm sorry I cannot tell you who I am. But it's important for you to know, Zeeta, that I loved your mother very much, even if we could only be together for one

night. I still love her. When I saw you, I knew you must be my daughter, Zeeta. You look like my sister—your eyes, the heart shape of your face. I am so proud. Yet so sorry that I could not be part of your life.

I never mailed these letters because I had no address for you, Layla. But I saved them in hopes our paths would cross again. Please do not try to find me. Please just know that you have always been loved. And Zeeta, know that you will always have the love of a father, even if you don't know me.

All my love.

My hand is shaking, my stomach doing cartwheels. I flip through the remaining letters. They're all addressed to Layla, dated throughout the year before I was born, and signed *J.C.*

My father's hands touched these papers. My father's hands were here, just beneath my own hands. He wrote these words.

I tuck the pages beneath my arm and stumble up the three flights of stairs.

FOURTEEN

Layla's on the roof patio, sitting at the table, making a mosaic with shards of a pot knocked over earlier by the wind. Our porch lamp bulb has burned out, so the only light comes from three candles in glass holders. Layla's neck is craned over her project as she strains to see in the dim light. "Hello, love," she sings when she sees me in the doorway.

"Layla," I manage to creak, holding out the papers.

Seeing my face, she drops the pottery shards. "What's wrong, Z?" She wipes her hands on her skirt and takes the letters, raising them to the candlelight. When she realizes what they are, her hand flies to her face. There her hand stays, over her mouth, as her eyes move over the words.

Meanwhile, I try to wrap my mind around what these letters mean. But I'm in too much shock to think straight. I can only feel the flames inside me, an inferno of unformed emotion. Something red-hot and burning. Raw fury. At Layla. At my *fantôme* father. At life.

And then come the words, the same ones, over and over, in wave after wave. *Not fair, not fair, not fair.*

Gradually, my thoughts take shape. For years, I desperately wanted to know my father. And now—*now*—is the time he shows up. Now, when I'm way too old to cuddle on his lap or sit on his shoulders or be spun around or dance on his feet. Now, when all that can happen is awkward conversation. I've spent years trying to fill the hole he left—forming friendships with Paloma's father in Guatemala, Gaby in Ecuador, Vincent and Madame Chevalier here in France, and so many others over the years . . . and now he drops into my life.

These gifts from him—they're taunting. They're cruel.

Finally, Layla has read through all the letters several times. She looks up at me. "Where did these come from?"

I force myself to form words. "My *fantôme*." I sink into a chair, my legs too weak to hold me anymore. I have the impulse to put the letters in the fire, let them burn up, turn to ash.

"Have you read them?" Layla whispers.

I manage to shake my head.

She pulls a chair close to mine and holds the first letter between us. I keep my hands in my lap in hard, clenched fists. The letter is not in French but in English. And it's dated nine months before my birth. I make myself read it silently.

> Lovely Layla,
>   You said you would write to me, and as I am too eager to wait for your letter, I shall write to you first. Why did you leave without saying goodbye? I woke up in the morning and you were gone, like an angel in a dream. Last night was the most beautiful night of my life. I can only wait for your letter from Italy, and hope it comes soon. Did you feel what I did last night?
>
>   Yours,
>   J.C.

The next letter is also written in English.

> Lovely Layla,
>   Your sunshine taste is still on my tongue, even after a month. I remember when I came out of the sea. You were sitting there like a mermaid in the moonlight. I thought I was dreaming you. And when we talked, you wove a spell over me. Perhaps we can meet in Italy? Oh, please write to me soon! I do not know where to send this letter. You

know how to find me, but I cannot find you.
I cannot stop thinking about you.

> Love,
> J.C.

* I hoping this leters have sence. My friend traslate for me. I am copy the leters. My Inglish riting is no good. Sory.

Layla has rested her hand on her chest. She's struggling to breathe deeply, but this is something too shocking for yogic breath to touch. She shuffles to the next letter.

Suddenly, my anger's directed toward Layla. I turn to her and hiss, "Why didn't you write to him?"

She shakes her head. "I don't know. The night was magical for me, too. But I wanted to explore, travel. I didn't want a man holding me back."

"But when you found out you were pregnant?" I push. "Why didn't you write him then?"

"I must have thrown away his address. I didn't think I'd ever see him again."

My fingernails dig into my palms as Layla rubs her temple, shuffling to the next paper. How would our lives be different if she'd written to him? If she'd gotten these letters? J.C. was in love with her. In *love* with her. It wasn't just a one-night stand for him. He *loved* her!

And now, in some kind of sick revenge scheme, he's teasing us with this.

I hate him. I don't even know him and I hate him. How could he give these to me and write that he won't meet me?

The final letter is in English too. I chew on my lip and force myself to read it.

> My Layla,
> I have left Greece. Every time I look at the ocean I see your mermaid hair tangled with sand, each grain a tiny star. It seems that night meant nothing to you. Your letter has never come. I have returned to France. I am tired of moving. Too heavy. Like a stone that can only sink. Farther and farther down. Here I will stay in Marseille, near the sea, where I can smell the salt and work on the water but not be haunted by the memories of our night in Greece. Forget about me. But you already have, no? And I will try to forget you. I still wear your Jimi Hendrix shirt. Perhaps someday I shall return it to you.
>
> Love,
> J.C.
>
> P.S. Make every day a song.

Layla speaks softly, in a kind of trance. "Marseille. He lived in Marseille. Right here in Provence." A sudden look of comprehension flashes over her face. "The List! J.C. must have been the one to recommend coming here. The first place on my List."

Barely registering her words, I grab the letters and stuff them back into the envelope. "He's a coward," I say. "A selfish, cruel coward."

"I'm so sorry, love." Layla tries to hug me, but I pull away.

We're quiet for a while. I let a kind of numbness settle over me. I hear a truck rumbling by. The neighbor boys laughing. A baby screaming. Some distant Middle Eastern music.

Then Layla starts crying, burying her face in her hands.

I crack, let my own tears spill over. I hate seeing her like this. And she's all I have. I lean my head against hers, try to still her shaking shoulders with my hands. Together, we sit under the stars, watching a silver cat creep across the roof, the blinking light of an airplane crossing the sky. My *fantôme* father is somewhere out there, hiding, and for all I care, he can stay hidden. Layla and I are fine on our own. We've always been fine.

FIFTEEN

My apartment buzzer rings just as the clock tower is chiming for the seventh time. Wendell is punctual. Seven o'clock on the dot, right on time for Illusion's dinner party. I grab my bag, call goodbye to Layla, and jog downstairs and out the door. It's the time of day when the sun's so low, the streets feel like deep, shadowy canyons. The angled light illuminates the treetops, the red-tiled roofs, the sheets and clothes hanging out fourth-story windows. But below, we're in the shadows.

Wendell can tell right away something's wrong. "What happened, Z?"

"My *fantôme*. I know who he is." My voice quakes. Wendell waits as I take a long breath. "He's my father, Wendell."

"Oh, God, Zeeta."

I summarize my *fantôme* father's letters. Even after I've had two days for this to sink in, I still think of him more as a ghost than my father.

After I finish, Wendell says, "I don't get why you're not excited about this, Z."

I whip around to face him. "Why would I be *excited*?"

"You thought you'd never find him. And now he's found you."

I shake my head. "He's skulking around, spying on me. He hasn't even introduced himself."

After a few paces, Wendell says, "Maybe he has a good reason. Maybe it took courage to give you those letters."

"Wendell, I can't believe you're taking his side!"

Wendell takes an Altoid tin from his pocket, offers me a mint.

I decline, walking faster.

"So what are you going to do?" he asks, struggling to keep up.

"Forget about him."

For a while we walk in silence. It feels too strange to hold Wendell's hand, so I keep both hands clasping the handle of my bag as I walk. We do not look like soul mates who've just been reunited after nine months.

After a block Wendell says, "Maybe he'll give you something else. Maybe he'll introduce himself. Maybe you just have to be patient."

"You know what? Let's not talk about this anymore. Anyway, here's Illusion's place."

We stop in front of Café Eternité and I press the ringer.

Someone buzzes us inside, and we go up a few flights of stairs, where Amandine is waiting for us with the door flung open. *"Entrez,"* she says.

Inside, evening sunlight streams through the floor-to-ceiling windows. I can see practically the whole apartment from this vantage point. It's sparsely furnished, with mostly bare white walls. The color comes from the giant backpacks and bags and piles of clothes pressed against the walls, wedged into nooks between furniture.

When Amandine kisses us both in greeting, Wendell turns his cheek the wrong way and ends up bumping noses with her twice. She laughs and leads us both farther inside, one arm around each of us, and introduces Wendell to Sabina and Julien. Smells of sautéed garlic and shallots and simmering wine fill the little space. Steam and smoke rise from pots on the stove, drifting around Jean-Claude's damp face as he empties a bowl of sliced zucchini into a pan sizzling with olive oil. From the kitchen area, he smiles and then bends down to adjust the heat.

Please don't kiss Wendell's cheeks, I silently beg. *And please don't kiss my cheeks in front of him.*

Thankfully, Jean-Claude simply waves to us but stays in the kitchen, apparently in charge of the cooking.

Sabina turns to Wendell and says in English, "So you're from Colorado? The mountains?"

They launch into a conversation about skiing, and Wendell throws in some garbled French here and there. He actually knows quite a bit, and I'm guessing that in a few weeks he'll be able to have a decent conversation. In the meantime, since Illusion speaks English, that's what we all use.

"Let me give you a tour!" Amandine says.

Wendell agrees enthusiastically. The apartment seems so tiny, I'm not sure where she'll take us. She leads us to the door of a minuscule bedroom, which can barely hold a twin-sized bed. "Julien and Sabina's room," she announces.

"And the rest of you?" Wendell asks, peering around.

"The sofa pulls out to a bed, where I sleep," she says. "The chair pulls out to another. That's for Jean-Claude. Tortue sleeps on the floor on a roll mat. He likes sleeping on the floor."

And to think I complain about sharing tiny apartments with Layla. "Where is he, anyway?"

She presses her lips together. "Not here." She hesitates, as if deciding how much to tell us. "He's in Montperrin."

"Where's that?" Wendell asks.

"It's a psychiatric hospital." She lets this fact sink in. "Not far. Just a couple kilometers away." Now that she's told us, she seems to want to talk more about it. "I've been asking him for weeks to check himself in, and he's finally done it. Probably not for long, just to get back on his feet." She folds her arms across her chest, hugging herself. A lonely, helpless gesture.

"Well," I say. "It's good he's getting treatment, right?"

Amandine shrugs, and then, shaking off her gloom, grabs Wendell's and my hands and skips to the bathroom. *"Regardez!"* This is what she really wants to show us, I realize. It's extremely tiny, just a single toilet. Barely enough room for the three of us to stand. Images from magazines are plastered over the walls and the ceiling. They're cropped in odd ways and arranged by body part—a bunch of knees in one area, armpits in another, a disconcerting collection of eyes in another.

"I'm getting ready to lacquer it," she says.

"Wow!" Wendell says, looking genuinely impressed.

Amandine smiles. "I leave my mark everywhere we live. The landlords let me. No one cares about the toilet room. Too small for them to decorate but perfect for me."

Even though we're crammed into an area the size of a dinky closet, Wendell wants to stay and talk about every single image. "Why did you choose to put this here?" "I love the juxtaposition of these two." It's like he's at a gallery opening, only it's just the three of us and we're squeezed into a one-by-three-meter space with flower-scented toilet paper.

"All recycled," Amandine says, standing with her foot pressed to the inside of her thigh, tree yoga pose. Her arm is stretched up, her hand leaning on the wall, crawling up like ivy. "I'm friends with the guy at the magazine kiosk on the Place de la Mairie. He gives me his old magazines, with the covers torn off."

Just when I'm thinking it can't get worse, Jean-Claude

appears at the bathroom door and sidles inside. And now he's kissing my cheeks and saying he's sorry he didn't greet me in the kitchen but his hands were full of zucchini. And I'm trying hard to pull away, but there's nowhere to go. Then he kisses Wendell's cheeks, and Wendell bumps noses with him, too, and now the bathroom smells like a suffocating mix of Jean-Claude's cologne and Wendell's cinnamon soap and the flowery pink toilet paper.

It's just too much. Gasping for breath, I push my way out the door, praying that this evening will end soon.

• • •

It's midnight, dark in Illusion's apartment, only the yellow glow of some candles, lamplight tinted red from a silk scarf draped over the shade, and a tiny bulb above the stove. We're four hours into dinner and there's no end in sight. The courses just keep coming and coming. I tried to excuse myself after an hour, after the first course of melon wrapped in prosciutto.

"Don't count on leaving before dawn," Amandine warned, her eyes twinkling. So far we've had aperitifs with olives and crackers, cherry tomatoes stuffed with fresh basil and goat's cheese, lemon sorbet to clean our palates, sautéed vegetables with *herbes de Provence* butter sauce, fish in béarnaise sauce, lamb chops basted in rosemary and olive oil.

The pattern became clear early on: each course lasts nearly an hour and gets its own plate. And each course comes with a splash of a particular wine that Julien has deemed appropriate—some white, some red, some rosé. The dinner lasts so long, and there's so much endless food, that the alcohol barely affects me—just adds to the smoky, steamy, surreal haze of the evening.

Amandine and Jean-Claude are glowing, obviously in their element, taking turns hopping up to wash dishes or get the next course ready in the kitchen. As they cross paths, they bicker over what kind of oil to use or what type of cheese to serve or just ruffle each other's hair. Now Amandine's sitting down, listening to Wendell talk about how he wants to be a photographer for National Geographic Explorer. He has a new camera this year, a fancy digital one with lots of lenses, which he uses to snap photos of each course before digging in. Amandine looks appreciatively at pictures he's already taken, admiring the angles. *"Ah, ça, c'est génial!"*

Meanwhile, I'm praying that the next course will be the last. Shouldn't midnight be a dinner cutoff time? Won't it spoil our appetites for breakfast after some point? It's not that I'm not enjoying myself. The food might be the best I've ever had. And the company is interesting.

It's just uncomfortable, the way Wendell and I left things undone. Actually, everything in my life feels as though it's been shaken up and spun around, especially my beliefs about my father.

When Amandine talks with Wendell about art, I have no choice but to talk with Jean-Claude. He quotes poetry and talks about the surrealists, symbolists, romantics. I write the names of the poets he recommends in my notebook, and match his quotes with verses from some of Layla's mystics. At one point, after the *endives au gratin*, I help him clear the table and prepare the next course, biting my lip when our elbows and hips graze each other in the small kitchen. When I'm holding a tray with a basket of sliced baguette and duck liver paté, he reaches over to move my hair behind my shoulder. On edge, I jump back, but he whispers, "*Calme-toi*, Zeeta. The tips of your hair were just falling into the paté."

Around one a.m., Jean-Claude pulls out his accordion and plays a reel before the next course. Over the music, he asks, "Whatever happened with that CD someone gave you, Zeeta? Ever find out who it was?"

Wendell and I look at each other.

Sabina chimes in, "What CD?"

Jean-Claude explains to Sabina and Julien that it was slipped into my bag. Amandine keeps her eyes on mine, watching my reaction.

I try not to let my emotion show. "He left some other things too," I say evenly. "Some letters. Turns out he's my father."

"Your father?" Sabina says.

"*Oui,*" I say. "And actually, I'd rather not talk about it."

Amandine wrinkles her eyebrows. "Why?"

"Because I'm not exactly happy my father's a weirdo who won't even introduce himself." I stop there. I'm flushing, starting to break out in a sweat.

"He could have a good reason," Amandine points out.

"That's what I said," Wendell agrees.

I close my eyes, wishing I were anywhere but here.

Amandine goes on. "Maybe he wants to connect with you but he doesn't know how."

Jean-Claude jumps in. "I'm with Zeeta. Parents are over-rated, anyway. Leave the past in the past."

Amandine shoots him a knife-sharp look. "You'd feel differently if your parents were dead."

"They are dead."

"*Oh, mon oeil!*" she snaps. "They're alive and living less than an hour away."

Jean-Claude stands up, almost knocking his chair over backward, and goes into the kitchen.

Amandine takes her last bite of baguette spread with paté, then stands up and clears this round of dishes. I hear her and Jean-Claude arguing in whispers in the kitchen.

I'm just about to stand up to leave, when Amandine emerges with a bowl of cherries. "Sit down, Zeeta!" she commands.

Over her shoulder, I see Jean-Claude pulling a tart from the oven, releasing a wave of buttery sweetness. He appears to be fuming. Even through the steam, I see that the expression on his face is rigid and cold.

"He'll get over it," Amandine whispers, pushing the bowl in front of me. "Have some."

I pluck a cherry from the pile and settle back in my chair for a few more rounds.

• • •

It's two a.m. when we finally leave. I'm exhausted but jittery in the aftermath of two espressos—the eleventh and
final course. Even though Wendell has a long trek ahead, all
the way to the outskirts of town, he walks me home. The
side streets are completely deserted except for a few random
passersby coming back from clubs.

We're quiet until Wendell asks under his breath, "What's
going on, Z?"

"What?" I say. "Nothing. What do you mean?"

"Z, you don't even want to hold my hand." His voice is
shaking. "You don't talk. You hardly even look at me."

My heart stops. It's like that moment when a glass slips from
your fingers and you know it will be a split second before it hits
the floor, not enough time to catch the glass, but enough time
for that cringing, blood-rushing feeling of *oh, no*.

"Z, can I ask you something?"

I dig my fingernails into my palms, bracing myself. "Okay."

"And you'll be honest?"

The eleven courses of food are suddenly churning in my
stomach. I nod.

"Is there something going on with you and Jean-Claude?"
Wendell's voice is vulnerable, something that could so easily
be smashed.

"No," I say automatically. Then, after a pause, I add, "Well,
we've been hanging out. But it's not just him." And then, in
one big, middle-of-the-night, espresso-fueled rush, all kinds
of things tumble from my mouth. "I'm—I'm confused.

About my *fantôme* father, about you, about me, about everything. I thought this summer would be like last summer. But it's not. I'm not the same person. Nothing stays the same. Not even my taste in dresses. Not my favorite colors." I'm rambling and I can't stop. "And now, with my father's letters, everything in my life is turned upside down."

Wendell's expression softens, tender with concern. "Z, of course you're the same. You might change a little, but—"

"I'm not the same Zeeta who fell in love with you." My eyes grow teary. "Everything's different from how I imagined."

He takes my hand. "I love you, no matter what Zeeta you are. I'm not worried about the future."

I wipe my eyes. "H-have you seen something?"

He pauses. "I see what's in front of me, here, now. You already know how I feel." A shadow passes over his face. "So it's up to you whether we stay together or not."

Until he says it, the possibility of breaking up doesn't seem real. But once it's out there, once the words are said, I can see that's where we're headed. "I don't—I don't know," I sputter. "I mean, I spent all year wanting to see you. And I love you. I do. But—I don't know." I look at him and whisper, "Nothing feels right."

He tucks some stray pieces of hair behind his ears. He speaks in a low voice that crackles with emotion. "Are you breaking up with me?"

"I—I guess so." I start crying again. "I'm so sorry, Wendell."

He backs away from me. If we hadn't just broken up,

he'd be holding me now. Instead, he rubs his eyes and turns to go.

"Wendell?"

"Good night, Zeeta." His voice is hoarse, full of pain, and he doesn't look back.

SIXTEEN

The pitter-patter of rain on the roof rouses me. I open
my eyes, taking in the pale, watery morning light. For a
pinprick of a moment, I consider falling back asleep. And
then all the events of the previous night rush back to me,
and there's no way I could go to sleep again, even though
I've only slept for five hours. Groggy, with eyes puffy and
red, I plop onto a kitchen chair and pick at some *mille-
feuilles* on the table.

Layla wanders in and pours herself tea. "Hello, love."

"Hey."

She opens a jar of lavender honey and takes a deep sniff
before spooning some into her tea. She splurged on the
honey at the market, spent as much as I'd budgeted for an
entire day's meals. She insisted she'd use it sparingly. "I'll

smell it and look at it through sunshine a lot, Z," she claimed. "Eating it's only a little piece of the pleasure."

As she's stirring her tea, she must notice my misery, because she says with concern, "What's wrong, Z? Are you still upset about J.C.'s letters?"

There's no easy way to break the news. I stare at the steam over her cup, avoiding her eyes. "I broke up with him."

Once she absorbs what I've said, she hugs me. "I'm so sorry, love." She seems sad, but not exactly surprised. Then, hesitantly, she asks in a low voice, "Is there someone else?"

I stare at the rain streaming down the pane, tiny silver pathways. "I don't know. I guess there could be." I'm reluctant to admit he's a nomadic street musician whose father figure is an eccentric clown. It would just be too in-your-face obvious that I'm following Layla's well-trodden relationship path. "I'm just like you, aren't I, Layla?"

"What do you mean?"

"Once I get close to one guy, I move on to another."

"You're nothing like me in that way, love."

"How can I not be? It's all I've ever known."

Her face falls.

I've hurt her. I stop myself from going farther down that road. I take a spoonful of straight lavender honey, taste its sudden sweetness filling my mouth. I swallow and ask, "So, Layla, why haven't you found the love of your life yet?"

"I have." She sips her tea.

"Really?"

Raising her teacup in a kind of toast, she says, "You, Z."

I make a face. "That's weird, Layla."

She bites into a *mille-feuilles,* and as a cascade of crumbs tumbles down her robe, she asks, "So who is he, anyway?"

This time I answer. "Jean-Claude. The accordionist for Illusion." I stand up, still looking away. If I see her face, all full of sympathy, I might start crying again.

She says in a soft, Rumi-drenched voice, *"This rain-weeping and sun-burning twine together to make us grow."*

• • •

From the vantage point of Madame Chevalier's window, the Place de la Mairie is a square, shiny lake speckled with sleek black umbrellas and people darting here and there, shielding their faces from the rain. I'm drinking peach tea with Madame Chevalier as we wait for Vincent to join us.

"There he is," I say, pointing to Vincent with his entourage of pigeons, Maude on his shoulder. Apparently, the rain doesn't faze him a bit. He waves and heads our way at a slow waddle.

Madame Chevalier peers at him through the binoculars, then, looking pleased, opens a little drawer in the table and takes out a silver compact and lipstick. With one slightly trembling hand she holds the mirror, and with the other she spreads on the lipstick carefully. Cotton-candy pink. Oddly girlish. She rubs her lips, then spritzes on a bit of jasmine perfume.

I smile at her. "You really like Vincent, don't you?"

"Of course." She twirls the binoculars cord around her fingers. "Maude is so fortunate to have him dote on her."

I like sitting up here with Madame Chevalier, an unseen spectator of life. "And how is your boyfriend?" she asks, patting her cheeks with rouge.

I press my lips together. "We broke up."

"*Mon Dieu!* How terrible!" She puts her hand over her heart, as if to calm it, and then whispers, "Why?"

I pause. I'm not sure how to put it into words. I'm not even sure I know the answer. "We're just too different" is the cliché I settle on.

She waves my reason away with a bony hand. "Oh, Vincent always said that about us. That I was a famous world-traveling artist, out of his league."

I raise an eyebrow. "But you're perfect for each other. The pigeons, the quest for the waters . . ." I trail off, studying her, trying to tell if she's blushing or if she just put on too much rouge.

"Well, *ma petite*," she says, closing her compact mirror and tucking it into the drawer. "Why don't you smooth things over with him?"

"I can't. We're broken up."

She looks doubtful. "At least you'll stay friends with him, won't you? He's essential to you finding the waters, you know."

I breathe out. "We'll see." I don't say more. I don't want to see her disappointment.

When Vincent arrives, Madame Chevalier fusses over him

and Maude, insisting they dry off with pink hand towels from the bathroom. Once she's satisfied they're warm, she tells Vincent about my breakup with Wendell. A grave expression falls over both their faces at this news. Apparently, they had high hopes that Wendell's divination powers would be the lucky break they needed. For a while, they stroke Maude sullenly.

They do brighten a little when I hand back the *Curiosités d'Aix-en-Provence* book and tell them about my trip to Entremont with Sirona and Layla. "I could just ask Sirona directly about the waters," I say. "That would be quicker and easier than this secret agent stuff."

"Oh, she won't tell," Vincent says. "You get smart after living for centuries." He taps a finger on his forehead.

Madame Chevalier nods in solemn agreement. "Or millennia," she adds.

"Oh, right," I say, trying to keep the sarcasm out of my voice. "I forgot about the accumulated wisdom of millennia." Today I seem to have less patience for indulging these two. I exhale slowly and ask, "So what's my course of action?"

"Just keep your eyes and ears open," Vincent says.

Madame Chevalier nods. "And when Sirona slips, you'll be ready."

Soon Vincent goes into the kitchen to make more tea, and I glance at the hallway lined with self-portraits. "You know, Madame Chevalier, you'd have an infinite number of hallways filled with paintings if you two get eternal life—"

"*Mais non, ma petite!*" she cries. "Remember what the book

says. Only those who drink regularly from the waters will have eternal life. One sip will simply heal you." She folds her hands, tucks them beneath her chin. "Oh, we only want a sip."

I survey the portraits and open my notebook. "What's the same about you in all these pictures? I mean, throughout all your travels, all the decades, what's never changed?"

A faraway look washes over her face. "Maude," she says. "Whenever I'd come back to Aix after a long trip, before my bags were even unpacked, I'd hear the lovely flutter of Maude's wings, see the glimmer of her feathers, feel her settle on my lap." She smiles. "And read the new message she carried."

I jot down her answers, and then, on an impulse, I lean forward and whisper, "Is it Maude you love, or the one sending the messages?"

Madame Chevalier puts her hand over her heart, her rouged cheeks turning pinker.

Vincent totters into the living room with a tray of teacups, clattering with each step. "Zeeta, I nearly forgot! Have you received any more mysterious gifts?"

"As a matter of fact, yes." I pull the packet of letters from my bag and translate the first one, my voice quavering with emotion. On the second letter, halfway through, I need to pause and take a deep breath to steady my voice.

After the third letter, I look up and see that Madame Chevalier's face is streaked with tears. "There's nothing sadder," she says, "than love that can never be realized, is there?"

I swallow, and say nothing.

"You must find this man, *ma petite.*"

I blink. "He doesn't want me to find him."

"Oh, I think he does," she says with confidence.

"Oui," Vincent says, nodding. "He does."

"Why would I even want to find him?"

Vincent strokes Maude's feathers before answering. "Because it's rare for someone to offer love like this. When it's offered, you take it. And if you have love to give, you give it."

Madame Chevalier looks at Vincent for a moment and reaches over to touch Maude's head. Her fingers graze Vincent's. Then she wipes her cheeks and says firmly, "You must go to Marseille, Zeeta. Look for clues there. Find your father."

• • •

An otherworldly bliss sweeps over Sirona's face as she plays the lyre. Her fingers skim the strings, almost of their own accord, while her mind floats away to another place and time. It's fitting that she's named after a water goddess. She moves like river currents: pure, effortless grace. In fact, all the members of Salluvii possess this elegance and ease. Damona's eyes scan the audience as she plays, interested and curious. Her gaze lands on Bormanus, who sends her a hint of a smile. Sirona's husband, Grannos, is subdued, relaxed, looking upward as he plays, to the tops of buildings, the sky, the birds.

I'm perched on the fountain in the Place de la Mairie, taking notes on Salluvii. When they started playing fifteen minutes earlier, Vincent ushered me out of Madame Chevalier's apartment, encouraging me to study the musicians up close. "Take notes in that notebook of yours!" he advised. I suspect he simply wanted time alone with Madame Chevalier.

The rain has let up, and weak sunlight is peeking through the clouds. I open my notebook, wanting to write about my father but not sure where to begin. Last summer, I translated letters that Wendell wrote to his birth father when he was younger, years before they'd ever met. Some letters burned with rage, others were light and casual, others full of yearning, and others simply grateful. Wendell said it was his way of making sense of his jumbled emotions in a powerless situation.

I turn to a fresh page and, slowly, write,

> Dear J.C.,
>   I got your packet of letters. At first I wanted to kill you. How dare you come into my life now? How dare you play games with my feelings?

I write two pages, until Salluvii stops playing. I feel a little better after venting, even though I doubt my father will ever read the letter.

After Salluvii's set, Sirona glides over, carrying her lyre. "*Bonjour*, Zeeta," she says, giving me two quick pecks on the cheeks and sitting beside me, bringing with her the scent of lavender and thyme, as if she's just emerged from a sunny field.

"*Bonjour*, Sirona," I say, closing my notebook, aware that Madame Chevalier is probably watching us through binoculars, speculating with Vincent on my conversation, cooking up some new, magical theory.

Sirona sets her lyre on her lap, absently plucking a few strings. In her calm voice, she asks how I'm doing. "*Ça va, Zeeta?*"

I hesitate, wondering whether I should confide in her. "Sirona," I begin. "Did Layla tell you about the letters from my dad?"

She nods. "What a shock for you. How are you handling it?"

"I'm thinking I might try to find him."

"Really?" She tilts her head. "Layla said you were angry, that you wanted to forget about him."

"Maybe I changed my mind," I say, glancing at Madame Chevalier's window, where she and Vincent sit side by side, watching me. Sure enough, the binoculars are half covering her face. I give her a small smile and turn back to Sirona. "What do you think about all this?"

She hesitates, running her fingertips over her lyre, bits of stardust. Then she leans in, close. "Zeeta, you wouldn't believe how much I've seen in my lifetime. And if there's one thing I've observed again and again, it's this." She pauses and lets her gaze sink into me. I imagine that Madame Chevalier and Vincent are waiting with bated breath, dying to hear what she's about to say.

"At the end of their lives," Sirona says slowly, "people usually regret what they *didn't* do, not so much what they *did* do."

I take this in. "And you think I'll regret not looking for my father?"

She nods. "Now, when he's so close, when he's reaching out. Now, when you have the opportunity. Maybe your only opportunity."

I turn her advice over in my mind, glancing up at Madame Chevalier in the window and then back at Sirona.

Both women are wise in their own eccentric ways.

Both have traveled the world.

Both have souls of artists.

And most importantly, both have given me the same advice.

• • •

It's rainy again today—just a light drizzle, but I'm wishing I had an umbrella. Layla doesn't believe in umbrellas. She insists that being caught in the rain is one of the greatest joys of being alive, and no way would she try to block it out. Since we've never had money for luxuries, I've learned to accept an umbrellaless existence.

I'm on Rue Granet, heading toward Illusion's apartment, since I have some extra time between tutoring sessions.

When I reach Café Eternité, I push Illusion's buzzer and duck inside the doorframe for shelter, shaking the rain from my hair.

Jean-Claude's head pops out the third-story window. *"Salut,* Zeeta!"

"Salut!" I call up. "Can we talk?"

"Bien sûr!" he says. *"Un instant."* He disappears from view, and two minutes later, he's downstairs kissing my cheeks, without an umbrella. Tilting his head to the sky, he lets raindrops fall into his mouth.

I'm guessing he feels the same way about rain that Layla does. "Do you want to go somewhere to talk?" I ask. "A café or something?"

"Ouais." He lightly takes my arm and we head down the street. "Let's go to my favorite fountain," he says. "It's hidden, just down there."

He leads us down a back street toward a small and simple rectangular fountain, just two modest streams of water falling from snake mouths. A few pigeons are clustered on the edge of the fountain, unbothered by the misty rain. The fountain is just in front of an abandoned-looking apartment building, boarded up, with broken glass and graffiti. Jean-Claude gestures to a stoop next to the fountain, under an overhang to keep off the rain.

I sit down, folding my arms across my chest, feeling chilled.

"Voilà!" he says. "A solitary nook. No tourists come this

way, or else the Aixois government would have fixed that window and cleaned up the graffiti." He leans back against the door and breathes in deeply. "I wish I could eat the smell of rain. I'd serve it at a feast. It would be a nice palate cleanser, like lemon sorbet without the tang."

It's starting to rain harder now, just a foot away from us, but I stay dry except for an occasional stray drop. The sounds of water surround us—the patter of rain on the street and in the fountain, the light rushing of water pouring from the snake mouths. The world looks blurry, subdued, the streets shiny and dark and empty.

"I've decided to look for my father," I announce.

He looks at me, surprised. "Last I heard, you wanted nothing to do with him."

"I'll regret it if I don't try."

He holds out a hand, cupping raindrops. "I told you my thoughts already. That parents are not necessary after a point."

"What happened with yours?" I hug my knees to my chest, shivering. "Why did you break with them?"

He shakes his head. "I leave the past in the past."

For a while we just watch the rain, and then I say, "My father lived in Marseille for a while. I think if I go there, I might find out something about him."

He gives me a sideways look. "What do you have to go on?"

"I think he might have worked on the docks sixteen years ago."

He raises an eyebrow. "There are over a million people in Marseille, Zeeta."

I take a deep breath. "That's why I was hoping you'd come with me."

He runs his hand through his hair, briefly revealing his scar. "Marseille is the setting for all my nightmares. I never go there."

I nod, biting my lip. "You're the only person I know from Marseille. It would really help if—"

"All right, Zeeta," he says abruptly. "I'll think about it."

"Merci." I hug my knees tighter and watch the raindrops land in the fountain, creating widening, intersecting circles. "Tell me one good memory of your parents in Marseille. There has to be something."

He gives a short bark of a laugh. A full minute passes before he says, "When I was little, we'd take a ferry to the islands of Frioul, just off the coast of Marseille. My step-father worked for the ferry company, so I got to sit up front, get royal treatment. They'd even let me work the controls sometimes. It was amazing for a little kid, to be steering something so huge. And then we'd get to the island and go swimming on the beach and have ice cream at a café on the docks. My dad would always bring along one of his instruments—and we'd sit on the towels and play together until the very last ferry left at sunset."

"Sounds good. Your parents sound great."

"You asked for a good memory."

"But there have to be more, Jean-Claude."

"Let's just say that the innocent boy steering the ferry is gone. And his parents are too." He traces the lines in the shattered glass, leaving a thick film of dust on his finger, which he wipes on his red velvet pants.

"Did something happen?" I ask.

He doesn't answer.

"Can't you tell me anything about your family, your past?"

"Like what?"

"Any brothers or sisters?" I ask.

"Julien and Sabina and Amandine."

"I mean real brothers and sisters."

"Dandelion seeds," he whispers.

"Where are they?"

"Wherever owls go in the daytime."

I think. I've never seen an owl in the daytime. "Where's that?"

"Exactly."

"Jean-Claude, why won't you tell me why you left home?"

"The past doesn't matter. There is only now. You. Me. The pigeons. The rain."

"What does that mean?"

"What does rain mean? What does a pigeon mean?"

"You're infuriating," I say, leaning back.

"*Désolé*, Zeeta," he says. Sorry. The word makes me think of desolate things, lonely and abandoned. I catch a glimpse of something vulnerable in Jean-Claude. Until now, he's always exuded confidence, charm, sparkle. But in this drizzle, his eyes reflect only the gray of wet stone. Even his red outfit seems subdued. It makes me think of Tortue's story of Harlequin, once the bad weather came.

Jean-Claude scoots to the edge of the stoop, into the rain, and closes his eyes, tilting his head back. I'm studying his face, trying to figure him out, when his eyes open and look into mine. He moves his face close. His breath is warm, his lips parted, coming closer to mine. I hold still, my heart pounding.

Suddenly, we're engulfed by the squawks of birds. There's an uproar among the pigeons, wild feathers flapping and beaks pecking and screeching. A pigeon fight.

I look at the pigeon that caused the commotion, its feathers still ruffled. There's a vial tied to its leg. I squint through the rain. There are only three salmon-pink toes on that leg. But even without the vial and missing toe, I could tell it was Maude, the way she prances around like a fussy old lady or a spoiled little princess. She gives me an impish look and ruffles her silver-flecked feathers.

It's as if Maude came to stop any budding romance between me and Jean-Claude. Maude, the cupid toting messages rather than arrows. Maude, the immortal protectress of true love. Maude, who has apparently decided that Jean-Claude is not *l'homme de ma vie*.

She wanders near my feet, and then flutters up, taking flight. She swoops down again, near my head, as though she wants me to follow her. This little back street isn't between Madame Chevalier's apartment and Vincent's shop. What's Maude doing here? And where is she headed? I remember Vincent's belief that Maude makes side trips to drink from the sacred waters. If that's true, maybe she's headed there now. I jump up, keeping my eye on Maude. "I have to go, Jean-Claude."

"Where?" he asks, bewildered.

"To follow this pigeon," I say with a wry smile.

His mouth drops open in confusion, but there's no time to explain. With a wave, I run down the street, after Maude.

SEVENTEEN

Maude is flying just fast enough to make me sprint at top speed. She sticks to the streets, never flying higher than the rooftops, making it easy to follow her. She turns right around the corner, leading me down another narrow side street. We're in the ancient part of town, where the streets are short and mazelike, where statues of saints and Virgin Marys perch in high-up niches on the corners of ancient buildings, where nearly every arched doorway is topped with a fantastical creature's face.

Within minutes, the drizzle lets up and the sun peaks out, gleaming off the wet pavement.

I'm breathless and starting to feel silly, considering giving up the chase, when Maude glides down. She lands on the head of a grumpy-looking seraphim protruding from a fountain, and takes a sip of the water spilling from its mouth. It's just a regular public fountain, though; there's no indication that it contains healing waters. "Why did you bring me here?" I ask Maude, slightly annoyed.

From behind, someone says, "You okay, Zeeta?"

I whip my head around. It's Wendell. He's sitting on a bench beneath a tree, his sketchbook on his knees. A cool damp lingers in the air, and the wet cobblestones are steaming in the sunshine. Droplets cling to tree leaves, draping them in crystals.

"Oh. Hi, Wendell." I try to catch my breath, glancing at Maude out of the corner of my eye. She's settled comfortably on the grumpy seraphim's head.

"Why were you running?" he asks.

"Oh." I titter. "I was running after that pigeon. Maude's her name." I gesture toward her. "Vincent and Madame Chevalier adore her. They think she's immortal."

He gives me a strange look.

"I know. It's ridiculous. But they have this theory she takes a detour at some magical waters. You know, the ones I told you about? One sip supposedly heals you, and if you drink from it regularly, you're immortal." I'm caught in a nervous stream of babbling, and I can't stop. "Maude here could have seen Cézanne painting over a hundred years ago."

Wendell gives a weak smile and looks back at his notebook, picking up his charcoal.

I know I should leave, but I hear myself keep talking. "Hey, how was your first day of classes?"

"Fine," he answers.

I gesture to his notebook with my chin. "What are you sketching?"

"The fountain," he murmurs. "Part of an assignment. Sketching all the fountains in Aix." He glances up briefly, not exactly avoiding my eyes, but not looking too closely. He looks at me as if I'm a casual acquaintance, nothing more. Even though I should be expecting this, I feel a stab of pain.

Ignoring my voice of reason—which tells me to leave him alone—I move closer. "Mind if I peek over your shoulder?"

"Go ahead." He pushes a strand of hair behind his ear. "Better you than my teacher. She's a tyrant."

He's not doing anything that shows he's upset. It's what he's *not* doing. He's not smiling the half-smile that I love. I loved. He's withholding those particular expressions that used to be woven into our every interaction.

I stand awkwardly, noticing that he hasn't invited me to sit on the bench beside him. I try to keep my voice natural. "How is she a tyrant?"

"She's always yelling, 'No outlines! Shadows only!' "

"What's that mean?"

"She says you have to train your eye to see light and shadows." He's looking at his page, not at me. "If you shade in the dark parts, then the areas of light will naturally appear. And as a side effect, the shape will emerge."

Hyper cool, I say, trying to sound enthusiastic, to break this tension. I stare at Maude, who's waddling along the edge of the fountain now, sipping at tiny puddles. I search for something else to say. I don't want to mention my *fantôme* father and my decision to look for clues in Marseille. Then I'd have to explain that I asked Jean-Claude to help me. Instead, I say, "I thought you were focusing on photography."

"I am. But the first half of the course is drawing and painting." He keeps his eyes glued to the page. "Everything's about light and dark. Learning in one medium transfers to another. That's what the tyrant tells us, at least."

"Can I see your other drawings?"

"Sure. There aren't many. Just a few from today." He tosses me the sketch pad, careful not to touch me. It's almost exaggerated, this lack of contact. As though if he accidentally brushed his hand against mine, we'd explode.

I sit down beside him and flip through the pages. "These are great."

"Not really. I have lots to learn." Another thing lacking— Wendell's spark. It's like he's reciting lines, only feigning interest in the conversation.

I hand back his sketch pad and ask, "Mind if I sit here? Write in my notebook?"

There's a long silence. Too long. Slowly, he says, "I don't think I can do this."

"What?" I ask, with a growing sense of dread.

"Be friends with you."

I swallow hard. "Why?"

"It hurts too much."

And what he doesn't say, but what we both know, is that

this means we'll never be friends. Because the reason he came here was me. To be with me this summer. And if it takes him the summer to get over me, then he'll go to Colorado and I'll be here across the ocean and then next year Layla will drag us somewhere else. And Wendell will be gone from my life forever.

There's an awkward silence. Maude flutters her wings and rises over the buildings, making a path over the rooftops to who knows where. I stand up, wishing I could follow her. My feet feel heavy as I head alone down the street.

• • •

Over the next few days, I fall into a routine, one from which Wendell is conspicuously absent. I fill my days tutoring the *lycée* students, buying food at the outdoor market, swinging by Les Secrets de Maude to see Vincent, having tea with Madame Chevalier in her apartment, hanging out with Sirona and Layla on the square. Nearly every day, I find time to sit at my favorite table at Café Cerise and write more letters to my *fantôme* father. With every new letter, I feel more determined to find him.

Which is frustrating, because Jean-Claude is set on delaying our trip to Marseille. Usually, at some point during the day, I run into Illusion playing in a square or on a side street. Between their sets, I have a *glâce* or an espresso with Jean-Claude. Whenever I ask him if he'll come to Marseille, he says something vague, like "Maybe next week," or "Maybe when the weather's nicer," or "Maybe after my cold goes away," as he makes an exaggerated sniffle.

Eventually, I pin him down. "Tomorrow morning," I tell him firmly. "That's when I'm going to Marseille. I'll come by your house around eight."

Jean-Claude nods, rubbing the scar beneath his curls. But he promises nothing.

The next day, I wake up early, butterflies in my stomach. I slip on a white sundress, put my hair in two braids, and tuck in some roses from our flowerpots. At the kitchen table, Layla's wearing her deep pink silk robe from Laos and smelling lavender honey before spooning it into her tea. "You look nice, love," she says in a scratchy morning voice.

"I'm going to Marseille today," I announce.

"Marseille?" She's surprised, which makes sense, considering I haven't mentioned my plan to her yet. I had a feeling she'd try to talk me out of it, so I've waited till the last minute.

"To see if I can find out something about J.C.," I say, slicing a leftover baguette and popping the halves in the toaster. "If he lived in Marseille and worked on the water there, someone has to know him."

"Why the change of heart, Z?"

I think about what Madame Chevalier and Vincent said. If love is offered, take it. If you have love to give, give it. Apparently not easy tasks, considering they haven't even tried to follow their own advice.

Finally, echoing Sirona, I say, "If I don't meet him now— now that we're in the same country—I might never do it. I might regret missing the opportunity." I grab the apricot jam from the fridge. "So, Layla, if you've remembered anything else about him, now's a good time to tell me."

She closes her eyes, breathes in the steam from her tea. "We've gone over this a hundred times, love. It was one single night. I was sitting on the beach. He came out of the water. It was like a dream. Just like he said in his letters. Like he was a sea creature turned human for a night."

I slam the refrigerator door, rattling the jars inside. "He wasn't some fantastical merman, Layla. He wrote those letters. He made me. He was real." I feel like shaking her. "Can't you remember his last name? What he looked like? Anything? There are over a million people in Marseille, so any way I can narrow it down—"

She twists her hair into a knot, then untwists it. "I wasn't thinking clearly, Z. I was intoxicated with moonlight. With the rhythm of the night waves. With the music of J.C.'s guitar."

I roll my eyes, spreading jam on the toast. I've heard all this before, all the various mythical versions of the night, tales that shift slightly depending on what kind of mood Layla's in.

"And the next morning," she continues, "I had to leave Ios. I'd gotten my boat ticket already. I never saw his face in full daylight. I can't even picture it. But you came from that magical night, Zeeta. Long ago, I accepted that we'd never know your father. But he'll forever be part of our own fairy tale."

Layla's quiet for a moment, finishing her tea. She sets her

cup decisively on the table and says, "I'll call in sick and come with you."

"Don't worry about it," I say, taking a bite of toast. "Jean-Claude's coming with me." Even though that's not necessarily true. He didn't exactly agree to anything.

"What about Wendell?" she asks. "Don't you think he'd be a good support? I mean, you helped him find his birth family, and he's—"

"Wendell doesn't even want to be friends with me, Layla." My eyes sting as I say the words.

"Oh," she says. "I'm sorry, love."

I force down the rest of my toasted baguette. Before I head out the door, Layla hugs me goodbye and says, "You don't have to do this, Z."

"Yes, I do, Layla." Suddenly, I'm more certain of this than ever. "Your fairy tale never satisfied me. I'm finding my father."

• • •

Outside, the sun is blazing, the heat already setting in. I pass through the Place de la Mairie, weaving around the potted plants and striped awnings set up for the flower market. The clean, light scent of thousands of petals mixes with the golden smell of warm baguettes.

A few minutes later, at Illusion's apartment, I'm just about to ring the buzzer when Amandine opens the door. She steps outside and cries, "Zeeta!" Kissing my cheeks, she says, "You look pretty."

At her heels is Tortue, in his usual mime costume. He

comes out onto the sidewalk, and says, in his soft voice, *"Bonjour,* Zeeta."

"Bonjour," I say, and turn back to Amandine. "Where are you going?"

Amandine looks at Tortue, who says hoarsely, "Mont-perrin."

"The psychiatric hospital on the outskirts of Aix," Amandine reminds me, holding eye contact with Tortue.

"I was checked in for a few days," he says. "Now I'm doing the day program."

Amandine links her arm in his, protectively. "And I walk him there every day."

"Oh, I see." I have no idea what to say. *Get well soon?* I offer what I hope is an encouraging yet sympathetic smile.

Taking a folded-up piece of paper from her bag, Amandine says, "Jean-Claude asked me to give you this, Zeeta."

I open the paper and read the message.

Chère Zeeta,
    I cannot bear to go to Marseille. Amandine will tell you why. My parents live at the address below. They live only a few blocks from the docks. My stepfather can probably help you. He worked for years as a ferry captain.

                                Bon courage,
                                Jean-Claude
    P.S. And tell my mother I'm fine.

My heart sinks. I'll have to do this alone. Apparently, Jean-Claude's fear of his past outweighs any willingness to help me. At least he gave me an address. Although who knows if I'll use it. Visiting his estranged parents has great potential for being incredibly uncomfortable.

I hand the note to Amandine. As she reads it, I ask, "So what happened to Jean-Claude in Marseille?"

She leans against the window of Café Eternité, the red velvet curtains inside the glass making her own hair gleam even redder. "He killed his brother."

"What?" Shivers run up my spine. I look at her and then at Tortue. He's standing against the wall, completely still, as if he wishes he could turn into stone.

"That's how Jean-Claude sees it," Amandine says. "He was fifteen and his brother, Thomas, was twelve. Jean-Claude took his parents' car without their permission, and drove with his brother to a nearby beach town. On the way back to Marseille, they got in an accident. Jean-Claude survived with just a gash on his forehead, but Thomas died."

I'm quiet for a moment. "But why doesn't he talk to his parents?"

"They went through a rough time after Thomas's death. Nearly separated. Jean-Claude was filled with guilt. He thought it was his fault that his brother was dead and his parents were in so much pain. Especially his mother. See, Jean-Claude's father had died in a car accident just before he was born. His mother was completely devastated by this second loss. For months, she was lost in grief. So Jean-Claude left. He couldn't bear the pain in his home. He decided to break from his past. Invent a new life. He never talks about what happened, except after a nightmare, when he needs comforting."

When she pauses, I ask, "And what do you think about all this?"

She answers immediately, as if she's already come to a conclusion. "That by refusing his parents' love, he's refusing anyone's love." Her lip quivers. "And by refusing to love his parents, he's refusing to love anyone." She blinks back tears, then looks at Tortue.

He puts his arm around her, a fatherly gesture, and kisses the top of her head.

"We'd better go now," she says, sniffling. "Tortue will be late."

They nod their *au revoir*s and walk away, leaning on each other like father and daughter.

I fold up the note and tuck it into my bag, wondering if I should go back home to get Layla. But she's probably already left for her classes. Instead, I head reluctantly toward the *navette* stop, despite the doubts creeping into my head. I don't know about contacting Jean-Claude's family. It might bring up old tragedies for them, not to mention entangling me in their messy relationships. My own relationships are messy enough.

• • •

In a kilometer, I reach the *navette* stop. It's a wide side-walk, crowded with people streaming on and off shuttles, dashing to catch a bus, or hurrying off somewhere. I scan the destinations shown in red lights on the *navettes'* electronic screens, trying to figure out which one to board. It's a chaotic scene, but less so than most bus stops I've encountered in South America, Asia, and Africa. Of course, I rode those buses alone all the time, and when I was years younger, too. So why is it I feel overwhelmed now?

I'm staring at the shuttles, when I notice something out of the corner of my eye. It's a strange sensation to see someone you know well in an unexpected place. First, before you register who the person is, you get a particular feeling in a primal spot in your brain.

The feeling I get comes in snapshots—a crystal cave by candlelight, a sunlit flower garden, a light-soaked field of corn plants. A comforting feeling fills me, then quickly shifts to a deep ache. It's Wendell. I broke up with him. And he doesn't want to be friends.

"Hi, Wendell," I say apprehensively.

"Zeeta?" He's caught off guard. "What are you doing here?"

"Taking a *navette* to Marseille," I say, trying to keep my voice steady. "How about you?"

"Going to art class." His words sound hard, distant. "What's in Marseille?"

"I've decided to search for my *fantôme* father."

He moves toward me, his face melting into concern. "Oh, Z!" And then, abruptly, he stops and folds his arms across his chest.

I fold mine as well, mirroring him. "I thought I could just forget about it, Wendell. But he loves Layla. He could love me, too. And for some reason, he's scared to show himself." I feel like sinking to the ground, right in the middle of these crowds rushing to and from the *navettes*. "You were right, Wendell. I have to find him."

Wendell sticks his hands in his pockets, looking awkward but worried. "You're not going alone, are you?"

I nod.

He looks at his feet, thinking, and then back to me. "I'm coming with you."

I have the urge to bury my face in his shoulder. "You have class. It's too much to—"

"You helped me find my father," he says firmly. "I'm helping you find yours."

And I know I should insist, *No, you don't owe me anything. Not after how I treated you.*

Instead, I say, "Thank you."

Eighteen

On the *navette* to Marseille, Wendell asks, "What made you change your mind about finding your father?"

"Something Madame Chevalier said about love. She's the artist I told you about, the friend of Vincent. One of my endearingly nutty elderly friends—the ones into pigeons and eternal life?"

"I remember you telling me about them," he says, and then, lightly, "Well, this lady can't be too nutty if her advice was good enough to change your mind."

"True," I admit with a smile.

An hour later, the *navette* stops right at the Vieux Port of Marseille, which makes it easy for Wendell and me. We simply walk off the bus and onto the docks, our destination. The bus pulls away, and as the exhaust fades, the salty, fishy sea wind wraps around us. Water laps against the pier, and my insides slosh around, wave after wave of jumbled feelings—excitement, fear, longing. For a minute I just soak in the brightness and blueness and hugeness. I watch the sunlight dance on wave tips, breathing in the ocean air and vast sky, listening to the hum of boat motors and seagull calls.

"Want to get something to eat and make a plan?" Wendell asks. He's beside me, a few feet away, snapping pictures. He was painfully careful not to touch me on the bus ride down here. Once, when he accidentally brushed my knee, he jerked away as though he'd been electrocuted. But here, now, the ocean seems to have calmed him, put some light back into his eyes.

"Yeah," I say, with a rush of happiness that he's here with me.

He tucks his camera back into the case, and into his backpack. Then we head across the street, toward the cafés lining the docks. We sit down at a little outdoor *crêperie* and order espressos and crêpes—lemon for me and Nutella for him.

Beyond the piers, the craggy hillsides are speckled with houses and buildings. This port is much bigger than I imagined. And very international. A mishmash of dozens of languages float past the café. There are African women swathed in colorful, wildly patterned cotton; veiled Middle Eastern women; camera-toting tourists from Eastern Europe and Asia. It's almost dizzying.

"So what exactly do we know about your father?" Wendell

asks. He seems solid and grounded with his logical questions. I feel another wave of appreciation for him.

"Well," I say, "we know English isn't his native language. And he has a dark complexion. But that wouldn't make him stand out here at all."

"True," Wendell says. "But we know he's a great guitar player. His initials are J.C. He probably looks like you. That's something."

I take a sip of espresso and say, "Thanks."

"For what?"

"I don't know." I stare at my drink. "For being here."

"Sure. No problem."

When I glance back up from my drink, he's looking down at his. "I know we don't have much to go on, Wendell. I think—" I hesitate, not wanting to say Jean-Claude's name.

"What?"

There's no way around it. It's our best hope for finding some clue to my father's whereabouts. "Jean-Claude gave me his parents' address. They live a few blocks away, and his stepfather worked on these docks for years."

"Sounds like a good connection," Wendell says after a pause.

"I know," I admit. "But I feel weird about contacting them. Jean-Claude ran away from home a few years ago. He doesn't even talk to them anymore. But I think they could give us a good idea on how to start looking." I pull out the paper and wait for Wendell's reaction.

He presses his lips together. "Okay. Let's go."

"*On y va,*" I say, relieved. We drop a few euros on the little silver tray and head down the sidewalk as the waves lap at the docks. The constant push and pull of the current makes me think of Wendell and me, moving toward each other for a moment, only to move away again.

• • •

After ten minutes of walking, Wendell and I arrive at the door of a gray stone building that matches the address Jean-Claude gave me. The name over the buzzer reads *Mme et M. Jorge Candelaria.* His stepfather must have Spanish origins, I note. I press the buzzer and wait, shifting from one foot to the other.

"*Oui?*" A woman's voice responds.

"*Bonjour.* I'm Zeeta. A friend of Jean-Claude's."

She pauses, then says, "Come in," and buzzes us inside.

She's on the first floor, the door on the right. When she opens the door, I immediately see her resemblance to Jean-Claude—the deep blue eyes, the dark, wavy hair. "I'm Clementine," she says in a warm, curious voice, not quite hiding a hint of anxiety. "Clementine Candelaria."

Wendell and I introduce ourselves, and then she leads us into a light, airy living room, where instruments are scattered throughout like pieces of furniture—a violin, a harp, a djembe drum, a guitar, a piano.

"Nice instruments," Wendell says.

"Thank you. We have a musical family. Most of the instruments belong to Jean-Claude's father—well, stepfather, really, but he was the only father Jean-Claude ever knew." She speaks slowly enough for Wendell to understand. "And that violin was Jean-Claude's. That's what he studied in school. And his dad—Jorge—played music with him for fun every night before bed. They would play, and Thomas and I would dance, for hours, here in this living room."

The room seems so empty now. I can hardly imagine how it felt filled with music and dancing and kids. I take in the white lace curtains, moving softly in the breeze, the white sofa and chairs, the glass table holding a vase of orange zinnias. Madame Candelaria's outfit matches the décor—a white linen skirt and tank and an orange silk scarf around her neck.

She sits us down on the sofa, then disappears into the kitchen, emerging minutes later with a tray of bottles and glasses, clinking together lightly. She pours us cool water with green mint syrup in tall glasses with no ice. And then, she leans toward us, across the coffee table. "How is my son?" she asks, obviously worried. "He's all right, isn't he? Did anything happen?"

"No, Jean-Claude's fine," I say quickly. "He knew I needed a contact at the port of Marseille. You see, I'm looking for a man who worked on the docks sixteen years ago. Jean-Claude thought his dad might be able to help us."

Madame Candelaria's face falls. "I'm sorry, *mademoiselle*, but you just missed Jorge. He left this morning on business. He won't be home for a month."

I sip my minted water, trying to contain my disappointment. Wendell gives me a sympathetic look.

Madame Candelaria reaches out her hands, imploring. "But please, tell me about Jean-Claude."

"He told me to tell you he's doing fine," I say, wishing his message had contained more emotion, even a hint of love.

But she looks pleased enough. With a wistful smile, she glances over her shoulder.

I follow her gaze. She's looking at a silver-framed photo of two boys posed in front of a boat, with blue sky and sea in the background. Their arms are slung around each other. The one on the right is a younger Jean-Claude, about fifteen years old. His face is softer than it is now, more open and innocent. And beside him is a boy who looks like a twelve-year-old version of Jean-Claude. It must be his brother. The picture must have been taken shortly before he died.

"That's a nice picture," I say.

"You know about Thomas?" she asks.

"Just a little."

"Jean-Claude felt so responsible for his brother's death. It was hard for all of us, of course. Maybe that's why we didn't see how much Jean-Claude was suffering. Before we realized what was happening, he'd shut himself off from us, from everyone he had ever known." She stops and takes a quivering breath. "We couldn't reach him. And then, a year later, he left home. I kept thinking he'd return, but it's been three years and he hasn't and he's all grown up now. It's like we lost both our sons—" She stops, unable to continue.

I don't know her well enough to hold her hand or put my arm around her. I glance at Wendell, who looks just as uncertain. One thing is clear: Jean-Claude's mother adores him. How could he reject so much love? I remember the sad, frustrated look on Amandine's face this morning. It's the same expression his mother wears now.

"I'm really sorry, *madame*," I say finally. "I think Wendell and I should be going. Thank you for the refreshments and your time." I stand up.

Wendell sets down his glass and stands too.

Madame Candelaria follows us to the door. "Tell Jean-Claude we don't blame him. Tell him we never did. Tell him we want to see him." She's crying now. "Tell him we love him more than anything."

Wendell reaches out his hand to hers and assures her, "*Oui, madame*. We'll tell him."

Just before the door closes she says, "*Bon courage*. And be sure to give Jean-Claude my love."

NINETEEN

Wendell and I walk toward Vieux Port, dodging clusters of people on the sidewalk as buses and cars speed down the wide streets. I'm quiet, until I finally burst out, "She was so sweet! And she loves him so much!"

Wendell nods. "Seems like his dad does too."

"I know!" I say. "I can't believe how Jean-Claude left things with them. It's so selfish, so immature."

After a few paces, Wendell says, "At least he's taking a baby step, Z."

"A baby step?" I can't keep the skepticism out of my voice.

"He gave you the address, Z. He gave you a message to give to his mom. And remember, he has pretty huge reasons for the way he's acted."

I find it interesting that Wendell is defending Jean-

Claude. It's almost . . . noble. But that's one thing I've always loved about him—how he doesn't judge people, how he tries to imagine what it feels like to be in their hearts, their heads. Inside Jean-Claude's head, there's probably a long list of reasons for refusing his parents' love.

And my father, my *fantôme*. If, by some chance, I find him, could I ever actually love him? Could I wade through my muddle of emotions to get to that place? And could I let him love me? It's too much to think about. Anyway, we're at the docks now. Time to form our plan B. I turn to Wendell. "So should we just ask around?"

"I guess."

Now, as I stare at the throngs of people and boats, some doubts creep in. Without a guide, the docks seem huge and intimidating, with dozens, maybe hundreds, of sailboats and ferries and motorboats. I take a breath and walk up to a friendly-looking, weathered old man standing in front of a small dinghy. *"Bonjour, monsieur."*

"Bonjour," he says in a nasal voice.

"We're looking for a man with the initials J.C. He worked here sixteen years ago and—"

The man cuts me off. "I wasn't here then. You want to talk with Maurice. He's worked here all his life. Knows everything about everyone. He's the man for you."

"Maurice," I repeat. The sailor's Marseillais accent is so thick I have to listen carefully to understand. "Where—?"

"Oh, he usually docks over there." The man squints in that

direction and says, "Looks like he's out on the water now. "Try Georges over here." He nods to the next boat over.

We approach Georges, a middle-aged man in a dark blue fishing hat and with an enormous mustache. "*Bonjour, monsieur.* We're looking for a man with the initials J.C. who might have worked here sixteen years ago. He liked the water, played guitar, had dark skin." I wish I knew more than this paltry collection of random details. "He's handsome," I add, because that's what Layla's told me, although she never saw his face in full light. "Sensitive, too," I say, thinking of his letters. "He lived in Greece at some point and traveled a lot."

I stop, embarrassed that this is the haphazard sum of what I know about my father.

Georges nods. "*Eh bien,* I do know a J.C."

"Really?"

"Jean Clément." The man rubs his mustache. "He had a boat here for a while, had dark skin. Don't know about the Greece part. What else did you say about him?"

"Um. Handsome?"

"Jean Clément was about as handsome as a dog's behind." Maybe Layla exaggerated. "Sensitive?" I ask.

"Hehehe. If you insulted him, the fists started swinging."

"Hmmm."

"He's in jail now after he killed a guy."

"Oh." I turn to Wendell and whisper, "Let's move on."

"*Merci en tout cas,*" I tell the sailor. Thanks anyway.

"*De rien, mademoiselle. Bon courage!*"

Once Wendell and I leave, we look at each other.

"My father couldn't be a sensitive killer who resembles canine buttocks," I say, only half kidding. "Could he?"

Wendell makes a show of thinking about it, then raises an eyebrow, amused. "Just how much wine did Layla have that night?"

I make a face. "She says it wasn't so much the wine. She was drunk on the moon's reflection."

Wendell nods, as if this makes perfect sense. "Yeah. I heard about binge moonlight drinking. It can really mess with your judgment."

I start laughing. That wild, deep laughing that happens when despair brings you to a raw spot in your center, a spot where laughter and tears both form. And you laugh so hard you can't stop no matter how ridiculous you must look.

Wendell watches me, letting one corner of his mouth turn up in the tiniest hint of a smile.

• • •

After three hours of walking around the docks, and still no Maurice, and still no leads on J.C., I feel thoroughly wind-beaten and sun-dried. Every conversation has been more or less the same. *Oui, I know a J.C. Jean-César. Jean-Charles. Jean Clochard. He's a priest. He's terrified of water. He's never left Marseille. He can't hold a tune. He's four feet tall. He's scared of women and lives with his mother. He only speaks Swahili. He's ninety. . . .*

By the twentieth time, the speech rolls off my tongue without thinking about it. After each failed conversation, Wendell makes some comment about the moon-reflection content in Layla's blood. *Maybe Layla's elevated moonlight levels made J.C. appear fifty years younger. Maybe her excessive moonlight imbibing added a few feet. Maybe that last shot of moonlight made the Swahili sound like heavily accented English.*

He offers these theories with a completely straight face, which sends me into fits of giggles.

When our stomachs start rumbling, we sit down and have espresso and Nutella crêpes.

"Want to keep going?" I ask Wendell.

"Absolutely." He tries to act energetic, but he looks beat.

"You sure?"

He takes a long breath. "We have yet to come across a polygamist cult leader J.C."

"Or a millionaire mafia J.C."

"Or a reincarnated Egyptian J.C."

Baby steps. Maybe that's what we're doing now, taking baby steps toward each other. For every wave forward, there's a smaller one backward. Maybe, just maybe, after this day is through, we can manage to be friends.

• • •

"Look, a blue dinghy!" Wendell gestures toward the water.

We've just finished another round of espressos and crêpes to regain some energy. We've been keeping an eye on the docks, waiting for Maurice.

Squinting, I let my gaze follow Wendell's finger. Toward the end of the pier is a small blue motorboat, and a man tying it to the dock.

Wendell shields his eyes and says, "Think that's Maurice?"

I stuff the last bite of crêpe into my mouth and down the final drops of espresso. "Let's go!"

We leave some money on the silver tip tray and dart across the street, half running up the docks, keeping our eyes glued to the sailor by his blue dinghy.

Up close, Maurice is a middle-aged man whose face is sunburned to the crisp reddish brown of bacon.

"*Bonjour, monsieur,*" I say, breathless and excited.

He eyes us curiously. "*Bonjour.*"

"*Monsieur,* we're looking for someone. And we heard you're the man to ask."

He grins, revealing a few gaps where teeth are missing. "*Oui,* that's true. And who is it you're looking for?"

I start telling him what we know about J.C. When I mention Greece, he stops me. "Greece, you say? Matter of fact, there was a fellow who worked here for a while. Years ago. His skin was pretty dark—but who knows how much of that was from being in the sun all day."

"What was his name?"

"Zhee-mee."

It takes me a moment to understand what he's saying. "Jimmy?"

He nods.

"He was American? British?"

"Oh, no. But he did speak some English, I remember. He could talk to the tourists, but it wasn't perfect. People called him Jimmy because he loved Zhee-mee Endreex."

"Jimi Hendrix?" Wendell interprets.

"*Oui!* You know, that guitar player. Jimmy wore a Jimi Hendrix T-shirt all the time! And he was as good as Jimi Hendrix too. The best guitarist I've ever met."

Wendell and I exchange glances.

"Where was he from?" I ask, excitement shooting through me.

"*Ouf,* who knows. He spoke a few different languages. Spanish, English, French. Probably some other ones too."

"Was he sensitive?"

Maurice laughs. "*Bien sûr.* You know how musicians are." He's quiet for a moment, searching his memory. "Ah yes, I remember now. He took a long trip to Greece one year. He couldn't get over some girl he met there. Kept writing songs about her."

I'm shaking. I look at Wendell to make sure he's understanding all this. He must, judging by how wide his eyes are.

Maurice scratches his head. "Had a little dinghy, this Jimmy, smaller than mine, and older. Not a very safe boat, but the tourists liked it. It was painted turquoise, the paint chipping off, their idea of what a Mediterranean boat should look like. For a while, he had the same job as me—taking tourists to the islands. Mostly to the Château d'If."

"The Castle of If?" I translate, in case Wendell didn't catch the strange name.

Maurice gestures to the widening expanse of water just outside the port. "The island right over there." Adjusting his hat thoughtfully, he says, "You know, Jimmy even worked there for a time. Maybe they have job records. Maybe they can figure out a last name."

My heart is thudding. "How do we get there?"

"Hop in. Fifteen euros there, fifteen back."

Wendell and I look at each other. *"On y va,"* he says.

I start climbing into the boat. My legs are so wobbly with anticipation that I lose my balance. I'm just starting to fall, when Wendell's hand reaches out to the small of my back to steady me. And then, the moment I've regained my balance, his hand is gone.

• • •

It's too loud to talk over the engine and wind, but halfway there, Maurice pulls over to a little cove and cuts the motor. "The Castle of If," he says with a dramatic flourish. "In the fifteen hundreds, it was a fort to defend the city. Later, it became a prison. It's famous for the story of *The Count of Monte Cristo,* written by Alexandre Dumas in the nineteenth century."

"Can you tell us the story?" I ask.

"Oui!" he says, looking pleased. "A few hundred years ago, a young man named Dantes is falsely accused of spying and thrown into a cell in the Castle of If." Maurice speaks slowly, savoring the story that he's probably repeated to hundreds of tourists. "But it is in prison that he learns of a buried

treasure." He rubs his whiskers thoughtfully and adds, "You know, it's not until one finds oneself inside the darkness of prison that one learns of hidden treasures."

I'm not sure he's speaking metaphorically. Maurice does look as though he could have gone to prison at some point. There's a toughness to him, an edge.

I translate for Wendell, but he seems to understand enough to follow on his own. "What happens next?" he asks.

Maurice smiles triumphantly. "He escapes and finds the treasure. Then he disguises himself as a wealthy count and sets out to seek revenge on those who framed him."

I jot down all this in my notebook, as sea spray speckles the pages. Maurice rambles on about Dantes's adventures— which sound like a fifteen-hundred-page soap opera. When Maurice is about to turn on the motor again, I ask, "What else do you remember about Jimmy?"

"*Ouf,* he didn't say much personal stuff. Nothing about his family or where he came from or his past or his plans for the future. But he was a great storyteller."

"Do you remember any stories he told?" I ask.

"*Oh la la la la.* It was a long time ago, but here's one I never forgot. It was late at night, Jimmy said, and he was walking on the docks. Did I mention he always had a guitar with him? Between customers he'd play. Beautiful music. Straight from the angels." Maurice looks dramatically to the heavens. "So Jimmy was getting ready to go home in the dark. The docks were mostly deserted. Then a gang of thieves surrounded him. They demanded his money, but he had only a few coins. They got angry, said they were going to kill him. So he said, 'Let me play one last song.' "

"I know a version of this folktale," I say, wondering if J.C. was the one who first told it to Layla.

"Oh, but this is not a folktale. It's a true story," Maurice says. "It really happened to Jimmy."

I look doubtfully at Wendell.

Maurice continues. "And the thieves said, 'All right.' So Jimmy played the most beautiful melody. He sang and he played and he brought them to tears. When it was over, they said, 'Another one, another!' And he played another. All night, he played to them, there on the docks. One by one those criminals drifted to sleep, and by dawn they were all sleeping like babies. And off Jimmy went, knowing that when things seemed bleakest, his song would burst forth and save him."

Maurice gives us a knowing look. "See what I mean about treasures?"

"Treasures?" I ask, confused.

"At the darkest times—in prison or trapped by ruthless thieves—that's when you find your treasure."

At that, Maurice starts the engine and takes off into the blinding blue, toward the Château d'If.

TWENTY

Beads of salty spray coat my skin and the hum of the motor fills my ears. Wendell and I sit side by side on the small boat bench, wrapped in damp, musty life jackets. The sea wind whips through our hair as we squint ahead at the Castle of If, growing closer and bigger. It fills most of the island, which is otherwise desolate, just a few sparse trees, sand-colored rocks and crags. The castle itself is a mammoth, imposing fortress—a heavy rectangle in the middle and two thick towers visible on either side. Stone walls surround the island.

When Maurice docks, we step off the boat. The water is brilliant, mesmerizing—translucent shades of green and blue, light and dark, swirling together. Close to the rocks, the water grows wild, churning, white foam slapping the stone violently. If you were an escaped prisoner, not the kind of water you'd want to jump into.

Maurice ties the boat to the dock and says, "I'll show you around."

"*Merci,*" I say, wiping trickles of sweat and seawater from my cheeks.

Inside the fortress walls, he leads us up the stone stairs. At the ticket booth—a small room just inside the walls—we discover that no one has worked there long enough to know Jimmy. Apparently, he worked there before they'd computerized all their payroll records. There's no record of him.

"Too bad he got fired," Maurice says, shaking his head. "Or he might still be working here."

"Fired?" I don't like the idea of my father getting fired. "Why?"

"I'll show you," says Maurice, leading us across a desolate stretch of weeds and parched dirt toward the castle. His short, thick legs don't seem well adapted to land. Under normal circumstances, I'd be asking this man questions about his take on life for my notebook. Sailors always have interesting perspectives. But now, all I want to hear about is my father. I want to squeeze out every last drop of memory of him.

Up close, I can tell from the tiny window slits that the château's walls are many feet thick. We walk through the giant doors, through a museum and gift shop, and emerge into a stone courtyard with a well at its center, surrounded by cells.

"There haven't been prisoners inside here for centuries,"

Maurice assures us, as if we're scared one might jump out at us.

The cells are refreshingly cool and dark inside. Scratched into the stone walls are words, symbols, names. Some etchings look ancient, some new. It's hard to tell where the genuine prisoner graffiti ends and the tourist graffiti begins. I run my hands over the walls, lingering on the words that look oldest, deepest, most worn.

"Names, mostly," Maurice comments.

"Makes sense," Wendell says. "You're stuck in here for years, you write your name to remember who you are."

"Or who you were," I add.

He nods. "Or who you might be if you ever get out."

"Come upstairs," Maurice says, and leads us up spiral stairs to the second story. We walk into a large, circular room inside one of the towers. A few slits in the massive walls form narrow windows—rectangular tunnels with patches of blue sky and sea at the end. Slivers of immense beauty.

Maurice peeks his head into the entrance of the tunnel-windows. "They say that homing pigeons delivered messages from the outside world. Those were the highlights of the prisoners' days, those little notes from the pigeons."

I study the window, just wide enough for a pigeon to fit through. Back in Aix, Madame Chevalier is probably sitting at her window, waiting for Maude's next message. Does Madame Chevalier feel she's in a prison? What's stopping her from leaving her post by the window?

Maurice comes over, standing beside me. "This was Jimmy's favorite cell. After closing time, he'd stay in here until he had to leave." Maurice drops his voice. "Then he started sneaking in and staying here overnight."

"Why?" This bothers me. It's creepy.

Maurice shrugs, surveying the wall. "It's around here somewhere," he mutters.

"What's around here?"

"The final straw! The reason why they finally fired him. He'd been missing work and coming late for a while, and then he did this thing. Imagine, a museum guard defacing a *monument historique!*" Maurice points to a spot on the wall, announcing, *"Et voilà!"*

Wendell flicks on his flashlight, the tiny LED beam casting a circle of white light on the stone. He moves the beam toward Maurice's fingertip. Now I can make out words scratched into the stone. They're hard to decipher but look relatively recent.

It's a list of some kind.

MAR
CIELO
MÚSICA

"It's in Spanish," I murmur. "Sea, sky, music . . ."

"Maybe his native language," Wendell says. "Can you make out the fourth word?"

I squint at it. It looks like . . . *Layla?*

"Layla?" Wendell whispers.

"It's really him," I manage to whisper. Any last doubt is gone. "My father. He wrote this." I run my fingers over the letters, tracing their smooth pathways.

Wendell pulls out his camera and starts snapping pictures. "But why this collection of words?"

"Maybe it's a list of beautiful things in life," I say. "Things worth getting out of prison for."

"But he wasn't in prison."

"Maybe he felt like he was. In his letters to Layla, he seemed really depressed after she left him."

"Understandable," Wendell says in a raw voice. I can't see his face, hidden behind his camera.

Suddenly, the darkness feels claustrophobic with its teasing slivers of blue light. I turn to Maurice. "Can we go on the roof?"

"Bien sûr." He leads us up another staircase, through the doorway, into sunshine and wind. The view over the wall makes me catch my breath—the expanse of water and sky and unfathomable openness. There couldn't be a more complete contrast, emerging from such darkness into such endless light.

I try to enter the state of my father's mind when he wrote Layla's name on the wall.

Sea, sky, music, and *Layla.* Were these his pigeons? His treasures? What gave him hope? What kept him going from day to day despite his sadness?

It's sunset as we putter back to the port in Maurice's blue dinghy. Golden orange light dances over the water, softly, gently, compared to the glaring light of midday. At the dock, as we climb out of the boat, I notice a word painted across the side in bright white letters. *Mercedes.* "Maurice, is your boat named after the car or a woman?" I ask.

He chuckles. "A woman. And not just any woman. The true love of Dantes, the one he was about to marry the day he was arrested. And nearly twenty years later, the only person able to see past his disguise as the Count of Monte Cristo, into his true self."

"Did they ever get together?" Wendell asks.

"Dumas leaves it open to interpretation. But if you ask me, they do." He winks. "True love is tough. It can survive for years and years, flowing underground like a spring. And now and then, you think it's disappeared, but it's been there all along."

We pay Maurice, throwing in a big tip. Wendell and I take turns shaking his thick, rough hand, thanking him. I write his number in my notebook in case we have more questions, and then make one last-ditch effort. "Maurice, are you sure you don't remember where Jimmy went? Or his last name? Anything else about him?"

Maurice thinks, studying his boat. "I'm sorry. It was so long ago." He squints at me in the evening light. "Can I ask, *mademoiselle,* who is this man to you?"

"I'm the daughter of Layla. She's the woman he fell in love with in Greece seventeen years ago."

He stares. "He's your—"

"Mon père."

Maurice closes his eyes for a long time, as though he's digging into every last cranny of his memory. "Jimmy wore a pair of silver sunglasses, the round kind. He kept a little Walkman clipped to his jeans. He wore his hair long and shaggy. Oh, and a necklace. Made of leather and shells and a nut from a tree. Said it protected him from the evil eye. Deer's eye, that's what he called the nut."

I memorize each detail to write later in my notebook. Each detail is filling out a little piece of my father, until I almost have a picture of him.

"Bonne chance, mademoiselle. Bonne chance. He's a lucky man, Jimmy. To have a daughter like you."

For some reason, these last words push me over the edge. *"Merci,* Maurice," I manage to say, just before turning to leave. Then the tears well up, warm and unstoppable, spilling down my cheeks. I walk faster and faster, wiping my face on my arm.

Wendell jogs beside me, trying to keep up. I wish he would put his hand on the small of my back, the way he did to catch me on the boat. I imagine his hand there, barely touching the curve in my back, as we walk in the dusk, toward the bus stop, keeping a meter's distance between us, a space wider than an ocean.

On the way home on the bus, Wendell and I talk in the gathering darkness. My tears have stopped but my head's still full of fuzz.

"So let's go over what we know," he says, in a reassuring, businesslike voice. "Maybe you should take out your notebook?"

I pull it from my bag and, feeling better already, turn to a new page. I write:

> My father Jimmy
> He loved Layla.
> He was a romantic.
> He played beautiful guitar music.
> He loved the water and the sky.
> His native language might have been
> Spanish.
> He wore a black Jimi Hendrix T-shirt,
> round sunglasses, and a deer's eye
> necklace.

We talk about the clues, examining them from every angle. Soon our conversation meanders, naturally and comfortably, to other topics—Madame Candelaria, Maurice, *The Count of Monte Cristo*.

"The Castle of If," I say, musing. "What a perfect name."

"Why perfect?" Wendell asks.

"A prison fortress made of *if*s. Made of assumptions. Like

the prison Jean-Claude's made for himself. *If* he talks to his parents again, all his pain and guilt will come back. Or *if* he tells his friends about his past, they'll think he's terrible."

Wendell nods. "Or *if* he lets himself love his parents, he'll lose them, too."

After that, we fall silent. I wonder which *if*s have formed my own walls. *If* I become closer to someone, it will hurt more when I lose him. *If* I break up with him before I lose him, maybe it will hurt less.

Wendell leans his head against the window, lets his eyelids fall shut. It's probably been hard, I realize, excruciating even, for him to be with me all day. He's been so careful not to touch me or look at me too long or too closely.

"I'm glad you're here," I whisper.

I don't think he hears me. Maybe he's fallen asleep.

My mind wanders to my father and his dark cell and his music that calmed the hearts of criminals. I wonder about his love for Layla, and Dantes's love for Mercedes, flowing underground for years. I wonder about true love, if that's what J.C. had for my mother, even after one night. I wonder about Vincent and Madame Chevalier, and what their lives would have been like if they'd admitted their love years ago. I wonder about eternal life, if it would get boring, if you'd get sick of yourself and your thoughts and the world . . . or if things would seem new and different every day. I wonder if living forever would be terribly sad, always loving people, then leaving them behind. I wonder how you'd survive so many losses and still be able to love.

I let my eyes linger on Wendell's face, which is only safe to do when he's asleep. His face looks tender with car headlights passing over it. I wonder what might have happened if I hadn't broken up with him. There are oceans of things I don't know about him, things I want to know. I watch him breathing rhythmically, a lock of hair fallen over his face. I look at him the way Vincent looks at his room full of dusty old treasures.

TWENTY-ONE

Steam rises from two small capuccino cups, swirling upward between Layla and me in the morning sunlight at Café Cerise. Layla's listening carefully as I read my notes about Jimmy. She's been unusually quiet since I came home last night. I gave her the highlights of my trip to Marseille, and her reaction was surprisingly subdued. She said she was tired, and I looked exhausted, and we could talk about it later.

After reading the deer nut necklace item, I close my notebook. "Any of that jog your memory, Layla?"

She licks some cinnamon-specked foamed milk from her lip and tilts her head thoughtfully. "Well, obviously, J.C. wasn't wearing sunglasses at night in the ocean. The necklace is a definite maybe. I *am* drawn to guys who wear necklaces."

I can't believe she's taking this so lightly. It's a huge, life-changing revelation. "But it has to be him, Layla! There's the Jimi Hendrix T-shirt. The Greece connection. Not to mention he was so in love with you he wrote your name on a prison wall!"

"Okay, Zeeta. So it's him. I'm just not sure what to say. You're not really any closer to finding him. Yes, it's nice he cared about me—"

"What if this was your shot at true love, Layla? And you missed it?"

"Oh, no. If it was true love, our paths will cross again."

"Shouldn't you *try* to make your paths cross?"

Layla fiddles absently with her tiny spoon, staring into space. "What if I try, and he's some stuffy businessman now? Or a cheeseball politician? I'd rather leave it up to the universe." She twirls her finger around her hair. "Anyway, we're fine how we are. Completely fine. We don't need a man to come in and ruin everything."

"How do you know he'd ruin anything?"

She rubs her temple. "What if he doesn't like how I've raised you, Z? What if he says I'm not a fit parent? What if he interferes? Tries to make you settle down somewhere? Makes me feel guilty for not doing it sooner?"

"Layla, he doesn't exactly seem too stable himself. A normal man would just introduce himself without playing games."

"But what if he has a good reason? What if he's spying on

us to see if I'm a decent parent? What if—" She looks at me, her eyes welling up.

I see it now. She's trapped in her own castle prison of *ifs*. "What if what?" I ask.

"What if he's everything you ever wanted in a parent? Everything that I'm not?"

• • •

In the weeks after the eventful day in Marseille, my days fall back into a pattern. I wake up early, which is easy since I go to bed early. Layla and I spend evenings together, making Provençal food or flower crowns or found-object mobiles or broken-pottery mosaics. Whatever she's in the mood for, I go along with it. Sometimes Sirona comes over and teaches us ancient Celtic dances or gives us basic lyre lessons. One night she lit a candle and recounted old Celtic legends in verse. Another time she described all Salluvii's seasonal festivals, showing us how to cook some traditional specialties. I take dutiful notes to share later with Madame Chevalier and Vincent, who can never get enough of this stuff.

In the mornings, Layla and I have breakfast together before she leaves for work. Her schedule is more demanding in France than it's been in any other country. She seems to genuinely enjoy the new challenge of teaching teachers how to teach English. And she's making more money than ever before, which we need to support our thirty-euro-per-day café habit.

She's acting more professional too, for a change. She used

to handwrite her students' worksheets, shunning any technology more complex than photocopiers whenever possible. But here, she's started going to Nirvana and typing out worksheets, a development that Ahmed finds thrilling, of course. Sometimes she even swings by Nirvana to just chat with Ahmed, enjoying the captive audience who hangs on her every word. Sadly, it's only a matter of time before she moves on to another man, leaving poor Ahmed alone, with only KnightQuest to comfort him. Still, he's much more stable and mature than most of her other flings, so I swallow my doubts and let it happen.

I try to focus on teaching, knowing I'll have to squeeze in as much tutoring as I can this summer, before school starts in the fall. The *lycée* students have warned me about the endless hours of studying I'll be doing once classes are in full swing. The students are friendly enough with me, inviting me to hang out with them after our sessions, but I keep the relationship professional.

After my morning tutoring, I usually go to Café Cerise and write in my ruby notebook—sometimes observations, sometimes interviews, and sometimes more letters to my *fantôme* father. I tell him my thoughts and memories, but mostly ask him questions. *When will you show yourself? What are you scared of?* And even though there are no answers, it feels good to ask. Somehow, I feel as though I know him better with each letter. And with each letter, more remnants of my anger fade, replaced by glimmers of empathy.

Most days, I cross paths with Illusion. They're on the

streets performing all day long. Apparently, this month is their peak season, when Aix is overrun with tourists here for the town's summer music festival. Jean-Claude always makes time for an espresso with me, even if it's just fifteen minutes.

I'd thought that my meeting with his mother might make him open up more about his brother's death, but he remains tight-lipped. When I told him about the visit, he appeared devoid of emotion. He listened, with an expressionless face, as I told him how his mother cried, how she and his father forgave him, how much they love him. When I demanded, "Don't you care that your parents love you?" he muttered, "It's too complicated for you to understand," and promptly changed the subject. Since then, our conversations have just skimmed the surface of impersonal things—music, poetry, books. It's frustrating, even infuriating at times, but probably for the best. The more time I spend with Jean-Claude, the more I realize that what we share is friendship, nothing close to *le grand amour.*

Three times, I've run into Wendell when he was sketching fountains. He's been a little friendlier to me since our trip to Marseille, but still guarded. Our conversation starts and stops in awkward fits, leaving me thirsty afterward, hungry, longing for something more.

In the afternoons, when I stop by Madame Chevalier's and Vincent's, they never fail to ask me about Wendell. Beneath their deliberately casual questions—about how he likes art class and how his French is coming along—is the one question they really care about: whether there's any hope we'll get back together. The very question I'm carefully avoiding. I don't tell them what I only admit to my notebook: that I miss Wendell. That I want things to go back to how they were before. And that I have no idea how to make that happen.

• • •

Out of the corner of my eye, I catch a flash of shimmery gold and red. I'm crossing the square toward Madame Chevalier's, just passing the fountain, expecting to see Illusion coming through the crowd, sparkling with their brass instruments. But it's just Amandine wearing a red leotard, a short, swirly skirt, and a golden scarf around her waist. She's walking, without her entourage of Illusion, across the square.

It's not until a split second later that I notice who she's with.

Wendell.

I wince, as though I've just touched fire.

They sit down at Café Cerise, smack in front of Madame Chevalier's window.

Amandine stretches her hands up like a cat. As Wendell talks, she listens attentively, her head cocked to the side. Wendell has an earnest way of talking. Some people just talk and talk and it doesn't really matter who's sitting there with them. But talking with Wendell is like weaving a rope together: you do a strand, he does a strand, and together you make something.

And I can see he's doing this with Amandine. Now she's

talking and he's listening. He's really looking at her, the way he distinctly *wasn't* looking at me on our trip to Marseille a few weeks ago. I can't see her leaf-green eyes from here, but I imagine they're locked with his. He smiles his half-smile and says something.

I realize my feet are stuck to this spot. And I'm gaping. I make myself look away. I can't believe I didn't see this coming. If anyone is *hyper cool*, it's the girl who casually does backflips in the street, who turns toilet rooms into art projects, whose flaming red hair could easily be the topic of any love song. The girl who is complicated, smart, talented, gorgeous, and hiding something.

I take a long breath and make a wide circle around the café, blending into a crowd of German tourists, hiding from Wendell and Amandine. Then I climb the stairs to Madame Chevalier's, my heart heavy.

• • •

Inside, I sit down on the blue velvet chair. Madame Chevalier has already set up the tea tray on the table between us. There's a pot of peach tea, a bowl of sugar cubes, and a pitcher of cream. Little rectangular butter cookies have been arranged with care on a rose-rimmed plate. On the table sits a blue glass vase of fresh flowers—lilies—probably from Vincent.

With shaking hands, Madame Chevalier stirs cream into her tea, the tiny spoon clinking against the china. "*Alors, ma petite*, why are you sad today?"

I glance out the window. There they are, Wendell and

Amandine, in perfect view. "I'm sorry, Madame Chevalier, but may I borrow your binoculars?"

With some effort, she takes the leather cord from her neck and hands me the binoculars. Her expression is sympathetic, but she doesn't seem surprised. She must have seen Amandine and Wendell already. She must have guessed how I'd feel.

Filled with curiosity and dread, I peer through the lenses. Amandine is leaning close across the table, listening to Wendell intently, her face soft and open. I notice the smattering of light freckles on her nose. It's strange seeing her so close up, as if I could reach out and brush her cheek.

And Wendell's face. I can see the fine hairs on his skin, his individual eyelashes, the tenderness of his earlobes. I'm lost in my intricate observations—well, spying, really—and wishing I could read lips, when Madame Chevalier moves her head close to mine and whispers, "You love him dearly, *ma petite*."

I lower the binoculars to my lap, breathing out slowly. "You don't know anything about—"

"It's free theater out there, Zeeta. I saw you two crossing the square one evening a few weeks ago."

She must have seen us coming back from the *navette* stop after our Marseille outing. Wendell had insisted on walking me home.

"I saw how he looked at you," she continues. "How he kept moving close to you, only to pull away again. You know, from up here I can't hear people's words, but I've learned to look deeper than words. I read their gestures, their gazes, their most subtle movements."

I shake my head. "Wendell's obviously moving on. It was my choice to break up with him. Now I have to deal with the consequences."

She nods. "You regret it."

"It's not easy breaking up with someone. It doesn't mean I regret it."

She peers closely at my face, as if she's reading it. "It appears that you do." She lays her hand on my arm, lets it rest there. "Now, what are you going to do about that?"

I try to steady my voice. "I'm not going to toy with his emotions. It wouldn't be fair." I pause. "*C'est la vie, non?*"

"We shall see," she says, patting my arm. "Remember his vision. You both, soaking wet. Perhaps it's your destiny to find these waters with him, *ma petite.*"

I bite into a butter cookie. "I'm sorry, Madame Chevalier, but I don't think so." I try to sound firm. "I can't ask him to help." I look up and see her expression—one of deep sorrow, something much bigger than simple disappointment.

She speaks in a barely audible voice. "I'd like you to ask Wendell. Do it for me and Vincent. Please." Her eyes gleam, reflecting tiny rectangles of light from the window. "For years," she says, twirling her necklace around her fingers, "we sent silly messages back and forth. And for years, I hid my true feelings. I had my career, my travels. I assumed he thought of me as no more than a neighbor, a friend. I never dared to show my true feelings. The years go by so quickly,

Zeeta. You always think there will be time. And suddenly you're old. And sick." She rubs her hand over her face. "Three months ago, I discovered I was dying."

Dying? I have no idea what to say.

"It's cancer," she says. "Lymphoma. When it sank in that I would die, I realized I was never able to be with my true love. Was never able to tell him. That is why now, the stories of the magical waters are no longer just an amusing pastime for us. Suddenly, they've taken on a deep importance."

I swallow hard. "How long . . . ?" I can't finish the question.

"Weeks, maybe months."

For a while, I'm quiet. She's waiting for me to say something. After a drawn-out, wavery sigh, I say, "Make every day a song."

She smiles sadly. "What wise person said that, *ma petite*?"

"My father." I look into her watery, clouded brown eyes. "You need to tell Vincent how you feel."

"I don't want to burden him with that. It would only make his mourning worse."

There's a flurry of wings, and Maude flutters onto the railing. Madame Chevalier takes the paper from the vial, brightening as she reads the message. She laughs for a while and passes it to me.

At the clear fountain
While I was strolling by

> I found the water so nice
> That I went in to take a bath

I raise my eyebrows, wondering if Vincent has gone off the deep end.

"A little inside joke that goes way back," she says. "It's a nursery rhyme called '*À la Claire Fontaine.*'" She pauses. "Mostly nonsense," she says, singing it softly, stopping after the refrain, which goes, "*So long I've been loving you. I will never forget you.*"

She breaks off a piece of butter cookie, feeding it to Maude, who sits comfortably in her lap. "Don't tell Vincent. He thinks cookies are bad for her *merde.*"

"I know," I whisper.

After Maude finishes the morsel, Madame Chevalier holds out her teacup and lets Maude stick her beak inside. Content with creamy tea and cookies, Maude settles back into her lap. Madame Chevalier pulls out a small piece of tissue-thin paper from a drawer beside her, and a paint tin, and places them beside the jar of water already sitting there.

"Is there a chance?" I venture. "Chemo or radiation—"

She shakes her head slowly. "The lymphoma was diagnosed two years ago. I had chemo, and it went into remission. The cancer came back this winter. There was more chemo, this time more intense, more poisonous. It made me terribly sick and tired, too weak to walk up my stairs. I stopped leaving my apartment. What's worse, the fumes from my oil paints made me nauseous, so I stopped painting canvases. And three months later, they still found cancer cells. I told my doctors I'd rather die than suffer through more chemo." Her voice crackles, her eyes grow wet. "And here I am, waiting to die. I don't go outside. I don't paint." She taps her tin watercolor case. "Well, except for these little messages for Vincent." She spreads out some newspaper from a basket at her feet and holds the brush, thinking.

"What are you going to paint?"

"What should I paint?" she asks.

"How about pink hearts and gold stars and exclamation points and *Je t'aime, Vincent*?"

She smiles, holding the brush with one hand and petting Maude's feathers absently with the other. I watch Amandine and Wendell pay their bill and walk away, outside the frame of the window.

I bring the dishes to the kitchen and wash them in the small sink. Before I leave, I hug Madame Chevalier goodbye, kissing both of her papery cheeks. "You really believe these waters exist?" I ask.

"I want to believe," she says. "So very much. I'd almost stopped believing. Then you came into our lives. That gave me hope."

"Then I'll keep searching," I tell her. "I can do it alone. I'll try my best."

She shakes her head, clucking. "*Ma petite*, you need Wendell."

"But he—"

"He will do anything for you." Her voice is so firm, I can't argue.

Instead, I respond, "And Vincent will do anything for you."

I motion to her brush and paints and the whispery thin piece of paper in front of her. "Tell him everything," I say, "just in case we can't find the waters."

Then, biting my tongue to hold back tears, I walk down the hallway, past all the Madame Chevaliers gazing at me. As I close the door, I look back to see the live Madame Chevalier picking up her brush and dipping it into the paint.

TWENTY-TWO

In the back street outside Madame Chevalier's apartment, I lean against the cool stone wall, listening to my heart-beat, breathing in the scent of buttery croissants and melting chocolate from the bakery around the corner, feeling very alive. But not in a good way. In a way that makes me think of all the smells and sights and sounds that Madame Chevalier will have to say goodbye to. All the things that will end for her.

I let the pent-up tears fall. Tears for Madame Chevalier. And for myself. I can't bear another goodbye. You'd think I'd be used to it by now, losing people I love. But it doesn't work that way. Every time I leave a country, it feels like a mass funeral, dozens of deaths every year. Deaths of friendships and daily rituals, favorite foods and special nooks. And then,

a plane ride later, I'm dropped into a whole new world of rituals and foods and nooks, while I'm still in mourning.

It's more painful with each new country. Each loss brings up
a string of past losses. The day I left Ecuador, Mamita Luz
packed me a bag of fresh-baked bread to eat on our series of
plane rides to France. Silvio gave me a crystal to protect me.
Gaby wrapped an indigo alpaca scarf around my neck. And the
girls filled my pockets with little treasures—nuts and pebbles
and wildflowers. Of course, we assured each other we'd keep in
touch, but I knew that after a couple years, our letters would
peter out. I knew I'd probably never again see the girls' chubby
cheeks or hear Gaby wheedling customers or taste Mamita
Luz's warm bread. Saying goodbye to Ecuador was saying
goodbye to a piece of myself.

I think again, of my prison of *ifs*, how part of me was
expecting my link with Wendell to die too, how, at the first
sign of trouble, I just cut things off with him, assuming our
relationship would end soon enough, assuming it might hurt
less if I did it myself. Then I remember something else from
that day in Marseille. On the boat, Maurice said that love
can flow underground, invisible, like a hidden spring. I think
of my love for Wendell, my father's love for Layla, Madame
Chevalier's love for Vincent. I think of this secret river,
always flowing, sometimes aboveground, sometimes below
the surface. And despite everything, I realize, I want to tap
into it.

Which means I need to look for the sacred waters. I need
to do it for Madame Chevalier. For her, the waters mean a

chance to fulfill a lifelong love. But beneath that, I need to find these waters for me. I'm not entirely sure why or how. All I know is that I *do* need Wendell's help. And if he's together with Amandine, I'll have to deal with that.

I take a few deep breaths, wipe my eyes, and walk down the alley toward the main street. I can almost hear Maurice's nasal voice, giving me a pep talk. If Dantes had never dared to escape prison, never dared to leap off the cliffs into the icy, raging sea . . . if he had never looked for the treasure and eventually let go of his bitterness, he would never have reunited, in the end, with the love of his life.

• • •

Back on the square, I glance up at the clock tower, noting that I have a couple hours before my English tutoring session, glad for the time to let my puffy eyes and blotchy face go back to normal. I'm heading to my apartment, just passing Café Cerise, when I catch sight of Amandine and Wendell, standing together and talking. I'd thought they'd left, but they must have been just outside of the view from Madame Chevalier's apartment. Before I can change routes or find some tourists to blend in with, Amandine catches my eye.

"*Salut,*" she says with two pecks on my cheeks.

Wendell just says, "Hi." It strikes me that he doesn't say my name, as if the word *Zeeta* is too intimate.

I raise a hand in a limp wave.

Amandine fills the awkward silence. "What are you up to today?"

"Just visited my friend. You know, that woman I told you about, Wendell." My tongue feels clumsy, my words choppy. "The artist. Madame Chevalier."

Amandine's eyes widen. "Violette Chevalier?"

"Ouais."

"You're friends with her?"

"Ouais."

"She's a famous painter. *Hyper cool!*" Amandine cries. "I studied her in school. Her paintings are in museums all over the world." She nudges Wendell with her elbow. "You'd love her work. Your art teacher would be so impressed if you met her."

She rambles for a while about Madame Chevalier as Wendell and I avoid each other's eyes. When the clock chimes, Amandine jumps. "Oh! I have to meet the band to get ready for a show tonight. It's in the basement club on Rue de la Verrerie. See you there, Wendell?"

He nods.

"You're coming too, Zeeta?" she asks.

"Oh, no . . ." I stall. "I have other plans," I lie.

She pecks us on the cheeks, does a cartwheel, and skips away.

Wendell and I are alone now. Stiffly, he asks, "Any more leads on your father?"

"Nothing."

After a pause, he says, "So, can I meet this famous artist sometime?"

I bite my lip. "Wendell, there are things you need to

know." I hesitate, unsure where to begin. "She and Vincent know about your vision of me. The one in the wet red dress."

"You told them?" he asks in disbelief.

"I—I'm sorry. It slipped." I take a deep breath. "I had no idea they'd get you involved. They're convinced that it's our destiny to find the waters together."

He tilts his head, confused.

"The supposedly magical waters I told you about," I clarify. "Remember? One sip heals, frequent sips make you live forever."

"Right," he says, still looking mystified. "I remember."

We step aside to let a group of tourists pass, and then I say, "I thought they were just two sweet old people playing this imaginary game, you know?" I pause, trying to keep my lip from quivering. "But now—" My eyes burn. I finish it quickly. "She's dying, Wendell. She has cancer. Lymphoma. She thinks the waters can heal her."

He blinks, then says, "Tell her I'll help you."

"Really?" I look at him more closely. "You don't think this is crazy?"

"Whether it's crazy or not, it means a lot to Madame Chevalier. It's her dying wish. We have to do it." He draws in a breath, looks over my shoulder. "But Zeeta, there's something else. I had another vision."

"What?"

He hesitates. "I don't want to freak you out."

"Tell me."

"You're—you're in some kind of danger. You're in that red

• 252 •

dress. It's wet and it's nighttime. There's a crowd of people around you. And there's a bearded man yelling at you, threatening you. You look really scared."

I take a moment to process this. "In this vision—where are we?"

He shrugs. "Outside at night. There might be firelight. I can't make out anything else."

"If it's dangerous, then maybe we shouldn't do this," I say. "Madame Chevalier will understand."

Some kids run by us, chasing a little dog. As their squeals and laughs fade, Wendell says, "I think we have to, Z. Both of us. I keep getting glimpses of something else, something . . ." His voice drifts off.

"Something you won't tell me," I finish.

"Right." He nods sheepishly.

A wave of frustration sweeps over me, but after a moment, I calm down. After all, he's agreed to help me. "Okay, I think we should meet with Madame Chevalier and Vincent together. When's a good time?"

He pauses, thinking. "I spend Tuesday and Thursday afternoons with Amandine."

I swallow hard. "Oh."

"She's doing all the art assignments alongside me—sketching the fountains, going to museums. And I'm teaching her what I learn every day."

"Why?"

"She can't afford art lessons, and she had to quit school to work."

A prickly heat moves up my neck.

"She's helping me with my French too." He shrugs, not meeting my eyes. "Plus, she's cool."

"Hmm." I feel nauseated. "Well, I have to go. I'm tutoring some *lycée* students soon."

Wendell tucks a strand of hair behind his ear, adjusts his backpack strap over his shoulder. "How about we meet Friday afternoon?"

"Okay," I say, disappointed that I'll have to wait a few days. "Meet me here at three."

"I'll be here."

There's a clumsy moment when he looks on the verge of moving forward to kiss my cheeks, and I step toward him to meet him halfway. Then a big group of women walk by, making us step aside, and when we look at each other again, the moment is lost. So off we walk in our separate directions. Still, it's *something*.

TWENTY-THREE

I peer into the courtyard of Les Secrets de Maude, looking for some sign of Vincent. Today the wrought-iron gate is shut, locked with a chain and padlock. He must be out. Too bad. I've just finished my tutoring session with the *lycée* students, and I'm craving Vincent's company. Lately, I've been picking up random objects in his shop—a rhinestone-studded candlestick or a Japanese doll in a genuine silk kimono—and he tells me the story behind them. Each piece of junk—or treasure, depending on how you see it—is a doorway to another world, like the 1920s Paris social scene or the nineteenth-century underbelly of London.

I'm about to leave when I hear a few guitar notes floating from the shadows of the courtyard.

"Vincent!" I call, looking again through the wrought-iron bars. It's hard to see past all the foliage and furniture.

"Bonjour!" a voice calls out. Not Vincent's voice, but a younger one. And then a head pops up. It's Vincent's son, Jean-Christophe. He walks toward me, ducking beneath huge leaves and stepping over pigeons and half-broken chairs and tables. He's holding a guitar.

"Bonjour, Jean-Christophe!" I say.

"Ah, it's you, *Mademoiselle* Zeeta," he says. "My father is away today, buying antiques in the villages."

"Oh, well, could you just tell him I stopped by, then?"

"Of course." He leans the guitar against the wall. "I'm headed to Marseille to sail off later today."

"Where to?" I ask through the bars.

"Oh, who knows, wherever the wind takes me."

"Bon voyage," I say, turning to go.

"Wait, Zeeta!" he says, his hands clutching the iron bars. "I'm sorry I didn't get to know you better. You're so kind to my father. And he adores you. I—I just want to thank you."

"No problem," I say. "Vincent's great."

"Really, Zeeta, it means so much to him. I'm his only child, you know. I feel bad I've never given him grand-children. He's always wished for them." His shoulders slump. "I love my father very much, but I haven't been a good son. I'm always leaving him. Perhaps I'm meant to be a solitary wanderer."

He reaches his hand through the bars.

Unsure what to do, I shake it.

"Zeeta," he says. "Thank you. I feel better leaving my father this time, knowing that you are here for him. It's his birthday on Friday. You'll give him good wishes, *non?*"

I don't know what to make of this man's speech, but I say, "Of course." With a smile, I add, "He'd make an excellent grandfather, you know." After wishing Jean-Christophe a good journey, I walk away, up the street as melancholy guitar notes drift along after me.

• • •

The antiques section of the sprawling outdoor market is just past the olive oil soap stands, in kind of a nook behind the cicada-print tabecloths. I wander through tables cluttered with crystal vases, doorknobs, gold-rimmed plates, lampshades, silver platters, marble busts, ceramic pitchers, old green bottles, paintings of flowers. Everything is worn, faded, rusted, and musty. It's hard to pick out a present for Vincent, who already has piles of this stuff in his shop. But today's his birthday, and when I meet him at Les Secrets de Maude in a few hours, I want to have some gift for him.

I run my fingers over the textures of the antiques, rubbing a lace ribbon, holding pink glass rosary beads to the sky, considering a pair of pig-shaped salt and pepper shakers. This whole time, I'm keeping a close eye on my bag, since this seems like a perfect spot for my *fantôme* father to slip in another gift. I linger at a table filled with crates of old books—coffee-table art books, gilded fairy-tale books, local history books. This stuff might be up Vincent's alley.

To the side of the table is a wooden box filled with old,

plastic-wrapped maps that catch my eye. They're mostly maps of Aix, some dated as old as the eighteen hundreds. I skim right over the ones that are priced over a hundred euros. The more recent maps—and the ones in worse shape—are much cheaper. My eyes scan the titles of the maps—*Churches of Aix-en-Provence, Aixois Gardens,* Hôtels Particuliers *of Aix, Cézanne in Provence.* The next title is harder to read. The paper is water-stained, torn in places, with faded script. I squint at the letters, and then freeze. *Les Eaux Sacrées d'Aix-en-Provence.* "The Sacred Waters of Aix-en-Provence."

I take the map from the crate and hold it to the sunlight, rereading the title in disbelief. But yes, that's what it says. The title appears to be handwritten onto the map in faint, old-fashioned ink. The map is about to fall apart, with holes and rips throughout. It looks as if it's been through floods and rainstorms, with all its yellowed spots and wrinkles and wavy, rough texture. It's in terrible condition, but perfect for Vincent.

On inspecting the map, I realize it doesn't even show the parts of town built in the past two centuries. How old is this map, anyway? I can't find a date on it. It's not expensive compared to the other maps, but still a lot of money for me. Fifteen euros—twenty dollars—is what I make in one tutoring session.

Quickly, before I can change my mind, I hand my money to the woman behind the table. With a satisfied smile, I roll up the map and tuck it into my bag. Vincent will be over the moon.

• • •

Vincent and I are making faces in a dust-covered, gilded mirror at Les Secrets de Maude. I'm showing him how to form the *r* sound in the middle of his mouth rather than gagging out the *r* from the back of the throat. He falls apart with laughter, and I force a smile, feeling nervous about Wendell's impending arrival. He should be here any minute. There's a whole shelf full of old clocks, but each of them says a different time, so I don't know how close to three it is.

If I thought the encounter with Wendell and Amandine on the square was awkward, my follow-up phone call yesterday was worse. When I found out Madame Chevalier had a home visit with her doctor this afternoon, I called Wendell to change our plans. I suggested he come to Les Secrets de Maude so that he could meet Vincent and celebrate his birthday. The phone conversation was going smoothly until Wendell agreed to pick up a lemon tart for the occasion. That's when I heard Amandine's voice in the background, recommending a good *pâtisserie*.

Now, every time one of the pigeons flutters up, my head snaps to the doorway to see if he's come.

"Red," I say to the mirror, exaggerating the *r* sound.

"Hed," Vincent attempts, making a guttural noise that leaves beads of spittle on the mirror.

"Red," I say again, waving away some pigeons so we can see our faces in the old glass.

"Hed," he says, then collapses into giggles. "You're making me act like Boofalo Beel!" He swirls an imaginary lasso over his head and makes some nonsense sounds, moving his mouth wide and making his lips slack and sticking out his tongue. He looks so ridiculous, I sputter out a small laugh. I'm guessing his idea of English comes mostly from old cowboy movies.

After ten minutes of practicing, Vincent still sounds as though he's hacking up phlegm, but I say, "Good job!" in English, trying to sound sincere. "You're improving!" It's true; he's moved from abysmal to just terrible.

"Zank you, Meez," he says, pleased, smoothing Irène's caramel-brown feathers. I can actually tell these pigeons apart now. I don't see Maude anywhere, though. As I look around for her, I spot Wendell in the doorway, holding a white cardboard bakery box. He steps carefully between birds, nodding at me in greeting, and extending his hand to Vincent.

"*Bonjour, monsieur.*" His *r*s are perfect, subtle and slightly raspy. His host family and Amandine are teaching him well.

"*Bonjour, bonjour!*" Vincent says, then rambles for a bit about how grateful he is for Wendell's assistance in our search.

When Vincent finishes his speech, I announce, "*Bon anniversaire!*" and on cue, Wendell opens the lid of the box, revealing a shiny yellow pie.

"*Tarte au citron!* My favorite!" Vincent clasps his hands together. "How did you know it's my birthday?"

"Your son told me."

A cloud passes over Vincent's face. "My son is an expert at

missing birthdays and holidays. He's always flitting in and out of my life." He shakes his head sadly.

Hoping to cheer him up, I pull my map from the bag and present it to him.

He puts his glasses back on. "Now, what is this, *mademoiselle*?"

"For you. I found it at the antiques market."

He unrolls the map. Wendell and I help him hold it up, the three of us crowded around the map. In this small space, Wendell's arm is just inches from mine.

"*Mon Dieu!*" Vincent cries. "*Les Eaux Sacrées d'Aix-en-Provence!*"

I turn to Wendell to translate, but he understands. "The sacred waters," he murmurs. "Where did you get this, Zeeta?" He speaks in French to keep Vincent in the loop. And he does a pretty grammatically correct job of it too.

"In the antiques market," I say, noting that Vincent is nearly bouncing out of his chair.

"*Ça, c'est incroyable!*" Vincent exclaims. Incredible! "What amazing luck!" Then, with a wink at me, he adds, "Or destiny." He positions a lamp close and points to an area not far from my neighborhood. "This map must be old," he says with reverence. "See? The walls are still intact around the city. And look! This map shows all the fountains, even the private ones, but you see, the nineteenth-century fountains hadn't even been built yet."

"What's that?" Wendell asks, pointing to a long, meandering blue line, so faint you could almost overlook it.

I squint. "How could you see that?" I ask.

"Light and shadows," he says. "I'm used to looking now." As his finger moves along the line, my gaze follows. It's a winding, haphazard path that crisscrosses the streets and goes right through houses.

"*Oh, la la la la,*" Vincent says, clucking with disapproval. "People can be so careless with valuable documents." He pulls out a magnifying glass from a drawer and studies the line. "*Attendez!*" Wait! He moves his head closer to the lens. "The blue ink looks very old. Maybe as old as the map itself."

"What do you think the line means?" I ask.

He puffs his cheeks with air, lets it out in a slow putter. "*Alors*, it's in the oldest part of town, the *quartier* where we are now. There are many underground rivers here. Perhaps the line shows a hidden spring."

Wendell reaches over again to the map, tapping at three separate spots. "Look at these. They're doodles or something," he says thoughtfully. "Symbols. Spirals."

And with his words, the spirals leap out at me. "Triple spirals!" I say. "Like the ones Sirona wears around her neck."

"Do they symbolize something?" Wendell asks.

"Triple spirals are special because they're one continuous line." I rack my brain for more details. "I think Sirona said they stand for eternal life." I look at Wendell. "And water."

"These markings are all deliberate," Vincent says slowly, stroking Juliette's milk-white feathers.

I nod, still staring at the map. Now that we've identified

the spirals, I can't understand how we missed them at first. There are three triple spirals total, at different places along the line, and each one falls inside a courtyard of a different building, all in the oldest part of town. "I wonder what they refer to," I say.

"You know," Vincent says, his face growing red with excitement. "If the blue line shows an underground spring, perhaps the triple spirals show where the waters come aboveground. In the form of fountains." He mops sweat from his brow with a handkerchief. "Now, over the years I've gone to all the fountains on the town registry. Even the private ones. The registry says nothing of fountains in those spots." He's headed toward a conclusion that, according to his bizarre logic, makes sense. "The blue line shows the sacred waters underground," he says, "and the spirals must show where they rise into fountains!"

I look at Wendell, wondering what he really thinks of this. After all, I'm used to hearing about the sacred waters, but it's the first time for Wendell. Still, he seems genuinely excited. "And we actually have addresses for these courtyards," he says, flicking a stray feather off his knee. "The perfect places to begin our search."

"*Oui!*" Vincent says, and then knits his eyebrows. "But how will you gain entrance into these private residences?"

Wendell gives a half-smile. "My art assignment is to draw the fountains of Aix. Extra credit for whoever gets the most sketches. Perfect excuse."

"Ah! Excellent cover!" Vincent says, nearly bursting with

giddy energy. His voice lowers. "Now, *garçon,* have you had any more visions of the waters?"

Wendell shifts in his chair. "No," he says, looking at me. "Just that one of Zeeta in the water in a red dress."

He must not want Vincent to know about the bearded man, the danger. Luckily, before Vincent can press further, Maude flies inside, landing on his shoulder. "Oh, we must tell Madame Chevalier about this map!" Vincent says, pulling a tissue-thin piece of paper from his pocket. He dips his fountain pen into a jar of ink, writes a message, and sends it off with Maude, as Wendell looks on, curious.

Afterward, we share the *tarte au citron,* and once we've had our fill of pie, Wendell and I say goodbye to Vincent, then wade outside through the pigeons.

Alone now with Wendell, in the stone courtyard, all the awkwardness rushes back. I fiddle with the strap of my bag. "Sorry I dragged you into this sacred waters weirdness," I whisper as we walk through the gateway, out onto the Place des Trois Ormeaux, where the circular fountain bubbles.

"No worries, Zeeta," he says. "It's fun."

There's something in his voice that makes me ask, "Do you think there's any chance these sacred waters are real?"

"They're real to Madame Chevalier and Vincent," he says. "That's all that matters. I mean, who am I to question what they believe?"

"True." I smile. If there's one thing my nomadic life has taught me, it's that strange things can happen. Mysterious things. Inexplicable things. "Hey," I say. "You want to go to

Madame Chevalier's now? Her doctor's probably gone. And then we can go to the spiral addresses. They're not far from her house."

"Sorry," he says. "I can't."

I wait for him to explain, and when he doesn't, I swallow and say, "Okay, well, maybe in a few days?"

"Let me talk to Amandine, and then we can figure out a time."

"Right. Amandine." I raise my hand in farewell. "See you later."

"Bye."

I sit on the fountain, trailing my fingers in the water, and watch him hurry down the street, off to meet Amandine. Escaping from my prison of *ifs* is considerably harder with a gorgeous, artistic, fire-dancing acrobat girl in the picture. And I didn't even see it coming.

• • •

"Aubergine," Layla says with a theatrical flourish. "It's a much more elegant word than *eggplant.*" She turns the deep purple vegetable over in her hands. "Don't you think, Z?"

"I guess," I say, chopping a zucchini.

We're making ratatouille tonight—the classic Provençal dish. I hoped all this chopping would be hypnotic, distract me from Amandine and Wendell, get my mind off the standstill in the search for my *fantôme* father. His guitar music is filling the apartment, because, as much as I try, I can't resist listening to the CD on repeat. The music takes on a whole new significance now that I imagine J.C. playing it. I can see his hands strumming, his fingers moving over the strings, the guitar resting against his Jimi Hendrix T-shirt. But above the neckline is empty space. No face to put there.

It's been weeks since my *fantôme*'s packet of letters, and I'm starting to worry that those might have been his last gifts. Meanwhile, I've continued to write letters in my notebook, which brings me closer to him than ever, in a strange, abstract way. I'm beginning to wonder if he's just as confused about love as I am.

"Can you pass me the garlic, Z?" Layla asks.

I check the wire basket dangling from the ceiling. Only a few wispy bits of garlic skin remain. "We're out, Layla," I observe. "I'll get some at the *épicerie*." I grab my bag and plunge my hand in to retrieve my change purse.

That's when I notice a small envelope marked with my name, written in that now-familiar compact script. My *fantôme*. But when? How? I've been so careful with my bag.

"Layla," I say, sinking onto the couch. "He left another gift."

She comes into the living room, knife still in hand, eyes wide. "What's it say?"

My hands are shaking. Maybe he's finally going to give his name, or address, or phone number. Maybe this time is it.

I open the envelope. Inside, there's a bookmark made of thick, brown, fibrous bark paper, painted with a golden, smiling sun on top and a pale, pensive crescent moon below.

The sun is surrounded with colorful flowers, the moon with silver stars. I remember this kind of thing from the tourist market in Guatemala.

The envelope also contains a piece of graphed paper, torn from a notebook. Taking a deep breath, I unfold it, revealing a short letter in French. Layla reads silently over my shoulder.

> Dear Zeeta,
>
> I know you were looking for me. I admire your spirit, your strength, your resolve to find me despite everything. I feel I owe you an explanation. It's not that I don't want to be part of your life. I'm working hard to become a father who would make you proud. Please be patient. I will try to find the courage to introduce myself.
>
> Love,
> Your father
>
> P.S. I notice you with your notebook. I thought you might like this bookmark.

I reread it a few times, then fold it up and put it back in the envelope, my heart sinking. I wasn't expecting this crushed, bruised feeling. Somehow, even though I've never met J.C., I've grown closer to him after the unsent letters

I've written, after visiting the Château d'If, after hearing Maurice talk about him, after listening to his CD a hundred times, after sleeping in his Jimi T-shirt.

Now, with this latest letter, I feel even closer. But in reality, I'm no closer to him at all. I don't even know what he looks like. I still don't know his name. These facts make my chest hurt.

Layla has the bookmark in her hand. She's rubbing the fibers, studying the moon and sun.

"Does the bookmark mean anything to you, Layla?"

She stares at it for a moment longer, then says, "No. But it looks Latin American, doesn't it?"

I nod. "You think he's from there?"

"Maybe." She kisses my hair. "Let's be patient, like he asked."

I tuck the bookmark in my notebook and stand up, unsure what to think.

Layla puts a hand on my shoulder. "I have to say, Z, he seems like a decent guy."

"I know," I say. His kindness makes it almost unbearable. It was simpler to just hate him. The tightness in my chest is making it hard to breathe. "I'm going to get some air," I tell Layla. "And the garlic, while I'm at it."

I walk downstairs, but instead of turning left to go to the *épicerie*, I turn right, on impulse, and jog to Nirvana.

"Zeeta!" Ahmed says as I jangle inside. "What a surprise!"

"*Essalam alikoum*, Ahmed," I say quickly. "I need to make a call to Wendell. Fast."

"And how is your lovely mother?" he asks.

"Good."

"Layla stops by sometimes to chat, you know. She loves swiveling in the chairs and giving me advice." He shakes his head, chuckling. "And she's always chiding me about my addiction to KnightQuest. You know, she's the only person I've met who knows as much about Rumi as I do. What a delight! What's she doing this evening, Zeeta?"

"Cooking ratatouille," I say, only half listening. "I'm supposed to get her garlic."

"Oh, she likes to cook?" he says thoughtfully. "While you're calling Wendell, I'll get a head of garlic from my apartment." He dials the number and then flips the sign on the door to Closed and disappears into a back room.

Miraculously, Wendell is the one who answers the phone.

"Hey, it's me," I say. Then I add, "Zeeta," since I'm not officially on a "me" basis with him anymore.

"Hey, what's up?" He sounds a little distant, and there are voices in the background.

I want to tell him about my *fantôme*'s latest letter, hear what he thinks about it. I want to explain how frustrated it makes me, how much it hurts, how it makes me feel as though I could explode. I'm about to let this all spill out, when I get the feeling Wendell's not entirely present. He's distracted, in the middle of something.

So I don't mention the letter, and simply ask, "Have you figured out when you want to meet? I was thinking maybe Sunday morning."

"Oh, right. Hold on a sec. Let me ask Amandine."

Amandine again? My chest tightens. "She's there?"

"Yeah. We're working on an art project. Hold on."

I shake my foot in an erratic, impatient rhythm.

"Hey, Zeeta," Wendell says, coming back on the line. "Yeah. Sunday around ten would work. Meet you at the fountain on Rue Mignet?"

"Okay, bye," I say quickly, and hang up.

Outside the phone booth, Ahmed is waiting for me with a head of garlic. "Zeeta, tell your mother that I would be happy to show her how to cook my mother's delicious Moroccan dishes. And please thank her for recommending I take a vacation. I'm planning one soon, you know—"

"Sure, Ahmed," I interrupt, taking the garlic and dropping some coins in his hands, then jingling out the door toward Layla and the ratatouille and my father's music.

TWENTY-FOUR

The fountain on Rue Mignet is an unassuming circular pool with a single spout spurting water from its center. It's such a small fountain that there's no edge to perch on, so I stand beside it, keeping an eye out for Wendell and trying not to tug at my red dress. Madame Chevalier reasoned that if—according to Wendell's vision—I'm going to find the waters in a red dress, I should increase our chances by pre-emptively wearing it. I've decided to humor her, although I secretly suspect she wanted me to get dolled up for Wendell—a futile attempt at matchmaking.

Yesterday, when I visited her, she was feeling weak and tired, so I only stayed long enough to tell her about the map of the sacred waters. That brightened her mood a bit, but I didn't want to exhaust her by having Wendell meet her today. We'll wait until she gets better, I decided. If she gets better.

Just as the clock tower starts chiming ten, Wendell appears around the bend, a mostly empty backpack slung over one shoulder. The morning sunshine backlights him, makes his hair glow. If I had a camera, I'd take his picture.

The first thing he says is, "Yep. That's the dress."

"I feel overdressed," I say, eyeing his jeans and plain white T-shirt. "Madame Chevalier made me wear it."

"It's nice," he says. "I mean, I told you before it didn't seem your style—" He stops, floundering. "But if your style changes, that's fine. Anyway, it looks really nice."

"Thanks," I say, suppressing a smile.

As we head toward the site of the first spiral from the map, I tell him about the latest letter from my *fantôme*. He listens closely.

"What should I do?" I ask.

"You could just wait, like he said."

"Hmm." Wendell makes it sound so simple. "But what if he never decides he's good enough to meet me?"

"Don't build yourself a prison of *if*s, Zeeta. Just trust that he'll do it."

"Okay," I say, thinking that it's much easier said than done. Still, I feel better after talking to Wendell about it.

Under a window box of red geraniums, he slows down and glances at the paper in his hand, then at the address over the door we're approaching. "Here we are, Zeeta!"

The building is buttery yellow, with an old wooden door carved with vines and flanked with potted roses climbing up a trellis. A glum stone face looms over the door—a thin man's face wearing a stylized crown and a small, neatly trimmed beard. He's frowning and sticking out his tongue as if he's gagging on some unsavory food. "He looks like he's just eaten a bad brussels sprout," I whisper to Wendell.

"Or duck liver pâté that's been left in the fridge too long," Wendell whispers back.

There are no buzzers, so we knock hard. I stare at my feet, waiting. And there, near my sandal, embedded in the stone, is a brass triple spiral, so tiny you could almost miss it.

"Look, Wendell!"

He crouches beside me to inspect it. "Maybe Vincent and Madame Chevalier aren't so nutty after all."

I knock again, louder now. Still no answer. The ground-level windows are shuttered, and the upper-level windows—some of which are opened—have lace curtains over them, blowing in the slight breeze. Outside, two of the window boxes are overflowing with red flowers. "Someone has to live here," I say.

"Maybe they're out," he says. "We can come back later."

As we leave, I take a last glance at the grimacing, gagging man over the door, who looks as though he's snarling at us to leave.

We walk down Rue Boulegon and turn onto Rue Matheron. Emerging from a tiny *épicerie* is the mime, in full costume, toting two bags of groceries.

I wave. "*Bonjour*, Tortue."

"*Bonjour*, Zeeta." As always, his voice sounds rusty. Strange that he even wears white face paint and gloves to run errands.

I introduce him to Wendell, then pull out my notebook. "Do you wear your mime outfit everywhere, Tortue?"

He gives a small smile. "When I'm in a depressed phase, I do. It's comforting, I guess. I don't have to be myself. I can disappear behind a mask for a while." He shrugs a shoulder. "At least, that's what my therapists say."

I figure since he's mentioned the therapy in front of Wendell that it's okay to talk about. "How's your treatment going?" I ask.

"*Ça va*," he says. "Little by little. No sessions on weekends, so I'm spending time with Illusion and doing some performing." He turns to Wendell. "And what are you two up to?"

Wendell looks at me. "Just taking a walk," he says.

"And how was your trip to Marseille?"

"Good." I don't know how much he knows about the situation, so I just repeat, "Good."

"I should get going," he says, holding up his bags of groceries as evidence. "*Au revoir*."

"*Au revoir*, Tortue," we say.

After the mime is out of earshot, Wendell says, "Tortue. That means 'turtle' in French, right?"

I nod. "Who knows how he got that nickname." I look

over my shoulder, watching him fade into the crowds down the street. "He's the deepest clown I've met so far. And as you know, I've met lots. It's too bad Layla's not into him."

"But doesn't he have emotional issues?" Wendell asks.

I laugh. "Out of all the clowns I've known, he's probably the most stable." I tilt my head. "Or he might be, if he ever took off that costume."

"Why isn't Layla interested?"

I blow a strand of hair from my face. "She says he's too serious. Not playful enough. She goes more for the Harlequin clowns—all flashy colors. He's a Pierrot—quiet and thoughtful."

"So she hasn't found any other clowns so far?"

"Miraculously, no. My friend who owns Nirvana is practically drooling over her, but even if she got past how clean-cut and responsible he is, she'd break his heart within a few weeks."

Wendell and I talk, lightly, joking about the guys in town who might make good matches for Layla. He comments on how much moonlight she'd need to drink to make them acceptable, which makes me giggle and reminds me of our day in Marseille.

A few blocks later, we've arrived at the second address, on Rue Epinaux. This door has a carved stone joker face over it. Or maybe it's a jester, or a demon, or an ancient Christian rendition of some pagan deity. He's laughing mischievously, his eyebrows raised in devilish delight. A bushy, unkempt beard frames his cheeks. His ears are pointed and his eyes impish.

"I like this guy better than Mr. Grumpers back at the last house," I comment.

"Definitely," Wendell agrees. "This one would be lots more fun to hang out with."

"Hey, look," I say, pointing to a small triple spiral in the stone on the sidewalk. It's easy to miss unless you're looking for it or staring at your feet.

"Two for two," he says with a grin.

Like the last building, there's no buzzer on this one. No one answers the door, no matter how loud we knock.

"I'm beginning to see a pattern here," I say.

"On to the third one?" Wendell asks, glancing at his watch.

"Plans with your host family later?" I ask, trying not to sound resentful.

"Amandine."

"Hmm." I want to ask straight out what's going on with them. If they're just friends, or more, or on the way to more. I clamp my mouth shut, because really, it's none of my business. Anyway, I'm having fun with him, and I don't want to ruin it.

The third house is just four meandering blocks away, on Rue du Gibelin. The face over this door is the nicest by far. It's a bashful lion, resting his curly-maned head on two cute paws. He looks painfully shy.

"This one is straight from *The Wizard of Oz*," Wendell says.

"Right! The cowardly lion. Only this was carved a few centuries earlier."

"True," Wendell says, and then, "Weird face over door? Check." He looks down near our feet. "Spiral in sidewalk? Check."

"Lack of buzzer?" I add. "Check." Then I knock on the door, expecting no answer. But on our third round of knocking, a head pokes out an upper window on the third story.

It's Damona. "*Bonjour*, Zeeta!" she calls out.

We call back up to her, exchanging pleasantries, and then giving our story about Wendell's art project. "We heard there was a fountain in the courtyard of this building," I shout. "Mind if we come in to sketch it?"

"*Bien sûr*," she calls back. "I'll be right down!"

I look at Wendell and whisper, "Incredible! It's Sirona's son's girlfriend. She's one of the band Salluvii. Which Vincent believes is *immortal*."

Wendell's eyes widen.

Damona and Bormanus appear hand in hand and greet us with kisses on the cheeks. "Come in," Bormanus says, leading us through a passageway that opens up to a courtyard filled with flowers and trees.

"Here it is," Damona says, waving her hand.

It's a rectangular fountain, featuring the face of a bearded man with his tongue sticking out. It's similar to the face over the first door, only this face has a giant beard, like Santa Claus. And his expression seems more lewd than grouchy. The hole where the water would come out is on his tongue. The basin of the fountain is dry, containing only a few spades, a rake, and a watering can. "We use it as storage for gardening tools," Damona says apologetically. "Will it still count as a fountain for your project?"

"I think so," Wendell says. He flips open his sketchbook and starts drawing. Shadows first, of course.

"Mind if I watch?" Damona asks, leaning over. The triple-spiral pendant slips from the neck of her tunic.

"Any other fountains or water sources here?" I ask. "Maybe some springs?"

"No. This is it," she says. Her gaze falls on Wendell's sketch pad. "You draw beautifully." She turns to Bormanus. "Look, isn't it lovely?"

And as the three of them talk about Wendell's art classes, I stand up and wander around the courtyard, scanning the stone walls for hints of water. I peek behind bushes and trees, through flowered vines, cracked clay pots, rusting garden shovels. Nothing unusual.

"So have you two lived here for a while?" Wendell asks. His French flows naturally now, getting better every time I see him.

Damona nods. "With Sirona and Grannos. We're always traveling, though. A couple months here, then we leave to play somewhere else. We have houses in a few different towns around Europe."

I wonder how they can afford a few different houses on a salary that consists of people's spare change.

"How long have you all been playing together?" Wendell asks.

"Oh, ages!" she says, smiling at Bormanus, taking his hand.

Once Wendell finishes the sketch, they lead us back to the entrance and out to the street.

Damona lingers, looking like she wants us to stay, but Bormanus waves and says, *"Au revoir."*

Damona adds, *"Bon courage."*

"Merci," we call out, walking away. *"Au revoir."*

"Au revoir." Arm in arm, they wave, finally closing the door.

Wendell and I walk around the bend, and when we're out of earshot, I burst out, "Wendell! I can't believe Salluvii lives there! This is too much to be a coincidence."

"Something's going on," he agrees.

"We have to get inside those other courtyards!"

He gives me a half-smile. "Snoop?" he asks.

I smile back, thinking of our detective work in Ecuador. "Snoop," I say. "How about tomorrow at three?"

"Sure. I wouldn't miss a chance to snoop with you, Z."

Our eyes meet for a stretched-out moment, and then we both start laughing, and it feels *hyper super cool.*

• • •

The next afternoon, Wendell and I knock on the doors under the gagging-man face and the devil face until our knuckles are bruised. No one answers. And no one comes into or out of the building either. Yet it's clear the buildings aren't deserted, because some windows are open. Not to mention that someone has to water those geraniums.

"Can we go to Madame Chevalier's?" Wendell asks, rubbing his knuckles.

"Sure." I stopped by her apartment earlier today and was relieved to see her back to her usual self. She assured me she'd just caught a little cold and was already feeling better.

"She won't mind?" he asks. "I mean, since she's famous and everything?"

I laugh. "Wendell, she can't wait to meet you. And don't worry about a thing. She already adores you."

"Really?" he asks, surprised. "Why?"

"Oh, um . . ." I hesitate, wishing I could cram my words back into my mouth. "Just—I guess because you've agreed to help." I flush. "And your art connection," I add.

An hour later, Wendell and I are in Madame Chevalier's tiny kitchen, cutting up a melon and rinsing cherries and arranging them on a china plate. Wendell and Madame Chevalier have hit it off right away, as expected. He raved about her self-portraits, taking a half hour to walk through her hallway. Unlike me, he immediately recognized that they were all pictures of the same person.

"It's amazing," he says, drying his hands on a towel. "In each painting, you can see the essence of Madame Chevalier, whether she's sixteen or sixty."

Vincent is sitting beside Madame Chevalier in the blue velvet chair by the window. They're pointing out the goings-on in the square to each other, chatting and laughing, and sinking into the little space they create together, a sunlit cocoon of jasmine perfume and butter cookies and milky tea and iridescent feathers and pigeon warbles. Their conversation meanders to Maude, cozy in Madame Chevalier's lap, to the soap opera in the square, to shared childhood memories, and back again to Maude.

"I can't figure them out," I say to Wendell in a low voice. Madame Chevalier's English is great, and she has sharp hearing.

"What do you mean?" he whispers, putting the remaining cherries on the plate with the melon.

"How happy they are together, but they won't admit it. They act like Maude's the reason they're even friends. And even with only a few weeks or months left, they still won't admit it."

Wendell picks up the plate of fruit. "It's not easy to see the truth about yourself." He looks right into my eyes as he says this. "They've been stuck in this pattern for fifty years. Maybe they're scared what would happen if they changed it."

"Mes enfants!" Vincent's voice comes from the living room. "Where are you? We have lots to talk about!"

Wendell grins and glances at them, there by the window. Even having barely met these old people, he feels real fondness for them. It's obvious. I can't imagine Jean-Claude looking at them this way, much less taking the time to indulge them in their sacred waters mission.

As soon as Wendell brings them the plate of fruit, Madame Chevalier pats his knee and says, "Wendell, dear, would you make me some tea, please?"

"*Oui.*" As Wendell goes into the kitchen, she leans in to me and whispers, "You know, the waters could help you, as well."

"I don't want eternal life. And I'm healthy enough."

"No! I mean healing you two. Your relationship."

Vincent murmurs, "Legend says the waters can give you clarity, understanding of yourself, of others."

Madame Chevalier nods emphatically. "They can even heal old wounds in your heart."

Before I can respond, Wendell comes back into the room with a tray of cups and saucers. "The water's heating up now," he says.

"Such a nice boy," Madame Chevalier says, tousling his hair as he sits down beside her.

"Let's figure out our next move," I suggest, trying to get us back on track. We've already told her and Vincent about the dry fountain at Damona's, and the spirals in the sidewalks, and how no one was home at the other two houses. "I still think we should just ask Sirona about the waters," I say. "She obviously has some connection to them. And she's a good person. We could just explain why we need them."

"*Mais non!*" Vincent bellows. "*Non non non non non!*"

Madame Chevalier is shaking her head and frowning deeply. "Oh, *ma petite,* how do you think they've been able to keep their secret for millennia?"

"By not telling a soul!" Vincent says. "Keeping it to themselves."

"With a secret so huge," Madame Chevalier adds, "you must see that they would do anything to protect it."

"Anything," Vincent agrees.

Madame Chevalier raises an authoritative, ring-adorned finger. "You must promise us you will not tell Sirona or any of them that you know about the waters. It could be very dangerous, life-threatening, even."

They're taking this conspiracy theory stuff a little too far. "Listen," I say. "Sirona's my mom's friend. She'd never hurt me. Or anyone, for that matter."

Vincent shakes his head. "Celtic priestesses could be ruthless at times. In battle camps, they'd ceremoniously slice the necks of the war prisoners and collect their blood in a bucket. They used the blood for prophecy."

Madame Chevalier nods. "My dear, you do not want to be a war prisoner of Salluvii, no matter how friendly they appear."

I barely suppress a laugh, imagining sweet Sirona wielding a bloody sword. I glance at Wendell out of the corner of my eye.

There's not a trace of laughter on his face. His eyebrows are furrowed together in concern. Then I remember his vision of danger. The man with the beard, threatening me.

Even though I'm certain Sirona would never hurt me, I suppose it's possible someone else might. Of course, ceremoniously slicing necks for prophecy seems utterly ridiculous. It's only Wendell's grave expression that makes my laughter inside fade, and a kernel of fear replace it.

TWENTY-FIVE

I keep glancing at Sirona, next to me on the sofa, trying to imagine her as a ruthless, two-thousand-year-old Celtic priestess, slitting throats and saving the blood. I stifle a laugh. Completely absurd. Sirona and Layla and I have just finished a dinner of leftover ratatouille, and now we're looking at pictures from Ecuador, which Sirona finds enchanting. "Oh, I like this one!" she says, pointing to a photo of me at the market, arm in arm with Gaby in front of her alpaca scarves. Gaby's kissing my cheek and I'm leaning into her.

Layla agrees. "You and Gaby simply exude happiness in this one," she declares.

Most of our pictures are from the album Wendell made for

me in Ecuador, which has photos of all our friends: the Quichua girls running through a horde of chickens, Mamita Luz kneading bread, Silvio in his candlelit curing room. And then there are pages of photos of me—in a cornfield, on a mountaintop, in a garden.

"Wendell's a great photographer," Sirona says. "When do I get to meet him?"

I shrug.

Layla nudges me gently with her elbow. "So you two have been spending lots of time together lately. Anything happening?"

I give another shrug. "We're friends again, I think." I swallow hard. "But he spends a lot of time with this girl, Amandine. I wish I hadn't—I want to be—close to him again. And now he's moved on. There's nothing I can do."

Sirona pats my shoulder sympathetically and then stands up, stretching. "I'll make more tea."

I keep flipping through the album. It's painful to look at these pictures, but I do it anyway. I love the way I looked at him through his camera lens. My eyes were naked and happy. I knew he saw me, really saw me. Knew he loved what he saw. If only I hadn't broken up with him, screwed it all up. If only I hadn't been so scared and stupid.

While Sirona's in the kitchen, Layla smooths my hair, gets on her Rumi-quoting face, and whispers,

"Your way begins on the other side.
Become the sky.

Take an axe to the prison wall.
Escape.
Walk out like someone suddenly born into
    color.
Do it now."

I roll my eyes. "Layla. First of all, prisoners don't have axes. Only flimsy fingernails. Second, the walls of the Castle of If are at least two meters thick. Impervious to the sharpest axes. Prisoners, by definition, are helpless. No chance of escape. You can go tell Rumi his advice is unrealistic."

Layla closes her eyes for a moment, then says, "There are easier ways." And she recites,

"Why do you stay in prison
When the door is so wide open?
Move outside the tangle of fear-thinking."

I should have learned by now. You can't win when you're up against thirteenth-century mystics. They always have the last word.

"Just look for the door, love," Layla says. "The wide-open door."

"If it were that easy," I snap, "then we'd all be happy, Layla."

"But it *can* be that easy!" she insists.

I slam the photo album shut. "I wish you'd given this pep talk to J.C. on the beach that night. Because it sure isn't easy for him to find the door."

She sighs. If she quotes Rumi again, I'll scream. Thankfully, she only says, "But you're different, Z. You're a seeker. Always have been. You, of all people, can find it."

• • •

Wendell and I have changed our strategy. No more fruitless knocking on the doors beneath the impish devil and the gagging man. Now we're spying, which consists of loitering down the street, just around the corner, and waiting for someone to come in or out. When they do, we'll leap into action. I've refused to wear the red dress this time, since it's a pain to hand wash. Today, I'm wearing jeans and a tank top, with my hair in a sensible ponytail. Wendell's leaning against a stone wall on Rue Littera, sketching something, while I keep an eye on the door below the gagging man's face.

"Still nothing," I say, peeking at Wendell's sketch. It's of a window with a skirt drying over the edge. Suddenly, I realize that he hasn't drawn me all summer. Or photographed me. He used to do it all the time in Ecuador. He must have thousands of pictures of me. But he hasn't taken a single one of me in France. I'm not aware I'm staring at him until he looks up. His expression is unguarded, and softens in response to my gaze.

"What are you thinking about?" he asks.

A breeze sweeps through the canyon street, whipping through my hair. I smooth it and say, "Do you think I'm a terrible person?"

Wendell looks at the sky. "I think you're made of light and shadow, like everyone."

"What do you mean?"

"If you were all light, you'd be flat. Boring. If everything always went happily, as planned, our lives wouldn't have textures or curves or hollows."

He's sort of evaded my question. "I really hurt you, didn't I, Wendell?"

He starts sketching again. "If I were happy all the time, I'd be flat too. It's the shadows that make you notice the light. Remember what Maurice said about finding treasures in prison."

I open my notebook and take out my pen. This is the first time I've asked Wendell a question for the ruby notebook. "If you took a hundred pictures of yourself, what essential thing would be the same in each one?"

He smiles. "You could answer that better than me."

"Really?"

"Z, you know more about me than anyone else. Last summer I showed you pieces of myself I'd never shown anyone. So you tell me. What am I at my core?"

"A crystal cave," I say softly. "At the center of a mountain."

Our eyes meet for a moment, then I look down at my notebook. We sit, and he sketches, and I write, peeking around the corner every minute or so. From time to time I ask him more questions, mundane questions now, like what he used to eat for lunch in elementary school. After I've filled up five pages of pure Wendell, I notice a man stopping in front of the spiral door, taking a key from his pocket. He's bulky and big, and carrying two shopping bags.

I slam my notebook shut and stuff it in my bag. "Come on, Wendell!"

We run down the street just in time to reach out our hands and catch the door before it locks shut.

"Bonjour!" I say, slipping inside the doorframe, into the dim hallway.

The man's thick eyebrows rise in astonishment, then press together in suspicion. A huge, coarse beard hides half of his face. His cheeks and nose are ruddy and slightly bulbous. His eyes are nearly lost in all the flesh. *"Bonjour,"* he grunts.

After I give him the story about Wendell's art project, he shakes his head and says in a gruff voice, "Our fountain is dry." He's blocking the corridor with his massive body.

Wendell hangs back, reaching for the door. "Zeeta. Let's forget it. Come on."

I hesitate. We've waited so long, and finally the man is here, and true, he doesn't seem too friendly, but I don't want to miss this opportunity. I plant a big smile on my face. "Doesn't matter if it's dry. He gets credit for that, too."

"I don't have time for this now." The words come out in a growl. He's more or less how I'd imagine an ogre to be.

"Oh, you can just leave us here by ourselves," I say breezily. "We'll make sure to lock the door on our way out." As I talk, I notice in the corner of my eye that Wendell looks scared. I meet his gaze. He shakes his head, slowly, almost imperceptibly at me. Something's wrong. I take one last stab. "So, do you mind if we look at your fountain?"

The man holds a fleshy hand out to Wendell. "Let me see your book."

Without a word, Wendell passes him the sketchbook.

The man flips through it. Our cover story must satisfy him, because he shoots both of us a stern look and says, "Ten minutes."

"Sure," Wendell creaks. "I'm fast."

As the man leads us down the dark hall toward the courtyard, Wendell grabs my arm and says through his teeth, "It's the man from my vision."

My heart starts thudding, but it's too late to turn around. We're in the courtyard now. Wendell crouches by the fountain, sketching quickly. Meanwhile, the man stands by the entrance and folds his muscled arms, leaning back and glaring. To cover my nervousness, I decide to continue my friendly act.

"Nice courtyard," I say, even though it's neglected, overrun with weeds and wildflowers and untrimmed bushes. In its center is a fountain starring a fat cherub, his chubby cheeks puffed out, and a spout emerging from his mouth. Dirt and dried leaves and dead insects coat the bottom of the basin.

The man grunts in response, still leaning against the stone wall like a bouncer at a rough bar.

"So, what do you do?" I ask casually.

He grunts again. In fact, he grunts in response to every question or comment I make. After five minutes of one-sided conversation, I still don't know whether he's from Aix, has a wife or kids, or works. He apparently cannot be cajoled into small talk.

Wendell finishes the sketch in record time and shows it to the man. Grunting, he walks us to the door. Once we're outside in the street, I reach out my hand and say, "Thank you, *monsieur.*" Reluctantly, he offers his giant hand, covered in hair, and that's when I see his ring, silver, with a triple spiral.

I push it. "To thank you, we could come back later. Wendell could do your portrait for free."

Wendell yanks on my arm, pulling me out into the street as the man slams the door behind us. Abruptly, Wendell drops my arm. "Um, Z. Need I remind you about these people's propensity for slicing enemy's throats? And the fact that this giant man was threatening you in my vision?"

I smile. He's called me Z again. And he's touched me. Sure, it was out of exasperation, but that doesn't change the fact that he did. It's reassuring, just having him here with me.

"Hey, did you see his ring?" I ask.

"The spirals." He looks at me. "Does he play in Sirona's band?"

"No." I hesitate, thinking. "I've never seen him before."

"Doesn't seem like a very social guy," Wendell comments.

Two houses down, one to go. The one with the impish devil laughing above the door. On the way I chat about Sirona and the ancient Salluvii. After a few blocks, Wendell stops, pulls out his camera, and takes a couple of pictures of a pigeon in an alcove, then some shots of the red geraniums spilling over a window box. And then, when I'm least expecting it, he turns to me and snaps a photo.

He lowers the camera, keeping his gaze on my eyes. "Zeeta, please. Be careful. In my vision—that man—he was terrifying."

"Okay, Wendell." I want him to keep looking at me this way, as though he cares about me more than anything.

He stuffs his camera into his backpack, his head down. "If anything happened to you, Z—" His voice cracks.

"I'll be careful," I say. "I promise."

• • •

Sunlight pours through the window, through the facets of a heart-shaped ruby on the gold ring on Madame Chevalier's finger. Held up to the sky, the stone casts a pool of red light onto my own bare hand in my lap.

"Isn't it beautiful?" she whispers, elated.

I nod. "Where did it come from?"

Like a giddy girl, she tells me how Vincent came into her apartment this morning, creaked down to one knee, and slid the ring ceremoniously onto her left ring finger. "A dream come true," she says.

My eyes wide, I glance at Vincent, who is just out of earshot, in the kitchen, preparing tea. "Are you—are you getting *married*?"

"*Oh, la la la la! Mais non!*" She lowers her hand, pressing the ring to her heart. "He said, 'Violette, will you accept this symbol of my true love?'" She giggles and looks toward the kitchen, where Vincent is clinking and clanking around. "I finally found the courage to take your advice, Zeeta. I decided to make every day a song, no matter how many songs are left for me. I painted him a message, like you told me, a silly, girlish thing with hearts and roses."

As if on cue, Vincent emerges with a tray crowded with a teapot and three cups, a little pitcher of milk, a sugar bowl, tiny spoons, and a small bowl of birdseed. As he walks toward us, he gazes at the ruby hanging loose on Madame Chevalier's gnarled old finger. "Looks lovely on you, *chérie*."

Madame Chevalier holds it to the light again and says, "Vincent, tell Zeeta how you found this ring."

"*Eh bien, dis donc!*" he says, setting down the tray and brushing a few pigeon feathers from his sleeve. "It's quite a story." He pours each of us a cup of tea, and offers Maude—who is perched on the railing—a handful of birdseed. Finally, he settles in his blue velvet chair, letting his short legs dangle there, not quite touching the floor. "Yesterday morning, Violette sent me this message." He pulls it from his pocket. "May I?" he asks Madame Chevalier.

"*Oui. Bien sûr,*" she says, blushing.

He hands it to me. It's a watercolor painting of his face and hers framed in a window with Maude on the railing and hearts and stars and roses floating around them and *Je t'aime* written at the top. *I love you.*

A smile spreads over my face.

Madame Chevalier matches my gaze, her eyes aglow. "I painted it weeks ago, after you urged me, *ma petite*. But it took a while for me to find the courage to send it with Maude's vial." She lets loose a laugh. "Tell her the rest, *chéri*," she urges Vincent.

"Well, I wanted to give Violette something special in return." He smiles at her adoringly. "So I dug out that old jewelry box—remember I showed it to you, Zeeta?"

"*Oui.* The one that plays *'La Vie en Rose.'*" I can picture it clearly: the red velvet inside and smooth dark wood outside, and how, when I opened it, the song burst out, in a sudden shower of tinkling notes.

Madame Chevalier begins humming the melody with her eyes half closed, the way old people sometimes do, as if they're waltzing in their minds. She keeps humming in a kind of dreamy sound track to Vincent's story. "Yesterday, I took out the jewelry box. I was cleaning the velvet inside when something rattled in there. I found my tweezers and pulled it out."

"This ruby ring!" Madame Chevalier bursts out, holding up her hand.

"In the shape of a heart!" Vincent adds. "The perfect thing to give to *la femme de ma vie*." He gazes at her face, as if he could never get enough of it. "So I shined it up and brought it here this morning."

Maude flutters onto his shoulder, looking satisfied. Madame Chevalier reaches out and sets her jeweled hand on Maude's back, gently.

Vincent rests his own hand over Madame Chevalier's, and Maude gives a sweet, warbly coo. "To think," he says, "all those years, this jewelry box was just sitting in my shop, and it took me until now to find the heart that was in there all along."

• • •

On the way out of Madame Chevalier's apartment, I think about hidden treasures, about all the different ways to make every day a song, about how maybe it's never too late. I think about the wide-open doorway out of my prison of *ifs*. There's no real reason I can't fix what I messed up. Even without magical waters. I have nothing to lose by telling Wendell how I feel. Telling him I might have a center after all, a constant Zeeta, one who loves him.

This decision leaves me humming, as though a thousand pigeon wings are fluttering inside me, about to take flight.

I will tell him. I will tell him. I will tell him!

He's probably out sketching fountains. I figure if I wander down enough side streets, I'll find him. The backstreets are mostly empty except for pigeons and gurgling fountains. Cheery flowers overflow from window boxes and music drifts out from open windows—Middle Eastern tunes with strong drumbeats that make me feel as though I'm dancing instead of walking.

I plan out what I'll say. I'll tell him about the hidden heart ring. I'll ask him to forgive me. We'll kiss and it will be all ruby sunlight and silvery feathers.

There's a tap on my shoulder.

I spin around. "Jean-Claude! You scared me."

"*Désolé.* Can I walk with you?"

"I guess. I'm just wandering. What about you?"

"I'm headed to Monoprix for toilet paper."

I laugh. Something has shifted. He would never have admitted going to the French version of Walmart to buy toilet paper to me before. It would have clashed with his troubadour image.

"Hey," he says. "Have you seen Amandine around? She's been elusive lately."

"No." I try to sound casual as my heart sinks. "She's probably with Wendell."

"Wendell?" He seems startled. "Really?"

"They do art stuff together," I say, keeping my voice steady. "Haven't you noticed?"

His face reddens. "She's too young for him."

Now, this is a side of Jean-Claude I haven't seen before. "She's the same age as me, Jean-Claude."

"It's different." Then he says, "It's just—not fair."

"Fair?" I give him a sideways look.

"It's that—we don't make as much money without Aman-dine. We take rent money from the change we collect, and she's not contributing when she's off with that guy."

I press my lips together. This is the most riled up I've ever seen Jean-Claude.

"*Pffft,*" he says, blowing air through his lips. "*Ça craint.*" This sucks.

"Yes, it does," I say, noting that his cool façade is com-pletely gone.

"Amandine's the heart of Illusion," he says, his voice heated. "She can't just run off. Why didn't she tell me?"

"Why do you think, Jean-Claude?"

After a few blocks, he calms down, but still seems dis-tracted. We head down Rue de la Verrerie, past cafés and pizzerias and seafood restaurants and *crêperies,* as he points out restaurants he likes. "The buckwheat crêpes there are the best," he says, gesturing to a hole in the wall with a yellow awning. "Try the chicken ones, with creamy béchamel sauce. And the cider is *trop top.*" Suddenly, he stops.

He's staring at something. At a couple, sitting on the side of a fountain.

Wendell and Amandine. A sketch pad lies open on Wen-dell's lap and a matching one lies on hers. Amandine's head is close to his, and she's whispering something in his ear. Now her hand is on his braid. And now on the small of his back. And now he's moving his hand to her back. They are kissing.

They are *kissing.*

I look at Jean-Claude. He's frozen.

Before Wendell notices me, I hurry away, in the opposite direction. Blindly, I turn down one side street after another, wanting to get far, far away from them. I don't know where to go, what to do, what to think. There's just this heavy feeling, a feeling that it's too late.

I turn onto a narrow street, deserted except for a silver cat. I sink onto a stoop, press my palms against the sobering, cold stone, and close my eyes. The words run loops in my mind. *It's too late. It's too late. It's too late.*

TWENTY-SIX

At some point, I hear footsteps approaching. I open my eyes and see Tortue standing a few feet away in his Pierrot costume, the perfect tear on his right cheek. He looks how I feel.

Somehow I'm not surprised to see him. Or embarrassed that he sees me in this state. He's almost familiar now. Like a piece of clothing you've had for a while that you think you don't like at first but that grows on you.

"Tortue," I say. "How did you know I was here?"

"I saw you back on Rue Granet. You looked upset, Zeeta. I didn't know if—" He hesitates. "Are you all right?"

"No. Actually, I'm not."

The look on Tortue's face is possibly one of concern, but it's hard to tell with his painted-on mask. He stays at a distance, looking uncertain. The bells of the clock tower chime. One, two, three, four. He takes his hands from his pockets, raises his palms. "Can I do anything?"

I shake my head.

Tortue sits on the stoop one door down from mine. He's so still, sitting there like a statue. He doesn't say anything else. I squint up at a rectangle of red fabric—a sheet, maybe, flapping like a bright flag in the breeze from a fourth-story window. I hear my breathing, ragged.

"You don't have to stay," I say finally.

He looks at his scuffed white tennis shoes. "I don't want you to feel alone."

I let out a slow breath, feeling just the tiniest bit better. I want to thank him for being here, for his quiet, earnest presence. Instead, I open my notebook. "Tortue, do you think there's a *grand amour* for each person?"

He pauses to think. Faraway sounds drift into the narrow street—the distant roar of a motorbike, children's shouts and laughter, a ball bouncing, rhythmically smacking the pavement. Finally, he says, "Yes. Sometimes I wish I didn't, but I do."

"And what if you screw up that chance?"

He's looking at his gloves now, tugging at the fingers. "We all make mistakes," he says. "Have regrets. Miss opportunities. Maybe the best we can do is learn from our past. Fix things if we're lucky enough to get a second chance."

I put my hand to my necklace from Ecuador, rolling the smooth seeds between my fingers, considering his advice.

"When I broke up with Wendell," I say, "I was confused. And scared. And momentarily dazzled by Jean-Claude." My voice is calm, assured, stating these facts that suddenly seem so simple. "I made a mistake. I was stupid. Wendell's the one I belong with. He's always been the one."

Tortue nods. "Jean-Claude is your Harlequin. And Wendell is your Pierrot."

"And I'm the fickle Columbine?"

"Maybe you've been exploring, trying things out, like she did." Tortue pauses, staring at green leaves peeking over the rooftop. "But I think we all have a Pierrot and a Harlequin inside of us. Perhaps Jean-Claude is a Pierrot to someone else. Our inner clowns emerge at different times, with different people."

I have to smile. Inner clowns. Layla would love this.

A trace of a smile peeks through Tortue's mask. "Now, me," he says, "because of my illness, I go for months feeling like Pierrot, months like Harlequin."

I'm still smiling, just a little. "And who is your Columbine?"

"I found her once and lost her. But it's not too late for you, Zeeta." And then, in a soft voice, he begins singing a kind of lullaby.

> "*Au clair de la lune,*
> *Mon ami Pierrot,*
> *Prête-moi ta plume,*
> *Pour écrire un mot.*

Ma chandelle est morte,
Je n'ai plus de feu.
Ouvre-moi ta porte,
Pour l'amour de Dieu.

"By the light of the moon,
My friend Pierrot,
Lend me your pen,
To write a word.
My candle is out,
I have no more fire.
Open your door to me,
For the love of God."

As he sings, I can't help but think Layla was right about clowns. I should give them more credit.

• • •

In my dream, someone is banging on a door, shouting for a pen, for fire. Gradually, I realize it's not banging and shouting, but buzzing from the doorbell intercom. Even after my eyes open, it takes me a moment to remember where I am. In my room, in my apartment, in France. The clock on my bedside table reads 3:00 a.m.

The buzzing continues, an urgent sound that shows no signs of stopping.

"Zeeta?" Layla calls from her room in a sleep-crackly voice. "You expecting someone?"

"No," I groan.

"Probably some drunks playing with the buzzers," she calls back.

But the buzzing grows more and more insistent until it's basically one long buzz. Groggy, I walk to the intercom by the door. *"Oui?"*

"Zeeta, *c'est moi.* Jean-Claude."

I blink and rub sleep from my eyes. What's going on? Is he drunk? But he doesn't sound drunk. He sounds worried, desperate even.

I buzz him up, splash my face with cold water, and throw on a robe. When I open the door, Jean-Claude's standing there, breathing hard, his usually perfect curls a frizzy, knotted mess, his eyes bloodshot, his face contorted in fear.

"Jean-Claude! *Qu'est-ce qui se passe?* Did something happen?"

From her bedroom, Layla shouts, "Everything okay?"

"Yeah," I call back. "It's just Jean-Claude. You can go back to sleep."

Meanwhile, Jean-Claude's eyes are darting around the apartment. "Amandine? She's not here?"

"Why would she be here?"

"You two are friends, *non?*"

Not exactly, I think.

He rubs his hands over his face. "The past few weeks she's been staying out late. Usually I wait up for her, but last night I fell asleep. I just woke up and she still wasn't home and—" His voice is rising in panic. He sinks down on the sofa, trying to pull himself together. "I had a nightmare and usually she—she sits with me and helps me fall back asleep." He looks at me, tapping his foot in a frantic rhythm. "Where could she be?"

I sit down next to him. "Jean-Claude, we both know who Amandine's with. We both saw them together."

Jean-Claude leans back and runs his fingers through his hair, revealing his scar. It's pronounced in the lamplight, almost luminescent, a sliver of moon. His matted curls stay off his face, making his scar look exposed. "What's Wendell's number?"

"We don't have a phone."

"I brought Julien's cell," he says, pulling a phone from his pocket.

I sigh. "Hold on." I shuffle through the papers on the kitchen table. "*Voilà.*" I hand him a sticky note with blue ink. "It's his host family's number."

Jean-Claude snatches the paper and dials.

After a moment, he says, "*Bonsoir, madame.* Yes, I know. I'm sorry. *Je suis désolé, madame.*" He must be talking with Wendell's host mom. I hold my breath, wondering if Amandine is there. "I'm looking for Amandine," he tells her. "A friend of Wendell's."

"*Non?*" He clutches his head, then he sucks in a breath. "Oh, I see." A pause. "*Ouais.*" The desperation on his face has turned into something else. Resigned misery, maybe. "It must be her," he says into the phone. "I'm sorry to bother you. *Au revoir, madame.*"

While he collects himself, I heat up water for tea. I take

my time getting out the mint tea bags, the lavender honey, the cups and saucers. By the time the water's boiling, he still hasn't said anything. I pour the water into the cups and let the tea bags brew. "What'd she say?" I ask finally.

"That Wendell and Amandine decided to take photos of some vineyard," he says flatly. "Pictures in the moonlight. For his art class. Since the buses don't run late, they're spending the night there. They left with blankets and coffee and food."

I can't find words. A vineyard in moonlight? With blankets? Spending the night together?

"I feel sick," Jean-Claude says, putting his head between his knees.

"Me too." I stir some honey into my tea, breathing in the minty steam, trying to make sense of what's happening. "You're in love with her, aren't you?"

Silence.

"Why aren't you with her?"

"She knows too much about me."

"Shouldn't that be a good thing?"

"Not in my case." He tugs hard on his hair, as if he wants to pull it out. "I've ruined everything in my life, Zeeta." Slouched on the sofa, staring at the ceiling, he says, "I'd just turned fifteen. I took our father's car without asking and drove with Thomas down to Cassis. I didn't really know how to drive, but I took the car anyway. On the way home, another car was switching lanes. I swerved out of the way, but right into a truck in the oncoming lane. It smashed the passenger side. My brother died instantly. But I survived with only a broken arm and a gash in my head." He rubs the raised white line on his forehead. "I killed him. And it nearly killed my parents, too." He buries his face in his hands, making his words come out muffled and soft. "I couldn't forgive the person who did that. So I re-created myself, became a wanderer without roots. A dandelion seed."

We're quiet for a while. Finally, I say, "That person is still inside of you." I look at him, sunk into the sofa, so vulnerable, his glimmery façade stripped away. If I'll ever reach him, now's the moment. I choose my words carefully. "Your parents forgave that person. Now *you* have to."

He makes a sound somewhere between a laugh and a moan. "That's what Amandine tells me." He pauses, thinking. "When I saw her and Wendell together, I wanted to scream. To punch something. To cry. To run to her and pick her up and just carry her away with me. To kiss her. An explosion of feelings I hadn't felt for years." He rubs his eyes. "Zeeta, she's everything to me. I don't want her to be with someone else. I don't want her to be my little sister. But she sees me as a messed-up, annoying older brother." He closes his eyes. "And she's with Wendell now. It's too late."

I shake my head. "I think you've been too wrapped up in yourself to see things clearly. To see how Amandine feels about you. Talk to her, Jean-Claude."

I'm not sure if he's heard me, or taken in a thing I've said,

• 307 •

but soon he stands up. "*Merci*, Zeeta. I'm going now. I'm sorry for waking you." And he's gone, leaving his cup of tea untouched and steaming in the lamplight.

· · ·

I stare at the two cups of mint tea sitting in front of me. I'm too awake to go back to bed now but not quite sure what else to do. Layla emerges from the bedroom in her pink robe and sits down beside me without a word. She sips Jean-Claude's tea, then adds a spoonful of lavender honey— smelling it first, of course. She tucks her legs under her and curls into the sofa cushions, looking cozy in the steamy golden lamplight. Together, in silence, we drink tea.

I think of my advice to Jean-Claude. And my advice to Madame Chevalier about Vincent. And her advice to me about Wendell. And even Tortue's advice. So much of the same advice floating around, and no one acting on it. It seems easier to do nothing, to just stay in the rut.

Halfway through my cup of tea, I whisper, "I'm not sure how to fix things with Wendell." I look at Layla. "I'm not sure it's even possible."

Her eyelids lower, her brows rise, and she says, "Remember what Rumi says."

"Walk out the prison door," I say in a glum monotone. "Well, I tried and it was locked."

"No, love. I'm thinking of this one: *Lovers don't finally meet somewhere. They're in each other all along.*"

I forgot about that one. It's nice enough, but doesn't

exactly give me direction. At least it's a short one and doesn't induce reflexive eye-rolling. "So who's the lucky lover hidden inside you all these years?" I ask.

She laughs softly. "I wish I knew."

"Well. We know he's probably a penniless clown." I sit up straight, inspired. "Hey, how about the mime?"

"You don't think he's creepy anymore?"

"Tortue's actually pretty nice. He's even changed my mind about clowns. See, I think you need a Pierrot clown instead of all the Harlequins you've been with."

She gives me a sideways look. "Are you trying to set me up with a clown, Z?"

"Maybe you have to go through all the clowns in the world before you find the right one, Layla. The one who's meant to be."

• • •

Late the next morning, my feet are dragging as I walk through the market stalls, past rows of truffle oil, vaguely wondering exactly what truffles are. Don't they have something to do with pigs? I'm moving on to the bins of olives, a dozen shiny shades of brownish green, when I glimpse a flash of sparkling red.

It's Amandine. Just on the other side of the olives. When she sees that I see her, she skips over and says, *"Salut!"* Her voice reminds me of wind chimes, and she shows no signs of sleep deprivation even though she was out all night with Wendell. She looks vibrant in a silky orange skirt and red top, with her hair in a braid that reaches down to the small of her back.

I let my knotted hair fall in my face, hopefully hiding the puffy circles under my own eyes. This morning there was nothing for breakfast, so I threw on some clothes, not bothering to brush my hair or my teeth, deliberately avoiding a mirror, and grabbed a market bag.

Amandine is holding a carton of strawberries. Of course, she doesn't eat them like a normal person. She plucks off the green part then throws the berry high in the air, several feet, and positions her mouth underneath, so that it lands on her perfect tongue. I can see why Wendell and Jean-Claude are smitten.

"*Salut*, Amandine," I say, keeping a distance.

"Have a strawberry, Zeeta."

I take one, accepting what might be a peace offering.

She smiles. "After I got home from my art thing with Wendell, Jean-Claude and I had a long talk."

"You did?"

"*Merci*, Zeeta!"

"For what?"

"For whatever magic you worked on him last night." She blushes. "When I came home at dawn, he was waiting for me. He told me he wanted to spend the day together. And he asked me to go to Marseille with him tomorrow!"

"Wow."

"We're going to visit his mother, then have a picnic on an

island he used to go to with his family when he was little. I'm buying the ingredients for it now!"

Jean-Claude did it. He actually did it.

She steps toward me. "And Zeeta, I have to tell you something. About kissing Wendell yesterday. I'm sorry."

I shrug. "It's not like he's my boyfriend anymore. He's free—"

"*Ecoute*, Zeeta. Here's what happened. Wendell and I—we were sketching together, and then I saw Jean-Claude and you coming down the street. I felt jealous. I wanted Jean-Claude to feel jealous too. So I picked that moment to kiss Wendell. He was surprised, but went along with it. Afterward, I felt bad, apologized to him."

This is a twist. "And what did he say?"

"That he just likes me as a friend. That his heart feels too raw right now." She looks at me, hard. "You know what we talk about most of the time, Zeeta?"

I shake my head.

"How we're really in love with other people."

I let this fact sink in.

She offers me another strawberry, then says, "I should get going. I just wanted to thank you. And apologize."

"*Merci*, Amandine," I say, taking a strawberry.

The berry's tart sweetness is startling. I watch Amandine skip away. She always seems to defy gravity, but today, she's positively flying.

With a sudden urgency, I half run toward Nirvana.

. . .

A faint stubble is growing on Ahmed's usually smooth-shaven face. His eyes are relaxed, happy, his skin tanned to a deep nut-brown, his hair pleasingly mussed, lacking its usual armor of hardened gel.

"Zeeta!" he calls out as I walk to the counter. "How is your lovely mother?"

"Fine," I say. "Welcome back. How was your vacation?"

"Refreshing! First Italy, then Greece." He rubs his stubble. "Look, I didn't shave. I thought your mother might like this look. Remember how you told me I'm too well groomed for her taste?"

I make a face, then say, "Well, glad you had fun."

"Oh, yes." He smiles broadly. "And how are you and *l'homme de ta vie?*"

"Actually, I broke up with him. But maybe we'll get back together."

"Really? So much happened while I was gone!"

"I'm going to ask him out tonight," I say, trying to sound confident. "To try to fix the mess I made." I stop. Something's strange about Ahmed, and I can't figure out what it is. Something more than his stubble, something about his eye contact, or . . . "Hey!" I say. "You're not playing KnightQuest."

He swivels around in his chair and pulls out a guitar. "Maybe I have you and your lovely mother to thank for that, Zeeta. You've reminded me of the free spirit I once was. So I took the holiday you suggested. Making music and traveling. There I was, on the beach, staring at the water, thinking of you two. And I decided maybe my young and crazy years aren't all behind me. Maybe life is short and I should spend it doing what I love." He plucks a few notes on his guitar and smiles.

A grin escapes me. Before sitting down at the computer, I say, "I'll tell Layla about your stubble, Ahmed."

I write an e-mail to Wendell. I know he's at class now, but I think he always checks his e-mail first thing when he gets home. *Can you meet me at Chez Gilles at seven tonight?* I quickly calculate how much tutoring money I've accumulated, then write, *My treat.*

Giddy and hopeful, I rush back home and spend the afternoon poring over last year's indigo notebooks, making something special to give to Wendell tonight.

TWENTY-SEVEN

The clock tower chimes seven times just as I'm walking down Rue Matheron toward the side street where Chez Gilles is tucked away in a romantic, ivy-covered hole in the wall. The fabric of my red dress soaks up the evening sunlight, nearly glowing. After trying on a dozen outfits, I settled on this one. My only real date dress.

Date. So I *do* think I'm going on a date with Wendell. I didn't use the word in my e-mail. In fact, I'm not even sure he got my e-mail in time. I'd intended to check back to see if he responded, but I spent all afternoon making his present. I went through my indigo notebooks, finding bits and pieces of notes on what I love about him. Then I copied the quotes onto small pieces of paper and bound them together with a red ribbon.

It took a long time. There are so many things, from how he sang "Head, Shoulders, Knees, and Toes" to our little kid friends in Ecuador, to how he used to trace the contours of my face, as though it was a landscape to explore.

I've put on lip gloss and blush, and twirled my hair up into a twist and put on dangling garnet earrings from Thailand. Walking past a used-book store, I spot Sirona. She looks more stunning than usual tonight, dressed in a long white tunic made of silky, flowing fabric, belted with a satiny red sash. She's carrying a large covered platter.

"*Salut*, Sirona!"

"*Salut*, Zeeta." She seems a bit flustered, or maybe she's just breathless.

"What's in there?" I ask, peeking under the lid. There's a heap of spiral cookies, hundreds of cookies.

"Have one," she says.

I bite into one. "Mmm. Good." But really they're too healthy-tasting, lacking sugar.

"They're made with honey and figs and nuts," she says.

That explains it. "Are you having a party?"

"Oh, no." Her eyes dart around. "Just, well, a little gathering. Nothing big."

Maybe she feels bad for not inviting Layla. I left her at home on the sofa reading. She said she might swing by Nirvana and hang out with Ahmed a bit, then go to sleep early. She hasn't mentioned anything about a party tonight.

Skilled at changing the subject, Sirona eyes my dress and says, "You look gorgeous, Zeeta. What's the occasion?"

"A date with Wendell." I grin.

"Oh! *C'est chouette, ça!*" She looks genuinely happy for me. "Have fun, Zeeta."

I watch Sirona hurry down the street and turn onto Rue Epinaux. Then I flip back through my ruby notebook and locate the list of Celtic holidays she described weeks ago. The holiday after the summer solstice is the festival of light, which falls on August first. That's today. I look at the notes I've jotted down beside it. *Harvest festival, music, dancing, food, flowers, handfasting.* I can't remember what handfasting means.

Wendell and I might have to skip dinner. It's too good an opportunity to pass up, a secret party with Sirona—and a big one, judging by the quantity of cookies. I slam my notebook shut, shove it in my bag, and sprint the last block to Chez Gilles.

• • •

At Chez Gilles, tables with white lilies and candles and tablecloths spill out from the tiny restaurant, onto the narrow cobblestoned side street. A blackboard easel lists tonight's menu in flowery cursive: roasted rabbit with rosemary and olives, tomato soup with goat cheese, eggplant au gratin, grilled asparagus with *herbes de Provence,* and strawberry mousse. Among pots of fragrant jasmine bushes, nearly each table contains a couple gazing at each other over elegant glasses of pink rosé.

I scan the faces for Wendell. There he is, tentatively sipping a glass of bubbly water topped with a wedge of lime. As

I walk toward him, he sees me and smiles. A natural, happy-to-see-you smile with maybe the tiniest hint of nervousness. Still, a smile that sends warmth through me.

"Hey, Z."

I wish we could sit here and have a real date with a romantic five-course meal topped with strawberry mousse. I wish we could sit here together and forget everything that happened this summer and just gaze at each other. But we can't miss this opportunity.

"Hey, Wendell," I begin. "Listen, I ran into Sirona on the way over. Something's going on—I think it might be a big, secret party for the festival of light. We might be able to get important information there."

"Where is it?" he asks, looking excited.

"I don't know. But I saw which way she was headed. We'll have to leave now to catch her."

"Let's go," Wendell says, dropping a few euros onto the table.

As we hurry away, down Rue Loubon, I glance longingly back at Chez Gilles, taking one last whiff of its atmosphere of pure romance, hoping I didn't just make a mistake dragging Wendell away from there.

We run back up the street and turn onto Rue Epinaux, where Sirona was headed. We're in the oldest part of town, the *quartier* where the spirals were marked on the map. We're nearly to the place with the impish devil face, when that very door swings open. I look at Wendell and we slow down, alert, our eyes glued to the door. We've spent hours watching that door over the past weeks, never seeing a soul coming in or out. But now, three women emerge, all wearing long tunics and bracelets on their upper arms, their hair in intricate braided knots, topped with flower crowns. They turn right, away from us. The door starts swinging closed behind them.

I leap to the doorway, reaching out my arm just in time for my hand to stop the door. I hold my breath, watching the women. They show no sign of noticing. They simply keep walking, lost in conversation. In Gaelic, I note.

Quickly, I slip inside, and Wendell follows.

"We have to be fast, Wendell."

He nods. "Let's check the courtyard and then catch up with those ladies."

We run down the dark corridor into the courtyard, a walled, square, grassy garden with a circular fountain in the center. It's made of worn stone, with a wide column jutting up from the middle. On one side of the column is a large brass disc—about a half-meter in diameter—and in its center is a snake with an open mouth, containing a spout where the water would come out. But, like the other two fountains we've seen, this one is dry.

I race around the edges of the courtyard to check for signs of water or anything unusual. Wendell, meanwhile, is standing motionless, close to the fountain, studying it. A look of intense concentration has come over his face, the same look he gets when he's sketching.

"Hey, Z," he says. "Have you ever seen a fountain with such a big metal plaque? Usually they're smaller, right?"

I consider his question. "I guess so."

He steps into the dry fountain and moves his face close to the snake plaque. Running his fingers over it, he says, "Feel this. There's a faint spiral pattern. Light indentations."

I climb into the fountain beside him and skim my fingertips over the plaque. "It's the triple spiral," I say, a thrill running through me. "With the snake right at its center."

Wendell points to the top of the circle. "And what's this?"

I move my fingers over it. "Seems like hinges," I murmur, my eyes wide.

"That's what I think," he says, pulling on the snake head, hard enough that he turns red with the effort. "Won't budge. Maybe it needs some oil." He takes a step back, staring some more.

"It could have some kind of latch," I say, feeling the cool copper with my hands, tracing the carvings in the snake's head. I try wiggling the snake from side to side. Nothing. Then I push it downward. There's a little resistance, but it creaks and moves a few centimeters, making a distinct click. Some mechanism inside has unlatched. Now the disc has separated at its base from the column. I push the disc upward.

That's when I realize what it is—a small, circular door, hinged on the top, and just big enough for a person to fit through. Wendell and I peer inside. A patch of daylight shines into the steamy darkness, illuminating a steep, spiraling stone staircase. The bottom isn't visible through the thick mist.

My mouth dropped open, I turn to Wendell.

A look of sudden comprehension sweeps over his face. "Zeeta. I finally understand a vision I had. It's darkness, with a fuzzy circle of white light in the middle."

"Like a circle of daylight?"

"No," he says slowly. "It's dark above. The light's from the moon, I think. A full moon."

"Tonight's a full moon," I note.

"Yeah," he says. "That's the circle of light. We're underground, looking up a tunnel. Like a well. It's fuzzy because of steam. I didn't understand it before—we're underground. We're in the waters underground."

"And I'm wearing the red dress," I say, peering back into the musty, damp darkness. "Tonight's the night, Wendell. Let's go."

Wendell grabs a fallen tree branch from just outside the fountain. "I'll stick this in the door to make sure it doesn't click shut."

I climb in first—a bit of a challenge in a short dress—and pull my bag inside after me. Wendell follows, then turns to adjust the branch and carefully lower the circular door. Now it's nearly pitch black, with only a sliver of daylight shining through.

I hear Wendell fumbling around in his backpack. Suddenly, there's the beam of a flashlight, a little LED light on the end of a key chain.

He shines it in front of us, but I can still barely see a few steps ahead in this dense fog. Wet moss makes the stairs slick. Holding on to the stone walls, which are also damp and coated in slime, I carefully step down, one stair at a time. A few times, I nearly slip in my worn leather sandals. Wendell reaches out an arm to catch me, his footsteps secure in his well-tractioned Tevas. The staircase is narrow, spiraling downward. The air grows warmer the farther down we go, and the mist grows thicker. From the ceiling, which is actually formed by the stones above us, water drips onto our heads, warm water, like tears.

Wendell's voice slips through the mist, comforting, the only familiar thing to hang on to. "See anything ahead?" he asks.

"No. Just steam and this spiral staircase."

We descend for what feels like a long time, although it might be just a few minutes, since we're going so slowly.

From time to time, Wendell and I call back and forth to each other. "You okay?"

"Yeah. You?"

"Yeah."

And just when I'm feeling that this staircase must spiral straight to the center of earth, I notice that the stairs are about to end, opening into a wide space. "Something's up ahead, Wendell."

When we reach the last stair, he puts his hand around mine. I hold on tightly, and together, we walk out of the narrow staircase passage into the open space as ribbons of mist rise and wrap around us.

At the same time, we gasp. It's as if we've entered another world.

· · ·

The chamber is round, with stone walls and a high ceiling. At the center are three circular pools, interconnected by short channels. A long channel on the far right side emerges from a tunnel, feeding into one of the pools. Another long channel on the left emerges from a second tunnel—this one steaming—and feeds into a second pool. Each of these pools flows into the third pool, a lightly steaming swirl of the cold and hot water. The water flows out along a third channel, into a tunnel.

Mist rises from the water, moves like phantoms around the room. In the flashlight beam, I can see individual droplets of water reflecting light. The chamber echoes with dripping and bubbling and flowing and gurgling.

"This must be it," Wendell whispers.

"I can't believe it," I murmur as we walk to the pools and peer inside by the light of his flashlight. Through the water, which seems alive with thousands of tiny bubbles, I can make out a spiral pattern of white pebbles in the pools' silvery floor. There's one unending line that branches into three spirals, one in each pool.

I crouch by the closest pool, which I'm guessing is a mix of the hot and cold water. Holding my breath, I plunge in my hand. The water's warm and tingly.

Wendell kneels beside me, dipping in his hand. "It's like a vat of seltzer water," he says.

"Or champagne," I say. On an impulse, I kick off my sandals. Before I think about what I'm doing, I've lowered my body into the water, letting the tiny bubbles engulf me, feeling the currents of cool and hot water swirl around my skin. I unclip my hair, close my eyes, and submerge my entire body, thoroughly soaking myself and my red dress. Underwater, I open my mouth, swallowing a small sip. Just in case. Then, in a rush, I burst through the surface.

"Come in, Wendell!" I shout, my voice and splashes echoing.

But once I make out his form in the darkness, I see he's already set down the flashlight, taken off his shirt. I catch my breath. I haven't seen him without his shirt for a year. Even in the dim mist, I can make out his broad shoulders, muscular chest, lightly rippled waist.

He lowers into the water a few feet away from me, a respectable distance. He's close enough that I see his arm muscles flexing, the water clinging to his skin. Slowly, his face relaxes, his eyes close. I'm glad his eyes are closed. This way, I can stare at him, unabashedly drinking in his face, his neck, his bare torso.

After a few minutes, my body feels as though it's completely dissolved into the water, as though it's made of a zillion floating bubbles. My insides feels different too, my feelings as clear as water. "Wendell," I say softly.

"Yeah?"

"Did you sip the water?"

He nods, smiling. "Just a little."

"Me too." I blow a few bubbles, then ask, "Hey, does this water make you feel different?"

"Like relaxed?"

"Something more than that," I say. "Things are clear."

"What things?"

"Everything. Including why I freaked out a few weeks ago. Why I broke up with you."

"Why, Z?"

I tilt my head back into the water, letting my hair fan out over the surface. "I was scared there wasn't one single Zeeta. Scared I had no core. Scared I wouldn't be able to love you. I felt like an empty box, one that's filled with whatever country I'm in, then emptied again the next time we move." I raise my head again, looking at him. "Do you understand what I mean, Wendell?"

He flips over onto his stomach, moves closer. He's looking at me now, really looking at me. "Remember what Vincent found in his empty box?"

I think of the ruby heart in sunlight, the tinkling notes of *La Vie en Rose.* "You know about that?"

He nods. "I ran into Vincent that morning, just before he gave the ring to Madame Chevalier. He wasn't sure if he should go through with it. He worried it might make her more sad, to feel she was leaving someone who loved her so much."

I swish my hands around, making spirals in the water's surface. "And what did you tell him?"

"I told him to risk it. I said that there will always be darkness and light. That she needs the ruby's light now, especially inside so much darkness."

I move closer to him, so close I could touch him if I extended my arm. Everything is so vivid to me now, despite the mist and steam. It's as though my mind can rise up to see the world from a pigeon's perspective. And what I see are questions, a whole landscape of questions I need to ask. "Wendell. Remember when you gave me those photos from Ecuador?"

"Yeah."

"And you told me you'd always tell me who I was? When I didn't know?"

He nods.

"Tell me."

He looks at me for a while, then says, "You're the Z sitting in the window, looking out with binoculars. Writing in her notebook. Observing, asking questions, noticing things that other people miss."

He moves even closer, his chest nearly touching mine. There's the faint smell of cinnamon on his breath, the droplets like diamonds clinging to his eyelashes, the water gleaming on his bare chest, beaded on his lips. "And more than that, Z," he whispers. "There's your music inside. A secret spring. A hidden ruby. There's *you*."

Our lips are about to touch, when there's a click. It's faint and far away, but a definite click. It echoes through the chamber.

"*Merde,*" I say under my breath.

"That wasn't the—" Wendell's eyes flick to the staircase.

"The door," I finish. "I think it was."

"Maybe it didn't latch all the way."

We scramble from the pool, and he grabs his flashlight. Barefoot, we head back up the staircase. "What if someone saw the door open and came in here?" I whisper, suddenly frightened. "What if it's that scary bearded man?"

"Then we're at his mercy."

We stay still for a moment, listening. No sound from above. We keep walking. When we finally reach the top, we breathe out sighs of relief. Just us. No one else has come in.

But then Wendell shines the flashlight on the circular door. It's shut.

"The stick must have fallen out," he says.

"Or someone took it out," I say, pushing on the door. It won't budge.

Wendell tries pushing on it with me. Nothing.

We scan the wall for latches or levers, anything, but the wall is smooth stone.

"No one knows we're in here," Wendell points out.

Panicked, I start banging on the metal, yelling, *"Au secours! Aidez-nous!"*

Wendell puts his hands on mine. "It's possible that if anyone does hear you, they're not going to be happy we snuck in here."

"Knife-wielding priestesses?" I say in a shaky attempt at a joke.

"Or giant bearded men," he says, half serious.

"So what do we do, Wendell?"

"Maybe there's another way out," he says. "Remember those tunnels leading to the pools? We could follow one. See where it leads."

I remember his vision of the fuzzy moon. Feeling a little hopeful, I head back down the stairs as he follows.

Back in the chamber, Wendell shines the light at the entrance of each tunnel. "Which one do we try?" he asks.

"You saw steam in your vision, right?"

He nods. "I think so."

"Then let's try the hot one."

Wendell picks up the flashlight and shines it on his backpack and my bag and sandals. "Let's leave our bags. We don't know how deep the water will be. If my camera gets wet, it's ruined. We'll just have to find a way out and get our stuff later."

"Okay," I say after a pause. I'm reluctant to leave my note-book behind, but at least this way, it won't get wet.

Wendell holds out the flashlight with one hand and puts the other hand at the small of my back. I wrap my arm around his naked waist, and side by side, we wade through the steaming water. When my bare feet slip on the slick stone, he's there to steady me. The water is waist high and hot but not uncomfortable. About the temperature of a hot tub. We take turns carrying the flashlight above our heads to keep it dry, aiming the beam ahead of us. There's nothing but tunnel ahead, disappearing into twists and turns.

We wade against the current until I'm breathless. We're at the point where we must have walked a kilometer, when I notice a light ahead.

Wendell does too. "See that, Z?"

"Yeah."

This gives me another wave of strength, and I wade faster. At the patch of light reflecting off the water, we stop, craning our heads back to look for its source. We're beneath a long tunnel stretching directly upward, with a circle of light far above us. It's a dim light, but it's there. And there's a bright white light at its center. The moon! And a rope hanging down, and a bucket, glinting in the moonlight.

Wendell looks at me. "So this is what it feels like at the bottom of a well."

"This what you saw?"

"Exactly."

Something rises over the sound of the flowing water. Music, floating in from above, echoing lightly off the tunnel walls. "Hear that, Wendell?"

He nods. "It sounds like harps and flutes."

"Salluvii's music." I strain to listen. There's laughter, conversation. And voices, too. "Think it's Sirona and her party?" I whisper.

Wendell turns to me, keeping his voice low. "I think we need to ask for their help."

"They might be angry. Remember your vision? That bearded man? Danger?"

"Yeah, but—"

A face appears, blocking the moon. A woman's face. She must have heard our voices or seen our flashlight.

Quickly, I turn off the light and grab Wendell's hand.

"Hé!" the woman yells. Now other faces are surrounding hers. In the dim light, and at this distance, I can't tell if they're angry or just surprised.

Wendell and I look at each other.

"There might not be another way out," he whispers.

Again the woman calls down. *"Montez!"* Get in! She's lowering the bucket, which clinks against the stone wall on its way down.

The bucket is dented and ancient-looking, copper, with greenish spots. I slip my hand out of Wendell's, grab the bucket, and inspect it with the flashlight. It looks solid enough, and the rope looks old but thick.

"I'll go first," I say.

"No, Z. It might not be safe. Let me—"

Before he can stop me, I climb into the bucket and grasp the rope. *"Allez-y!"* I call out.

Instantly, I'm heaved up, in jagged fits and starts, my shoulders banging against the slimy stones lining the well. I take a last look at Wendell's face growing smaller and smaller; then I focus on the incredulous faces framed by moonlight, growing bigger and bigger.

TWENTY-EIGHT

It's uncomfortable to be pulled up in a wet dress with an ancient copper bucket digging into the backs of your thighs. Not to mention terrifying. A fall from this height could kill me. I swing back and forth, clutching the rope, near panic.

And I'm up.

I'm up and entering a nighttime world lit by torches, a dreamlike world filled with tall bamboo stalks and tropical trees and exotic flowers. Not plants you'd expect to see in France. From somewhere behind the leaves drifts harp and flute music. Clusters of voices come from here and there. In the distance, through shadows of petals and branches, I can make out the ghostly forms of people moving and dancing and eating and drinking. Pools of torchlight swim over the grass. Stone pathways meander and disappear into the darkness. I glimpse a fountain beneath rising steam, and hear its faint gurgling and trickling. The scent of tropical night-blooming flowers saturates the air. Smoke and steam mingle together, and I can't tell how far the trees and bamboo stretch. It can't be too far, I realize, because the stone walls of houses rise on all sides. We must be in a large courtyard.

People stand around the well, quiet and cloaked in mist. They watch me, their faces bewildered, with traces of concern and curiosity. They all wear the raw cotton, hand-dyed tunics I've seen on the members of Salluvii. Bangles and bracelets snake up their arms, on both the men and women. Each person wears a triple-spiral symbol, either on a pendant, a ring, earrings, or a bracelet. Now that I'm looking closely, I notice that from the belts around their waists hang leather pouches containing large daggers and swords.

The silver-haired woman unfastens a thick brass pin from her red cloak, takes it off, and wraps it around me. The rough fabric scratches my damp skin, but I'm grateful for the gesture.

"Merci," I say.

She nods, lowering the bucket again, her triple-spiral earrings dangling. She speaks in French. "Shall we pull up your friend?"

I peer into the well nervously. Here in the light, I can see that the rope is waterlogged and frayed and rotted in places. "Is it safe?"

"Yes," she assures me.

I call down, "Ready, Wendell?"

"Go ahead!" he shouts back.

Two women and two men help pull him, turning the crank slowly. I hold my breath and chew on my lip until Wendell's up.

He climbs out, looking around with a dazed expression. "Where are we, Z?"

"I don't know," I whisper.

Wendell squeezes out his long hair, then takes my hand. He doesn't have a shirt on, I realize, and offer to share the cloak. Together, we huddle under the scratchy fabric.

Suddenly, through the small crowd, the bearded man appears. The burly one from the courtyard. From Wendell's vision. I press myself to Wendell, keeping my arm tight around his waist. He returns the gesture, his hand firmly on my hip.

With a flash of recognition, the bearded man narrows his eyes. Firelight washes over his fleshy face, which is twisted into a scowl. "How did you two get here?"

"Through a tunnel," I say, trying to steady my voice. "It led to this well."

"Were you at the sacred pools?" he demands, his hand on his dagger.

I hesitate, then say, "Yes."

"Which entrance?" He barks out his questions like an interrogator.

I glance at Wendell. I can't outright lie. That might get us in more trouble. "The snake fountain in the courtyard on Rue Epinaux."

He raises an eyebrow. "That's what you were doing with that art project, wasn't it? Trying to find a way into our courtyards."

Wendell and I nod, giving each other rueful glances.

"How did you know about the pools?" the man growls.

"An old book I read," I say. "And a map I found at the market." I'm determined to keep Madame Chevalier and Vincent out of this.

The bearded man glares at me for a moment, then turns to confer with the others in Gaelic. Wendell and I stand together, waiting for our fates to be determined. The bearded man's voice grows louder as his face reddens. Spittle flies from his mouth.

The silver-haired woman tries to calm him. I wonder if she's one of those priestesses who cut the throats of their war captives. Finally, the woman turns to us and says solemnly, "You have trespassed in our sacred place. You have intruded where you were not invited."

She unwinds a long scarf from her waist. Slowly, she removes the holster containing her dagger, and hands it to a man beside her. She gestures to another woman to do the same.

Wendell keeps his arm around my waist, drawing me closer. I'm grateful he's here with me, but feel terrible that I've gotten him into this mess. Who knows what these people are capable of? There are many ways they could kill us. They could slice our throats and save our blood for prophecy, then dump our bodies into the well, never to be found.

I take a deep breath and scream. A split second into my scream, the bearded man's hairy hand clamps over my mouth.

My scream must have attracted attention, because now people are streaming toward us from the shadows, men and women, the youngest around our age, the oldest white-haired, all dressed in long cotton tunics and cloaks.

Wendell and I are far outnumbered. Now I know how the guitar-playing troubadour felt. I wish I played guitar angelically so I could trick them into keeping us alive. Maybe I can try anyway.

I dive deep, through all the layers of myself, all the countries, to the source, the spring inside me that makes music, the one that sings the clear, flowing truth. And what it says is this. *I love Wendell. I want to be with him.* And we've barely had a chance to start. There's so much I want to do with him, discover about him. A whole lifetime of things.

The man's hand is still over my mouth, but not as tight now that I've stopped screaming.

"Please don't shout," the silver-haired woman says quietly, and gestures for him to let go.

Slowly, he releases his grip.

"Don't kill us," I blurt out. "Please."

The silver-haired woman looks at me, amused, and hands us each a scarf. "We won't kill you. Please put on the blindfolds."

Holding the scarf, I take a last look at Wendell. He's looking at me, his expression intense. I try to silently tell him how I feel. *I love you I love you I love you.*

Suddenly, a woman breaks through the crowd, and people part for her passage.

Sirona!

She stands in front of us, like a beautiful phantom in the steam rising from the well. She's wearing a crown studded with glittering stars, what seems like hundreds of them. "Zeeta?" she cries.

I throw myself into her arms, inhaling her sunny scent of lavender and thyme.

"You know her?" Wendell whispers.

I nod, dizzy with relief. "Sirona, this is Wendell. Wendell, this is my mother's friend—and my friend—Sirona."

Sirona says something in Gaelic to the others, then turns back to me. "So, Zeeta, what brings you two here?"

I take a deep breath and let everything spill out in an incoherent jumble. "We were looking for the sacred waters and got trapped and followed a tunnel from the chamber, the one with the spiral pools, and we had to find a way out so we waded up a tunnel until we saw the moon in the well, and they pulled us up and now they're going to blindfold us and—oh, please, help us, Sirona."

Another flurry of conversation in Gaelic sweeps through the crowd. Sirona keeps her arm around me the entire time. Finally, she turns to me with a sigh. "You are indeed a seeker, aren't you, Zeeta?"

I hold on tight to her arm. "I'm sorry, Sirona." And then, as my stomach contracts with fear, I ask, "What are they going to do to us?"

"Well, they were planning on leading you home blind-folded so you wouldn't be able to find your way back here."

"That's it?"

"What did you think?" She looks at me, suppressing a smile. "Now, why were you searching for the waters?"

"I have two friends—older people—who've always believed that there was a magical spring under Aix. A spring with heal-ing waters. One that could give eternal life. And these friends—they asked me and Wendell to find it for them."

Sirona nods thoughtfully, smiling. "So that's why you were asking me about immortality." She gestures to the people around her. Her voice turns serious now. "It's our duty to pro-tect the sacred waters. We—and our ancestors—have kept the waters pure and safe for thousands of years. And now that you two have discovered our sacred pool, you share our secret. And you share our duty to protect the secret."

I don't get it. Does this mean the water really has healing powers? I'm about to ask Sirona if we can take some water for our friends, when Wendell says, "We understand."

Sirona talks with the others again in Gaelic. She's obvi-ously a person of great authority here.

The group seems to have reached an agreement, nodding in consent. Sirona turns back to us and announces, "We've decided that you and Wendell may stay for tonight's festival as our guests."

Wendell and I exchange glances.

"But," Sirona continues, holding up a finger, "you must promise to take nothing of ours when you leave at dawn. And agree that you'll keep our secret—and the waters—safe."

Which means that we can't ask for the water for Madame Chevalier. I nod, swallowing my disappointment. Wendell looks at me, and then answers, "Yes, we promise."

Sirona kisses our cheeks lightly and says, "Enjoy the party." And with a sly smile, she adds, "The handfasting will happen soon."

"Handfasting?" I ask.

"Yes," she says with a wink. "You and Wendell might be interested in it, you know." She walks away, drifting toward a grove of bamboo, and calls over her shoulder, "As your mother would say, *make this night a song.*"

• • •

The crowd dissipates, moving along stone paths into groves of trees. People must have been told to leave us alone. Wendell and I explore this strange courtyard, wandering in and out of shadows and torchlight, following the paths that branch here and there in a kind of labyrinth through the mist. It's hard to tell how big the courtyard is. The foliage hiding the walls gives it the feel of a forest that stretches forever. Clusters of bamboo stalks and trees divide the space into smaller clearings. One clearing contains a fountain, a large stone covered in moss, dripping and steaming into a circular pool, enveloped in a lacy fog. I'm guessing it draws from the same waters as the well—the sacred waters.

Wendell and I drift through more clearings and groves, passing by couples and small groups, some standing, some sitting on blankets, others eating, talking, or dozing. A few people are playing instruments—lyre, trumpet, horns, flutes, timpans—in melodies familiar to me from Salluvii's songs. We wander into another clearing, this one featuring a large stone table holding a heap of flowers and silver satin cords.

"Where do you think we are?" I whisper, brushing my fingers over the petals, smoothing the mysterious cords.

"We must be somewhere in *le centre-ville*," he says, "or nearby, if they were planning on having us walk back."

I nod. "And we couldn't have gone more than a kilometer or two in the tunnel. Probably less with all those twists and turns." I look around, soaking in the steam and moonlight and flowers and rustling of leaves and harp music. "But doesn't it feel like we're in a different world? I mean, if we're in Aix still, why are these plants you'd find in a jungle?"

Wendell thinks. "Maybe the warm waters and steam just keep this courtyard tropical year-round."

"Maybe." But I can't help feeling as though we're in another world. A thoroughly magical one. A world where I never broke up with Wendell, where we can start over. Where nothing can be destroyed, nothing can die. Where everything can be healed. Everything gets a second chance.

We're quiet for a while, listening, strolling, watching shadows of people through the trees. Soon we come across another clearing. In the center of this one is a stone table covered with food—piles of fruit, nuts, figs, cakes, cookies, pitchers of golden liquid, and a giant pot of stew that smells of lamb and garlic and rosemary.

"Hungry?" Wendell asks.

"Yes!"

We pile our plates, then sit at the edge of this clearing, on a patch of velvety moss beneath a tree. The food is delicious. Even the honey cookies that tasted too healthy on the square are scrumptious now. Wendell and I are sitting close but not touching. I want to hold his hand again, or slide my arm around his waist, his shoulders, but somehow it seemed easier when we were in danger of death. His chest is bare again, now that I'm wearing the cloak. He's assured me he isn't cold anymore.

After I finish my last cookie, I ask, "Wendell, can you give me a second chance?" I lean closer to him, still not quite daring to touch him. "Can you still love me after what I put you through?"

He leans toward me. "Actually, I talked to Vincent about that."

"You did?"

"That morning when he brought the ring to Madame Chevalier. He told me you still loved me."

"He said that?" I don't know whether I want to kill Vincent and Madame Chevalier or thank them.

Wendell nods. "But I told him that you'd hurt me too

badly. That the easiest thing would be to leave France after my classes were over and never see you again."

I suck in a breath. "And what did Vincent say?"

Wendell gives a half-smile. "He told me the story of a famous homing pigeon named Cher Ami. The bird lived here in France during the First World War and worked with the American army. Want to hear the story?"

"Yeah," I say, curious how Vincent managed to connect a pigeon soldier to my relationship with Wendell.

"So, there was this bloody battle," Wendell begins, "and two hundred American troops were trapped behind enemy lines in a ditch without food or ammunition. Their allies didn't know they were there. They were accidentally dropping artillery on them. The trapped soldiers sent a desperate message with Cher Ami. He flew through enemy fire but got shot down. Just when the soldiers thought all hope was lost, the pigeon rose up again, triumphant. He got to the army base covered in blood, with his leg hanging by a tendon. He'd been shot in his breast and blinded in one eye. But he did it. He delivered the message in time to stop the Allies from killing their own troops. That little pigeon saved two hundred lives. The army medics operated on him and carved him a little wooden leg to replace the one he'd lost."

I'm confused. "So love's a bloody war?"

He laughs. "Well, according to Vincent, love is a devoted homing pigeon. It solves misunderstandings. It saves you. It survives. It's something you don't give up on. If it's missing a leg, you make it a wooden one."

"Or you heal it with magical waters." I meet his gaze. "Does this mean I get another chance?"

I'm waiting for his answer when three people emerge from the trees and walk down the path toward us. It's Sirona, her son, Bormanus, and his girlfriend, Damona. "Ready for the handfasting?" Sirona asks.

"*Oui,*" Wendell says, and I go along with it.

"*Oui,*" I echo.

As we follow the three of them along a path, Wendell whispers, "What's handfasting?"

"No idea," I say, grinning.

We stop at the flower-covered stone table, where a crowd is gathered. Sirona places a garland of flowers around Damona's neck, then puts one around my neck, scattering more flowers at our feet. She moves along to other young women, encircling their necks with garlands from the heap on the table.

Sirona says something in Gaelic, and four young couples step forward. They look just a few years older than me and Wendell. Sirona walks up to the first couple and rests her hands on their shoulders so that they face each other. She takes the young woman's right wrist and with a silver cord, ties it to the young man's right wrist. Then she does the same with their left wrists. In the end, the couple's arms are crisscrossed, forming a figure eight, an infinity symbol. Looking elated, the young man and woman nod to Sirona in a gesture of thanks, and retreat to the trees at the edge of the clearing.

As Sirona does this with the remaining three couples,

Damona comes over to me and Wendell, and whispers, "The silver cord binding shows that they're a couple. They'll stay together for a year and a day to try it out. And then the next year, they come back and declare whether they want to stay together or separate." She pauses and looks at us. "Would you two like to join them?"

I flush, glancing at Wendell. "It's up to you."

"Yes," he says, smiling. He moves his lips close to my ear and whispers, "I saw this in a vision, the silver cord binding us. I didn't understand it, but I knew I wanted it."

"Me too," I say, picturing a battered little pigeon rising bravely up and up and up.

Damona gives us a small shove forward into the middle of the clearing. Sirona has a pleased expression on her face as she positions Wendell and me in front of each other. I bite my lip, watching him press his lips together, both of us trying not to laugh. I hold out my right hand, and he holds out his right hand, crossing his wrist over mine so that we're barely touching. Sirona binds our right wrists gently with the cord, then moves to our left wrists. The cord is cool and silky and light on my skin. It feels right. Not like a heavy chain but like something whispery thin, yet strong. Something like spider's silk.

Wendell and I lock eyes, and then, following the lead of the other couples, we retreat into the trees. The silver cord makes walking tricky. He ends up walking backward, pulling me with his wrists, as I try to steer him between trees. We're laughing and tripping over each other, and eventually fall down in a soft, mossy spot. We lie beside each other, our wrists still bound together, pressed between our chests. Our faces are moving closer, and soon our laughter turns to kisses, and we dissolve into each other's skin, each other's lips.

TWENTY-NINE

A while later, I let my eyes float closed and tuck my face into the crook of Wendell's neck. We must be near the fountain, I realize, as its gurgling sounds lull me toward sleep. I'm nearly asleep when I hear something.

The coo of a bird. A splash. The flutter of wings.

I open my eyes and squint through the mist. A pigeon has landed at the edge of the fountain and started drinking the water. I stand up and walk toward the fountain. The pigeon looks at me in a kind of greeting. As I'm closer, I notice the vial around her left leg, and the distinct lack of a fourth toe.

"Maude!" I whisper. This fountain must be one of Maude's secret little detours. "Maude, *viens ici*, Maude."

She waddles to me and settles in my lap. I tap my finger on her vial, an idea forming.

Wendell raises his head and looks around, confused. When he sees me, and the bird nestled in the fabric of my dress, his face breaks into a smile. "Maude?" he says, standing up and walking over.

"Look, Wendell!" I whisper, pointing to the plastic vial. "Think it would hold water? Should we sneak some water out with Maude?"

Wendell tucks a strand of hair behind his ear. "But Sirona trusts us," he says slowly. "Wouldn't this be a betrayal?"

"We won't break the promise, Wendell. We *will* leave empty-handed. And think about Vincent and Madame Chevalier. It's just a little vial. And it might not even do anything. But it would make them so happy, give them so much hope."

Wendell strokes Maude's feathers for a moment, then says, "Okay. But let's just uncap the vial and dip Maude's leg into the pool."

I take a furtive glance around. Only a few people are in the clearing, lying at its edges beneath trees, asleep on the moss. Even awake, it would be hard for them to see us with most of the torches burned out. And the steam over the water is so thick, it forms a protective veil around the fountain.

Maude doesn't protest as I twist off the cap and gently dip her leg in the water. After the vial fills, I cork my finger over the top and settle Maude back into my lap. I screw the cap back on, and then, with a grateful kiss on her head, set Maude back on the fountain's ledge.

"Think it's too heavy?" Wendell asks.

"She can do it," I say, confident in Maude. "Remember

Cher Ami? And Maude won't have anyone shooting at her. Anyway, it can't be more than a kilometer or so to Vincent's." I watch Maude, hoping she'll fly away. But she stays there, drinking.

I'm about to pick her up and toss her in the air, the way Vincent does, when some branches rustle.

At the edge of the clearing, Sirona appears through the leaves.

Wendell grabs my hand, pulls me away from the fountain. I try to paste a casual, innocent look on my face, to act as though we're simply strolling. What if Sirona sees the vial of water on Maude's leg? What if she figures out we did it? What will her people do to us then?

"Dawn's coming," Sirona says, glancing at the lightening sky. "Did you two have a nice time?"

"Yes," I say quickly, praying Maude will fly away. She has to leave before it grows much lighter, before anyone notices the vial of water. *Go, Maude, go!*

A few other people appear on the path through the trees— Bormanus; Damona; Sirona's husband, Grannos; the bearded man; and a few others. They gather around us.

Maude, meanwhile, is taking her time flapping around in the water, raising a ruckus. Of all times to take a noisy bath, she chooses now.

Sirona glances at her. I squeeze Wendell's hand. But then Sirona looks back at me, showing no sign of having spotted the vial. I keep my hand tight around Wendell's, silently pleading with Maude to fly away.

"Now, Zeeta and Wendell," Sirona says, holding out two silk scarves. "Close your eyes."

Damona wraps one scarf around Wendell's eyes while Sirona wraps the other around mine. I feel her tie it securely in back, then adjust it to completely cover the area from my forehead to my nose. No light comes through. I'm blind. With the scarf on, I'm extra aware of every sound: the voices in Gaelic, the water gurgling, a few birds singing, Maude splashing. I notice the feel of things—the light breeze on my skin, the rustling of leaves, Wendell's hand, warm in mine.

Suddenly, from the direction of the fountain, I hear a flutter of wings, close at first, then fading. I hold my breath, waiting and listening for some sign we've been caught. But the voices continue talking in Gaelic as before, no alarming change in their tones. I breathe out in relief.

A man's voice says, "Wendell, I'm just going to check your pockets." It sounds like Bormanus.

Damona asks, "You don't have any pockets on that dress, do you, Zeeta?"

"No."

"Are you two ready, then?" Sirona asks.

Wendell's voice is strangely solemn in the darkness. "Yes."

"Yes," I say.

"Remember," warns a gruff male voice. It must be the bearded man. "You may never return. And you will keep our secret safe."

Here comes Sirona's voice again, brighter in contrast, with a smile in her words. "And remember to choose your meeting place to complete the handfasting. In a year and a day, you'll decide whether to seal the bond."

Wendell squeezes my hand. I squeeze back, and move my other hand to my neck, where I've tied the silver cord.

Damona puts her hand on my shoulder, ushering me out. "This way, Zeeta," she says. "Watch your step."

I walk tentatively along a stone path. Soon I hear the creak of a door. "Step up here," Damona says. She leads us through an indoor area, where the air is more still and smells slightly musty. Under my bare feet, the tiles feel cold and smooth. I hear other people's footsteps, soft in their leather sandals. There must be a small group with us, judging by the number of footsteps.

We turn a corner, step over what must be another threshold, and go down two stairs. There's the sound of a key in a lock and another door creaking open, and once again we're outside in the cool, light breeze of dawn.

Now there's pavement beneath my feet, occasionally something sticky. I trust Damona to lead me around any piles of dog *merde*. I pay careful attention to everything, trying to construct a map in my head. But at each turn, she spins me around and around until I have no idea which way we're going. After a few minutes, we pass a fountain that must be big, judging by the deep sounds of water falling from multiple spouts.

Damona unties my blindfold.

I blink, shocked.

We're in the Place de la Mairie. At the fountain where

Vincent feeds pigeons. The air is the blue-silver of dawn, bright compared to the darkness of my blindfold. Damona and Bormanus kiss our cheeks goodbye, and Sirona cups my face in her hands, then does the same to Wendell, a kind, motherly gesture. "I'm glad our paths have crossed, Zeeta and Wendell, if only briefly. I wish you both well."

"Thank you, Sirona," we say at the same time.

And then she murmurs to the others in Gaelic. They split into four pairs, each pair heading down one of the four streets that leave the square.

THIRTY

On the way to my apartment, Wendell and I pass the street cleaners with their hoses, the *boulangerie* cashier going to work, a sleepy-eyed man walking his tiny dog. Each one tosses us a curious glance. We're probably a strange sight—Wendell without a shirt, me in a bedraggled red dress and bare feet. We stop at a public pay phone and Wendell leaves a voice mail for his host family.

Then we head to my apartment and collapse together on the sofa, too tired to pull out the bed. We're lying down, squished together on the cushions. His eyes fall closed, and his fingers brush idly over the skin of my shoulder, landing on the silver cord around my neck. He laces it in his fingers and says, "I'm so happy, Z."

"Me too," I say sleepily. "Happy and complete. Nothing's missing."

He strokes my hair. "Even though we haven't found your dad?"

I nod, yawning. "I still haven't given up hope. In the meantime, I have you and Layla and all the friends who come and go in my life. They're all still part of me. And there's Vincent and Madame Chevalier and Tortue and Sirona and . . ." I'm falling asleep. My eyelids feel impossibly heavy, even though part of me is still humming with excitement.

Wendell kisses my earlobe. "Think Maude's back at Vincent's with the water?"

"Probably. Let's go there after we sleep a little."

There are so many more things to turn over in our minds, to tell each other, ask each other, so many things. I brush my lips over his neck, his cheeks, his lips, and soon our murmurs melt into the sighs and breaths of sleep.

• • •

My eyes open to sunlight streaming through the window, illuminating dust motes and pooling on the tile floor. Layla's clinking around in the kitchen, making tea in her pink robe. I raise my head. She meets my gaze, curious, then glances at Wendell, who's still sleeping. I know she's dying to quote some Rumi.

In this bright sunlight, last night, with all its water and torchlight and mist and moonlight, seems like a strange dream. I extricate my limbs from Wendell's and sit up, yawning.

At my movement, Wendell opens his eyes and smiles. He pushes up onto his elbows and stretches. Looking around, he says, "Hey, Layla." His voice is scratchy and low, and his hand rests on the back of my neck, underneath my hair, his fingers twirling around the silver cord. Our only tangible proof that last night really happened.

"How was your night?" Layla asks.

"Good," we answer at the same time.

"Anything dazzling happen?"

I look at Wendell. "Nope," we say in unison.

Layla's face falls. She wants, somehow, to be part of our happiness.

"Hey, Layla," I say, feeling generous. "What's the Rumi quote about the spring and dawn?"

She gives me a stunned look. It's been years since I actually requested Rumi. But she doesn't question my motives, simply gets on her Rumi-quoting face and says,

"There was a dawn I remember
When my soul heard something
From your soul. I drank water
From your spring and felt
The current take me."

"Thank you, Layla," I say, explaining nothing, leaving her mystified but content.

After breakfast, Wendell throws on a gray T-shirt that

belonged to one of Layla's ex-boyfriends. Together we walk toward the square, where the golden, buttery, chocolatey smells of early-morning Aix waft from the *pâtisseries* we pass. The sunlight is fresh and lemony yellow, warming the stone streets. In the Place de la Mairie, we're greeted with flowers of all colors, spilling out from beneath the striped awnings of the flower market. A light breeze plays with the petals, nudging them here and there. The entire square looks alive, shimmering.

We're heading across the Place de la Mairie in the direction of Les Secrets de Maude when I notice a crowd of pigeons by the fountain, pecking at birdseed. Through the feathers, I make out Vincent. He's standing beside something large—an artist's easel, it looks like. I see the back view of a woman in a purple dress sitting on a stool facing the canvas. At first I don't recognize her here by the fountain, not framed by her window, without binoculars around her neck. I can't believe it. Madame Chevalier is *inside* the square. Not just observing it at a distance. She's inside life, with Maude on her shoulder like a little guardian angel.

"Wendell, look," I say, pointing.

"Is that Madame Chevalier?" he asks. "Outside? Oil painting?"

We walk closer. Vincent is scattering birdseed while Madame Chevalier is painting and watching him and laughing. When we reach them, Madame Chevalier stands up and kisses us both emphatically on both cheeks. She still seems weak, but something has shifted. Not only is she out-side, and painting, but there's a lightness to her movements that wasn't there before.

Vincent embraces us next, wraps us up in his smells of pi-geons and dusty old things. "*Merci, merci, merci, mes enfants!* Maude brought me a special delivery this morning"—and here he winks—"and I sent it straight to Madame Cheva-lier!"

Madame Chevalier sits back down on her stool and says, "Tell us how you found it!"

Wendell and I exchange looks.

"We have to tell them," I whisper in English.

"But we promised—"

"Come on, Wendell. You know the secret's safe with them. They deserve to know."

"Okay," Wendell says. "Let's tell them."

After making them promise not to breathe a word about it, we describe our night, starting with the snake fountain in the courtyard at sunset and ending with how we were blind-folded and brought back here at dawn. The only thing we leave out is the kissing, by silent agreement.

Vincent clasps his hands together. "This morning when I set out birdseed for Maude, I noticed her acting different, excited. And I saw the vial of water, and I knew! I knew!"

We sit on the edge of the fountain and listen to his story, trailing our fingers in the water, our hands touching each other.

"It was early, barely sunrise," Vincent says. "I'm an early

riser, you see. I knew Maude would fly faster than I could walk, so I sent her with a note taped to the outside of the vial that said *Drink me.* Then I got dressed and went to Violette's house as fast as these old legs could carry me! And by the time I got there, she'd already drunk the water. She was dressed and had coffee ready for me, and oh, I couldn't stop looking at her face, all rosy and beautiful. I could actually *see* the color coming back into it."

Madame Chevalier takes over. "Vincent said, 'Let's go to the fountain!' And I said, 'Why not?' and he helped me down the stairs. Then he went back up to get my easel and here we are!"

Vincent gazes at Madame Chevalier, and Maude gives a satisfied coo. Inside the fountain's water, my hand joins Wendell's. Madame Chevalier must notice, because she says, "I see the waters worked their magic on you two, as well."

· · ·

By the time we make it back to the apartment, it's midafternoon. Wendell and I lounge on the sofa, kissing and talking and napping and kissing some more, until Layla breezes in, carrying a crinkly white bag from the *boulangerie.* "Spinach quiche!" she announces.

As we set the table, she says, "Oh! Guess who stopped by while you two were out?"

Wendell and I look at each other. "Who?"

"Sirona. She came to say goodbye. She's leaving town with the rest of Salluvii."

"Really?" I sink onto a chair.

"Yeah," Layla says, frowning. "I'm bummed. She was my best friend here. Although I got the feeling there were things she didn't share with me."

I nod. "So . . . what did she say?"

"She dropped off your bag, love. And your backpack, Wendell. Said you left them somewhere. I put them in your room, Z."

Wendell tries to act casual. "Where's Sirona going?"

"On tour around Europe," she said.

After the quiche, Wendell and I go into my room to get our bags.

I pull my notebook from my bag. Sweet relief. A rush of gratitude to Sirona.

"Everything there?" he asks, poking around in his back-pack, making sure his camera didn't get wet.

"I think so." As I shuffle through the other contents of my bag, my hand rests on the little book bound with red ribbon that I made Wendell. I hand it to him.

"What's this?"

"A present for you," I say. "You gave me all those photos in Ecuador, and I realized you should have something from me."

"Thanks, Z," he says, surprised.

As he leafs through it, I root around in my bag, looking for lip balm. My hand touches something hard and round and small, attached to a cord. Some kind of necklace. I pull it out. It's a tree nut hanging from a worn leather cord. A tree nut that looks just like a deer's eye, a circle of black surrounded by a brown band. Taped to the cord is a piece of paper.

"Wendell. My *fantôme* left me something else."

Wendell moves close to me on the edge of the bed, putting his arm around my shoulder. Together, we read it.

> Chère Zeeta,
> Before I can be a father to you, there's something I must do. I need to answer some questions that have haunted me for twenty years. And the answers lie far away, across the ocean, in the place I was born and raised. Once I find these answers, I hope I will be a complete person, good enough for you. I don't know how long this will take me. I will contact you when I feel ready. Please forgive me.
>
> > Love,
> > Your Father

I read it three times. "He's leaving."

Wendell strokes my hair. "But he'll contact you."

"If he ever becomes perfect. Which will never happen."

• • •

I'm not exactly sure why I'm wearing my *fantôme*'s Jimi Hendrix T-shirt. Maybe because even though I'm frustrated with my father, I still love him. Maybe it's my way of telling him I'll wait for him to be ready to love me. The shirt is comfortable, the fabric smooth and soft, so threadbare I have to wear a black tank underneath. Wendell keeps poking his finger through the holes to tickle me. I laugh and slap his hand away, secretly waiting for him to poke me again.

A day has passed since we came back from the courtyard party, and we're walking hand in hand down Rue Mignet, headed toward Les Secrets de Maude to visit Vincent. At the Place des Trois Ormeaux, I catch sight of red sparkles. It's Jean-Claude, walking beside Amandine. We say our *bonjour*s and kiss each other's cheeks. Amandine looks sad—a huge change from the last time I saw her, at the food market.

Before I can ask her what's wrong, Jean-Claude says, "I didn't know you and Tortue were friends."

"What?" I have no idea why he's bringing up the mime.

"His Jimi T-shirt. He gave it to you before he left?"

"What?"

"That's Tortue's shirt, right?" Jean-Claude steps closer. "*Oui. C'est ça.* I'd recognize it anywhere. He sleeps in it every night. Right, Amandine?"

Amandine says nothing. She looks pale, her eyebrows knitted together.

Gradually, the significance of this sinks into me. Tortue.

Tortue, invisible beneath his mask of paint. Soft-spoken, quiet Tortue. So easy to overlook. I think of that day on the side street, when he noticed I was upset, when he comforted me simply by being there. I think of the tenderness in his voice as he sang *"Au Clair de la Lune."* It was a kind of lullaby, just what I needed, just what I would have wanted from a father.

What was he thinking? Was he wishing he could have sung it to me years ago? And why would he think he wasn't good enough to be my father?

And that day at the market, when he told Layla and me the story of Harlequin and Pierrot. Was he still in love with her? Does he believe Layla is his Columbine?

All these questions are making me dizzy. I lean into Wendell for support. "It's Tortue," I say under my breath.

Amandine is staring at me. *She knows. She's known all along.* She must have been the one to put the things in my bag. The *fantôme*. Tortue's accomplice.

Jean-Claude looks confused. "What's going on?" He's obviously been left in the dark.

For a while, Amandine and I look at each other, so many secrets passing between us. Wendell squeezes my hand, a gesture of solidarity.

Finally, I turn to Jean-Claude. "*Ecoute,* I have to talk to Tortue. Where is he?"

"He's gone."

My heart sinks. It's too late. He's already on his way across the ocean. "Are you sure?"

"He packed his bags and left without a goodbye. Just a note." He puts his arm around Amandine's shoulder, draws her in to him. "Amandine's really upset."

"What did he say in his note?" I ask Amandine.

Her eyes spill over with tears. "He went back to his child-hood home. To face problems he'd left behind." Wiping her cheeks, she takes a long breath. "His therapist encouraged him. He's been on new medication that's lifted his depression. He said things are clear to him now. Said he has to take this trip. To become the person he wants to be."

"Do you know where he went?" I ask, my voice shaking.

"Mexico," Amandine says, sniffling. "On the coast, somewhere in the south. He's mentioned the place before, but I don't remember anything more—"

"Do you have his address? A phone number? Anything?"

She shakes her head. "He said not to worry, that he'd contact us when the time was right."

"But he doesn't know how to contact me."

"Yes, he does," Amandine replies. "From when you signed up for Illusion's mailing list."

Jean-Claude gives me a confused look. "Why do you suddenly care so much about Tortue?"

Slowly, I say, "It appears that he's my father."

Jean-Claude stares at Amandine, his mouth dropped open. "And you knew this, Amandine?"

"I'm sorry," she says. "He made me promise not to tell anyone." She turns back to me with a wavery sigh. "He asked me to put the stuff into your bag, Zeeta."

I think of Amandine's backflips, her cheek kisses—perfect distractions while she was slipping things into my bag.

"So, Amandine, you knew from the beginning?" Wendell asks, looking a little hurt.

Nodding, she turns to me. "Tortue saw Layla in the square and recognized her right away. He wanted to talk to her, but he didn't know how. Then, when he saw you, Zeeta, he said you look just like his younger sister."

An aunt. I have an aunt. It really hits me now. And probably there are more aunts, and uncles, too. It's overwhelming, this tidal wave of information.

Amandine takes a deep breath and continues. "He suspected you were his daughter. When I found out more about you, and your birthday, he was sure of it. And that made him happy and terrified at the same time. He wanted you to know that he existed, that he loved your mother, that he cared about you two. I pushed him to introduce himself. I was hoping he'd do that at the dinner party. But he could only work up the courage to leave you the letters and gifts."

So many questions are churning inside me, I don't know which to ask first. "What's his real name?" I whisper finally.

"José Cruz," Amandine says.

My heart sinks. It's one of the world's most common names.

Wendell tightens his arm around me, comforting me. "It's something," he says.

I shake my head. There are probably thousands of José Cruzes in Mexico. I don't even know his second last name. And since he hasn't lived there for years, there probably wouldn't be any useful records. No phone, no address, nothing. I try to wrap my mind around the idea that my father—who I finally feel as if I know, finally feel ready to love—has just disappeared across the ocean. "It's not fair—it's not—"

"You know what's not fair?" Amandine snaps. "It's not fair that he's your father instead of mine. It's not fair he's not psychologically stable. It's not fair he has unresolved problems in Mexico."

I've been selfish, I realize. "I'm sorry, Amandine." In some ways, this man is more her father than mine. "So why is he called Tortue?" I ask softly.

"I think he got the name Turtle a long time ago. In Mexico, it was *Tortuga*. Here it's *Tortue*. I guess he's always loved sea turtles. Even worked with them when he was younger."

I close my eyes for a long time. "Did he say anything else?"

She pauses to think. "I don't think so. Well, just that— when I tried to convince him to tell you, he said he felt ashamed."

"Why?"

"He said, 'What would Layla say if she found out her daughter had a crazy clown for a father?' "

I put my face in my hands and groan. "Somehow, I don't think it would bother her." I look up. "I'm going to find him, Amandine."

"How?"

"I don't know yet. But I am."

THIRTY-ONE

The water is so blue, such a deep, delicious, clear blue, and so full of light, I can't stop looking at it. We're on the upper deck of the ferry in the Vieux Port of Marseille, headed out of the harbor, past le Château d'If, toward the chain of islands to the right. Les Iles de Frioul is where Illusion is going to play tonight at a music festival. It's also the island where Jean-Claude and his family used to go to the beach, where he and Amandine had their picnic with his mother a few weeks ago. His mother and stepfather are sitting beside him and Amandine, talking and pointing at the islands in the distance. Every once in a while, his mother leans over to kiss his cheek or touch his hair, as if to convince herself he's really there.

Amandine and I have formed a tentative friendship, although we're still far from being sisterly. Next to her sit Sabina and Julien, nuzzling each other, as usual. And beside them are Layla and Ahmed, who've been spending more and more time together lately. He's brought his guitar, since Illusion invited him to be their guest soloist for a few songs. His stubble is even longer and more scrappy-looking now, just the way Layla likes it.

When I told Layla the news about Tortue, she promised that if he hasn't contacted us by the time her teaching contract is up at the end of the year, we'll go find him. Near Layla, over by the railing, stand Madame Chevalier and Vincent, his arm around her shoulder. Three weeks ago, her nurse made a home visit to her apartment and noticed she was looking significantly better. She brought her to the hospital for tests, which revealed not a single cancer cell. " 'Spontaneous remission' is what the doctor said," Madame Chevalier told me with a girlish laugh.

I lean my head against Wendell's as we peer over the opposite railing. "Don't you wish we could dive right in?"

He smiles his half-smile, which I will never, ever get tired of. "We will. Next summer."

My eyes widen. "You see us?"

"We're underwater, Z. Swimming together. It's the bluest, greenest water I've ever seen. And there are thousands of silvery fish around us."

My gaze moves back to the water below us, here and

now—a liquid green gemstone, impossibly bright and dark at the same time, sunlight dancing on the surface, while deep blue shadows stretch far below. Our ferry hums through the waves, swirling together the darkness and light, making its way toward the open sea.

GLOSSARY AND PRONUNCIATION GUIDE

* The *r* in French is a raspy *h* sound formed in the throat with the back of the tongue.
* The *n* sound at the end of a word is very nasal, made with vibration in your nose, not with your tongue. (But if the *n* is followed by an *e*, it's a regular *n* sound.)
* For French vowel sounds that don't exist in English, I gave a rough approximation. For accurate pronunciation, listen to an online dictionary (or find some French-speaking friends!).

2eme (deuxième) étage	DUH-zee-em ay-TAZH	second floor (for Americans, third floor)
à la claire fontaine	ah lah CLAYR fohn-TEN	at the clear fountain
Ah bon?	ah BOHN	Oh really?
Aidez-nous!	EH-day-NOO	Help us!
Aix-en-Provence	EX-ahn-proh-VOHNS	city in southern France
allez-y	ah-lay-ZEE	go ahead
alors	ah-LOHR	well/so

Amandine	ah-mahn-DEEN	female name
amant	ah-MAHN	lover
attendez	ah-tahn-DAY	wait
au clair de la lune	oh CLAYR duh lah LEWN	in the light of the moon
au revoir	oh ruh-VWAHR	goodbye
Au secours!	oh suh-COOR	Help!
bac	BAHC	an important French exam
béarnaise	bay-ahr-NEZ	type of butter sauce
béchamel	bay-chah-MEL	creamy white sauce
bien sûr	bee-EN SYUR	of course
bizarre	bee-ZAHR	weird
bon anniversaire	BOHN ah-nee-vayr-SAYR	happy birthday
bon courage	bohn coo-RAHZH	good luck
bon voyage	bohn vwah-YAZH	happy travels
bonjour	bohn-JOOR	hello
bonne chance	bun SHAHNS	good luck
bonsoir	bohn-SWAH	good evening
boulangerie	boo-lahn-ZHREE	bakery
ça craint	sah CRAHN	that/this sucks
Ça va?	sah VAH	How's it going? or It's going (fine).
café au lait	cah-FAY oh LAY	coffee with milk
Café Cerise	cah-FAY suh-REEZ	Cherry Café
cave	CAHV	basement
centimes	sohn-TEEM	cents
c'est ça	say SAH	that's it
C'est chouette!	say shoo-ET	That's great!
c'est la vie	say lah VEE	that's life
C'est lui pour moi. Moi pour lui.	say loo-EE poor MWAH. MWAH poor loo-EE.	He's for me. I'm for him.
c'est magnifique	say MAHN-ee-feek	that's wonderful

charcuterie	shahr-kew-TREE	butcher's shop
Château d'If	shah-TOH DEEF	Castle of If
chère, chérie	SHAYR (shayr-EE)	dear
Chez Gilles	SHAY ZHEEL	restaurant name
Comme elle est belle!	COHM el ay BEL	How beautiful she/it is!
crème brûlée	CREM brew-LAY	creamy, sweet dessert
crêperie	crep-REE	crepe shop
crêpes	crep	crepes (thin pancakes)
curiosités	CEW-ree-ah-see-TAY	curiosities
cybercafé	SEE-behr-cah-FAY	Internet café
de rien	duh ree-EN	it's nothing/you're welcome
désolé(e)	day-soh-LAY	sorry
écoute	ay-COOT	listen
eh bien	ay bee-EN	well then
Eh bien, dis donc!	ay bee-EN dee DOHN	Well then, how about that!
enchanté(e)	ahn-shahn-TAY	enchanted/nice to meet you
Entremont	ahn-truh-MOHN	an ancient Celtic-Ligurian settlement near Aix
entrez	ahn-TRAY	come in/enter
épicerie	ay-pees-REE	small grocery store
éternité	ay-ter-nee-TAY	eternity
excellent	ex-uh-LAHN	awesome, great
excuse-moi	ex-CEWZ-MWAH	excuse me
extraordinaire	x-TROHR-dee-nayr	extraordinary
fantôme	fohn-TOHM	ghost/phantom
fête	FET	party
flics	FLEEK	cops
fou	FOO	crazy

française	frahn-SEZ	French
garçon	gahr-SOHN	boy/young man
génial	zhay-nee-AHL	cool/nice
glâce	GLAHS	ice cream
gourmands	goor-MAHN	food lovers/gourmets
herbes de Provence	AYRB duh proh-VAHNS	herb blend of Southern France (rosemary, thyme, basil, marjoram, savory)
hyper cool	EEP-ayr KEWL	really cool
illusion	ee-lew-zee-OHN	illusion
Imagine!	ee-mah-ZHEEN	Imagine!
incroyable	ehn-cwah-YAH-bluh	incredible
insupportable	en-soo-por-TAHB-luh	too much, unbearable
je ne sais quoi	zhuh nuh say KWAH	a special, indescribable something (literally "I don't know what")
je suis désolé(e)	zhuh swee day-soh-LAY	I'm sorry
je t'aime	zhuh TEM	I love you
Jean-Claude	ZHON-CLOHD	male name
la femme de ma vie	lah FAHM duh mah VEE	the (female) love of my life
la vie en rose	lah VEE ohn ROHZ	life in rose/pink (colored glasses), a song recorded by Edith Piaf
le centre-ville	SAHN-truh-VEEL	downtown
le grand amour	luh GRAHND a-MOOR	true love
les eaux magiques	layz OH mah-ZHEEK	magic waters
les eaux sacrées	layz OH sah-CRAY	sacred waters
Les Iles de Frioul	layz EEL duh free-OOL	Islands of Frioul
Les Secrets de Maude	lay suh-CRAY duh MOHD	Maude's Secrets

l'homme de ta vie	LOM duh tah VEE	the (male) love of your life
liberté absolue	lee-bayr-TAY ahb-so-LEW	complete freedom
lycée	lee-SAY	high school
ma petite	mah puh-TEET	my little (one)
madame	mah-DAHM	ma'am, Mrs., Ms.
Madame Chevalier	mah-DAHM shuh-vah-lee-AY	Ms. Chevalier
mademoiselle	mahd-mwa-ZEL	miss, young lady
mais	MAY	but
Mais non!	may NOHN	But no!
Marseille	mahr-SAY	big city on the Mediterranean coast of southern France
Maude	MOHD	female name
merci	mayr-SEE	thank you
merci en tout cas	mayr-SEE ahn TOO CAH	thanks anyway
merde	MAYRD	shit
mes enfants	mayz ahn-FAHN	my children
mille-feuilles	MEEL-FUH-yuh	type of pastry (literally "a thousand leaves/papers")
mon amour	mohn ah-MOOR	my love
Mon Dieu!	mohn DYUH	My God!
mon oeil	mohn UH-yuh	yeah, right (with sarcasm) (literally, "my eye")
mon père	mohn PAYR	my father
monsieur	muh-SYUH	sir, Mr.
Montez!	MOHN-tay	Get in!
monument historique	mohn-ew-MAHN ees-toh-REEK	historical monument
navettes	nah-VET	shuttle buses
non	NOHN	no

On y va!	ohn ee VAH	Let's go!
ouais	oo-AY	yeah
Ouf!	OOF	Phew!
oui	WEE	yes
parfait	pahr-FAY	perfect
pas de problème	PAH duh prohb-LEHM	no problem
pâté	pah-TAY	ground liver or meat spread
pâtisserie	pah-tees-REE	cake/pastry shop
pistou	pees-TOO	French pesto (ground garlic, basil, olive oil, Parmesan cheese)
Place de la Mairie	PLAHS duh lah may-REE	Town Hall Square
Place des Trois Ormeaux	PLAHS day TWAHZ ohr-MOH	Three Oaks Square
Qu'est-ce qui se passe?	kes KEE suh PAHS	What's going on? What's wrong?
regardez	ruh-gahr-DAY	watch (a command, formal/plural form)
rouge	ROOZH	red
rue	REW	road/street
salut	sah-LEW	hi
s'il te plaît	SEE tuh PLAY	please
super cool	SEWP-ayr KEWL	really cool
tarte au citron	TAHRT oh see-TROHN	lemon tart
tarte aux fruits	TAHRT oh frew-EE	fruit tart
tortue	tor-TEW	turtle
tout à fait	TOOT ah FAY	exactly
très amusant	TREHZ ah-mew-ZAHN	very fun
très intéressant	TREHZ ahn-tay-reh-SAHN	very interesting
trompe l'oeil	TROHMP-LUH-yuh	painting that creates the illusion of depth

trop top	TROH TOHP	great, awesome (slang)
un moment	un moh-MAHN	one moment
vâchement cool	VASH-mahn KEWL	really cool
Venez!	vuh-NAY	Come (here)! (formal/plural form)
Viens (ici)!	vee-EN ee-SEE	Come (here)! (informal, singular form)
Vieux Port	VYUH POR	Old Port
Vincent	vahn-SAHN	male name
voilà	vwah-LAH	there you go